indra's net

BY BRAD BRYANT

Alec + Kathy,
Pretty soon, you'll have a whole collection of
signed first editions by obscure writers.
Thank you so much for dinner and a
long-term friendship.
At least this isn't in classical
Greek.

Best,
Brad & Sharon

Numerous translations exist of the Zoroastrian *Gathas*. The Humbach and Ichaporia version - cited at the end of this book - is a good example. In Chapter 11, I have paraphrased from several stanzas of Song 3 from the original while attempting to retain its intent and flow.

The short passage from Lao Tzu's *Tao Te Ching* found in Chapter 15 represents yet another paraphrasing of words from that ancient Chinese text which also has been translated hundreds of times into Western languages. One of the better translations in my view is that done by John Wu and cited at the end of this book.

Cover design and interior layout by Gretchen Long.

To Fathers and Sons, Mothers and Daughters,
Brothers and Sisters
… and to Sharon

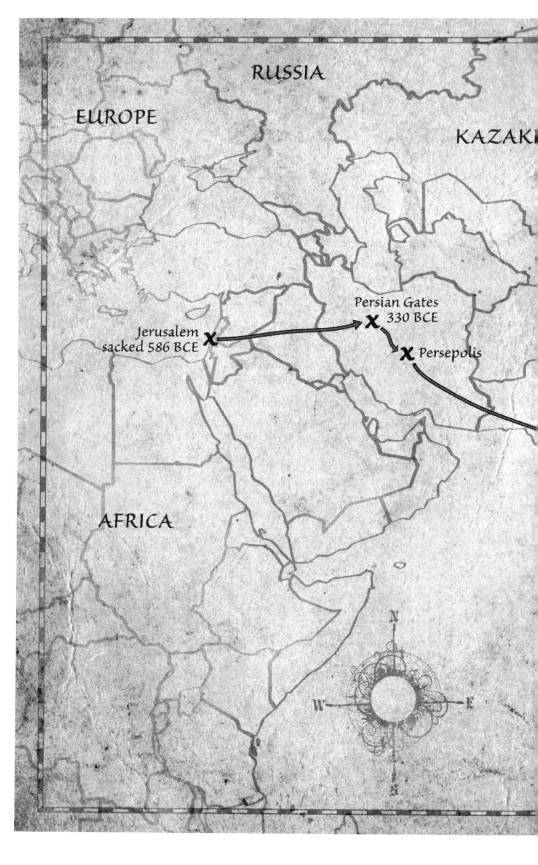

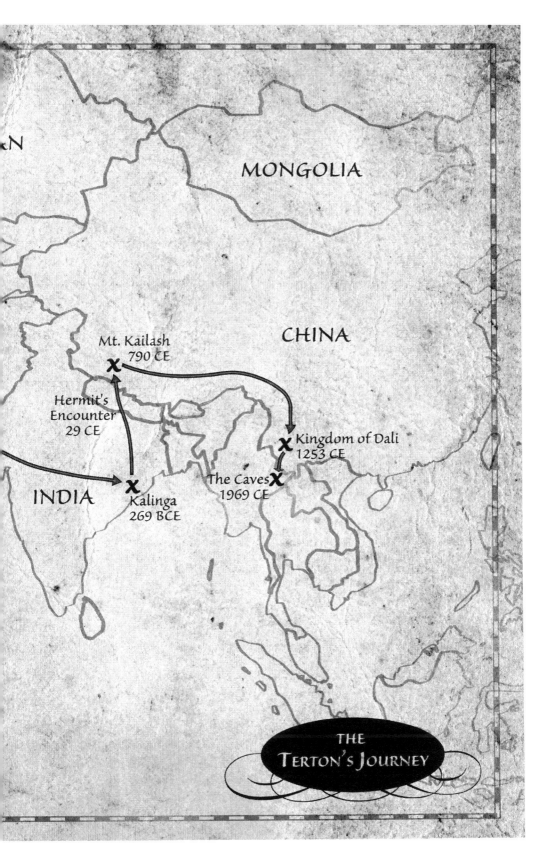

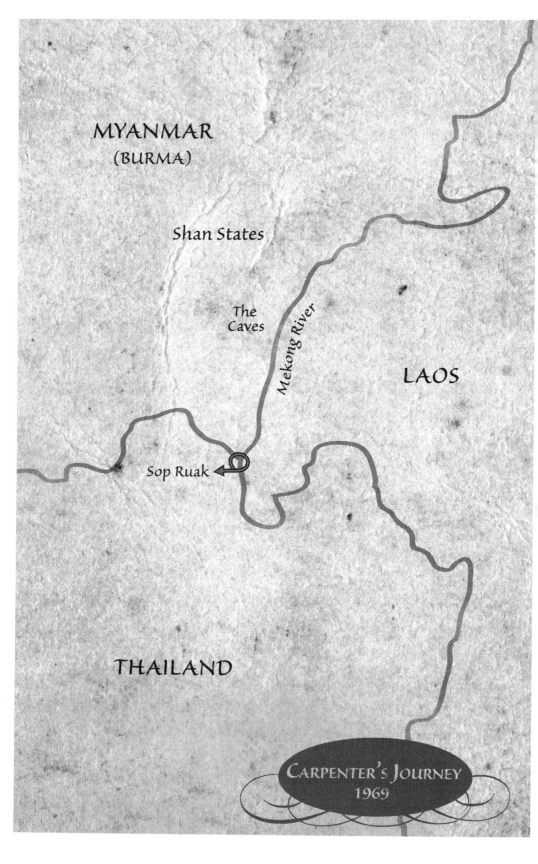

HISTORY

Dreams shape the journey through time and geography described in this book. While the dreams are imagined, their historical roots are not. Here are a few.

Human sacrifice of the kind described at the beginning of the book is alluded to in the Jewish Torah and in several places in the Christian Old Testament. In the latter work, such sacrifices are associated with idol worship and straying from a more righteous path. Specifically, there is mention in 2nd Kings, Chaper 17, Verse 17, which includes these words:

> *And they burned their sons and their daughters as offerings ('passed them through the fire'), and used divination and sorcery, and sold themselves to do evil in the sight of the Lord....*

The sack of Jerusalem and destruction of the temple referenced in Carpenter's dream on the train with Kohein (which name, like 'Aaron', means 'priest' in Hebrew) took place in 586 BCE during what is typically referred to as the Babylonian exile or captivity. Nebuchadnezzar II was king of Babylon at the time. Chaldean soldiers were used to siege and assault the city. A final battle was fought on the plains of Jericho in which there was great slaughter. Many of the elite of Jerusalem were made captive and brought to Babylon. The Jewish king, Zedekiah, was captured and blinded after being made to witness the execution of his sons.

The Persian Gates are located in what is modern-day Iran. In the winter of 330-331 BCE, Alexander the Great's Macedonian army threatened the Persian capitol of Persepolis. Alexander was opposed by a Persian army led by Ariobarzan at this narrow defile in the hills. The Macedonians were trapped and defeated there but soon took Persepolis anyway, which they eventually looted in an orgy of destruction. Legend has it that in his campaign eastward, Alexander entered Judah and left it in peace after Jewish leaders acknowledged his supremacy and possible recognition by the prophet Daniel.

Sir James George Scott was a British journalist who in the mid-19th century argued for the colonization of Burma to prevent further French expansion in the region. Scott traveled extensively throughout Burma and became the first colonial governor of the Burmese Shan States. Though Scott was an excellent observer and writer, the journal alluded to in this story is completely fictional. The people to whom his fictional letter is directed, however, were actual persons. E.B. Gould was British Vice Consul in Chiang Mai. Lord Salisbury, despised by Scott, was the British Foreign Minister at the time. L.T. Leonowens, son of the famed Anna (of Anna and the King of Siam), headed the Borneo Company trading post in Chiang Mai during the same period.

King Ashoka the Great ruled a vast empire from 269 to 232 BCE which included most of the Indian subcontinent, extending from present day Pakistan and Afghanistan east to Assam and south as far as the modern Indian province of Kerala. The early part of his reign was bloody. After conquering the state of Kalinga with devastating loss of life, he embraced Buddhism and sponsored its spread throughout the region and beyond. His stone Edicts, erected after his brutal ascension to the throne, portray him as a gentle father figure. He is highly regarded today as a patron of Buddhism.

Guru Rinpoche, an Indian monk, was a key figure in the establishment of the Vajrayana or Tantric branch of Buddhism in Tibet in the 8th century CE. He is credited with secreting various *terma* or 'treasures' in caves and other remote places that were to be uncovered later by 'truth revealers' or *terton*. Adherents consider Guru Rinpoche to be an emanation of the Amithabha Buddha of the Pure Land Sect.

The Kingdom of Dali was established in 937 CE in what later became the Chinese province of Yunnan. It became a devoutly Buddhist kingdom in its middle years with half of its rulers leaving their thrones to become monks. Dali maintained its independence for several centuries until it was conquered by the Mongols in 1253 under Kublai Khan, founder of the Yuan Dynasty in China.

Indra's Jeweled Net is referenced in the Avatamsaka Sutra or "Flower Garland Sutra". It represents the thinking of the Chinese Huayen school of Buddhism, which scholars consider to be a mixture of Taoist and Buddhist thought. The Flower Garland Sutra began to be committed to writing sometime around the 2nd century CE. Huayen flourished during the Tang dynasty (600-700 CE) and had a profound influence on the development of Buddhism in East Asia. Indra's Net is a central Huayen image representing the inter-connectedness of all things.

indra's net

In the Heaven of Indra, there is said to be a network of pearls, so arranged that if you look at one you see all the others reflected in it. In the same way each object in the world is not merely itself but involves every other object and in fact IS everything else.

— Sir Charles Eliot, **Japanese Buddhism**
describing an image from the Chinese 'Flower
Garland Sutra' (approximately 2nd century C.E.)

The metaphor of Indra's Net may justly be called the first bootstrap model, created by the Eastern sages 2500 years before the beginning of particle physics.

— Fritzjof Capra, **The Tao of Physics**

All men are caught in an inescapable network of mutuality, tied in a single garment of destiny.

— Dr. Martin Luther King, Jr.
Letter from Birmingham Jail

He had drunk the soma and walked unaided in ritual procession to the sacred grove. He had laid himself on the altar stones, on the pyre which the king had commanded them to erect in all the high places and under every green tree throughout the land. The air was heavy with incense and with the blood-stench of burnt sacrifice and the sour fragrance of his own fear. Surely his father would not cause him to be passed through the fire to feed the union of Sun and Moon. Surely the harvest would come.

He watched his uncle struggle as if from a great distance. Saw the hands of his father's men holding him back. Heard the angry shouts from lips used to laughter; the rash demands to take the place of the first-born son.

He saw his beloved teacher turn away in disbelief and shame, tears spilling from gentle eyes. The tough little sergeant, his friend and childhood protector, stood nearby dismayed at his mentor's grief and struggling to contain his own.

He studied his brother's mask of resigned righteousness and piety concealing smug satisfaction. Priest more than brother, next in line to rule. His bearded chin jutted forth in official judgment tinged with private disdain. Father's chief advisor stood at his brother's elbow, secret delight dancing in cold eyes beneath a cruel and hairless brow.

He sought his mother's smile, the comfort of her gentle eyes and iron will. He could not find her.

Now the ropes were wound around his body and his hands and feet were bound with wetted leather. The crescent horns of the god framed the noonday sun overhead. The rough bark of cedar logs scraped against his back. Smoke gushed from the torch in his father's left hand. Sharp reflections danced from the jeweled knife in his right. He turned wide eyes to his father, to the face of his executioner and priest. The face whose cheeks ran with anguished tears, but whose jaw clenched in dread purpose.

He swallowed against the desperate plea building in his throat despite the power of the drug. "Please, Father! Please..." But the eyes that turned away were the eyes of a priest. They dragged themselves upward to the sun, husband to the moon. The left hand lowered torch to tinder. Flames leapt from bundled straw to dry branch. A quaking voice rose above the smoke in fevered prayer. The blade swept downward as flames rose to drink his blood. "Please, Father! Please..."

Bangkok

NOVEMBER 1968

ONE

PANICKED AND DRENCHED IN SWEAT, he startled awake to the crackle of a thin metallic voice.

"… seatbacks up and ready for landing. The local time is 2:00 p.m. Thank you for traveling Pan Am." His eyes opened to the glare of the overhead reading light. His breathing slowed as he fled to the moment and the familiar nightmare image began to fade. Was the dream simply a ghost of anxiety or something more? Why did it come with such intensity, such clarity? Why did it feel more real than imagined? He pulled his long frame forward in the cramped seat. Back to earth … literally, and with relief.

The plane banked steeply left and Carpenter leaned to watch a spiral of golden sunlight sweep across flooded squares of green paddy. Gray streets and buildings circled into view, obscured by vegetation and split by the broad black waters of the Chao Phraya as it snaked through the center of the city. A network of canals crisscrossed the landscape and spread like dark capillaries from the river to the land. For one dramatic moment, a flash of reflected light knit the whole into a single dazzling web of emerald brilliance. Carpenter breathed slowly in and out, filling his mind with the waking image and banishing the shadow of what could only have been a dream.

The thump and screech of rubber on concrete brought him fully awake. He stretched for a long moment, arms overhead, and extracted his legs from under the seat in front of him. He placed his disembarkation card between the pages of Jung's archetypes, shouldered his backpack and waited for a place in the crush of exiting passengers. He stepped to the cabin door, suddenly nervous at the prospect of this first conscious view of his long-forgotten birthplace.

Heat. Unbelievable heat… an assault. He ducked through the exit and onto the stairs. The weight of the air slapped him hard across the face and squeezed sweat from every pore. Asia. The tropics. Bangkok at the beginning of the 'cold' season, just before the harvest. A year already began to seem like a very long time.

At 19, James Carpenter felt a wave of near-panic and unbidden nostalgia for the cool, familiar breezes of home. The brave face he had presented at departure in Seattle melted to a pool of doubt in the pit of his stomach. Waves of thick air shimmered over the tarmac. White glare stabbed his eyes like needles. He squinted against the light. No sunglasses.

Towering over the other, mostly Asian, passengers, Carpenter ducked through the exit, down the stairs and across the concrete struggling for breath in the toxic mix of jet fuel and tar. He followed through the terminal door and up a short flight of steps to where a stern-faced immigration official stood behind a sort of lectern in what looked like military dress.

"Patpot!"

"Excuse me?"

"Patpot! Patpot! *Phood Thai mai pen, le*? You no sapeek Thai, you sapeek Angrit, yet?"

"I'm sorry, I don't understand."

The official pointed impatiently to the passport in Carpenter's hand. "Patpot! You gib me patpot now, OK?"

"Oh, yes, of course. I'm sorry. " Carpenter handed over his passport and yellow International Health Certificate.

"You Amelican, uh?"

"Uh, yes, American."

"No look *farang*. Look Thai. Too big Thai."

Carpenter understood *farang*... foreigner. "Well, part Thai or something - and part *farang*."

"Hap-hap, uh? Mommy Thai?"

"Uh, I don't really know. I don't actually know my real parents." How did the conversation get here so fast?

A quizzical look, then a merciful return to official business. "Nebah mine. OK, Amelican.

Purpot you wisit?"

Carpenter shook his head in confusion. "I'm sorry?"

"Why you come Thailan, huh?"

Another complicated question. Carpenter hadn't expected to be confronted so early on with the true fundamentals. Of course, that wasn't what was being asked here. "Umh, I have an internship for the year with an aid organization? In the North, with hill tribes in Chiang Rai? I'm doing graduate work ... cultural anthropology, ethnography, that kind of thing. You know, group identity, differentiation, social evolution..." Carpenter stumbled on, knowing they both were lost.

"What you do? You wok? You tourit?"

"No. I mean, yes. I'll be teaching English part of the time. You know, at a school? It's a special program from my college?" As if any of this would be of remote interest, let alone comprehensible.

A frown, almost a scowl, then a broad smile of understanding. "Ah, you teacha. Bery good. OK. Dirty day." With a flourish, the official pounded a visa stamp into Carpenter's passport, quickly scrutinized the health document and handed both back with an air of accomplished nonchalance.

Could he have said thirty days? Carpenter decided to worry about that later. Father Wilkins had said he would take care of visa problems once Carpenter arrived in Chiang Rai. Right now, he wasn't even sure how to find his suitcase. "OK, yes. Uh, thank you very much." Carpenter carefully replaced his documents in the black travel billfold his mother had given him, stifling an irrational fear that his passport – perhaps his entire identity – might somehow disappear if he failed to clutch them with both hands. He bowed slightly to the official and waited for direction.

A benign smile. "Wehcum Thailan! You go dah way".

Carpenter followed the other passengers to the baggage claim area and stood waiting alone beneath a slow-moving ceiling fan. He watched the swarm of activity around him, conscious of amused and appraising looks from passersby. At over six feet, he had begun his journey as tallish and emerged as a giant. But still a mongrel - even here - he told himself.

Don Muang airport most resembled a small-town American bus station. Checkered linoleum floors peeled at the edges. Cigarette butts, plastic bags and paper trash pooled around the base of a single stained and overflowing bin. Uniformed officials with epaulettes and military-style caps hurried past stone-faced soldiers in olive drab, M16s clutched to their chests. After a half-hour, several carts appeared pushed by lean, sweatless men with knotted muscles and sun-darkened faces. Carpenter's one bag appeared beneath a cascade of other luggage. He hefted the weathered suitcase his father had lent him for the trip and flushed briefly at the memory of their argument over what Carpenter really needed for this 'useless trip'.

Suitcase in hand, he shouldered his carry-on backpack and proceeded to the customs line. He pictured an eruption of books and clothes as laughing officials held up a copy of the *Tao Te Ch'ing* next to a pair of underwear. Instead, he passed quickly through the line without so much as a glance from the bored agent who waved him on without a word. At the exchange window, he turned twenty-five American dollars into four hundred eighty-five Thai baht, keeping his remaining $75 in reserve.

Feeling more composed, he looked around for a bathroom. No urinals, no commodes. Stalls without doors, each with a small floor-level oval with a hole in the center and footrests on each side. Squatters. No toilet paper, just a small bucket of water to the side presumably doubling for flushing. Sinks, but no soap. He turned a faucet... no water. Strange, lethal germs.

Outside, the sun beat without mercy against the glass doors and sidewalk. Carpenter dropped his suitcase and wiped oily sweat from his forehead. Immediately a half dozen nimble men mobbed him shouting offers of "Taxi, taxi!" and "Numbah 1 hoten, numbah 1 girn!"

One stepped forward, meeting Carpenter's gaze like an old acquaintance. "Where you go? You Japan?"

"To the Orchid Hotel in Bangkok. No, I'm not Japanese."

"Ah, Amelican, uh? Numbah 1! Orchid Hoten no good. No loom."

"No room? How do you know?"

"I know. Orchid all foon. No good. I got numbah 1 hoten. You come!" The man took Carpenter's hand and gestured toward a small blue Toyota covered with mud and rust.

Carpenter pulled his hand away in reflex, feeling the muscles in his neck stiffen. He forced his voice down to a normal register. "How much?" He clutched the Thai baht in his pocket.

"Cheap-cheap! You come!" The driver tugged insistently on Carpenter's hand. "One hundet baht taxi. Two hundet baht hoten, OK?"

"I'll give you 50 baht for the taxi and one hundred for the hotel." Carpenter had been told he must bargain for everything here.

"OK, OK. You pay me taxi now, OK?"

"OK. You got a deal."

"Dean? What dean? You go?"

"What? Dean? No, no, I said a *deal*. You know, a *deal*, an agreement." Carpenter's voice rose with his frustration.

The driver frowned. "You go?"

"Uh, yes, OK. I go."

"OK. Come, come!"

Carpenter tossed his bag into the taxi feeling like a complete foreigner ... the ugly American he so resented. The one he had vowed never to be.

The taxi ride was like no other automobile experience he had ever had. The driver roared down the two-lane highway toward the city at top speed, slicing past slower vehicles and into the path of oncoming traffic as if blind to the possibility of collision. Carpenter gripped the seatback in front of him in white-knuckled fear. A broad black canal choked with hyacinths ribboned by on the left. A naked boy rode a water buffalo into a deep ditch of thick muddy water. Groups of farmers in wide conical hats stooped knee-deep in flooded fields. Pigs and chickens rooted under wooden houses built on stilts five and ten feet above the ground.

Then the rough outskirts of Bangkok itself. A city of four million growing in great leaps and bounds fueled by the influx of American dollars for the war effort to the east. Thousands of GIs in country to support the air war. More each day on leave from Vietnam and possible oblivion. The capitol of an ancient civilization. A westernizing boom town. The "Venice of the East" whose picturesque canals were being filled and replaced by concrete and pavement to accommodate huge numbers of inexpensive Toyotas and extravagant Mercedes flooding the crowded streets.

The driver slowed only by necessity. Traffic coagulated, then stopped altogether. Huge potholes rippled with brown water in the middle of narrow streets. The rainy season had passed, but not the short downpours that came in torrents most afternoons. The streets were clogged with an array of vehicles... motorcycles and pushcarts, limousines with chauffeurs, Japanese compacts in every state of disrepair. Brightly painted trucks with golden angels and silver demons squeezed into impossible alleys. Black exhaust poured from a melee of tailpipes. Horns blared. Music rose from every cinderblock shop front. Temple roofs glistened red, yellow and green in the setting sun. Vendors shouted their wares of jackfruit, papaya and sweet tea in plastic bags with ice. There were people everywhere... moving, sitting, laughing, dancing, singing, scolding, buying, selling. Pungent smells mixed in the air. Charcoal and garlic, onion and coriander, jasmine and rotting garbage. Bangkok. Carpenter swallowed and fought a sudden flush of dizziness.

The hotel was on the Strip. In this chaotic year of 1968, Petchaburi Road was new, without sidewalks, badly paved and lined with bars and short-time hotels. Neon signs flashed from cheap board and block structures with names like *My Blue Heaven, San Francisco* and *Pussy Cat*. Half-naked girls from subsistence farms upcountry danced awkwardly in the windows to the thump of American Top 40 and acid rock. Carpenter climbed from the taxi and dropped his bag in the red dirt in front of the new two-storey *Massachusetts Hotel*. A heavyset American in uniform passed with a slight young girl laughing and clinging to his meaty arm. Carpenter turned away. Above him, towering white cumuli glowed orange and gold. Looking down Petchaburi, the twin frenzies of war and commerce offered a disturbing counterpoint to what otherwise might qualify as a sense of almost spiritual adventure. Was this home?

At the desk inside, he paid the 150 baht demanded, lacking energy to bargain further. First night on the other side of the world and he had ended up at a hooker hotel named *Massachusetts*. His inner judge ran commentary. "Great. Right where all the new babies like me are made." So much for reclaiming his Asian roots.

The girl was sitting in the one chair in what passed for the lobby. He had hardly noticed her when he entered, preoccupied with the prospect of negotiating an acceptable price for his night of lodging. She approached as he started for the stairs.

"You GI? You wanna gullfen?"

"Oh, no thank you. I'm just getting in. It's been a long trip."

"You no wanna gullfen? I Number One gullfen."

Carpenter felt a hot blush redden his face. And something else, something electric and unbidden.

"No, really. Thank you." He hastened up the stairs. At the door to his room, she was still behind him, leaning against the rail on the outside landing facing the street. The glow from the sky bronzed her coffee features and wreathed her black hair in a subtle halo of golden light. Carpenter fumbled with the key.

"Really. Thank you." Carpenter unlocked the door and escaped into the room. A flood of cool air wrapped itself around him. Air-conditioning. A Western-style bathroom with a commode and a shower. Hot water and soap. He rushed to the sink and washed his hands for a full minute. Safe… from dream and reality. For the first time since landing, he felt a guilty measure of relief.

TWO

CLEAN AND COOL, CARPENTER EXAMINED THE FACE IN THE MIRROR. Maybe a shave would feel good. But no need to shave, really. Another dubious advantage of whisker-free genetics.

He opened his eyes wider and pushed lightly with his forefingers at the corners - a ritual repeated countless times to simulate his adoptive parents' 'American' look. He relaxed his fingers. They were Asian eyes, close-set and intense, almost predatory. A startling green rather than the brown they should have been. Thin arching brows over a narrow nose that hooked slightly where it had broken. Smooth brown skin... definitely not in need of a shave. Dark hair but with a hint of auburn and near blonde at the temples.

'What are you, anyway, some kind of Chinese or something?' Yeah, like Bruce Lee, so piss off or learn Chinese the hard way. Carpenter took a deep calming breath to still the boyhood voices that had never gone completely away despite a late growth spurt and years of self-discipline. This is a different place, he reminded himself. Different voices... another language altogether.

He stepped to the window to survey the landscape. As he pulled back the curtain, a small green lizard scurried out and across the wall. Carpenter jumped back, adrenaline racing through his chest. Cute. Probably doesn't bite. Just eat bugs, he assured himself, trying to calm the lingering jangle of nightmare anxiety.

A different place for real. A world to rediscover. He pulled on a T-shirt, shaking his head slightly at the sight of the nametag sewed into the neckband. Overtime mothering. Embarrassing and reassuring. He placed his billfold in the front pocket of his jeans for safety, grabbed his room key and stepped out onto the landing.

She was standing at the railing looking out at the Strip. She turned immediately, an anxious smile forcing its way onto her face. "Where you go?"

"Uh, just for a walk. Maybe get something to eat. Look around a little."

"I go. I show you ebyting."

"Um, no thanks. I think I'd really just like to look around for myself a bit, you know. Just check it out on my own."

She looked closely at him as he spoke, as if analyzing each word and tone. "OK. Maybe latuh, you come back. I be heah."

"Uh, sure. Maybe." He moved on down the steps, nervous and expectant, ignoring a tiny thrill of shame.

Outside, he turned left toward the sweep of lights further down. Cabs and three-wheeled *tuktuks* – motor scooters with small canopied cabs stretched over the driver and a narrow bench in the rear – beeped and smoked along the broken concrete. Psychedelic colors flashed from the dark interiors of a dozen ramshackle bars. A group of small boys sighted him as he passed an establishment bearing the name, *The Soul Shack*. "You! One baht! One baht!"

Carpenter patted his pockets. "Sorry. I don't have change." At least, not enough for everybody.

"You gib me ten baht. I go get chain." A huge white smile flashed out from the largest boy along with a thin brown hand.

I can't really say I don't have ten baht. Carpenter dug into his pockets, avoiding the telltale lump of the billfold. "Hold it. Let me check again. OK. Here you go. Here's one baht."

The leader quickly pocketed the coin as the other boys chorused, "One baht! One baht!" in protest.

"Sorry. That's all I have. Sorry." Carpenter tried to walk past. The boys raced ahead and in front of him shouting, hands out, faces darkening now at the injustice. Other boys down the street looked up and started toward the scene. Carpenter looked around as if for an exit. He couldn't push past. He only had a few coins. He pulled them from his pocket. "Here. This is all I have."

Small hands darted forth. "Gib me! Gib me!" Carpenter poured the coins randomly into palms and fled inside the closest doorway.

The aroma of fried chicken, pork fat and greens filled his nostrils as he closed the door behind him. Across the room someone shouted, "Hey Jimmy, you got any more of that sweet potato pie?" Carpenter turned to see a dozen black faces glance at him dispassionately and return to their private conversations.

To his right, a large man with a balding head and a stained apron looked up from behind a counter. The apron read, "*Jimmy & Noi's Soul Shack* – Best Grease in Town".

"Can I help you?"

"Uh, yeah. I guess so. I just got here." Carpenter felt awkward, torn between entrance and exit. He had planned to eat Thai food for his first meal. To avoid the familiar.

"So I noticed. How can I help you?" the man named Jimmy asked again. "That is, besides offering refuge from that angry mob outside?" He nodded toward the window framing the street where the crowd of boys already had begun to disperse. A slow smile spread across the man's face. "I hope they left you some money, man, 'cause I ain't feeding no white boys for free."

Carpenter felt himself blush in embarrassment. "Yes, I'm sorry. I mean I just got here – you know, to Bangkok – today." The man's smile stayed in place – amused but friendly. Carpenter began to relax. "And, yes, I kept a few baht and yes, I am hungry. It feels like I haven't eaten for about a week."

"Well, come on in then and take a seat. You've come a long way for some down-home cookin'. Where you from... you don't look like no G.I. In fact, you don't look like no white boy either. You American?"

Carpenter bristled involuntarily, then managed, "Yes sir. I'm here for a year from grad school, kind of a work-study thing."

"College boy! You hear that fellas? Finally got an educated man in here." Jimmy addressed the room in general, then turned back to Carpenter. "I guess we can at least feed you, son, as long as you drop the 'sir' bullshit. I ain't that old. What'll you have?"

The food was delicious and comforting. Alone at a small table near the counter, Carpenter hardly looked up from his plate of chicken and greens when the chef took a seat across from him. "So, your first day in country. Ever been here before?"

Carpenter put down his fork to examine the face opposite him. "I'm told I was born here."

"Yeah? Told by whom?"

Carpenter's eyes narrowed as he hesitated, hoping to avoid the unwanted expressions of sympathy he had come to expect. "My parents," he said finally, looking directly into the man's eyes.

Jimmy held Carpenter's gaze and raised his palms in a gesture of gentle submission. "Hey, sorry, Chief. Didn't mean to pry. Just curious about new customers visiting from the World."

Something about the man felt safe. The intelligence in his eyes. The warmth in his expression. Carpenter looked away. "Sorry. I guess I'm feeling a little weird."

"A lot of that feeling weird going around." Jimmy nodded briefly toward the rest of the patrons whose shouts and laughter filled the room with an almost manic electricity. "Most of these guys just got here from Nam for a little R & R. They don't know for sure if they'll make it home. This place is the closest some of 'em may get to the old neighborhood."

"Yeah, I guess I'm pretty lucky. A couple of friends from high school got drafted. One dropped out of college and enlisted … ended up Special Forces in Nam." Carpenter's voice faltered for a half-beat. The image of another open dark face came to mind. Reginald 'the King' Kingston – as he had been dubbed by local sports writers. Bigger than life. Scholar, athlete, protector of the weak and different. Missing in Action before he could vote.

Carpenter remembered his useless arguments with Reggie about enlisting after Tommy Cook was drafted and killed. Carpenter, exasperated, had challenged him. "Why blow your scholarship? One stupid death is no reason to make it two."

Reggie had held up a big hand and stared him down. "Listen, JC. My daddy used to say that a black man in this country is always suspect. He can be a thug or a deadbeat, but not a patriot. Daddy understood that. That's why he went to Korea. Never came back. And my granddad got it too… which is why he ended up on the Burma Road. *He* never came back either. It's in my family, man. I'm not riding this fight out on some deferment I got because I can run with a ball. Not when I got friends getting killed over there."

Carpenter looked up from his private thoughts to see Jimmy watching intently but without judgment. "Yeah, some of us are luckier than others. I made it through two tours myself. Couldn't work up any enthusiasm for going home. Then I met my wife over there…" He motioned toward a thin Thai woman carrying a tray of sausage biscuits to a nearby table. "We opened this place and here I am. I'd call that lucky."

Carpenter rebounded with a relieved grin. "Lucky for me too. I might have starved."

"That's right, we saved your damned life. So, where you gonna be? Here in Bangkok? Up-country?"

"Chiang Rai province. My uncle… he's a Catholic priest… has a small school and sort of a mobile clinic and a church for hill tribe people."

"Chiang Rai, huh? The Golden Triangle itself. That's quite a place. You're talking jungle now. Giant teak trees. Elephants, tigers, King Cobras. Opium poppies and heroin factories… nasty business. A dangerous area, my man. You ready for all that?"

"Actually, I'm more worried about whether I'll have to go to Mass. I'm kind of a recovering Catholic… it's been a while. Anyway, I guess I'll find out." Find out a lot of things, he thought to himself. He'd always wondered about the place, dreamed about it even. Chiang Rai was where his uncle had found him – maybe where his real parents are… or were.

Jimmy seemed to sense something behind Carpenter's words. His response was gentle, non-invasive. "So what's your uncle like? He gonna try to make you into a missionary?"

"I don't think so. I don't really know him… but he *is* a priest. He's kept in touch with my folks and we've written some, but I haven't seen him since I was so little that I don't remember. He's been over here for a long time… with the Columbans and in the army before that in Burma during World War II."

"He Burmese?"

"Burmese? No, he's American." Carpenter recognized the nature of the question now. He felt a familiar rush of shame, a sense that he was somehow flawed at the core, less than other, normal people. Anger followed close behind. Carpenter paused, his bottom teeth clamped on his lip. "He's white, actually." He looked up in defiance to meet Jimmy's eyes. "I'm adopted. He was the one who found me, over here. Nobody seems to know where I'm really from or who I am." Carpenter looked down, pushed out a breath and swallowed to master himself. He struggled to add a note of nonchalance to his tone. "So, it's kind of a mystery since I don't look totally Asian."

Jimmy held Carpenter's gaze and nodded slightly, his expression blank, without judgment. He started to speak, stopped himself, then cocked his head and smiled. "No, you're a mongrel all right. Me, I have so many different genes in my blood I'm like a walking U.N." The conversation lightened up. "But you are a *young* mongrel, whatever your pedigree is. What are you doing in graduate school? You probably can't buy a beer back in the States."

Carpenter relaxed. "I started college early, finished pretty fast. So I still have my deferment. I'm doing kind of a mixed degree in anthropology and sociology and a little evolutionary biology. I'm interested in origin myths, group identity… stuff like that."

"Like how do people get to thinking they're so special, huh?" Jimmy grinned.

"Yeah, like that." Carpenter grinned back. "My father doesn't think it will earn me a living. He's probably right, though I wouldn't give him the satisfaction of hearing me say it. I got a grant from a private foundation so I'm taking advantage of the opportunity to be here."

"An egghead, huh? Actually, social anthropology was my favorite subject at Xavier. Might have got into the Master's program at Tulane if I hadn't got drafted first. Maybe I'll go back and do it someday, who knows? This is an amazing place to be if you're into that kind of thing - especially the North... the foothills of the Himalayas, really. Lot's of different tribal groups, languages, customs."

"Sounds like you got the bug too."

"Oh, I definitely been bit." Jimmy glanced again at his wife who was serving another table and aiming a pointed look in his direction. "Like the song says, 'there's nothing like the real thing'." The big man pushed back from the table. "But, as my dear Noi so often remarks, I tend to talk too much and work too little. I better get my ass back behind that stove before she uses it for a public kickboxing demonstration. Anyway, good to have a fellow student in country. Just one more thing..."

"Sure, anything." Carpenter had deepened his estimation of the man in the stained apron.

"What's your name, Chief? I'm James LaFontaine... Jimmy. Also a recovering Catholic, by the way." A large hand reached across the table.

"Oh, sorry. I'm Carpenter, also James. Pleased to meet you. You know, you remind me of a friend of mine."

"He must be a prince of a guy," Jimmy offered with a laugh.

Carpenter paused, feeling the spread of a slow smile. "Yeah, a king, in fact. Thanks for the down-home Thai dinner."

"Like it says..." Jimmy patted his apron front, "best grease in town."

THREE

NIGHT HAD FALLEN OUTSIDE, though the small breeze it brought did little to cool the thick air. Carpenter felt lighter despite the meal, the heat and the unreal, hurly burly atmosphere of Petchaburi Road. His first friend in Bangkok – a Vietnam vet. "Expect the unexpected, A-Man," Reggie had advised in one of the letters he had written after hearing that Carpenter would be coming to Southeast Asia. 'A-Man' was Reggie's nickname for Carpenter. A fitting counterpoint, he would claim, to his own more relaxed disposition. "Man, you are one hundred percent Type A. You don't get nothing *but* A's. You always angry - with a capital 'A', so you generally are ready to *kick* some 'A'. And you are Always Awake – that's two 'As'. Oh yeah… definitely type 'A'."

Reggie would lean back with a lazy grin. "Now me, I like my sleep. Just check me out in class, man. I take it easy. I'm catching Zs. Fact, you could say I'm more of a type 'Z' myself. You and me are like bookends, you understand? We got the alphabet covered between us… A to Z."

"Yeah, A to Z," Carpenter repeated to himself, wishing he knew what had happened to the other bookend… where he was, whether he was even alive.

Caught up in thought, Carpenter decided to check out the opposite side of the street on his way back to the hotel and nearly stepped in front of a 10-wheeled truck by looking left instead of right for oncoming traffic. He knew Bangkok streets moved on the British model, but habit trumped knowledge. He drew back just in time, cringing at the blast of an air horn. Cars, trucks and small motorcycles – some carrying whole families – whipped by at a variety of speeds. An opening appeared behind another 10-wheeler and Carpenter dodged safely across.

Hendrix boomed from the open doorway of the *Angel Baby* bar. A hand-printed sign promised 'Topless Go-Go' to the tune of 'Purple Haze'. Ahead, crowds of freshly scrubbed young GIs gawked and swelled as nightlife began to erupt in earnest along the Strip. Carpenter stopped in front of the *21 Club*, musing over the possible meanings of the promise of 'LIVE FLOOR SHOW' displayed prominently in the window. The whole scene was off somehow. Like a slumber party at a carnival. He turned at the sound of shouting above the general din.

"Bull*shit*, man! I don't owe you shit!" A crew-cut young man in bellbottoms was shouting at a *tuktuk* driver, who listened impassively to the tirade. Several other GIs started over to the scene, hands outstretched in gestures intended to restore calm.

"Hey, easy man, easy. What's the problem?"

"This motherfucker is trying to rip me off, tha's the problem!" The young man slurred the words slightly.

"He owe 20 baht." The *tuktuk* driver held his ground.

Carpenter approached, looking for a way around the scene. Unable to pass to the left, he stepped around the *tuktuk* and into the street. A horn and a shout blared immediately as a motorcycle screamed up from behind. Carpenter flung himself back in a rush of adrenaline and collided with the angry young soldier who staggered against an onlooker, almost falling, then wheeled on Carpenter in a full-out rage.

"Motherfucking gooks! You are dead meat!" Bellbottoms rushed forward, fists clenched, arms swinging.

Carpenter's reaction was immediate and instinctive. Always younger and smaller, always different, he had put up with years of taunts and bullying before finally putting on size and the need to defend himself physically had started to wane. Before that, he had hounded his parents until they agreed to pay for judo and karate classes at age 9. He had proven to be a prodigy. Fighting had saved him, empowered him. It came naturally and with a ferocity he struggled to control.

Carpenter blocked the first wide blow with a forearm and ducked easily under the next and stepped away. The force of the swing propelled Bellbottoms forward and to his knees. Wild now, he pushed himself to his feet, panting. Carpenter breathed and focused, mentally clearing the red from his vision, determined to control the urge to hurt and punish. He mastered his initial reaction and prepared for the next rush. Bellbottoms lowered his head and drove forward, only to find himself again on the ground with Carpenter standing quietly over him.

"Do we really need to do this?" Carpenter spoke to the man on the ground, while checking his periphery as well. Bellbottom's friends so far had made no moves.

With an angry grunt, the young man was on his feet again, hands positioned for serious combat. He moved warily to his right, then pivoted on his left leg to send a high kick toward Carpenter's head. Carpenter ducked inside the kick, bent low and took the attacker's support leg out from under him with his own low sweep. Once again, the young man hit the ground, harder this time. Carpenter stood and stepped back lightly, eyes still surveying the gathering crowd of military. To his right, the *tuktuk* driver now stood with a small knot of his fellows. A larger melee was brewing.

"Are we finished here?" Carpenter addressed the man on the ground, but let his voice travel to take in the entire scene. The *tuktuk* drivers drew in closer to him. Young GIs edged forward, faces clouding up.

"With style, friend, with style." The deep voice cut through the tension with an air of confident authority. "You have just saved Corporal Kline here from a serious ass-kicking. Old *tuktuk* here would have finished him with some *muaythai*." The remarks clearly were directed to the man on the ground. "Get up, Ben, and thank the man for doing you a favor."

Unsure of this unexpected intervention, Carpenter swiveled to look around for the source. A large crewcut man with a pink face and a broad toothy grin stepped into the open space between the two groups, thick arms spread palms-out in a gesture clearly intended to minimize threat. "Don't worry, friend. It's over. Ben has had too much to drink and he's lost his pointy little head. We're all fresh from the jungle... nobody's thinking too much, least of all Ben here. Sorry... but then Ben's the one owes you an apology."

'Ben' - a young corporal - rose slowly to his feet, rubbing dirt from his elbows and knees. "Christ, Sarge, I dunno what got into me. I jus' lost it." He shook his head and looked from the sergeant to Carpenter and back again. "Man, I'm strung out bad." He looked down at his feet, swallowed and moved his head again slowly back and forth as if in denial. Then, without looking up, voice cracking, "I am completely fucked up... completely." He buried his head in his hands, shoulders shaking, tears dripping through his fingers like rain.

The sergeant wrapped a stout arm around the younger man and extended his other hand to Carpenter. "How about a drink, Champ? I know Ben here could use some more practice."

Carpenter just wanted to escape, but the sight of the young soldier crying and the sergeant's gentle insistence left him feeling awkward and ashamed. Would a 'regular' person get caught in a scene like this? Why was anger so easy and compassion so hard? Now he somehow felt responsible for the whole ugly scene and allowed himself to be led inside.

The *21 Club* was loud and busy. Pairs of freshly scrubbed GIs and mini-skirted bar girls danced beneath strings of Christmas lights as a Thai rock band pounded out a local version of *Mother's Little Helper*. Five quart bottles of ice-cold *Singha* beer stood in the center of the table – one for each of the men seated around it. The sergeant sat to Carpenter's left. Ben Kline – head down, face red - to his right. Other members of the unit completed the quintet.

"Name's Barley," the sergeant began after glasses had been filled. "Let's drink to the World... and getting back to it." Everyone raised his glass. "*Semper Fi!*" Four glasses tilted and drained. Carpenter felt compelled to follow suit. The rich, cold liquid went down easily and hit the spot. Barley refilled his empty glass as soon as it banged down on the table. "So, what's your name, partner, and where did you learn to fight like that? You Special Forces?" Barley turned to flag down a waitress to order another round.

"No, just some training I got when I was a kid." Carpenter left out mention of obsessive training, tournaments won, trophies on the mantel. "I'm James Carpenter. I'm, uh, not in the military, actually. Just here to teach. I have a friend in Special Forces, though," he offered weakly, looking for some common ground.

"You hear that Kline? A goddamn teacher. American, right?" Barley asked, scrutinizing Carpenter's features.

"Yeah, American." Carpenter stifled an automatic reaction, deciding to keep his story as short as possible.

"God bless America! *Semper Fi!*" Barley drained his glass, followed quickly by the rest of the unit.

Carpenter drank again, already beginning to feel the effects. "I'm not much of a drinker. This is pretty strong."

"Oh, yeah. Thai beer has some punch. Not like the weak piss we get back home." Barley looked across Carpenter to Kline. "You hear what the man said? He's not much of a drinker either. You two are practically brothers. Peas in a pod. Pups from the same litter." Barley raised his glass again, "*Semper Fi!*"

Carpenter lifted his again.

"So, how about that apology, soldier? You still seeing gooks, or is that just another ol' dog sitting next to you?" Barley's voice was gentle but direct.

Carpenter was embarrassed for both of them. "Hey, Sarge, it's OK. It's already history, you know."

Barley kept his eyes fixed on Kline. "True. But the thing about history, a man's got to deal with what's happened before he can let it go. Can't just chase the dragon and hope it'll go away." Carpenter could tell the remarks were directed at Kline, not at him. "Dragon'll turn on you when you're not looking. Bite you in the ass. Isn't that right, son?"

Carpenter didn't know what to make of the sergeant's comments, but kept a careful silence, waiting for some sign as to if or how to respond.

Kline kept his face down, eyes closed tight. "Bitch has some sharp teeth." He looked up toward Carpenter, almost meeting his eyes. "You ever have a puppy, man?"

Caught off-guard, Carpenter managed to toss off a response. "No, but my best friend used to call me a dog. I guess that's close."

The attempt at humor didn't seem to register. Kline went on, looking into space somewhere over Carpenter's head, his voice low as if talking to himself. "We used to raise puppies, you know. Labs mostly, and Pointers."

"Yeah?"

"Yeah." Kline glanced quickly at Carpenter's face, then away. "You ever shoot anybody? With a machine gun?"

The table went silent. Carpenter could not reply.

"It's like shooting puppies, you know? They keep on coming up the hill and you keep on shooting and they keep on falling..." Kline's voice trailed off.

Barley reached across Carpenter and took hold of Kline's arm. "Now say you're sorry, son," his voice a near-whisper.

Kline didn't move, though a new stream of tears ran down his cheeks. Carpenter could hardly hear him. "Sorry, man. I'm just all fucked up. I'm trying to get straight, but it's not working too good."

Carpenter's chest tightened. The situation seemed unreal, almost like he wasn't there. He felt awkward and guilty. "Hey, you know..." No other words came. He patted Kline's back, hoping to make up for whatever he should have said. "No problem. It's history..."

"*Semper Fi!*" Barley shouted again.

Carpenter looked around at the chorus line of raised glasses. "*Semper Fi!*" he shouted, and drank.

Toasting continued unabated for another hour. Carpenter finally pulled himself unsteadily to his feet. Kline sat, zombie-like, staring into space, head dipping periodically in a parody of sleep. Sergeant Barley was wide-awake, apparently unaffected by the extraordinary amount of drink he had put away.

"I think I've learned what they mean by *toasted,* " Carpenter quipped as he fumbled for his wallet.

"Put that away, my man. The unit is picking up the tab here." Barley patted Carpenter's chair. "This is no time to quit, Champ. Sit back down."

"I'm sorry, Sarge. I can't do it. I've been in transit since yesterday. I need to find a bed before I crash like Kline there." Carpenter's last ounce of adrenaline had washed away in a tide of cold beer. "Let me pay my share while I can still stand."

"No way, partner. It's on us." Barley looked around the table and back at Carpenter. "We got too few days and too much money. We've got this one. Right, gentlemen?"

Semper Fi! rang out again in ragged unison.

"Well, thanks, guys. Good luck to you. And tell Kline 'so long' for me, alright? Maybe next time, we could start out with a simple handshake, huh?" Carpenter slapped hands all round, stopping at Barley to say, "I appreciate it, Sarge. You could have taken it in a much different direction, I know that."

Barley squeezed Carpenter's hand. "Worked out for everybody, way I see it. We're trying to get the kid straight before we go back – but drinking makes him half-nuts even if it takes the edge off, know what I mean?"

Carpenter frowned and shook his head, "Not really, Sarge."

Barley paused, considering. "Listen, you're a civilian. Probably no way for you to get it, no matter what I say. Maybe I shouldn't say anything at all. But what the hell." Barley shrugged and emptied his glass. "Let's just say there's a lot of ways to get hurt in Nam, son. Not just bullets and mortars. Kline's been smoking too much shit and now the dragon's chasing *him*. He's just a farm boy. Didn't know shit when he got drafted and didn't know shit when he hit the ground six months ago. We're trying like hell to keep him alive, but it may be a losing battle. Double U-O Globe's like a trip to heaven… but with hell to pay."

"Drugs?" Carpenter asked, feeling stupidly naïve.

"Number 4 heroin, son. Pure white flake. Stronger than hitting up on street smack back in the World. One toke, you choke. Kid's been trying to obliterate his memories since our last little picnic in the jungle."

"Shouldn't he be getting medical help or something? I mean, isn't it dangerous to try and fight like that?"

Barley exhaled a deep breath. "Sure it's dangerous… but so is 'getting help'. You might get hospital or you might get the brig. Anyway, he's not alone. Too many like him for the military to deal with. As long as he can point a gun at the enemy, he's good to go."

Carpenter started to respond, then realized he could think of nothing to say.

Barley was shaking his head, "Forget it, kid. Nothing you can do. We'll take care of him ourselves. Home remedy… feed him some speed to keep him going and alcohol to take the edge off. Family that strays together stays to-gether." He pursed his lips and seemed to will the wide grin back onto his face. "Enough of this sad shit! This is R &R … we're on vacation, son! Like I said, it all worked out fine. Kline needed something to move him forward."

He nodded down at the younger man's sleeping form. "Your approach beat the hell out of stepping in front of a bus… or a *tuktuk* driver." Barley looked back to Carpenter and extended his big hand again. "You done alright, kid … good luck." He pounded Carpenter's back in an attempt at light-hearted ban-ter. "And watch your ass, hear?"

Carpenter turned for the door. As it banged shut behind him, he could hear Barley calling for another round amid a hoarse chorus of *Semper Fis*.

Carpenter had to re-orient himself as he faced the street. Vendors squatted by the roadside in pools of harsh light selling fresh flowers, sweet pineapple and grilled squid, calling out to GIs and their escorts as they passed by. An enor-mous yellow moon shimmered overhead, competing with the artificial glare. Blue exhaust mixed with smoke from charcoal stoves and trash fires in a slow, humid swirl. The air smelled of gasoline, cooked fish and gardenia. Gardenia close by. He turned his head toward the fragrance.

"Where you go, sugah?" A broad-faced girl in a tight pink dress stood just behind him, a white blossom tucked over one ear.

"Just trying to figure that out, as a matter of fact." Carpenter swayed slightly on his feet. A slender palm braced him gently from behind then slid slowly around to the front. Carpenter felt himself respond.

"You like Thai girn?" The voice teased as the hand slipped inside his shorts and down past his navel. "Oo! You like me, huh?"

Carpenter blushed and shivered. Gently moving her hand up and away, he turned to look down into a strikingly beautiful face oddly twisted into a doll-like pout. "I like everybody," Carpenter replied. He dropped her hand, bowed awkwardly and turned left up Petchaburi toward the hotel.

The road rose and fell in gentle waves as Carpenter negotiated his return. He skirted puddles and eased past clumps of revelers with careful, measured steps. Spying the hotel across the street, he stood to look each way a half-dozen times before setting out. He crossed without mishap and mounted the steps to his room with arms stretched across the narrow stairwell for balance.

She stood leaning against the railing in the harsh light of a single fluorescent bulb just outside his room where he had left her. "You see I wait you. Wehcome home, nah?"

"Uh, good evening." Carpenter patted his pockets to find his key, avoiding her eyes. No key. Locked out. Nowhere to go. A frantic, lost feeling started in his chest. He frowned as he forced himself to look up. "I can't find my key…"

The girl stepped forward and placed her hand over the pocket holding his billfold. "You put heah." Carpenter patted the pocket, feeling only the wallet's flat surface. "Heah. You gib me." She slid her hand gently into his jeans pocket beneath the billfold and withdrew the room key. Without comment, she turned to unlock the door. Taking Carpenter by the hand, she pushed it open and began to lead him inside.

He pulled back at the threshold. "Listen, I can't do this. I'm sorry."

Confusion. "You no like Noot? You no like girn?"

OK, now I know her name. Carpenter struggled for clarity and control. "Uh, hello, Noot. Yes, I do like girls… and you're very pretty. I just can't do this. It's complicated."

Her expression was blank. "You no wanna make lub? No money… flee, flee. Noot numbah one make lub."

She tugged again at Carpenter's hand until he had joined her inside. The door clicked shut. She slipped the short dress from her shoulders and dropped it to the floor. Naked now, she stepped close, pressing her slim body to him. Carpenter's right hand moved to her breast as if drawn by some unseen force. The other slid down the smooth curve of her back.

She whispered, "Ah, you like, na? You make lub wit Noot na?" Her hand reached for his belt.

Carpenter shook himself and straightened. "*Mai dai. Mai ow. Mai dee.*" I can't. No good. The only Thai words he could think of for the situation.

"*Mai ow, lyr? Mai dee, lyr?*" Her face showed hurt and anger... and something else.

"No pay, OK? No worly." There was a hint of desperation in her voice.

The tone sobered him. He stepped back. "Listen, I don't get it." He drudged up some more of the Thai he had been studying over the past year. "*Mai khawjai. Thammai, khrab? Raw mai rujak gan.*" I don't understand... why? We don't know each other."

She pulled away startled and looked at Carpenter as if for the first time. "*Phood Thai pen, ry? Thammai mai bog?*" You speak Thai. Why didn't you say so?

Carpenter realized he would soon be out of his depth. "No, I don't speak Thai – just *nit noi*, a little bit. I'm just trying to talk to you like a person, you understand?"

Noot bent to pick up her dress and held it against her small breasts. Carpenter tried to keep his eyes on her face, despite the magnetic pull of hormones. She stretched to draw the dress back over her head, exposing the graceful contours of her body from the neck down. Carpenter wrenched his eyes free and swept the room at random to divert his attention. His suitcase lay half-open on the small bed. A sheaf of light blue paper peeked out from beneath a stack of neatly folded clothes. Letters from Reggie.

"My fren gone. Noot no hab loom." Her eyes were downcast as she spoke.

Carpenter thought at first she had read his own thoughts, then realized she was attempting to answer his question. The confusion helped his resolve. "You don't have a room?"

"No loom, my fren stay wit her GI."

Carpenter regained full control of himself. Great. My first night in Thailand and here I am in a short-time hotel ready to buy sex with a night's sleep for a homeless hooker. Maybe make another baby like me.

He spoke gently. "Look, you can stay here, OK? I'll sleep on the floor. You can have the bed."

Noot frowned in confusion. "You no wanna make lub?"

"Of course I do," Carpenter started to explain, then gave it up. "Never mind, it's too complicated. I just want to get some sleep." Maybe without a nightmare sacrifice this time.

She met his eyes and smiled. "OK, never mind. You take bed. I take bath." Problem solved, she turned abruptly and disappeared into the bathroom, leaving Carpenter wondering if he would find things out about himself here where he began that he hadn't expected and didn't really want to know.

FOUR

THE NIGHTMARE CAME AGAIN TOWARD DAWN. Anger. Heat. Terror. But now he watched from a distance, as if standing over the altar pyre, his vision blurred by tears. Flames enfolded his body as it struggled against its restraints. His own voice called out to him in desperate supplication. Profane lips whispered soft assurances in his ear. Depthless shame engulfed him like a crematory fire. Then, through the swirling smoke, another face. Indistinct, but still strangely familiar – like a memory hovering on the edge of recollection. A woman. Her dark eyes bore into his with an intensity that rivaled the flames, cooled them. Her voice soothed and guided. "Nothing has power beyond what you choose to give it. Accept what cannot be changed and move on." The words merged with the sound of chanting voices and crystal chimes echoing gently through hollow rock and tumbling water.

Sunlight struck Carpenter's eyelids like searchlights in a manhunt. He opened his eyes, then shut them quickly against the ungodly glare. Lurid images lingered there. Why did this nightmare keep coming back? Why did he feel it this way? He opened his eyes again and yesterday's events rushed forward. Dream images lifted like morning fog. Thoughts of Noot rushed in to displace the fantasy-woman's face and voice. He sat up to look around the empty room. The girl was gone. Relief and regret mixed in equal measure with the pain in his head. He laid back for several minutes to give his body time to recover and his mind a chance to find the moment.

How had it all happened? An acutely private person spilling his guts to everyone he met. A street fight his first day in the land of Buddha. Drinking to the greater glory of the Marines in a war he hated. Very nearly abandoning conscience for sex. Of all people, James Carpenter of the slanty green and badly bloodshot eyes. The motherless child … ready to become another father rushing for the nearest exit. So ready to blame everyone but himself. He swung his feet over the edge of the bed and sat up. He breathed and stretched. He fought a familiar sense of shame. Good old Catholic guilt… move on.

He showered and dressed. The journey was hardly over. He still had to make his way north to Chiang Mai to meet up with Father Harry, then on to Chiang Rai and finally to the mission further on. As he gathered his things to re-pack, the bundle of Reggie's letters fell from his suitcase and spilled across the floor. Carpenter knelt to retrieve the scattered papers, then sat on the bed to put them back in order. He scanned the familiar pages as he re-shuffled them.

October 16, 1967

JC,
Sorry I haven't written before now. Just getting here and getting oriented has been insane. There's a lot of us coming in and it feels crazy – like someone sent an invitation but didn't expect so many to show up.

The first thing, it's hot. I mean H-O-T. I told you Basic was bad down in North Carolina, but that was nothing compared to this. This isn't even the hot season according to locals. Rains every day. Huge downpours, then it gets hot again. They say the cold season comes in a couple of months. We'll see. I doubt it will be a white Christmas.

Most of the regular Army guys are right out of high school. Drafted and scared shitless. It didn't take long before we saw some body bags. I feel like an old man and I get carded trying to buy booze back in the world. That's what they call home, by the way – the 'world'. Anyway, I'm one of the few with some language training, so the other guys tap me for inter-preting, especially with the ladies. Could have stayed home to pimp.

Will probably move into the hills after some time in the field down here in the plains...

Carpenter pulled another page at random.

December 1, 1967

Merry Christmas,
Just a quick note. Made it to the cold season and still waiting for the cold. We're back out on patrol tomorrow after a week in Saigon. Unreal. Seems like half the Army is high. Weed is strong and they sell heroin in noodle shops and roadside stands like lemonade. Can't wait to move north. The war here in the lowlands is a complete mudfuck. Been working on lan-guage and should be up with the Hmong in a couple of months if I don't get shot in the ass.

And another.

July 22, 1968

JC,
Just finished many moons in the Central Highlands. A much better duty – amazing even. Definitely better than down in the cities where you're not sure who the enemy is. The hill people have their own thing going – not really into 'nationalism' – just their own tribe and village. They are minorities here and don't get a break from the lowland Vietnamese or the government. Finally feel like I'm fighting for something that matters. It's surprising how fast you can learn a language if nobody else speaks English.

You'd love it here - except for the war part, of course. The Hmong have their own distinctive dress – beautiful embroidery. The women wear pleated skirts they make by sewing in the pleats and soaking and drying the cloth, then taking out the stitches. They make the cloth themselves by hand from cotton they grow. And dye it with colors they make from plants. You'd be in your element – plenty to study.

I start a new assignment soon. Can't say much about it except it will still involve contact with Hmong, but not here in Nam. I'll be in the mountains some. The air war is heavy duty and we are losing planes and copters and pilots. A big fiasco last April when a spotting site got overrun in Laos. So probably will be involved in some rescue ops.

Congratulations on the fellowship! I may be at Nha Trang but could be in northeast Thailand too. Udorn airbase is huge, about a hundred klicks from the Lao border. So, I may be closer to where you'll be. Maybe we can hook up in Bangkok. Or maybe I can get over to Chiang Rai. Can't really say – even if I knew.

And then the last one.

September 14, 1968

JC,
Not sure when this will get to you. Not even sure you'll get it or if it will get "edited" before you do. I'm sending it out by the friendly skies of a local airline, which shall remain unnamed. If it smells like poppies, just think of them as the flowers I forgot to send you for Valentine's. Ha ha.

The country we get into is incredible – very remote, steep hills and deep valleys. I think I could get used to living here except I would miss a hot shower and a hamburger now and then, not to mention a good night's sleep. Lots of strange dreams lately – waking up every night trapped in someone else's battle, but mad as hell. I swear the pictures in my head feel more like memories than dreams. I see my granddad working on the Ledo Road, then my daddy somewhere in Korea. They talk to me, but I can't understand what they're saying. They're just over a hill that I keep climbing but never cross. Funny what can float to the surface when you're out of your depth, like me sitting here in the middle of nowhere.

Almost a year now, but it feels longer. Not so sure what to make of the current assignment. Some weird shit going on. Can't say much about it. I think I'm starting to understand your point of view – you always were the smart one. Not so sure who the good guys are anymore. I'll tell you about it when I see you. Got your letter and asked about Sop Ruak in Chiang Rai. It's way the hell north in the Golden Triangle on the Mekong. Hope you know what you're doing. Anyway, I probably can make it there if we can't meet up in Bangkok.

That's it for now, little brother.

Amen A-Man,
Reg

P.S. My mother said you stopped by – thanks. Ricky's getting into some trouble hanging out with older kids. Sounds like he's getting into some serious drugs, though she would never say it right out. If you get a chance to beat some sense into him, be my guest. I'd do it myself, but I'm kind of tied up for the time being.

Carpenter thought back to his visit with Reggie's mother and her desperate concern for Reggie's younger brother. In a way, maybe it was better for Reggie to have gone missing. It would have killed him to hear what finally happened. He folded the letter back into its envelope, bundled it together with the others and placed the packet between layers of clothing before shutting the suitcase. No more letters, no word at all. Simply 'missing' according to the official words of the military.

Carpenter settled his bill at the front desk and asked the young man there to put in a call to the church at the provincial seat of Chiang Rai. Father Wilkins was supposed to be there today to take his call. There was no phone at the mission or in the town of Sop Ruak. Carpenter gave the clerk the number and waited for the connection to go through. After a short wait and an exchange in Thai, the young man handed Carpenter the receiver.

"Hello? Father Harry? Harry Wilkens?" Static, then a thin voice crackled across the line.

"Paw Harry mai yoo, khrab. Krai pood?"

"I'm sorry. I don't speak much Thai. This is James Carpenter calling from Bangkok. Do you speak English?"

"Oh yeah. Almost like a native... South Boston, actually. How you doing?"

Carpenter laughed. "OK, thanks. Who's this?"

"Brother Joe Mallory. Welcome to Thailand. Harry said you'd be calling. He's not here right now. I came down from the mission to be sure someone answered when you called."

"Oh... well, thanks. Pleased to meet you. I'm actually getting on a train today – the 12:10 to Chiang Mai from Bangkok. Father Harry said to call when I was about to leave. I'm not sure when the train will get in. The guy here said something like 20 hours. Could that be right?"

"Sure, if all goes well. Of course, then there's the ride up here to Chiang Rai and then north to Sop Ruak and then up into the hills to Sangor and the mission. Listen, Harry was due a couple of days ago from the sticks, but he's not back yet. So if he doesn't show in time, one of us will be at the railroad station to pick you up tomorrow... if the Land Rover is running. I think Brother Edward is planning to go down to Chiang Mai, so don't sweat it. If it's me, I'll be the short fat white guy in the blue shirt. He'll be the short fat brown guy with an Indian accent. One of us will be on the platform or just inside the station, OK?"

Carpenter liked Brother Joe already. "Great, thanks Brother Joe."

"Just Joe will do. Whadda I call you?"

"Carpenter is good."

"And good enough for our Lord. See you when you get here. Listen, there's a phone at the station in Chiang Mai if you need it and if it's working. And there's the one at the church here in Chiang Rai too, which is where I'll be if I can't get the Rover running. So you can try to call here if you don't see one of us in Chiang Mai."

A comforting thought. "OK. Uh, how far is it to Chiang Rai?"

"Oh, we're another couple hours or so from Chiang Mai, if it doesn't rain too bad, which it shouldn't since we're past the real monsoon season. But we can worry about that once you make it to Chiang Mai."

"Thanks. I guess I'll see you tomorrow, then." Carpenter began to feel a leaden weariness settle into his bones.

"Let's hope so. The power of prayer and all that. Listen, I hope you're not tall. Are you?"

"About 6'3". Why?"

"Sweet Jesus. Never mind. Try to find a seat by yourself so you can stretch out, alright? At least it's not the bus or you'd feel like a goddamn pretzel by the time you got here… sorry, Lord." A long-suffering sigh. "Good luck, kid."

The line went dead. Carpenter looked at the receiver in his hand, wondering if Brother Joe had hung up, been cut off or struck down by the hand of the Almighty. He passed the phone back to the clerk, hefted his bag and headed into the morning heat to find a cab big enough for a goddamn pretzel.

FIVE

HUALAMPHONG RAILWAY STATION WAS A WORLD IN ITSELF. Its huge arc of roof curved over the flat Bangkok skyline like an overturned oil drum half-buried in a child's sandbox. Carpenter paid his 10 baht taxi fare, dragged his battered suitcase to the curb and turned to survey the hangar-like space.

Fruit and drink vendors dotted a wide paved area leading to a bank of open doors. Along the ground, mounds of purple mangostene, green papaya and spiky red rambutan lay heaped on straw mats like daubs of color on a Gauguin palette. Sarong-clad women and tiny children wove through the crowds of arriving and departing passengers bearing baskets of grilled chicken, fish cakes and fist-sized portions of sticky rice wrapped in banana leaves. There were no other Westerners in sight. Rail-thin dogs cowered at the edge of the crowd, outcast and scavenging, but somehow more a part of the scene than Carpenter felt himself.

He began to work his way toward the station doors, fascinated by the riot of sights and sounds. Stepping to avoid the edge of a vendor's mat, he tripped and nearly fell as his left foot snagged on something solid but yielding. He caught himself and glanced back. On the ground, legs spread wide for balance, a person of indeterminate gender sat holding a small child in one arm and a wicker basket in the other. Toeless feet protruded from a tattered sarong spread over short legs. Milky eyes stared up from a ruined face whose nose seemed to have melted away to little more than a lump of flesh with breathing holes. Carpenter drew in a quick breath, took a step back and stopped as the blunt gaze locked him in place. The basket moved toward him clutched in a tightly clawed hand.

"*Khoa tang noi, na kha*". The basket moved with a sense of righteous urgency. Horrified, Carpenter fumbled in his pocket and gently placed a fistful of *baht* in the basket. "Um, I'm sorry. Please… excuse me. I'm sorry…" He turned quickly away toward what seemed now to be the distant station doors.

Inside, a vast umbrella of structural steel and soot-blackened plastic panes arched over half a dozen train tracks that stretched straight out into the blaze of morning light like ladders to infinity. Carpenter stood, arms drawn in tight, trying not to obstruct the river of humanity flowing past from all directions. Occasionally, he caught a word or phrase of the language he had studied during the year before but could not now begin to comprehend. He looked around for a ticket booth. Signs dotted the walls and track heads, but all displayed only the exotic but otherwise impenetrable Thai script.

A hand tugged gently on his sleeve. "Excuse me. Might I be of help?"

Carpenter turned toward the deep voice which, to his surprise, belonged to a heavyset middle-aged man whose dark eyes and face were nearly level with his own. The man's elegant dress distinguished him from others in the passing crowd. His English was flawless; British-inflected and with a slight guttural accent. A thick black mustache framed purple lips stretched across large white teeth in an amused smile that brought such a rush of déjà vu that Carpenter found himself at first unable to respond. The voice continued. "Please forgive the intrusion. I couldn't help but notice that you seemed a bit confused."

Recovering, Carpenter answered, "Oh, sorry. I just had one of those feelings… I mean, yes, thank you. I was looking for a ticket booth, actually. I don't really speak much Thai and can't read the signs at all."

"Of course. And I wasn't certain whether or not you were Thai, though you hold yourself rather like an American. Amit Kohein…" the speaker said, offering a hand adorned with two very large rings set with some sort of precious stones.

"James Carpenter. Good to meet you Mr. Kohein."

"Yes. Well, where are you headed young man? I speak the language and perhaps can be of some assistance."

"Chiang Mai, actually. The 12:10 train."

"Ah, Chiang Mai. My destination as well, as luck would have it. Track 6 is ours. Tickets may be purchased on board, you know." The man glanced down at a heavy gold wristwatch. "And we may very well be leaving on time. Shall we proceed?" He stooped to pick up a richly oiled, loose leather bag set down across his feet to protect it from the grit-blackened floor. Carpenter followed to the Track 6 platform and the two walked together toward the front of the train.

"Were you planning first or second class? I prefer third myself in preparation for the less accommodating amenities available in Chiang Mai… and elsewhere," he added rather curiously. "The price is difficult to beat, although it does become rather crowded."

"I'm on pretty limited funds, actually." Carpenter realized he was embarrassed at having to mention cost, given the stranger's obvious wealth.

"How does sixty baht sound... three American dollars?" Kohein responded easily, without a hint of condescension.

"Just sixty baht? Oh, that's great! I can certainly manage that." Carpenter began to relax.

"Then, perhaps you would care to join me? I welcome the opportunity to speak English, though I do have a tendency to prattle on if you'd rather a bit of quiet."

"That'd be great, Mr. Kohein. But I may drift off at some point. I just got here yesterday and my clock is kind of out of whack."

"I'm likely to do the same. It's rather a long trip. And please, you must call me Amit."

"'Amit'. Is that like 'Ahmed', or am I totally off?"

"Well, yes, the sounds are quite similar. I had several friends named Ahmed as a child in my country." Kohein gestured to the entrance of a car near the front of the train. "Shall we?"

Carpenter shrugged sideways with his pack and suitcase and followed Kohein down a narrow aisle to a pair of bare wooden seats facing each other toward the rear of the carriage. The interior looked like something from an Agatha Christy novel. Rich teak paneling graced ceiling and walls. Handrails and luggage racks shown like brass. The wood-framed windows, Carpenter saw, could be raised to allow passengers to lean out and call to vendors on the platform below. He wrestled his suitcase onto the overhead rack and took a seat facing front. Kohein eased into the opposite place, resting the leather bag close to his side.

Settling back, Carpenter looked across to his new traveling companion. "So are you from the Middle East?" he asked, curious if Kohein were Arab and wondering how he had come to be in Thailand.

"Yes, Iraq, actually, but not Arab if you are wondering. Simply another wandering Jew, if you will. 'Amit' actually is Hebrew for 'friend' while 'Ahmed' is short for 'Muhammed'. The sounds and in some cases even the meanings of words are often shared among Semitic peoples... and beyond. Interesting, yes?"

Carpenter began to respond, but Kohein continued on, clearly delighted at the prospect of conversation. "Did you know, for example, that the Thai word for 'friendship' has the same root sound as 'Amit'? *Mitrapaap* is 'friendship' in Thai, likely derived from the original Sanskrit. And *pen mit gan* means 'to be friends'."

Carpenter grinned. "Makes me want to break into a verse of 'What a Friend We Have in Amitabha!'"

Catching the reference, Kohein laughed in turn. "Indeed, indeed. I see you have stayed with me here, despite my wandering references. I also see you recognize the Amitabha from the Pure Land Sect of Mahayana Buddhism. Perhaps you have read the relevant *sutras*? The root '*amida*', you know, can be traced back from the Japanese and Chinese to Tibetan."

Carpenter remained still. Kohein clearly had plenty to say... probably on almost any topic.

"We know the Amitabha Buddha promised eternal bliss to his devotees. What greater 'friend' could there be, I ask you?" Kohein's eyes widened in mock discovery of a new world of possibility.

Carpenter laughed, delighted. "There is also the French for 'friend' ... as in '*mon ami*', or 'friendship' – *amitee* - which is like the word 'amity' in English – both derived from Latin, I believe."

"I confess I had not made that particular leap. But it follows the same reasoning – whimsical though it may be." Kohein cocked his head as a new thought sprang up. "Isn't it interesting that 'amity' sounds so much like 'enmity'?" Kohein shook his head and directed a resigned look at Carpenter. "And so we have the sad and contradictory history of my homeland... really of this struggling world itself... reflected in what might once have been a single undivided source."

Kohein took a quick breath, ready to go on, then stopped to give Carpenter a self-conscious smile. "Speaking of history, this must qualify as the most complicated answer to a simple question in all recorded time. Forgive me, my mind tends to race at times - and to run away with my tongue."

"No, no, please! Don't apologize. The world truly is a maze. Maybe I should say 'amazing' just to keep the ball in the air," Carpenter offered a playful laugh. "But, seriously, I do love to follow the pathways – even if I tend to get lost in them. Like with the Amitabha. I'm not Buddhist, but I've done a lot of reading on Buddhism and other religions though I don't have anything like your obvious familiarity with it. Are you a professor or student yourself?"

Kohein lowered his eyes, embarrassed. "Oh, no. Not a scholar, but a student of sorts, I suppose. I do have a particular interest in the Huayen School - and in various Tibetan traditions. But I am purely self-taught, I'm afraid. I simply am blessed – or cursed - with what I have been told is a rather pernicious sense of curiosity. I can only hope that intellectual acrobatics serve to keep the mind limber rather than causing permanent injury. No, I am not a professor or scholar, but merely a humble merchant and tradesman."

Carpenter was fully engaged. "Well, however you have managed it, your scholarship is impressive. I'm a student myself, in anthropology."

"Ah then, another intrigued by the mystery of the human journey. And there is much to learn in this particular region, I have found."

"So you come here frequently?" Carpenter asked.

"Oh, yes. My business – I have a modest jewelry shop in Bangkok - brings me here several times a year to find product. Burma – just across the border - is a major source of stones, though it is a difficult and rather dangerous place to travel. There is, however, a great deal of traffic of one kind or another across the border in the more remote parts of the two countries… due mostly to the drug trade, I must say. So I have had opportunities to see territory that most travelers do not."

Kohein dropped his voice and looked around nervously as he spoke. "But the rewards can be worth the risk, if you are careful and circumspect. And…" he began to proceed, then checked himself without offering further detail. His hand came to rest on the satchel at his side. He sat back, resuming a more normal volume of speech. "But I burden you with petty commercial matters. What is particularly interesting in the North is the extraordinary proliferation of ethnic groups – a veritable Galapagos of humanity, as it were. But please, tell me about yourself. How have you come to be here?"

Carpenter wondered again at the frequency with which his own origins had edged into otherwise superficial conversation since his arrival. He felt a real, if unmerited, comfort with Kohein despite their short acquaintance. He decided to bring the issue to the fore himself rather than let it sneak up on him later. "Well, I'm from here originally… born in the North, as far as I know, adopted by an American couple and raised in the States. An American priest, my mother's brother actually, found me when I was a baby."

Kohein betrayed no reaction to the mention of adoption. "And you are on the way to visit him, I presume?"

Carpenter felt a degree of excitement talking freely like this about personal issues. Perhaps because Kohein was a stranger. Perhaps because he did not seem like one. "Yes, he's still in Chiang Rai province, in a small village called Sangor near Sop Ruak on the Mekong River. He arranged a teaching job for me and I'll also do a small study involving some of the tribal peoples in the region – their origin myths and how they define themselves."

Kohein's response reflected an appreciation for levels of implication rather than a penchant for judgment. "Ah, so your journey combines the personal and the academic. I see now why your looks and manner portray such contrasts. A brave journey for such a young man. I salute you."

"Of course, there's no guarantee I will learn anything about my own antecedents, but my uncle definitely knows more than anyone else – more than I do anyway – about where I come from. He's been in the area since World War II... all through Burma and Laos. He speaks several of the languages."

"Excellent. And what peoples will you come to know?"

"Father Wilkins - that's my uncle - works with Akha and Meo tribes now, so I should have opportunities to spend time in some of their villages. I did a good bit of reading on the ethnology of the region last year and would love to learn more about the Chin as well. But, of course, they are mostly further west in Burma and northern India."

"Yes. As it happens, I have friends among the Chin and Kachin, and the Shan, as well as the hill Chinese and others. I share your interest in the Chin. Did you know some branches claim a distant connection to the Jews?"

"Actually, I do. I read something to that effect about the Minoche branch in northern India. Apparently some of their customs and rituals bear resemblance to Jewish practices. An elder claims they are descendants of one of the so-called 'lost tribes'."

"Precisely. The entire area is a patchwork of humanity stretching along the ancient Silk Road from the Middle East to China. All of northern and northeastern Burma – like northern Thailand and western Laos – is just such an ethnic wonderland. A pity travel is so risky, but of course it is the risk and the remote nature of the region that help preserve its character... and its mystery."

Carpenter could not help but ask. "I'm probably being too forward, but I wonder if there would be any chance that I could accompany you on one of your trips into the less traveled areas? I mean... if it wouldn't be too much of an imposition?"

Kohein's lips drew together in a brief grimace. "You understand, of course, that my travels are of an ... ah, unofficial nature? It would be difficult, to say the least, to bring others along – not simply for the risks involved, but because my contacts are rather suspicious of strangers... often with good reason."

Carpenter immediately regretted having spoken so completely on impulse. "Mr. Kohein – Amit – I'm sorry. Please forgive me for even asking. I really over-stepped there."

Kohein's expression relaxed. "Please. No need to apologize, my friend. You are, after all, both young and American. Really, it is I who should apologize for speaking of it at all. As much as I would welcome your company, I'm afraid it would be impossible to invite you along. I'm very sorry."

"I didn't mean to presume."

"Not at all. I am flattered by your interest. But you see, the area is particularly dangerous at this point in time. The poppy trade has blossomed, so to speak, with the growth in heroin consumption in your country and, I'm afraid, among your military in Vietnam."

"I ran into some American soldiers last night. They were on R &R from the war." Carpenter paused, considering. "They mentioned the drug problem in Vietnam, too. And a friend of mine in the Special Forces said heroin was everywhere there. Like it was an open secret."

"Well, the trade certainly has flourished in recent years. It lines a number of influential pockets. The 'Golden Triangle', as it is called, is golden for some and quite wild, I'm afraid. Lawless... but for the simple rule of survival of the fittest or best-armed. Much of the opium is grown in Burma. The profits help finance various armed struggles against the government. There are remnants of the Kuomintang Army there that fled after their defeat in the Chinese civil war. They now control the drug trade, though others are involved as well... Shan rebels, the Burmese Communist Party, even Red Guards from Yunnan province. And there are the Wa and the Kachin who have revolted and need arms and the money to purchase them."

"I didn't realize how complicated it is."

"Nor, I'm afraid, has your government," Kohein replied, then paused to consider whether or not to proceed. "Forgive me, politics is a minefield – not a good topic for new acquaintances seeking to become friends."

"That's OK, I won't be offended." Carpenter attempted to ignore an urge to defensiveness, despite his protest to the contrary.

"Yes, well, America is a great empire. Great empires often mean well – or convince themselves they do - even if their actions seem to contradict their stated intentions. Laos, for example – the poorest country in this struggling part of the world - is being devastated as we speak, though I'm afraid your leaders deny it altogether. But bombs are falling there, not dominoes."

"Do you think the whole 'domino' thing is manufactured?" It seemed so obvious to Carpenter that the domino metaphor was an easy one to make once the players had accepted that the pieces were all black and white.

Kohein thought for a moment. "No, but I do believe it is about fear. The irony, if you will forgive what surely sounds like preaching... the irony is that your people seem to fear the rest of the world despite your strength. Perhaps because you know so little of it." Kohein finished, shaking his head slowly, then seemed to come to himself again. "Ah, but the point here was travel into Burma. I seem once again to have wandered rather far afield. Forgive me. I'm afraid I am given to strong but weakly managed opinions."

"Not at all. I understand, really." Carpenter took a deep breath. "In some ways, you know more about my own country than I do."

Kohein raised a hand in gentle dismissal. "Not at all, but I do believe I know more about the rest of the world than your country does about us. The world pays attention to America. It must. We admire you, you know, or envy you at the very least. You, on the other hand, sometimes seem not to notice that the rest of us exist. I fear some day you will be forced to do so."

Carpenter began to respond and Kohein raised his hand once more.

"Perhaps that is enough of politics, my friend. We have only just met and are barely acquainted, though I feel that I have known you for some time. Perhaps we were intended to meet. I must admit I felt an odd connection when I first saw you in the station." He nodded to himself. "Indeed. How fortunate to find a kindred soul in such an unlikely place."

* * * * * *

The train moved slowly northward through what seemed to Carpenter like a storybook landscape. The low central basin of the country - it's great, fertile 'rice bowl'- stretched away from Bangkok in vast open flats of wetland and networks of thatched roofs, dirt tracks and shallow waterways. Every hour or two, the train groaned to a stop amid the shouts and bustle of vendors bearing baskets of food and drink and hurrying to negotiate a sale through the carriage windows before the behemoth jerked forward once again.

Sometimes at a distance, but often very close to the tracks, Carpenter could see the dazzling red, green and yellow-tiled roofs of temples glistening in the tropic sun. Several housed huge sitting Buddhas of shiny brass or bronze, some sparkling with hundreds of tiny squares of gold leaf pressed and fluttering against the base. Saffron-robed monks sat beneath shade trees in quiet conversation or droned Pali chants in the cool air of open-sided pavilions.

Here and there along the narrow canals, fishnets fixed to bamboo frames hovered over the water like giant storks dipping for fish and eels. Dreamy-eyed water buffalo cast their indifferent gaze at the passing train, submerged to their necks in brown water, huge curved horns and broad snouts shiny slick with mud. Small villages dotted the sweep of green fields like tiny islands in an undulating sea. Women in dark tops and long *sarong* worked side by side with men in loincloth *pha khawma* as they bent to the harvest. More than once, a still landscape sprang to life as human figures seemed to emerge fully formed from the dark soil of ditch and dike. For Carpenter, the scene was at once breathtakingly exotic and peacefully mundane.

Hours passed with Kohein in conversation that swung from the philosophical to the personal. Kohein explained how he had learned to make and market jewelry from his father. Then of the deep conflict in that relationship over Kohein's determination to marry his first love, an Arab girl. Then of his increasing sense of isolation in a land grown hostile to Jews after 1948 and the Palestinian exodus from Israel. He spoke fondly of his childhood friends – Arab Sunnis and Persian Shi'a – and with regret at the distance that had grown between them despite the common struggles their families had shared.

Kohein was unlike anyone Carpenter had encountered before, despite the inexplicable sense of familiarity he felt with him. Impulsive, even rash, but with the courage to act decisively without hesitation if need be. Kohein's decision to leave his home for a country he had only ever read about struck Carpenter as both brave and dangerously naïve. He listened, amused, at Kohein's tales of family life in Bangkok with his Thai-Chinese wife and in-laws, of his utter devotion to his three children and to a business that had boomed with the influx of American soldiers and dollars.

Despite his struggles to remain awake, Carpenter at last sank into exhausted sleep as the sun began to dip behind the rise of hills forming in the distant west. Kohein continued to hold forth, moving from topic to topic with complete personal and intellectual abandon. Carpenter was able to make out one last musing before slipping into unconsciousness.

"Of course, we Jews are everywhere by now after so many years of exile and escape. But are we not all members of some lost tribe? Lonely seekers running from ourselves while joined at the hip by Creation itself? There must be something like God at work within each of us. But if we truly are made in His image, my friend, then I doubt that He sits idly on some heavenly throne. No, if He made us as Himself, then the word 'God' itself must be a verb."

SIX

HE OPENED HIS EYES TO DARKNESS. *Had he dozed off? Night had descended on the city. Enemy campfires burned like candle flames in a circle beyond the city's walls. He watched through a sentry's nervous eyes from atop the inner-most enclosure. Clearly, peace could not be purchased again. Jerusalem would not be spared. Neither gold nor blood would satisfy the wrath of Nebuchad-nezzar. This time, the holy city would die.*

His uncle pulled his large frame to the top of the ladder, an amused smile gleaming white through black mustache and purple lips. "Hunger has left little strength for fighting, nephew, and I am too much a coward. I see no path for escape. Zedekiah is too proud to lead us into exile. I say give Nebuchadnezzar his victory and find a way to survive."

He heard himself speak defiance. "The tyrant will either kill us in battle or take us as slaves in surrender. I will fight so long as I can stand."

The beat of massive oak against the gates pounded like thunder. Wood shat-tered and split. A deep voice rang out from below. "You up there! Down... quickly! The gate is breached. Follow me. Muffle your weapons and make no sound!"

A rapid descent down a steep ladder. Swept up in a crowd of soldiers moving toward the King's gardens. The scholar's hand on his shoulder pulling him to the side in the shadow of a stone archway. "We must not allow the remaining wealth of the temple to be taken, nephew."

"What are you doing?" he hissed, feeling a warrior's heat.

"I mean to bring the jewels from the temple... and the scrolls. I will not see them stolen. One bears the riches of this earth. The other carries the word of God."

A rush of fear and anger. "Are you insane? We have no time to strip the temple of its treasures. You would bury us with your fascination with wealth and your passion for words. Leave them! There is no time for either!" He looked anxiously down the cobbled street toward the sounds of shouting and struggle. The scholar paused, considering, then slid away into the darkness of the temple entrance. The warrior raced after him.

Inside, a jewel-encrusted cabinet glittered in candlelight. The scholar pried at the stones with his dagger, then reached inside for the stack of scrolls within. "Save these treasures. Help me, nephew!"

He felt a shout rise from his stomach. The enemy was nearly upon them. "Impossible, Uncle! We can't begin to carry this weight! Bring some token if you must, but come now while you still can!" He grabbed a single scroll and stuffed it into his uncle's satchel. "This is the only treasure you can salvage. Except your own life… and mine!"

"I cannot leave these precious gifts! They are holy. They are ours alone!" The scholar reached for another scroll.

"Enough!" Tears streaming down his face, he drew a short sword and held it to his uncle's throat. "I will kill you myself before I leave you to be savaged by beasts."

Outside, he pushed his uncle on, half leading, half driving. Narrow streets rushed past filled with the fearful eyes of the people… the wives and children and aged parents. At the King's house, they entered and circled to the rear where the warrior's squad waited near a thicket of vines and overgrowth. He ducked to bend past the brush and through a small garden door that opened onto the space between the double walls. He felt his breath raw in his throat. He followed through an opening in the outer wall… and ran.

They ran through the night. By dawn they had reached the plains of Jericho. He lay on the ground as in a trance, staring at the waking sky and deaf to all sound but his own labored breathing. Beside him, his uncle clutched his satchel close, his own strength used up by the flight and by the burden he had chosen to shoulder.

The King stood before them, defiant still, as if his kingdom could be called back by a single blast from the ram's horn. Zedekiah feared no man, no battle. He could not flee, not to save himself or his army when Jerusalem itself called to him for protection. Courage was his strength and his curse. Zedekiah the King shouted the men to form. Together they faced the army of Babylon. Together they died.

"I am no warrior. Let me die… there is no place for a scholar or a coward here." His uncle shrank behind his nephew's shield against the onslaught. Wave after wave. The warrior spun to slash at the scarred, grizzled face of a Chaldean foot soldier then back at the sound of a cruel thud. His uncle lay fallen, arms pinned by the twists and folds of his shoulder bag and anchored by its weight.

He stood over the scholar and among the bodies of his comrades, fighting on with hands and feet, possessed now by blood lust and the fierce thrill of battle. His body became a blur of deadly motion, striking and recoiling like a serpent until at last and alone he fell exhausted across his uncle's body. He sheltered it with his own, the satchel hidden beneath the still form.

He lay silent among the dead. Those who survived were bound as slaves and marched in broken columns up to Nebuchadnezzar at Riblah where he sat in angry judgment. Proud Zedekiah the king was made to watch his sons die as Nebuchadnezzar bent to the whispered urgings of a fawning advisor. Then Zedekiah's own desperate eyes were put out and he was led away to Babylon in chains.

But the warrior lived, lying in fear and angry silence among his broken comrades until darkness hid his escape. Carefully he felt beneath him for his uncle's satchel … the anchor his uncle had dragged to this place only to lie with it clutched in dead hands. What good is ink and stone to you now, Uncle? Can you see the words? Do they ring in your dead ears? Can you hold the jewels to the light?

He nearly left the bag and all its contents with the corpse that had carried it. In the end, he emptied it on the bloody ground, keeping only the largest of the gems his uncle had collected. He bent to the scroll and rolled a small portion onto an end and cut it free. The stone and the hide parchment would serve as tokens of his beloved uncle and of the so-called treasure that had cost him so dearly.

He stood to scan the surrounding area for movement. A pale naked figure danced atop a pile of corpses in the near distance. He shouldered the satchel and turned away from the west and away from Jerusalem and its doomed temple. He walked, no thrall to Babylon, but never to turn homeward again. Not for all his days nor those of his children or his children's children.

SEVEN

CARPENTER STARTLED AWAKE IN THE DARKNESS AS THE TRAIN HISSED TO A SLOW STOP. Images of death and war crowded his mind. The dream clung to his consciousness with a tenacity much like the tortured nightmare that had haunted him for so many months. Across from him, Kohein jerked upright and shook his head as if to clear it. What visions had crept into *his* mind?

"Did you dream?" Carpenter's question carried more anxiety than he wished to express, but the images that still resonated included a face too like his companion's.

"Dream! My God, I hardly know where I am," Kohein answered. "I feel like a time traveler."

Carpenter's breath caught. He leaned across the short distance separating the two seats. "Really? Why a time traveler?"

"Such a strange and troubling dream – quite vivid…" Kohein squinted, struggling to recall. Carpenter could see his companion's eyes move beneath closed lids as if looking for something hidden just beyond reach or sight. "But it is gone already, I'm afraid." He shook his head again, then pressed his fingertips against his eyes as if to protect against the intrusion of unwanted memory.

Carpenter reached a hand to Kohein's knee and stared intently at the older man. "What was it about? You must be able to remember some part of it, can't you?"

Kohein caught Carpenter's look. His dark eyes narrowed, head tilted a degree sideways in curiosity. "Very little, really… mostly the feelings. But I believe you were in it and we were in a terrible rush. Likely a reflection of my own fear and foolish anxiety about this trip. I tend to obsess about risks, you see… risks both to myself and to whatever of value I possess." He straightened as if to shrug off a fixation. "Not to worry, of course. Just another dream."

Carpenter's mouth opened slowly and shut again. He sat back. "I don't know. I was dreaming too and you were in it and we were in a holy city under siege and we were running away and there was a battle and I escaped, though the king was taken and blinded. And jewels and scrolls were lost, though something was saved …" Carpenter looked at Kohein as if for confirmation, omitting reference to the scholar's death.

"My word! That sounds very like the Babylonian captivity. You clearly possess an exquisite and detailed imagination, my friend." Kohein seemed to strain to achieve a normal, lighter tone. "One can only wonder what you might have dreamed had your traveling companion been a Greek jewel merchant. Perhaps you would have found yourself with Alexander conquering the known world and amassing a great fortune."

The train lurched suddenly and Carpenter's backpack fell to the floor, interrupting the conversation. Carpenter retrieved the bag from where it had slid beneath Kohein's seat. Kohein checked his watch. "We are slowing. We must have reached Lamphun – it's nearly dawn. Not long now to Chiang Mai. Can I buy you breakfast?"

The question turned Carpenter's attention to his empty stomach. "Now that you mention it, yes. I am incredibly hungry. But I can pay for myself, really."

"*Mai pen rai* as they say here – 'never mind'. The cost is negligible. Would you like something sweet or something more substantial?"

"I'm real hungry… I could eat most anything."

"Let me caution you to be careful with such statements here unless you have an extraordinary capacity for spicy food."

Kohein stood to lean from the open window and beckon with his hand. "*Nu, Nu! Ja syr gai yang noi!*" Here, little mouse. I would buy some of your grilled chicken. He turned back inside to Carpenter. "You will eat grilled chicken, yes?"

"You bet! Thanks."

Kohein handed Carpenter a crisp brown chicken leg and thigh on a bamboo skewer. "This is a Northeastern specialty, actually, but popular everywhere… and not so spicy to start the day with."

Carpenter bit into the tender meat and closed his eyes in pleasure.

Kohein bent to pick up his leather case. "And I shall make use of the facilities, such as they are."

"I'll watch your stuff," Carpenter volunteered, still chewing.

Kohein hesitated, turning in both directions to survey the length of the carriage. "I have some personal articles in my satchel, but please do watch the larger suitcase, thank you." Kohein shouldered the smaller bag and set off toward the rear.

Carpenter was stiff after the night's cramped slumber. The feel of the dream crept back into his consciousness. Real... more like a memory. He recalled Reggie's last letter and his reference to dreams that felt more like recollection than fantasy. "Funny what floats to the surface when you're out of your depth..."

Carpenter stretched and went back to his breakfast. He took his time finishing the chicken, then stood to look for a trash container. Seeing none in the immediate vicinity, he turned in the direction Kohein had gone. A hiss of steam announced the train's imminent departure as he neared the connecting platform between cars. At the end of the next carriage, he caught sight of Kohein facing two men and clutching his bag to his chest. The three were engaged in animated conversation, as if acquainted but not necessarily friendly. Carpenter hesitated, then tossed bones and bamboo from the open carriage door and moved toward them.

As he approached, Carpenter could hear raised voices speaking in Thai, but more quickly than he could follow. One of the men reached for the satchel. Kohein slapped his hand away and turned as if to flee. His eyes met Carpenter's and he paused, right hand gripping the open door jam of the carriage. Carpenter sprang toward him and was flung further forward as the train lurched sharply into motion. The two assailants staggered backward into the adjoining car and away from Kohein, who turned and ducked quickly past them and out through the exit door to his left.

Carpenter let the force of the train's sudden movement accelerate his advance. He stood braced at the door to the next car before either of the two men had fully recovered balance. The first began to push past. Carpenter's long frame blocked his exit. The man looked up in surprise, eyes narrowed and threatening.

"*Og pai, rew!*" Carpenter stood over him expressionless, unmoving. "*Pai sa!*" the man repeated his order to move and started forward again. The train jolted as it gained speed. Carpenter placed his hand on the man's chest as if to steady himself, but added his own momentum to the physics of the train's motion. The man sat abruptly on the floor at his companion's feet.

"Oh, I'm sorry! Man, it's really hard to stay on your feet when these things start moving isn't it?" Carpenter leaned to offer his hand to the man, at the same time keeping a careful watch on the companion. The first man scrambled quickly to his feet, eyes blazing but confused. He seemed to study Carpenter for a beat, then turned abruptly and with his companion raced back the length of the car. They disappeared – also to the left - jumping just as the train cleared the station platform in departure and began to pick up speed. The image of the man's grizzled face remained in Carpenter's mind. Had he seen it before? Or was it simply the scarring around the man's eyes and nose that told a familiar tale of ring battles won and lost? A fighter of some kind… most likely a Thai-style boxer.

What about Kohein? Carpenter stepped quickly to the open carriage door and looked back toward the Lamphun station, visible now only in miniature as it receded into the gray morning light. Too late now to jump from the train. And what to do instead? How to explain what had happened and to whom? And in a language he spoke only haltingly at best. He struggled to summon the words for 'theft' and 'bag', able at last to cobble together only idiot phrases, *"Phyan mii krabow. Khaw wing. Phu chai song khon wing duay"*. My friend has a bag. He runs. Two men also run. Oh yes, and see Spot run…

'My friend has a bag…' The phrase caught in Carpenter's mind. He remembered Kohein's suitcase – and his own – both unprotected in the luggage rack back at their seats. Continuing to mull avenues of action, he moved quickly forward to his seat and was stunned by what he found. Alone on the bench opposite Carpenter's, Kohein's fine leather satchel sat upside down, missing only its owner.

Chiang Mai

EIGHT

CHIANG MAI IS THE CAPITOL CITY OF A PROVINCE BY THE SAME NAME IN THE
NORTH OF THAILAND, about 435 miles from Bangkok as the crow flies. Nestled
in folds of blue-green mountains that rise and ripple upward toward the high
peaks of the Tibetan Plateau, the topography surrounding this once independent kingdom forms the jagged perimeter of an ancient tectonic collision. To
the west and north of the city lies Burma – sometime enemy, sometime protector. To the north and east is Laos, whose language roots it shares.

Chiang Mai is a walled city about a mile square with moats on all sides. Four
gates face the cardinal directions following the Hindu-Buddhist design placing
Mt. Meru – dwelling place of the gods – at the center. The city rests on a river
– the Ping – itself a tributary of the Chao Praya whose muddy waters run
south to and through Bangkok on their way to the Gulf of Siam. Located
strategically on this major waterway, Chiang Mai became something of a commercial center for goods transported throughout the area, attracting traders
from south China and linking to the great Silk Road itself. While traditionally
Buddhist, Chiang Mai – town and province – also is home to tribal animists,
Moslem Hill Chinese and small communities of Christians. The city boasts
mosques and churches as well as Thai and Chinese Buddhist temples.

But the city's most prominent landmark is the temple or 'Wat' Prathat on the
hill of Doi Suthep overlooking the city from the northwest. Legend has it that
the site for this holy construction was selected by placing a relic of the Lord
Buddha on the back of a royal elephant that was then loosed to wander until
it circled, laid down and died on the spot where the temple was built. In a
parallel often seen in Buddhist and Hindu cosmology, Lord Indra – king of
the gods - is typically pictured like the Buddha astride a royal elephant. As
one looks out across the fertile green plain of the Ping River Valley from the
mountaintop at Doi Suthep, a magical kingdom ruled by gods may not seem
so very far away.

******

Carpenter had thought sleep impossible after the excitement at Lamphun. He woke gradually to the slowing cadence of the train as it approached Chiang Mai and watched, half-asleep, as the surroundings took shape.

The land here was different from the central plain. Open fields rose and fell in gentle undulations toward a horizon guarded on all sides by dark forested hills partially obscured by blue haze. A shallow river hurried past the train to the left, headed south and away from the approaching city. Tiled rooftops and golden domes flashed against the mid-morning light, framed by clusters of low palm and flowering shade trees.

Full consciousness came slowly. Carpenter found himself wrapped in dream cloud. A vague tinkle of chimes became the high-pitched grinding of brakes to still his reverie and complete his wakening. He sat up quickly, gathering his bags and Kohein's close around him.

Carpenter began searching the platform as the train screeched slowly to a stop. He scanned the platform from his window seat, hoping to catch a stranger's eyes doing the same. Smiling friends and relatives crowded forward to greet passengers as they descended. Carpenter hung Kohein's leather satchel around his neck and dragged the larger pieces of luggage to the exit. He surveyed the platform again, this time locking onto a pair of staring eyes above a narrow, bearded face that immediately disengaged and melted into the shadow of the overhanging roof. Carpenter struggled down from the car as quickly as he could manage and looked over the heads of the crowd, seeking to confirm the contact. A hand pulled gently on his left sleeve at the elbow.

"James Carpenter, yes?"

Startled, Carpenter jerked quickly away, then looked down into a pair of round black eyes set in a round black face and framed by a fringe of dark curly hair beneath a shiny dome. "Yes! I'm sorry, I somehow thought you had gone inside. You must be Brother Edward?" Carpenter offered his hand.

"Oh, yes. That would be me." The smaller man grasped Carpenter's hand for a long moment, slowly examining his face as if for clues to a puzzle. Then, realizing himself, he beamed a huge smile. "Please excuse me. Your face is… very interesting, you know. Yes, I am indeed Brother Edward or 'Kumar', if you prefer. I will answer to most anything, you see, if food is offered." He patted his midsection.

Carpenter laughed. "Thank you Brother Edward…uh, Kumar. Thank you so much for meeting me. You don't know what a relief it is. It's been a pretty strange trip."

"Well, I must hear all about it. But let us get you settled and fed. Brother Joe is waiting outside with the Land Rover. He was able to get it started, but didn't feel comfortable turning it off again." Kumar reached for Carpenter's suitcase. "Here, let me help you with your luggage. It must have been a challenge to manage them all," he offered diplomatically.

"Oh, yeah, for sure. But that's part of the strangeness. Half of these bags aren't even mine."

"Really? Shall we wait then for a traveling companion? Or perhaps hurry on before we are apprehended?" Kumar winked.

"No, the owner has disappeared, in fact. I'm pretty sure he was trying to get away from two other guys … I saw them all together. He was being attacked or threatened somehow. He jumped off the train at the last stop and left his bags." Carpenter patted the leather satchel squeezed against the pack at his shoulder. "I know his name and I know he has a jewelry shop in Bangkok. We talked for a long time during the trip."

"My word! A strange trip, indeed. And rather alarming, I should guess. You say he left the train at Lamphun? Come, we will notify the local police, then I will make some phone calls from the House. We will find this man, or some-one who knows him. Have you checked his belongings? And what did you say his name is?"

"Amit Kohein. I would have told someone but I didn't know how to explain what happened. And I didn't really know what to do. The train was already moving pretty fast…" Carpenter stammered, anxious and ashamed for aban-doning his friend.

"Amit is it?" Kumar's expression showed surprise and concern. "But I know this man! I haven't seen him in donkey's ears, of course, but he travels here in the North rather frequently. We share an interest in hill tribe culture. You say he jumped from the train? An impulsive, if risky gambit… much like Amit."

"He did it to get away from these two men who seemed to know him. I saw them arguing and one of them tried to take this from him." Carpenter nodded to indicate the bag at his shoulder. "He slapped the guy's hand away and jumped off the train as it was starting to move. I ran back to where they were and kind of blocked the two guys from chasing him. When I got back to our seats, this was there – upside down on Kohein's side. I think he must have run past and thrown it back through the window."

Kumar rubbed his chin. "Perhaps it would be best to keep this to ourselves. You say Amit appeared to have escaped successfully?"

"Well, he had a pretty good lead on the guys."

"Amit is, shall we say, a resourceful man… quick-witted, if a bit rash. He must be, given his less than sterling business associations. If he was able to get free, he likely has been able to remain so. We can make some inquiries here before involving the police, who at times can create additional confusion. Did Amit say where he was planning to stay in Chiang Mai?"

"No, I'm sure we would have gotten to that, but the conversation was more about politics and philosophy; then he was gone."

"And the satchel? Have you looked inside to see if there is any indication of where he might be found?"

"No. I felt funny about opening it. He kept it close the whole trip and seemed pretty concerned about it. I just didn't feel comfortable looking in it, to tell you the truth."

"Yes, admirable. But it would appear that Amit trusts you with it, you see. Why else would he place it in your care? Perhaps there is something inside that would help us return it to him?" Kumar straightened and turned toward the station exit. "Think about it at any rate. Clearly it is yours to decide. Meanwhile, we should find Brother Joe before, as you Americans say, he blows a gasket. He does so, you know, with some frequency… and with surprisingly little assistance."

Carpenter followed Kumar through the station building and out the front door. The street was crowded with motorbikes, small cars and *samlor* or "three wheels" – bicycle-drawn rickshaws. As he followed Kumar past the waiting vehicles, Carpenter felt the odd sensation of eyes watching. He turned back toward the station, but saw nothing to confirm the feeling. As he stood looking, a loud voice cut through the street noise.

"All right, all right. Let's get a move on, kid. I'm triple parked out here!"

Carpenter swiveled to where Kumar stood at the open door of an aging beige Land Rover. Next to him, a short white man with bulging tattooed forearms was gesturing impatiently. "Come on kid. These *samlor* drivers are killing me here. And the engine's going into the red zone!"

Carpenter hurried over to the car, hand extended. "You must be Brother Joe. I didn't expect you. Thanks for the limo service."

The little man's grip was vise-like. "Yeah, well I actually needed to get a couple parts for this piece of … junk," he said slapping the hood of the vehicle. Looking up at Carpenter, he froze and stared. "Jesus Christ," he crossed himself twice, then rushed to add "… is our true Lord and Savior". Then, "Do you have any idea who you look like?"

NINE

"ITS NAME ACTUALLY MEANS 'NEW CITY', but Chiang Mai lies at the center of one of the oldest of all independent Thai kingdoms. Along with Sukothai to the south, it was the first Thai kingdom to break away from Mon-Burmese influence on the west and Khmer domination on the east sometime in the late 13th century. At the time, various internal pressures caused the Burmese to pull back from their frontiers even while the vast Khmer empire that produced ancient Angkor fell into decline. Angkor itself, of course, eventually was swallowed by jungle."

Carpenter listened to Kumar's enthusiastic account as he leaned from the left-hand passenger side of the Rover to view the approaching city. Tall brick walls and golden spires could be seen through the foliage as the car wove its way west along a street crowded with carts, bicycles and pedestrians. Open food stalls hung with fresh vegetables and plucked chickens crowded alongside small shops selling cloth, hand tools and simple manufactured goods from Japan. Over all, a heady bouquet of garlic, chili pepper and diesel exhaust laced the air. Kumar kept up his steady flow of travel narrative while children crowded close to laugh and point whenever the vehicle slowed to match the decidedly rural rhythms of local traffic.

"That is where you would catch the bus to Chiang Rai had Brother Joe not succeeded in his repair efforts."

"Don't jinx us now, Kumar, for Chri … um, please." Brother Joe gripped the wheel with fierce determination as if to keep the vehicle running through sheer force of will. "Stifle the enthusiasm until we're back at the House, OK?"

Kumar responded with calm good cheer. "Certainly, Brother. I am simply grateful you have such prodigious technical skills, unlike the rest of us. Thank God for your valuable experience."

"It was God … well, you and God… got me out of the frigging Merchant Marines before all that valuable experience nearly killed me. So thank you both."

"You were in the Merchant Marines?" Carpenter asked, curious.

"Yeah, up until a couple years ago. That's where I picked these up." Joe raised his hands briefly from the wheel to show the scroll of tattoos winding up both forearms and disappearing along huge biceps into the upper arms of his short-sleeved shirt. "You could say I was down and out in Bangkok. I ended up at a Catholic church and managed to pass out on the steps. Kumar found me and convinced the priests to take me in." Brother Joe glanced quickly at Kumar. "I owe him big time."

"But then we owe Brother Joe as well," Kumar replied lightly. "He came to us with a most colorful and extensive vocabulary. He has taught us a great deal over the past few years."

"Yeah, my ass. I've been a corrupting influence on these jokers, but at least they manage to keep their own language clean."

Joe looked over to Carpenter to make a serious point. "If Kumar hadn't found me down in Bangkok, I'd be dead by now, no kidding."

At the eastern wall to the old city, Brother Edward pointed out huge wooden rollers built into the bottom of massive gates guarding access to the kingdom's center. "This is the Tha Phae Gate - one of four set in the walls that form a square of defense around the old city. Ancient Chiang Mai was a jewel, blessed by the rich influences of its trading partners and threatened by its enemies – who were one and the same. The rollers were needed to close the doors quickly in case of attack and to open them again for commerce. In that sense, Chiang Mai seems much like the Vatican, I would say, mixing defense and invitation. A Buddhist kingdom, yes, but with a very catholic – that is, universal – dilemma."

Carpenter was surprised and delighted by the comparison, which seemed to hover just beyond the edge of orthodoxy in metaphor, if not in principle.

"This is the kind of … stuff I gotta put up with all day." Brother Joe threw up his hands in mock despair. "I can't think of enough words, and he knows too many. He can't help himself, kid. He's a heathen at heart and a Buddhist in his head."

The Rover passed through the gate and proceeded westward through the city. Elegant houses on stilts with ornately carved teak exteriors and tiled roofs alternated with scrap wood shacks topped with thatch or tin. Temple ruins and aging monuments dotted groves of coconut and palm. Brother Edward kept up his commentary. "This is Radchadamnern Road, one of the main thoroughfares. It extends most of the way through the city, but ends just ahead there at Wat Phrasing."

Carpenter leaned forward in his seat to take in the extraordinary temple complex spread before them. A veritable sculpture garden of wood carvings and white masonry extended across his vision and back into the shade of spreading trees. Behind the teak structure of the main sanctuary with its red and gold tiled roof, the white spire of the largest of many stupas ascended in diminishing spirals against a deep blue sky. Before it all, on either side of the grand arched entrance to the complex, two giant white griffins stood in fierce silence guarding against any evil that might attempt to breach the ornate walls.

"My God!" Carpenter moved his head slowly side to side in disbelief. "Incredible."

"Yes, and that is only the exterior," Brother Edward continued. "There are many *viharn* - or sanctuaries as we would call them. Inside each are exquisite images of the Buddha. The largest, the *Woramaha Viharn*, has dozens of the bronze figures clustered together and ranging in size from two stories high to smaller than a child."

"You see what I'm talking about here? He loves this stuff like the heathen idol worshipper he is." Brother Joe kept a straight face as he turned the Rover right to pass the temple entrance, then left to skirt the perimeter of the complex which extended for several city blocks in all directions. Emerging through the west gate at the far side of the city, they crossed the canal moat and turned north onto Arrak Road, then west again toward the mountains. On the distant hillside ahead, the temple at Doi Suthep gleamed gold and alabaster in the green of the surrounding forest.

The Rover passed Wat Suan Dok on the left with its sweep of white stupas arrayed in myriad shapes and sizes against the backdrop of the main *viharn*. Near the new university grounds, they turned right into a pleasantly shaded compound with a circular drive and large fountain in the center. Just beyond the fountain, what appeared to be a Buddhist temple rose in quiet relief against bordering flame trees. A single, large cross on the face of the structure signaled its purpose. Brother Joe followed a side track to a group of low dormitory-style buildings and parked near the largest.

He turned in his seat to grin at Carpenter. "Welcome to Suan Dok Gnam – or as we hillbillies call it, the holy Hilton. Hope you like it. It's probably the last running water you'll get before we head north."

TEN

"JUST LEAVE THE BAGS IN THE TRUCK FOR NOW. You'll be in the teachers' dorm over there." Brother Joe gestured to a squat rectangular building behind and to the right of the Rectory. "This is our place here. Come on in and meet the people while I get some water for the friggin' radiator, OK?"

Carpenter climbed down from the Rover and followed inside to a small foyer. Three wicker chairs formed a sitting area next to an old fashioned wooden desk facing the entrance. A large crucifix hung on the wall above with a pale, thorn-crowned Christ draped down its length. Behind the desk, a young Thai man in jeans and a white T-shirt sat hunched over a pile of papers.

"Joe! Edward! What a treat! God bless you! Good to see you." The young man stood smiling and approached with arms outstretched.

Kumar accepted the hearty embrace while Brother Joe held his hands out in mock protest. "What's with the hugging, Anond? All the time hugging. It's already strange enough you're living in a house full of men. What's wrong with a simple handshake?"

The younger man took one of Brother Joe's defending hands, gave it a firm shake, then drew the shorter man playfully to him. "Well, I see the hills haven't changed you, Brother. Still starved for affection." Turning to Carpenter, he asked, "And who have you brought with you?" Not waiting for an introduction, he extended his hand. "Anond Sansaniyakhunvilai. Pleased to meet you... and welcome."

"This here is Father Anond, who you can see is a little shy. Spent too much time in the States... ruined him for good." Brother Joe turned to the priest. "And this here is James Carpenter, Harry's nephew. He's gonna be helping us out up north. He just got in. We fired up the Rover and came down to get him."

"Good to meet you, Father," Carpenter said releasing his grip.

"Anond will do unless you prefer. I'm still getting used to being called 'Father' by old *farang* guys like Joe." Anond hesitated, then continued. "I somehow hadn't expected you to be Thai, or Asian, or whatever.... You're Father Harry's nephew, right?"

"Yes. But I'm adopted." The statement came more easily now. "Father Harry is my mother's brother. I may be Thai, but I've been raised *farang*. I think that's why Brother Joe has taken such a liking to me." Carpenter grinned over at Brother Joe, who feigned shock.

"Kid's a smart ass, just like Harry. Whaddya gonna do?" Brother Joe threw up his hands in pretend despair.

"Well, welcome to the club," Anond replied. "My father's Thai, mother's French-Vietnamese and I studied in the U.S. So I guess I'm also part *farang*, at least by training." Anond winked broadly. "Which is probably why Joe is so partial to me, too."

Brother Joe rolled his eyes.

Anond turned to the two Brothers. "We knew Brother Edward would be coming today, but we hadn't expected to see you both. How long are you down here for? You're at least staying the night, of course."

Brother Joe answered. "Yeah, well. It's kind of up in the air right now. Harry was supposed to be back a couple of days ago, but he hasn't showed yet. I was hoping he would be here to greet the kid and decide on the itinerary. And to meet you, while he was at it."

The priest's face clouded in concern. "Should we be worried? Do you think he's OK?"

"Yeah, I think he's alright. You know, he takes these trips into the hills and it's never real clear exactly where he's going or how long he'll be gone. He doesn't know what he'll run into and, let's face it, uh... stuff happens."

"Well, you know you're welcome here as long as you can stay." Turning to Carpenter, he continued. "I've heard about your project, you know, though I'm pretty new here myself. I'm a Bangkok boy. I can guarantee you there's plenty to see in Chiang Mai before you head north. The old city is beautiful and Brother Edward has all sorts of contacts in the villages in the area. Right, Kumar?"

"I do, and James is most welcome to join me if he likes. I believe it would be best for him to spend a few days here at any rate while we wait for word from Father Harry." With a slight bow in Carpenter's direction, he added, "I am planning a trip tomorrow, in fact, to a Meo village near the temple at Doi Suthep, if you'd like to come along?"

"Oh, that would be great! Thank you," Carpenter replied immediately.

"Holy shit!" Brother Joe quickly crossed himself. "I left the Land Rover running. I gotta go give it a drink so it can make it up the mountain and back tomorrow." He disappeared into the interior of the building, returning quickly with a large earthen jar which sloshed water generously onto the floor as he hurried out the front.

"Well, why don't we follow Brother Joe and get you settled into the dorm?" Father Anond led the way out to the parked Rover, where Brother Joe was gingerly unscrewing the radiator cap with a dirty rag. A gust of thick steam hissed forth as the cap loosened and Joe backed away.

"OK, OK. Just grab the bags and go while I try to get this mother into the shade to cool off. Too bad we don't have a spare thermostat..." Brother Joe gestured vaguely toward the dormitory building while continuing an angry conversation with the vehicle's engine.

Bags in tow, the three headed for the smaller building which sat in the shade of several broad flame trees. Inside, the dim space resembled a military barracks. Wooden sleeping platforms topped by colorful woven mats were arranged on either side of a central aisle along the concrete floor. The room was empty save for a lone occupant at the rear who kneeled at the side of a bed, stiff-backed and head bowed. The figure was square and young, although a bushy red beard gave the thin-necked countenance something of an elderly air. He did not seem to notice the arrivals, but continued to rock slowly back and forth on his knees, clutching a string of rosary beads in steepled hands. After the bags were deposited next to one of the sleeping spaces near the front, Father Anond spoke in a low voice.

"That's Paul Hemple," he said. He sniffed and swiped at his nose, then nodded toward the figure. "He also is newly arrived... came a few days ago hoping to find Father Wilkins." His voice betrayed the smallest hint of uncertainty.

"Paul is with IVS in Laos – that's the International Voluntary Service – though his passion clearly is for missionary work. He has been corresponding with your uncle, who seems to have agreed to help him establish a small school across the river in Laos. He has a letter from Harry to that effect. He's quite devout, really. Quite, uh, enthusiastic about his faith. So, you'll have some company while you're here anyway. The dorm can be kind of dreary, I'm afraid."

Father Anond turned to Kumar. "Maybe we should give James a chance to clean up and settle in?" Then, back to Carpenter. "We'll give you a few minutes to get squared away. The bathroom is in the rear. We'll be at the rectory. Come over and have some lunch when you're ready. Take as long as you like. Bring Paul along with you – he eats like a horse when he gets the chance."

Carpenter thanked them both again and turned as they left to consider the mass of luggage piled on and against the bed frame.

"You'll never pass through the eye of the needle with all that, you know. You must be new to the country."

Startled, Carpenter swiveled toward the high-pitched and unusually loud voice just behind him.

"Paul Hemple." The young man from the rear of the room had made his way forward without a sound. He seemed pleased at Carpenter's discomfort. "I was referring to scripture, of course. About the narrow path we must negotiate if we expect to enter into the kingdom of heaven. I believe you'll have to pare down a good deal if you hope to enter, friend." A thin red smile opened in the tangle of beard, but failed to reach the close-set eyes that perched bird-like behind heavy framed glasses.

Carpenter swallowed against a surge of irritation and extended a hand. "Pleased to meet you. I'm James Carpenter. And these," he said, gesturing toward the bags on the floor next to them, "mostly belong to someone else. I'm looking after them for the time being."

"The same could be said for our immortal souls." Hemple took Carpenter's hand with a hint of triumph. His grip was surprisingly strong, forcing Carpenter to squeeze back reflexively to avoid pain.

Carpenter met the challenge in the other man's eyes until Hemple glanced away. "So, what are you in for?"

"In? You mean like in jail?" Hemple's eyebrows shot up, slightly scandalized.

"Yeah, like that. It was a joke, sorry…" Carpenter released the other's hand and nodded toward the large empty room. "I mean, it *is* kind of Spartan, you know?"

"Well, luxury is not required for those doing the Lord's work. Unlike some of the priests and brothers here, I prefer to live like those I have come to help."

Carpenter went for a safe response. "How do you like it here? I'll be in-country for a year, doing some teaching, once Father Harry gets back from his trip."

Hemple's face brightened with excitement. "Father Harry Wilkins? He's why I'm here! I haven't met him yet, unfortunately, but he and I will be working together very soon. We share a mutual calling." Hemple stepped back to look Carpenter over, frowning an appraisal. "How were *you* able to join his mission? Are you from a tribal area? You look like you could be, but you *sound* American…" An earnest, almost accusatory tone.

Carpenter breathed. When does it stop? He decided to cut the conversation short. "Great. Sounds like things are going well for you, then. I'm sure I'll like it too." Carpenter turned away toward the pile of luggage. "Father Anond invited you to lunch by the way, in case you're hungry. Meanwhile, I think I better get this stuff organized first before I lose my shot at heaven, huh?"

Behind him, Hemple's response was stiff with formality. "Well, I certainly didn't mean to offend you. I was simply referring to scripture. After all, we are here to do God's work, aren't we?" He stood, waiting.

Carpenter heard the challenge in the voice. The judgment lying in wait of a wrong answer. Back still turned, he replied. "Actually, I'm just here to do some research. I'm afraid you'll have to handle God's work on your own… unless you get a little help from those pesky priests and brothers." He tossed a glance over his shoulder. "Nice to meet you, Paul," and turned again to the task at hand.

Hemple stood silent for a moment, speechless, then managed a barely controlled, "God bless" before returning to his own bunk to kneel again, rosary in hand. He was still keening and rocking ten minutes later when Carpenter let the front door slam as a call to lunch.

* * * * *

The meal was an odd mixture of east and west. Rice, of course, with a green curry. A mysterious lunchmeat from an olive green tin and crackers from another. A stringy orange marmalade on the side.

"Somrak, our cook, is great with Thai food, but she's still trying to figure out what to do with the C-rations we get from the American military." Anond nodded toward the back of the rectory kitchen where a plump Thai woman of middle years smiled broadly as she stood chopping greens near the screened door. The priest sat at the head of a square table spread with a worn red and white-checkered oilcloth. He continued to detail the origins of the meal as Carpenter, followed shortly by Hemple, took seats opposite Brothers Edward and Joe.

"The U.S. military drops surplus stuff off for us at our House in the Northeast where most of the airbases are. The worst of it makes its way here after the guys in Bangkok pick through it," Anond explained, referring to the priests at the Order's main House in the capitol. "The Americans like it, I guess, right Joe?" Brother Joe shot him a baleful glance, looking up from a plateful of green curry. "I think this meat is some kind of Spam. The crackers come with it. Kumar makes the marmalade himself. It won't kill you, though you might want to be careful of the curry if you're new to Thai food."

Carpenter swallowed a spoonful of curry. He felt the fire immediately and rushed to gulp ice water as his throat seized up and eyes and nose began running fast.

"Aha! A second monsoon!" Brother Joe teased from across the table.

"You may find that rice is a bit more effective than water as a palliative," Kumar suggested politely as Carpenter drained his glass and reached desperately for the pitcher for a refill.

Between fits of coughing, he managed to apologize. "How do you ever get used to it? I can barely breathe."

"Time plus hunger. That's the basic equation." Brother Joe spooned a mound of rice and curry into his mouth with evident relish, head bent over his plate while he looked up at Carpenter through bushy eyebrows. "Works for profanity, too." His eyes twinkled as he spoke.

"I wonder when exactly it will start working for you, Brother." Hemple's tone was polite but off-hand, his eyes looking down the table as if searching for a dish.

The twinkle left Joe's eyes as he sat up straighter in his chair. "It's working right now, as a matter of fact, pal." His gaze remained on Hemple who continued to ignore him as though preoccupied with other matters.

Kumar interceded. "So, James, you will join us tomorrow? It should be an interesting day. As I said, the village itself is on the side of Doi Suthep - the mountain we saw as we drove in. A *doi* in Thai is a hill. The temple on Doi Suthep – Wat Phrathat - is quite famous. We can stop there on the way if you like. It's well worth seeing. The village is not far from there as the crow flies, though quite a distance in other ways."

"For sure, I'd love to go along. I've studied hill tribe cultures, but it's all been from books and journal articles. It would be an amazing opportunity for me if I wouldn't be in the way."

"Not at all," Kumar replied with a smile. "It will be good to have your company."

"There would be room for another, wouldn't there? I'd certainly like to go along. I may not have Carpenter's academic background, but I am always ready to witness for the Lord with the hill people." Hemple's red beard jutted forward as he spoke, so that his comment took on the character of a demand rather than a request.

Kumar glanced quickly to Brother Joe at his side. "Certainly. I'm sure we can all fit in the Rover, wouldn't you say?"

"Yeah, sure. If the damn thing goes at all, it'll carry everybody. Saints and sinners alike. It's always good to have a spare saint along in case we need a miracle." He rose, looked hard at Hemple, and dropped his napkin in his plate. "I'll go work on it. I still have the time, if not the hunger."

"Well, I have some things to do before evening." Hemple stood to leave. "Thank you for the lunch, Father, and for the invitation, Brother. I assume we'll be leaving after morning Mass?"

"Actually, I was planning an earlier start, which would mean missing Mass," Brother Edward replied. "Would that pose an inconvenience?"

Hemple straightened. "Actually it would, Brother. I try to make Mass every morning. I hope you won't mind leaving a bit later. After all, the service - as I'm sure you know - is early enough. And, I would venture to say, not without its benefits for those of us who need the Eucharist."

"Of course," Kumar nodded politely. "We'll leave after Mass, then."

"You are a patient and a gracious man, Brother Edward." Anond addressed Kumar after Hemple had gone. "I do hope Father Harry is aware of what his commitment to Paul may require." Turning to Carpenter, he offered, "I'd be happy to show you around the complex, James, if you like, but I know you must be beat. If you'd rather nap or even turn in, you're welcome to."

"To tell you the truth, Father, I feel like I'm fading pretty fast. Just getting a little food into my stomach seems to have knocked me out. The idea of a bed is pretty appealing."

"Then why don't you relax a bit. We'll have dinner around 7:30. Come on over when you've rested."

Carpenter rose to thank his hosts and proceeded toward the rear kitchen door. As he passed the cook, she turned to him with a curious smile. "*Aroi, mai kha?*" Was it tasty?

Carpenter had learned this much Thai in his year of study and replied as clearly as possible, "*Aroi maak, khrab. Khop khun.*" Very delicious, thank you.

"*Oho, pen khon Thai chai mai, kha? Chan khid wa yang nan.*" Oh, you are Thai then? I thought so. Carpenter understood this too, but not what followed.

Somrak surveyed his face, moving her head slowly side to side and clucking her tongue. "*Dae nadaa myan Khun Phoa duay, na kha. Myan jing jing. Pen yaad gan mai, kha?*"

Carpenter shook his head to show he didn't understand. "I'm sorry, I don't really speak much Thai. I just got here."

Somrak laughed. "Nevah mine. I think you Thai man. You sapeek Thai sound like Thai man." She paused to consider the English words. "I say you face look like Fahduh, you know?" Somrak looked around toward Father Anond and Brother Edward. "*Jing, na kha!*"

Kumar rose quickly and approached. "She likes your face, you see. She said it looks like Father's. That's a loose translation, at any rate". Kumar's expression betrayed a slight embarrassment.

"Well, I guess it's a compliment to look like her father, right?" Carpenter turned to Somrak. "*Khop khun maak, khrab.*"

The cook twisted her head to the side and gave Kumar a puzzled glance. Then, with a nod and a gentle smile, she responded, "*Mai pen rai, kha. Mai pen rai.*" You're welcome, quite welcome.

ELEVEN

CARPENTER WAS ASLEEP ALMOST BEFORE HIS HEAD TOUCHED THE THIN PIL-
LOW. He felt himself fall through a thick mist. Faces swam past in a confusing jumble. He floated down.... and down.

He watched as a ghostly shroud of morning mist lifted dreamlike to reveal slick rock on both sides of a deep chasm. The Macedonians would enter at the beginning of the Persian Gate. The way was wide there, offering broad paths and reasonable footing on both sides of the small river, even in winter. They were many. Their numbers would crowd both sides and bunch up as the passage narrowed further on. But the track would close slowly, swallowing the Greeks and forcing them ever closer together even as it turned their faces into the rising sun. They would be trapped by their own numbers, unable to move forward quickly enough to avoid the rain of boulders and arrows from above and blocked from retreat by the multitude behind. Many would surely die, though the survivors would still vastly outnumber the Persian defenders.

He was a mercenary like so many of his forbearers. Wanderers and fighters... sometimes merchants or scribes... but often mercenaries. His family could trace its long journey from the sacking of Jerusalem. From a single warrior fleeing captivity down through ten generations that spread across a loose empire stretching east from the sea to the far satrapies bordering India.

He bellycrawled through the crusted snow to the edge of the steep cliff wall and peered down through the shadows at the narrow passage below. He shivered at what he saw. Cold rock cliffs in a bare and angular landscape made more forbidding by the crystal layers of ice along the river's edge and by the low whistle of a bitter winter wind. The captain touched his leather pouch for luck, though he had little faith in such things. The gem inside of course had value, but the ancient scrap of hide parchment was nearly blank, the original char-acters rubbed off by time.

The captain assessed the trap set for his current enemies. Perhaps he would prove to be not simply the latest but the last in this line of warrior priests. But then the tight canyon began to echo with the sounds of armored men and horse. The captain felt the familiar red flush of fear and excitement that preceded battle. He crept back from the cliff edge to where his small but fierce sergeant stood growling his men to silence, thick tattooed arms held high for quiet.

"Soon now, soldiers of Persis. Alexander comes." His hoarse whisper echoed low and hollow from the bare rock. All along the rim of the defile, archers stood ready with bags of arrows at their feet. Stacks of boulders the size of sheep balanced at the end of levered platforms waiting to be released. Boys braced themselves behind piles of smaller stones that, at this height, would crush a man's skull and smash bones.

The Macedonians crowded together and moved, unsuspecting, toward the newly raised wall waiting to block their progress. On they came, closing tighter and tighter on each other as the rear continued to march forward, pressing against the backs of those in front. Cavalry horses whinnied and rose kicking, terrified at the suddenly close quarters. Spearmen raised shields to ward themselves, further closing the narrow space as the column slowed, then halted. Those blocked in front were pinned by the force of those behind. Panic spread quickly. Phalanx leaders shouted their men to calm, only to deepen the chaos as their commands mixed with cries of fear that echoed through the canyon like the screams of a thousand tortured souls.

Then the killing began. Platform supports were pulled. Boulders fell like the earth had shaken, crushing men and beasts in a turmoil of blood and agony. Unchallenged archers loosed steadily on the defenseless troops below, who clawed at each other seeking escape. Clouds of cold dust rose up from the floor of the Persians' Gate to obscure the sight of a ravaged army and muffle the echoes of the wounded and dying. The captain felt no joy of battle now. He watched as from a distance, as if he were someone else, then turned away sickened by the bloody work.

But even this uncelebrated victory was brief. Prisoners taken before the ambush led the Macedonians through hidden passes to the Persian rear. Caught between the teeth of Alexander's larger force, the Persians fought as men possessed. Some, left without weapons, even managed to drag their attackers to the ground and kill them with their own knives as if to cleanse their souls with untainted blood and free themselves from a darker stain. The captain was among these, sword and spear broken, fighting only with hands and feet, leather pouch bloody and slung across his chest.

After, bound and penned with his sergeant and a few remaining troops, the captain was called before Alexander who greeted him with respect despite the

Macedonians' terrible losses. The captain was curious at this treatment though grateful that he had not yet been put to the sword or worse. The pouch, taken from him when he was subdued, lay open before the king. The gem and the parchment rested alongside.

"You are not of Persis, your fellows tell me." Alexander's strong brow knitted in curiosity. "You are of Judah and worship the one God. You are a priest, perhaps?"

"You are correct, Lord. I am a Jew, though not a rabbi. I am late of Persis. My people have wandered far since the days of Nebuchadnezzar and the destruction of Jerusalem."

"And you fight for those who pay you," Alexander challenged. The hint of a smile played at the corners of a broad mouth beneath a thick straight nose. His face, though not ugly, was bull-like and set above a broad neck and heavily muscled shoulders.

"Yes, Lord. I earn my way as a soldier."

"Explain this," Alexander demanded, nudging the rolled parchment. "What does it say? It appears to bear writing."

"Like the stone, it is merely a token from the ancient temple in Jerusalem before its destruction. My family could not save the scrolls of sacred writing, so they took a gem from the temple and this piece of parchment as a remembrance before the temple was looted and destroyed. I believe the first entry on the piece of scroll is, 'In the beginning...' But in truth, the letters are more memory than fact after so many years."

"And where does eternity begin?" Alexander spoke almost to himself, then continued to the captain. "So, the beginning has been lost, has it? Perhaps it is to be invented anew by those of us bold enough to believe it possible." Alexander's smile was sharp. "I see an omen in this." The Conqueror paused for a long moment, then leaned forward, intent.

"I came through Judah, you know. I did no harm there. Your rabbis showed me the teachings of your prophet, who foretold my coming." Alexander's eyes sought a response. Seeing none, he continued. "Some call me the son of Zeus. Yet, the Jews do not recognize Zeus. What say you to that?"

"My own people have traveled far from Judah, Lord, though I suppose we still are Jews by tradition if not by practice. As for Zeus, there are many names for God. The Persians have Ahura-Mazda as he is called here. By whatever name, if there is a Creator, he is father to us all. And surely to one prophesied by Daniel."

"So you know of the prophet, but do not pretend to knowledge beyond our ken. Nor do I. I seek what I do not profess to know, though the prophets guide." Alexander straightened now. *"Troops from the armies we have defeated serve with my own Macedonians. Together we will march to the end of the world. Not to destroy, but to build and unite. We will create the world anew. Another beginning. We fight for something beyond ourselves."* Alexander's eyes again sought the captain's as if searching for acknowledgement. *"Will you join me as a fellow seeker? Join me, and you and your men who are willing to serve will have equal standing among us. You have my word."*

The captain could scarce believe his ears. *"I grow weary of war, Lord, but I too would hope to build rather than tear down. Forgive my boldness, but I also must tell you that I will serve as a free man, but not as a slave. My family has refused to be bound in slavery, no matter the cost."*

"As I thought, a kindred spirit." The king now bore a satisfied expression. *"You will be a free man, Captain. Should you find that I have spoken untrue, I give you leave to go where you will if first you simply come to me."* He handed over the purse and its contents.

The captain found himself in the ranks of his enemies, marching with Alexander to the capitol city of Persepolis, his sturdy sergeant at his side. There was peace in that great city, for Alexander had hurried there to prevent looting. In the palace of Xerxes in the east of the city, the captain and sergeant were assigned the task of cataloguing the royal archives which contained works older even than the captain's own scrap of hide. They discussed the teachings of Zarathustra with the magi from Medea who served Ahura Mazda and performed funeral rites for the royal family.

Both were drawn especially to one priest whose gentle black eyes glowed with wisdom and compassion and who took contagious delight in knowledge. The mage could recite whole passages from the sacred scriptures in a voice that soared like a bird in flight but landed softly on the fertile earth. The captain was moved and enlightened; the sergeant even more so. He covered his tattooed arms and abandoned his suspicions and muttered profanities. He began to hope for a new and better life immersed in learning and mentored by his teacher. The little sergeant vowed everlasting allegiance to the priest and attended to him as closely as a brother.

Through the mage's wise instruction, the captain grew and changed. He came to view the origins and destiny of the world in terms of choice rather than fate or divine decree. He studied and admired the "Gatha" - lines written by Zarathustra himself. He was impressed in particular by the teachings offered regarding Choice:

Hear with your ears that which is the sovereign good;
With a clear mind, look upon the two sides
Each man and woman must choose for him or herself
Between good and ill

The words on his scrap of hide were all but invisible now. Across the faded scratching of the older entries he wrote, "... each must choose."

The captain understood now that freedom could neither be given nor taken away by any man, save himself. Not even by a king or an emperor; not even by death. So long as he could choose, he was free to create his own future simply by the way he faced it. And there was always choice – no matter the weight of its burden, no matter the terror its exercise could inspire.

He came to this realization during the early months of occupation of the city. As with his sergeant, a life of scholarship seemed possible... certainly preferable to war. But the peace that Alexander had imposed, Alexander chose to end. His army had grown impatient with ideals and hungry for the spoils of war. An obsequious counselor pressed his pale face to Alexander's ear and whispered the dangers of passion thwarted and victory blunted by generosity of spirit. To placate him and them, the king allowed the city to be looted and in the orgy of drunkenness that followed, the palace of Xerxes and all its treasures burned.

The teacher was not spared. His tender heart was too weak to withstand the brutality and the loss. He was trapped in the flames. The little sergeant, frantic with grief, threw himself into the inferno to save his friend and mentor only to perish at his side.

After, the captain begged audience with the king. When he approached Alexander, he quoted the Ghata and said, "I thank you, Lord, for sparing my life when it was yours to take. You gave me the choice of freedom then, which I accepted not realizing it already was mine. Now I choose it again. I seek your blessing, though not your permission. I leave you, Lord. If I must purchase my freedom, then take this if you will." He held out his palm with the ancient gem gleaming in it.

A chastened Alexander reached out a hand and folded the captain's fingers over the jewel. "I would rather you stay than go. Lacking that, I would rather keep my word to you than take your treasure. Go, then, with my blessing if not my permission."

The captain went out of Alexander's presence alone and away from the charred city of Persepolis, walking east toward the sunrise with no destination but the dawn.

TWELVE

SHADOWS DANCED ACROSS HIS EYELIDS AS DAWN FLICKERED THROUGH THE LEAVES OUTSIDE THE DORMITORY'S EAST WINDOW. His feet were tired and sore, his throat dry, his heart heavy with loss. A pale face whispered and mocked from the flames. Rage and terror burned in Carpenter's mind. He lay quiet and momentarily confused. This dream, too, held the frightening intensity of his repeated nightmare and of the vision that had invaded his sleep on the train. He started at a rooster's crow somewhere outside. His heartbeat slowed. The roar of inferno gave way to other sounds. A radio blared a tinny version of a popular Thai song. He thought incongruously of Rudy Valley with a megaphone and opened his eyes.

"I hate to wake you, but we gotta get on the road, kid!"

Carpenter opened his eyes to see Brother Joe at the foot of his bed. "Really, kid, I know you needed the sleep, but 15 hours is gonna have to do it for now. Sorry…"

Carpenter sat up quickly and shook his head. "Are you OK, Joe?" He paused, confused by his own words. "Wow, I had a crazy dream. I think you were in it. I didn't mean to sleep like that. It must be tomorrow, huh?"

"Well, your 'today' was yesterday about 6 hours ago. If you keep sleeping, it'll turn into tomorrow before you know it. And yeah, I'm fine, thanks, except for a crazy nightmare of my own. Woke up in a sweat and couldn't get back to sleep… weird."

"You had a nightmare too? What was it about?" Carpenter scrambled to a sitting position to hear Brother Joe's reply.

"I can't remember much detail, but it scared the hell out of me. Smothering in smoke, couldn't breathe. Kumar was in it… lost him. That was the worst part. It killed me… I'd never admit it to his face, but he's the best man I've ever known. Anyway, I was glad to wake up." Bells tolled to announce the beginning of morning mass. "Of course, he slept like a baby himself. Look, he's getting ready to go. You still want to come along, right?"

Anticipation pushed dream images to the background as Carpenter recalled the trip planned for the Meo village. He took a deep breath to clear his head completely before replying. "Oh, yeah, definitely. Do I have time to wash up?"

"Sure, don't sweat it. Mass just started. We'll wait for 'Saint' Paul." Brother Joe's eyebrows shot up and he looked side to side as if in fear of being over-heard. "I swear, I don't know why Harry invited this guy along. Must be some kind of penance."

Carpenter bit back a sarcastic reply. "He's already helped me exercise my own self-control."

"Yeah, me too. Probably good for me. Anyway, you should have time to bathe and get a little bite before we take off." Brother Joe tossed a wide length of black and red checked cotton cloth onto the bed. "Here, you can have this *pha khawma*. The shower's outside in back." He gestured toward the rear of the building. "Guys here wear one of these when they bathe. Keeps everything private, you know? Just wrap it around your waist like a towel. No hot water out there, but hey, it's wet." He headed for the door, then turned to say, "Oh, and the shower actually is the big jug … should have a little bowl in it. You'll figure it out. Help you wake up real quick."

Carpenter padded down the length of the dorm to the washroom, holding the *pha khawma* around himself with one hand, carrying soap, towel and tooth-brush in the other. He brushed his teeth with the boiled water inside, then looked out through the screen door to the bathing area - a concrete slab en-closed by a neat fence of woven matting hung on bamboo poles planted in the ground at regular intervals. Short benches lined the fence. A large earthen *ong* jar filled with water stood waist-high under a spout protruding from the rear wall. A shiny aluminum container the size of a cereal bowl floated on the surface. Carpenter twisted the ends of the *pha khawma* together to secure it around his waist, and pushed through the squeaking door and into the dap-pled light. He tested the water with his hand… cold, but he already could feel the heat and humidity of the day beginning to build.

He scooped water with the bowl and poured it tentatively over his calves and feet, then took a breath, filled the bowl again and dashed the contents over his head and body. He soaped from head to toe, then dipped water again from the *ong* jar to pour over his head to rinse. Warm sun filtered through the leaves of a shade tree. Carpenter closed his eyes and lifted his face. Light and shadow played across his eyelids while a small breeze slowly lifted moisture from his drying skin. He felt rested and alive.

A sweet chirping song. He opened his eyes. Overhead, a small bird sat motionless, watching him from the safety of a low branch, its miniature frame silhouetted against a single gold blossom. Its head was a dazzling emerald blue. A pattern of white and dark blue stripes stretched horizontally across its chest. Carpenter whistled softly. The tiny creature cocked its head, then whistled a reply. Carpenter closed his eyes again and breathed deeply. He realized it had been days since he had done this with any awareness. He sat and continued his morning breathing ritual, focusing on the bird song and the sense of connection he felt with the singer.

He rose and faced east. Regular stretching had become an integral part of his daily routine since taking up judo and karate years before. Yoga had drawn him as a supplement to martial arts training. He had discovered a book of postures one day as a child on his own in the library. He actually had begun practicing *asanas* and breathing sometime in grade school. He couldn't explain the attraction at that age, beyond the likely explanation that all things Eastern had been discouraged at home – his parents' well-meaning attempt, he realized now, to make his obvious difference disappear. He had wanted to experience something related to who he was, not to the person his parents wanted him to be. Their cheerful efforts to discount how he looked and how others saw him had left him feeling almost invisible at times and fiercely angry – especially with his father who seemed most intent on denying Carpenter's true origins.

Long hours of repetition and practice, his special refuge, had left him supple and expert if mechanical. He placed his palms together to begin the *suriya namiskar* with the same *wai* gesture used in the traditional Thai greeting. He bent forward at the waist and grasped his ankles, noticing the strain in the back of his legs. He slowed to pull himself down more gradually until his forehead rested against his knees. He breathed in and out in time with the melody that continued to float on the breeze.

"Lean into the pain, do not avoid it. Let it lead you. Be gentle with yourself, but never timid."

Startled, Carpenter broke his pose and looked around for the source. But it was not outside. The voice was soft and internal, comforting and strong. As if a part of his own breath and motion. Familiar, like he was simply talking to himself. Yet, he realized as he returned to his pose, not *his* voice, but *hers*. A woman's voice - one he couldn't identify beyond vague memory - offering guidance he somehow recognized but did not recall ever having heard.

Carpenter held the posture to complete the *hatha* sequence. After, he stood quietly for a moment and let his thoughts go. The voice had been more than internal dialogue. It had timbre and volume as if spoken by someone very near. But it was not sound in the way the constant bird song was. He opened his eyes. The empty branch was dipping slowly in the breeze.

Now I'm hearing voices. Next, I'll be seeing things. Carpenter let go of his internal dialogue, smiling to himself as if fooled by his own magic trick. Dry now, he opened the door. The grating sound of a rusty spring overcame the remainder of the moment. As he passed through the washroom, he heard the front door slam shut. The big room was empty as he made his way back to his bed. His suitcase and Amit's leather bag, which he had placed under his bed on arrival, now lay on top and open.

Carpenter hurried to the front door. No one within sight. Church bells rang across the empty yard announcing the end of mass. He cinched his *pha khawma* tighter and returned to the bed. Items from both bags had spilled onto the covers. Loose papers lay on top as if dropped in mid-perusal. Carpenter recognized the thin blue pages of Reggie's aerogrammes, no longer bunched neatly together. A rush of anger tightened his chest. No one else staying in the dorm but Paul Hemple.

He began to gather the stack of Reggie's correspondence. Doing so, he noticed a small leather-bound journal hidden beneath the sprawl of paper, several thick sheets protruding separately from its cover. The yellowed pages were covered in a flowing handwritten script and headed, "November, 1889 – eastern Shan area near Mekong". Carpenter hesitated, then picked it up and read.

Dear Gould or Whomever May Receive This Missive,

I send this diary with Haw traders, who assure me they will carry it to safety in Chiang Mai. I have paid them well in rupees and promises – rather more of the latter, I'm afraid. They are well-armed and likely to avoid danger from local villagers or from the rare Siamese official tasked with governance in this remote region. I have asked them to deliver it to you, our Vice Consul, or to Leonowens at the Borneo Company.

In this journey through Upper Burma and the Shan hills, we have found numerous shrines located in the limestone caves – some with exquisite images of the Buddha and related artifacts of no small value. We also have encountered a host of strange and miraculous tales that, while wondrous, hold little credibility beyond their contribution to one's understanding of local custom and belief. Among them are stories of wizards and witches, spells and counter spells, alchemy and boundless treasure. One legend from the Thaungthut area describes a mountain cave inhabited by magicians. The sick and cursed travel there to be healed, but few return. Quaint and colorful, but certainly well beyond the realm of credibility.

I say this as a pragmatist and something of a non-believer. I feel no compulsion to assure the conversion of the Burmans, for example, as their Buddhistic system has much to recommend it. Having said so much, I am most intrigued by a particular tale that has begun to offer proofs beyond the superstitious or purely speculative.

Local legend has it that there is a cave high in the steep hills nearby which offers entrance to the sacred mountain, dwelling place of the gods. It is said to be home to Indra, originally king of all the Hindu deities, but now subordinated to Buddha. Elephants are said to guard the portal, behind which is a hidden treasure they refer to as a 'terma' – a name, by the by, with which our multi-lingual friends among the Haw are decidedly unfamiliar.

Curious, I inquired the meaning from village leaders, who in turn appeared anxious that I might prove to be someone sent to reveal the treasure, as they put it. They had a word for such a person, which sounded quite like 'turtle' to be honest though I chose not to take offense. Again, the term is not one known to the Haw despite their fluency in Burman, Shan, and most of the other hill languages of the area.

Whatever the nature of the 'hidden treasure' and the lucky lad sent to reveal it, the locals ascribe the cave itself a floor of emerald and walls formed only by an endless net of pearls or clouds of jewels, all of which emit fantastic, mesmerizing music and the fragrance of heavenly blossoms. They claim it to be inhabited by witches so that none who venture there ever return.

Utter nonsense, of course, except for this. Higher up, we came to a village and encountered a shaman who claims to have been to the cave, or at least to have traveled there in a dream. He showed us a ruby the size of a walnut which he claims to have brought back from the cave himself... no mere dream, that. He refused to lead us there despite offers of reward. We spent a day scouring the hills – all quite steep, I must say, but revealing nothing.

But dreams abound. I have had several in the past few days that are particularly intense and disturbing. I hesitate to mention them, as you may well discount this entire tale as a result. But in them, I see a mountain and a cave with a sort of guardian image with an elephant. The interior is entirely of jewels in which reflections dance across time and space as if neither existed. Even in waking hours, I and my companions must admit to having heard a faint, but unmistakable echo of drums and crystal chimes. All in all, a rather disturbing phenomenon, I dare say.

This must sound preposterous, of course. I swear I have not come down with fever, as you will surely by now suspect. Regardless of my mental state, however, this land clearly is rich with deposits of precious minerals which we should protect and exploit. The local tales may even have a rational explanation, or at least prove valuable as a guide. Dreams aside, I shall continue on, but send my account of this single portion of the journey as a record separate from other, more 'official' notes. I expect to solve the mystery one way or another before a week is out and proceed eastward toward the Mekong and the French weasels on the other side of the river. I would offer coordinates, but my compass has inexplicably stopped working. Last reading put us around N20°50-60' E100°15-20'. If, for whatever reason, I should not return, I leave this with you to follow up on behalf of the Crown.

Yours truly,
J. G. Scott

P.S. Please do not involve that idiot Salisbury, as he likely would offer whatever treasure may be found to the bloody French.

Carpenter sat for several moments holding the letter in his hands. If genuine, the item was some 80 years old. A valuable piece of history, regardless of authorship. Its age alone helped explain Kohein's protectiveness. Carpenter placed the letter and journal back into the satchel and scooped together the remaining contents of Kohein's bag. The last item was a map of northern Thailand showing portions of Laos and Burma... the 'Golden Triangle' region.

An oval had been drawn in pencil around an area of the upper Mekong stretching from the border of Yunnan in China down to the town of Sop Ruak in Thailand and including portions of eastern Burma and western Laos on either side of the river which formed the border between the two. Further down and to the left, "Chiang Mai" itself was circled. A line connected it to the bottom margin and the penciled words, "Ban Haw Msq."

Carpenter puzzled over the lines for a moment, then shook himself. None of it made any sense to him, though the reference to 'crystal chimes' produced a curious thrill. The only piece of information that might offer a clue to Amit's whereabouts was the reference on the map to 'Ban Haw Msq.', whatever that was. Chiang Mai was circled, so that place name was at least familiar. He was sitting in Chiang Mai, after all. He refolded the map and tucked it back inside Kohein's bag, then snapped the clasps into place with extra pressure as if to close the contents to his own curiosity.

"OK, kid! You now have time maybe for a coffee and a banana. Put some clothes on, we gotta go." Brother Joe was shouldering his way through the front door, hands swathed in a dirty rag, dark grease smudges mixing with the red and blue ink decorating his swollen forearms. "Don't worry about your stuff – it's safe here."

Carpenter's head jerked toward the door. "Hey, Brother Joe. Actually, I think someone's been going through my things. I found these two open on the bed." He gestured to his suitcase and Kohein's satchel.

"No shit... I mean, no kidding? Anyone else here?"

"No one I saw, but these were here like this when I came back from the shower."

"Jeez. Let's take the stuff over to the House, then. We can lock the bags in Father Anond's room. Just take your pack."

"I think I'll take this, too." Carpenter patted the leather case. "I feel like I ought to keep a hand on it until I can get it back to Amit – the guy on the train."

"Sure... whatever. Bring 'em both. I'd help carry, but I've been doing surgery on a hopeless patient. Lucky for us, Anond offered us his Jeep." Brother Joe turned to leave. "But get a move on, OK? We need to leave before he changes his mind."

"Brother Joe?" Carpenter stood and held up a hand to slow him. "Do you know what 'Ban Haw' with the abbreviation 'Msq.' after it might mean?"

Brother Joe turned back. "You mean do I know *where* it is? I'm pretty sure the place you're talking about is in town, off Charoen Prathet Road. How come?"

"It's a place?" Carpenter asked, puzzled.

"Yeah, a mosque, which is probably what 'Msq.' stands for. It's the oldest one here. It's formal name is Matsayit Chiang Mai, but it's usually just called the 'Ban Haw mosque' because it was built by the *Jin Haw*... about a hundred years ago or so, I think."

"*Jin Haw?*"

"The Hill Chinese. There's a lot of them up here – all through the North actually... in Laos and Burma too. They're Muslims, you know. Brother Edward can tell you all about it. He knows all that stuff. Like a walking encyclopedia. Guy's amazing."

"I definitely need to talk to him, then. There's a note in Kohein's bag that must refer to the mosque."

"Yeah? So maybe that's where he hangs out, or someone knows him there."

"Yeah, maybe. But how did an Iraqi Jew get hooked up with Chinese Muslims… in Chiang Mai?"

THIRTEEN

"I SUPPOSE ONE COULD SAY IT WAS BECAUSE OF KUBLAI KHAN." Kumar was sitting in the back seat of the Jeep with Paul Hemple and describing the history of the so-called Hill Chinese. "The *Jin Haw* – or the *Hui* as they call themselves more often – have been here for centuries. You may recall that the Mongols under Kublai Khan conquered China in the 13th century. And most of Central Asia and the Middle East as well."

"But the Chinese didn't become Muslim," Carpenter responded.

"No, no. That is, the majority *Han* Chinese did not convert. But you must realize the Mongol empire stretched through most of the known world at the time. Kublai Khan followed the time-tested Chinese practice of using 'barbarians to control barbarians'. Uzbeki warriors in this case. Fierce fighters from Bukhara… Muslims."

"I know something about Kublai Khan, but to tell you the truth the first thing that comes to mind is Coleridge and the 'stately pleasure dome' that Kublai Khan decreed. I don't really know much detail when it comes to Chinese history." Carpenter felt under-educated.

Kumar warmed to his narrative. "In the mid-13th century, Kublai Khan used his Uzbek fighters to subdue the south of China – the kingdom of Dali in what became Yunnan. They were then given control over much of the province – roads and communications primarily – which put them in position to become very successful tradesmen. They were sent also to pacify Burma where they established themselves as the primary middlemen in the area."

"But it seems odd there would be enough *Hui* here in Chiang Mai to support a mosque," Carpenter mused.

"Actually there are nearly a dozen mosques in the city. Ban Haw is the oldest but not the only. The *Hui* in Yunnan rebelled against the Ch'in Dynasty, you see, in the mid-19th century. The revolt was put down rather brutally. There were massacres. Many *Hui* fled south to safe spots where they had done business for centuries. Chiang Mai is one such place. The *Hui* have prospered here."

"And they speak Thai, then?"

"Oh, yes. And Yunnanese and generally several other languages as well. Though not their original Turkic tongue. That, I'm afraid has been forgotten. They are quite assimilated at this point in their various adopted homes, including China. Perhaps because Kublai Khan was wise enough to provide them with Chinese wives."

"Disgusting." Paul Hemple spoke for the first time.

"Sorry?" Kumar turned to face the younger man whose face was set in a deep scowl.

"I said, 'disgusting'. It's disgusting that any man, even a heathen, would stoop to such tactics. There are so many good, Christian Chinese, despite the communists. I know... I have worshipped with them." Hemple's back straightened, whether out of pride or defensiveness – or both – it was hard to determine.

"Indeed! As have I. And, I would add, there are rather a decent number of Chinese Muslims as well. More, in fact, than can be found in Iraq or Syria or Libya for that matter. Some of them good, no doubt, despite the sad error of their ways." Kumar's tone was matter of fact, his face utterly devoid of sarcasm.

"Misguided..." Hemple mumbled and went quiet.

"Yes, well, good guidance is sometimes hard to come by." Kumar allowed generously. "But not today, as luck would have it. We are blessed with the stout heart and steady hand of Brother Joe himself!"

The atmosphere inside the car lightened.

"Don't start with me, Kumar. I know what 'stout' means." Brother Joe assumed his role of beleaguered soul with the skill of a true professional. He patted his midsection. "And it took a lot of Stout to build this, you know, back in my misguided days." He sat up straighter behind the wheel. "But you're the guide today, Kumar, not me. Where to first? I told the kid we might stop at the temple on Doi Suthep if there's time. Whaddya think?"

"The temple certainly is a sight one should not miss. And the village is very near. On, I say, driver, on to the temple."

****

Carpenter stood at the base of the steps leading up to Wat Phra That perched on the ridge above. Red brick stairs angled steeply up and into the overhanging foliage. Towering over him where he stood, the multiple heads of two giant snake-like creatures flanked the base of the entrance, mouths agape, long teeth smiling in triumph... or threat.

"These, of course, are the Nagas which one sees here in the North on either side of steps leading to the central *viharn* of the temple. According to legend, the giant serpent sheltered the Buddha while he meditated. One often sees images of the seated Buddha backed by a many-headed snake. One cannot help but notice, however, that the same Naga appears in Hindu mythology – also as a protector, but of Shiva rather than the Buddha." Kumar clearly was relishing his role as educator and tour guide.

"There is a saying about Thailand – about the whole of the Indian-influenced countries of Southeast Asia, really – that is, I believe, quite accurate: 'Scratch a Buddhist and you'll find a Hindu. Scratch that Hindu and you'll find an animist.'"

"And if you scratch a Christian?" Hemple, standing between Carpenter and Kumar, appeared ready to do battle.

"Ah, Christians simply bleed, Paul ... particularly we Catholics, given our peculiar tendency to treat guilt with pain. So, Western Christians bleed. Local Christians, on the other hand, are very much like their Buddhist brethren, I should say. Cross yourself on Sunday and try to keep the local spirits happy during the week."

"I'm surprised to hear a Brother make such a statement." Hemple's voice rose an octave.

"Ah, but you see, my young friend. I am not Western, after all. I am cursed with a near pagan sensibility that tends to distort the much clearer view you bring to these things." Kumar's tone was relaxed and inoffensive as he turned to include Carpenter. "But, I delay your heavenward journey. I shall not accompany you to the summit. My heart, while pure, is not up to the strain of the 290 steps. Brother Joe and I will wait for you here and watch the bags. It would be most helpful if you are able to return to meet us at the Jeep within the hour. We will want some unhurried time at the village." Kumar backed away from the steps, nodding a mischievous smile to Carpenter and leaving Hemple red-faced and speechless.

Hemple turned to Carpenter, brows knotted in indignation, thin lips compressed to form a small O-shape buried in a tangle of orange beard. Seeing Carpenter's amusement, he snorted a dismissal, turned to the stairs and started up. Carpenter followed, slowly at first. Then, impatient at Hemple's progress, he lengthened his strides to span two of the broad steps at a time. As Carpenter drew abreast, Hemple increased his own pace.

Carpenter's first impulse was to pull ahead, which he did in short order. Thirty feet further along, however, he realized the competition was depriving him of the very experience the temple offered. He slowed to a walk. The forest nestled in around and overhead. Bird song mixed with the clear, sweet chime of temple bells drifting down from the grounds above. The green-scaled undulations of the *naga* bodies bordering the stairs seemed to fuse with the landscape. Carpenter stood and breathed. Hemple puffed past without a glance, head lowered, jaw out-thrust.

At the summit, Hemple stood rigid, chest still heaving, his expression forced to unconcern. He turned as Carpenter reached him. "Tough climb." Superior, but magnanimous in victory.

"Beautiful, actually." Carpenter's breathing was even and deep, his quiet passage up through the dense slope had filled him with a sense of peace. He was at ease now with the prospect of walking the grounds with Hemple, or alone. He took off his shoes before stepping onto the tiled surface above the stairway and set off to the right where the ridge sloped away toward the city. Hemple did not seem inclined to separate. He followed a few paces behind Carpenter out onto the broad veranda surrounding the *bot*, *viharn*, and other monastic structures.

The temple was a jewel set beneath a towering sky. It gleamed red, gold and immaculate white in the morning sun. Ornate gilded carvings graced the rooflines of buildings at once both elaborate and subtle. Slender birdlike *chofa* images, their bells tinkling in the wind, stretched upward from the corners of the tiered roofs as if readying to depart this world for another. Carpenter wandered across the veranda studying the temple's carved bas relief or staring out across the broad river valley that stretched in shades of green to the far blue hills lining the horizon. Orange robed monks, heads shaved, feet bare, moved slowly through the crowd of visitors, stopping to speak with whomever approached. The devout knelt to place smoking *joss* sticks at shrines containing images of the Buddha or of venerable monks from times past. The fragrance of incense mixed with jasmine in the quiet air. Carpenter stopped at the main *cedi*, a huge golden *stupa* rising toward the heavens as it narrowed to a point and disappeared.

"I don't believe in the worship of images." Hemple stood just behind him.

"OK." Carpenter had no desire for conversation.

"It's all just hocus pocus, if you ask me."

"So, I won't ask you."

"What, you believe in this? I thought you were Catholic."

"Recovering Catholic, actually." Carpenter finally turned to face Hemple. "I don't find these pieces of architecture any more or less meaningful than the images we pretend not to venerate. Do you know what the *cedi* represents?"

"No, and I don't care."

"Really? In its own way, it's about the struggle to attain heaven. Not so far from what we have been taught... what we all seek in one form or another. It's an architectural metaphor for the diminishing of desire and attachment in the course of spiritual evolution."

"I don't believe in evolution. It's a denial of God and Creation."

"Or simply another way to describe both. The *cedi* stretches back past Buddhism to its original roots in Hindu cosmology. It represents Mt. Meru at the center of the universe, home of the gods and dwelling place of Indra himself."

"Ridiculous primitive stories. I don't understand how you can take any of it seriously, if you do."

"Stories are what we have, Paul. They're all just approximations, reflections. It's too bad, in my opinion, that we get so attached to just one story and ignore the rest."

"I have no interest in stories – only the truth. And the notion of a mountain ruled by gods is childish and absurd whether you're talking about Zeus or Indra, or some other pagan deity." Hemple sniffed, his tone derisive.

Carpenter had had enough of intellectual jousting. The morning's discovery weighed heavy and unspoken. He felt a strangely cold and satisfying anger take hold as he stepped closer to Hemple and held his eyes with his own. "I'm surprised, Paul. Judging from your reading habits I would have taken you for a devotee of the Lord Indra yourself."

Hemple flinched. A small tic fluttered his right eyelid. "What are you talking about? What would you know about my reading habits, anyway?"

"I know you have an interest in letters and old diaries... and other people's stuff, generally." Carpenter was looking directly at Hemple, brows raised in innocent inquiry. "Isn't that why you went through my things... looking for reading material?"

Hemple's response was exaggerated. "I don't know what you're talking about. I did not go through your suitcase or through the leather bag, either one."

"So how did you know those were the two pieces I'm referring to? I had several bags under the bed, Paul... too many, I believe you pointed out, to get through the eye of the needle with, right?"

Hemple looked away as if hoping for rescue. He had known this moment would come, but had no ready answer. He went with simple denial. "I'm no thief. You have no right to accuse me."

"This isn't an accusation, Paul... it's an observation. Am I wrong? Or maybe you're saying I'm lying?" Carpenter mastered an impulse to slap Hemple's frightened face and reduce him to tears. He jabbed a finger into Hemple's chest hard enough to cause him to take an involuntary step back. "Either way, you touch anything of mine again and you will need a lot more than prayer to save your sorry ass. You would be wise to file that advice under the category of revealed truth."

"Are you threatening me?" Hemple's voice cracked as he struggled to maintain a semblance of dignity.

"Definitely." Carpenter nodded and held Hemple's eyes waiting for a challenge. None came. A rush of shame rose to dilute the undeniable pleasure he felt at the prospect of causing Hemple pain. Carpenter breathed and stepped back. "But out of deference to the peace of the Lord Buddha, I'm going to let it go right now... as long as you find someplace else to be and someone else to be with."

Carpenter turned his back to gaze up at the *cedi*. He could feel Hemple behind him for a moment, then heard the soft padding of his feet as he moved away. Carpenter stood alone for several minutes more waiting for a sense of peace to return. The energy of the confrontation faded, but something else remained. He sensed it in the back of his neck and head. A sense of being watched. He turned around and found himself looking into the dark eyes of a sharp and lightly bearded face. The same face, he realized, that he had first seen at the train station as he disembarked yesterday.

The stranger held Carpenter's gaze for a startled moment, then stepped back into a knot of worshippers. Carpenter started forward and the man bent and disappeared around a corner. Carpenter followed, tentatively at first then faster as the likelihood of simple coincidence receded. When he rounded the corner himself, the man was gone. Carpenter did a slow 360 to check the entire area. Groups and individuals paced quietly about the grounds. The face was nowhere to be seen. Paul Hemple, however, stood stiff and alone at a stone balcony looking out over the city.

Carpenter approached. Rage had faded now along with the guilty thrill of impending violence. "Listen, Paul. I've said what I needed to say. As far as I'm concerned, it's over. I'm heading down now if you're ready."

Hemple turned, his expression like a chastened child's. With effort, he managed, "I am not a thief." He swallowed hard. "But I admit I opened your things." There, he had said it.

"Why?"

Why indeed. There was no answer but the simple truth. "I wanted to know more about you."

"Did you consider just asking?"

Hemple swallowed again and straightened himself like a man facing a firing squad. "I am not good with people... you may have noticed. I say the wrong things. You're different. Everyone seems to like you right away." He looked down at his feet and spoke without meeting Carpenter's eyes. "So I wanted to know more about you without having to say anything." His voice trailed off. "Before you decided to write me off." Hemple pulled his head up and resumed a semblance of dignity. "I thought you would be longer. I wouldn't have taken anything of yours. I'm not a thief."

Carpenter explored Hemple's face for a long moment. He nodded slowly. "OK, I'll buy that. You ready to go?"

They returned to the long stairs, retrieved their shoes and descended in silence through the trees. Hemple refused to look at Carpenter, who directed his attention to the steps below for a glimpse of the mystery watcher.

Kumar waited at the bottom smiling in anticipation. "Well?"

"Beautiful, exquisite." Carpenter grinned in response. "Thank you so much for stopping here. I wouldn't have wanted to miss it."

"Yes, an experience," Hemple mumbled and looked away.

"I'm happy you could enjoy it. I only wish I were still capable of the climb myself." Kumar motioned up the hill to his left where Brother Joe stood next to the Jeep. "Shall we proceed, then?"

The three set out for the vehicle. As they walked, Carpenter asked Kumar, "Did you happen to see a guy with a beard come down the stairs while you were waiting for us?"

"A bearded fellow? No, I'm sure I would have noticed. There are so few beards to be seen here except for the Sikh merchants and among the *Haw*. And Paul, of course. Why do you ask? Did you meet someone of interest?"

"I *saw* someone of interest, but didn't actually meet him." Carpenter briefly described the man and the encounter from the day before.

"Most curious. But, no, I saw no one of that description, I'm afraid. I certainly will keep a 'lookout' as they are so fond of saying in your movies."

Brother Joe waved a greeting as they approached and climbed into the Jeep. At Kumar's direction, he turned around and headed back down the steep incline for barely a quarter mile, then, again following Kumar's instructions, turned off the paved road to the right and onto a clay track leading into the forest.

"This will take us directly to the Meo village," Kumar announced. "However, we may need to leave the vehicle some distance from the village itself. The path becomes narrow and quite steep."

"We better not screw up Father's Jeep." Brother Joe spoke without taking his eyes from the rutted path ahead. "Or get it ripped off. I can stay with the car and the bags."

"The Jeep should be safe here, though I would hesitate to leave anything inside." Kumar leaned forward to address Carpenter. "Can you bring both bags, James? I think it would be wise to do so."

"Sure, the satchel has a shoulder strap. I can hang it on my backpack."

"I can carry something if you like." Hemple spoke to the ceiling of the vehicle, his tone disinterested.

Carpenter swiveled in his seat. "That's very generous of you, Paul. Thank you."

"You're welcome." Hemple's gaze remained fixed on the ceiling.

A mile further on, the forest closed in dark and thick around them. "The land drops off rather steeply just ahead," Kumar warned. "Perhaps we can walk from here?"

"It's OK to just leave the Jeep in the middle of the path?" Brother Joe was dubious.

"Yes. I have done it before. We can rest assured we will not be impeding the progress of other vehicles that come along. None will, you see." Kumar opened the rear door and stepped out as Brother Joe set the parking brake. "It's best to leave the doors unlocked so the curious may examine the interior without doing damage."

Brother Joe nodded, strode to the front of the Jeep, lifted the hood and leaned in. A minute later, he straightened, holding a rotor in his left fist. "That should discourage anyone looking to take a joy ride."

Carpenter handed his backpack to Hemple and shouldered Kohein's case. "Here you go. Careful with how you hold it. My things seem to have a tendency to fall open unexpectedly." He softened the comment with a grin, then followed Kumar and Brother Joe forward through the shadows and dense growth.

The forest opened onto an outcropping just above the village. The dirt track they had been following curved sharply down and to the right, then meandered left again through a collection of small wood and bamboo structures topped with thatch that stretched along the zigzag path and back up the hillside. The fronts of the houses bent forward at a down-slope angle, their roofs hanging low and close to the ground. Children whooped and cried in the pounded dirt, chasing each other round and round, dodging among chickens and pigs and laughing at the short-haired brown dogs barking at their heels.

As they entered the village, they were greeted by a thin, middle-aged man dressed in a loose black cotton shirt and indigo breeches, a chain of small bells circling his neck. Several women of varying ages stood behind, two bearing infants or young children on their hips. Sunlight glinted off their tall headdresses, which were adorned with silver coins and tassels. Kumar stepped forward to greet the man.

After a short exchange, Kumar turned to the others. "This is Mr. Vang and his wives. He is patriarch here. " Kumar turned to Mr. Vang and, in Thai, introduced each of the visitors in turn. Introductions complete, Mr. Vang spoke to Kumar, apparently offering a question. In response, Kumar delved into his own shoulder bag and produced a large manila envelope. The family members quickly gathered around him as he pulled a sheaf of glossy color photos from the envelope. "I took these on my last visit here. They are most impressed with photographs – especially these large colored prints."

As if understanding Kumar's comment, Mr. Vang held up a photo of himself dressed in a beautifully embroidered jacket and posed with a flintlock rifle held to his eye, aiming at a target somewhere off to his right. He patted his chest and nodded vigorously as if to confirm that the image was, indeed, himself. After several minutes admiring the pictures, Mr. Vang offered Kumar an awkward *wai* – a Thai gesture, but one that communicated appreciation in their common parlance. He spoke then at some length, expression turned serious, eyes revealing sadness and concern.

"One of his sons is ill," Kumar translated without turning away from the speaker. "The child has been unable to keep food down for more than a week and is running a fever. Mr. Vang regrets that he cannot spend time today to tell me more about life in the village – particularly about how others are adapting to his conversion."

Hemple, who had been gazing absently around the village, swiveled toward Kumar immediately. "He has converted? He's Christian?"

Without turning, Kumar answered. "Yes, Catholic. We have been discussing how this change has affected him and his family and relations among others in this village and nearby."

"Well this is wonderful. Praise the Lord! I ..." Hemple spoke loudly, and over the quiet words of the sad father.

Kumar glanced back quickly, his expression sharp and commanding. "Do not speak now." He turned back to Mr. Vang, his expression compassionate, head moving slowly side-to-side as he listened.

Hemple reddened, but stopped abruptly.

"There will be what they call a *hu plig* to consult the spirits about his son. Something like a séance or even exorcism." Kumar continued to listen. "We may attend if we wish. He hopes our prayers will add to the power of the ceremony."

Hemple could not contain himself. "I thought you said he was Christian – Catholic. This is witchcraft!"

Mr. Vang looked up at him in alarm, then continued addressing Kumar. Kumar took his hand and spoke briefly to him. Then turning to Hemple, Kumar spoke in a low, clear voice. "You are not obliged to attend this ritual, Paul. Actually, you are not invited. You may wait here or return to the Jeep – whichever you prefer."

Hemple started to protest. Kumar held up a hand, his black eyes steady above the command of his brown palm. "Now is not the time to debate theology. This man is desperate to do whatever he knows to do to save his son. You certainly have a right to your opinions, but at the moment I'm afraid there is no place for them here."

Red-faced, Hemple handed Carpenter his pack and began the walk to the Jeep, back straight and chin thrust forward in an attitude of quiet defiance. But as he walked, he kept up a steady stream of self-criticism. Why had he spoken at all? Kumar was less devout than he. But he had succeeded where Hemple could not even manage a simple introduction. He marched on, looking neither left nor right until he reached the Jeep, where he sat in angry silence waiting for the next calamity and hoping he wouldn't be the one to cause it.

FOURTEEN

THE BUILDING WAS ROUND AND STOOD AT GROUND LEVEL, sided in split bamboo and roofed in a thick thatch spread over wood and bamboo supports. The floor inside was clay. Kumar, Brother Joe and Carpenter sat on a low wood bench to the left of the entrance. Sunlight cast a rough rectangle on the brown floor just inside the doorway. Otherwise the interior was dark and unlit.

A small boy clad in black, hair cut close to his scalp except for a foot-long topknot hanging down his back, sat wide-eyed and silent on a short stool set three or four feet in from the doorway. Facing him at the far end of the room, a rough wooden altar sat bare save for a collection of smoking *joss* sticks set in tin cans at the base of the structure. Cotton strings tied to the boy's wrists connected him to the altar and ran along a shallow trench that had been scraped in the dirt. Occasional grunts and scratching sounds came from the far side of the room where a makeshift pen and woven reed cage sat together against the wall. Carpenter shivered and shook off a sense almost of foreboding.

A wrinkled black-clad man bent near the altar holding a looped device roughly the size and shape of a ping-pong paddle and strung with what appeared to be seed pods. His voice rose and fell in a chanting cadence punctuated by the rattle of the seed pods as he began to circle the room in a slow dancing motion. The ceremonial atmosphere was oddly offset by the activity of an older woman calmly sweeping the dirt floor near the doorway with a stiff broom of bound twigs. To Carpenter, the shaman's movements seemed somehow familiar, perhaps recalling the ceremonial dances he associated with American Indians. The shaman wove his way about the room, raising his knees high, shifting weight from one foot to the other, and ignoring the boy each time he came near.

"He is beginning to call out to the spirits," Kumar whispered. "He will eventually fall into a trance while he travels to the spirit realm where he will attempt to bargain for one of the boy's souls. The child has many, but one has been captured – possibly while he was asleep. It seems they are readying it to feast upon. This is the cause of the boy's illness."

Carpenter blinked away a blurred double image of the child that pulsed with his accelerated heartbeat.

After making several circuits, the shaman walked across the room and past the woman, who continued sweeping as if nothing out of the ordinary were taking place. He stopped and picked up a white porcelain bowl, then turned to the cage set against the wall. He lifted the basket top, reached in and withdrew a large red and brown hen which he brought along with the bowl to set near the boy's feet next to the trench.

Kumar was writing busily in a thick notepad he had drawn from his bag. The shaman paused to look up sharply, shaking his head and speaking urgently. Kumar quickly closed the notebook and put it back into his bag. The shaman cast a wide-eyed glance at Carpenter as if warning him to manage his companions. He returned then, chanting, to the task at hand.

Crouched before the boy, he produced a short curved blade from the folds of his jacket and drew it quickly across the chicken's throat. The creature shrieked and struggled for a few moments, then collapsed twitching into the shaman's hands as its dark blood spurted into and around the white bowl. The shaman scooped blood-wet earth into the bowl, his voice rising and falling, his body trembling as if possessed. Beginning at the boy's feet, he stooped away trickling a thin stream of dark red along the trench toward the altar.

Moving again to the far wall, the shaman set the bird's carcass near the basket cage and returned with a small pig kicking and squealing in his grip. He held it aloft and spoke, then bent again at the boy's feet and quickly drew the blade across the animal's throat. Its scream was horrific, almost human. It struggled and kicked frantically in the shaman's grip until its life had drained away. The white bowl overflowed in red. The shaman poured its steaming contents slowly into the earth all along the trench and onto the strings connecting the child to the altar.

There was silence in the room, save for the incongruous scratching of the old woman's broom across the clay. The shaman stood shivering and quiet, head cocked as if listening, the body of the dead animal motionless at his feet. Carpenter, realizing he had been holding his breath, let it out in a single long whoosh that seemed to echo through the room like a low wind.

The shaman swayed and moaned, eyes closed, lids flickering. He mumbled quietly for a moment then seemed to come awake. He opened his eyes and looked around the room as if re-orienting himself, caught Carpenter's glance again, then bent to grasp the pig by its front and rear legs. Lifting, he carried it over to the far wall where he laid it next to the stiff form of the lifeless bird. He returned then to the boy, gently untied the strings from his wrists and cupped his small face tenderly between calloused hands. He spoke a few quiet words, raised the boy up and walked with him through the doorway and into the bright sunshine outside.

The three observers rose without speaking and followed. Brother Joe hunched his shoulders and shook his head as he exited the hut. He looked at Kumar and Carpenter. "Don't try *that* at home…" He took a deep breath and shook his head again slowly.

Near them, the boy was nestled close in his father's arms. Mr. Vang conferred with the healer while nodding anxiously and stroking the child's back. The shaman spoke reassuringly, gesturing with his fingers and hands and seeming now and then to refer to the three observers. At one point in the conversation, he turned to nod toward Carpenter, his voice rising momentarily in pitch. The conversation drew to a close and the shaman ducked back beneath the low roof, glancing once again in Carpenter's direction before disappearing inside.

Mr. Vang came over to Kumar and spoke at some length, looking occasionally at Carpenter. Kumar nodded and listened, then turned to translate. "The healing appears to have been successful. The spirits accepted the offerings in place of the boy's soul. We are invited, by the way, to help consume the earthly remains which the shaman keeps as a sort of fee for his services."

Kumar's tone changed. "Something else. There was apparently a surprise during the ritual. Most unusual, it seems. The shaman claims that in his journey to bargain for the soul of the boy, he encountered spirits who asked after you, James. They asked specifically for the '*terton*' - a term even the shaman did not understand. I add here that if he were Tibetan, the word would have some meaning. There, a '*terton*' refers to one who unearths a treasure hidden in years past – a '*terma*', I believe it is called. This *terma* is intended to be found years later when most needed.

"At any rate, the spirits appeared to recognize his confusion. They explained that you are well-acquainted with sacrifice and the need to heal and make whole again. They were most amenable to the shaman's request on the boy's behalf, given his association with you."

Carpenter could find no reply.

"He assumes you also are a healer and spirit traveler; that you too journey across time and space. He reports, however, that the spirits warned of danger in your current quest. He referred specifically to a Being he called simply 'the demon'." Kumar's expression was a strange blend of sincerity and amused disbelief.

"Ordinarily, the shaman would not offer a feast after an exorcism. However, he is prepared to share the fruit of the sacrifice with you as, I suppose one would say, a professional courtesy." Kumar ended, brows raised in a 'Can you belief this?' expression, then looked to Mr. Vang to indicate he had completed the translation. Vang smiled and nodded enthusiastically, as if to show his agreement.

Carpenter was stunned. He felt an odd mix of excitement over the special status he seemed to have been accredited and an unsettling sense of disquiet. He tried to discount both. "Well, I am honored by the recognition, however misplaced... and by the invitation, of course. I'm sorry that the shaman - or the spirits, perhaps - appear to have mistaken me for someone else. I *am* a recent traveler, but by airplane rather than spirit."

Kumar translated. Vang replied with a knowing look and spoke briefly.

"He says the shaman told him the same thing – that is, that you fly. He understands that you wish to protect your secrets and thanks you for your intervention. He swears not to reveal your identity to your enemies."

Kumar waited a beat to allow Carpenter to reply. Hearing no response, he went on. "We should perhaps indicate whether or not we intend to accept the shaman's invitation. He waits inside. Unfortunately, Paul also waits for us and he is not as welcome a guest as you."

"Uh, well... in that case, I suppose we should thank the shaman and Mr. Vang for their extraordinary hospitality and generosity, but regretfully decline their invitation. Maybe you could say we have a journey ahead of us and must be on our way... something like that?"

Following Kumar's translation, Vang nodded and bowed, then stepped inside the shaman's quarters. After a few minutes, he re-emerged with the shaman, who bowed to Carpenter and spoke through Vang, who then translated his words into Thai, which Kumar then put into English. The process was disjointed, leaving Carpenter frustrated at his inability to communicate directly. Kumar stood before Carpenter and Vang, Brother Joe and the shaman to the side. Vang's son had put his head down on his father's shoulder and appeared to be sleeping.

"The shaman has been honored by your visit and regrets that you cannot stay to share the remains of the sacrifice. He wishes you, his brother, safety in your journey." Kumar looked a question to Vang, who turned to the shaman.

The shaman stepped past Vang to place a hand on Carpenter's shoulder. He looked into his eyes, speaking confidently as if expecting the younger man to understand. He held the gaze for a long moment then stepped away.

Vang hesitated, evidently considering, then spoke. Kumar nodded and turned to Carpenter. "I have no idea what this means. In Thai, he said, '*Haa phoa, jyr luug.*' Literally, this translates as 'Search for father, find offspring' – probably 'son' in this case. So, 'Seek father, find son'. The language offers no verb tense or qualifier to add specificity – leaving considerable room for interpretation. Vang seems satisfied that it is an allusion to his newfound faith, but the shaman, of course, is not Christian. Does any of that make sense to you?"

Carpenter shook his head. "Nope. None whatsoever."

****

Kumar, Brother Joe and Carpenter stood on the ridge above the village looking back down on a scene from an innocent travelogue, musing on the unexpected twists their visit had produced.

"This is perhaps the most interesting and certainly the most surprising of all the trips I have made to the hill tribes in the last decade." A long note of astonishment lingered like an echo in Kumar's voice.

"Certainly not what I had expected, to say the least," Carpenter agreed. The encounter continued to resonate with a sense of almost physical impact – not exactly a bruise, but tender to the touch.

"I must say, I had not until now fully appreciated the protection offered by the anthropologist's role. We seem to have moved well past the concept of 'participant observer' to simple participant. Particularly you, James, though I doubt 'simple' would begin to describe your own experience."

"Well, it describes *me* well enough." Brother Joe observed. "Simple is what I'm feeling... as in 'simpleton'. I don't know what the hell that was all about, but it gives me the friggin' creeps, I'll tell you that."

They turned together toward the path back into the forest.

"I assume Paul decided to return to the Jeep and wait there, rather than enjoy the hospitality he so quickly earned." Kumar's tone was characteristically neutral despite the sharp edge of sarcasm the comment implied.

"Well, unless he can hot-wire a handicapped engine, he's either waiting for us at the car or walking the road to Calgary by himself," Brother Joe offered innocently. "I guess he wasn't interested in carrying anything with him - no cross, no bags."

Brother Joe moved forward into the tangled shadows. Carpenter shouldered his pack and Kohein's bag and followed behind Kumar into the bush. The late afternoon sun deepened the shade, lengthening the dark patches created by overhanging vegetation. Little direct light penetrated the canopy, though occasional glimpses of the western sky revealed a stronger glow ahead than behind them as they walked single file along the narrow path.

Rounding a sharp turn on the uphill side of the track, Brother Joe stopped short and raised a hand. "Hold it, we have a little problem here." A mass of brush lay across the path ahead, blocking progress. Brother Joe moved forward to consider a way around. "This wasn't here when we came this way before." He peered into the foliage beside the path. "This is weird. These bushes didn't drag themselves here."

Just then, Carpenter heard a snap of branches from behind. He spun around to see two short, burly men step onto the path from either side. Each held a thick wooden stave like a bat at the ready. He turned back toward Brother Joe as two more men stepped onto the path in front of the makeshift barrier. One carried a stave, the other a machete unsheathed and held high as if ready to swing.

"*Ya khid maag, na?*" A fifth man emerged from behind a large, elephant-ear bush next to the machete-bearer. Carpenter recognized the scarred and grizzled face of the boxer from the train. Then, to the rear, another voice. Carpenter turned to see the second man from the train move onto the path. Six altogether.

"Basically, that means, 'Don't try anything'." Kumar said evenly, facing the man in front.

"*Kho krabow noi, na khrab,*" the boxer said with singsong politeness, indicating the leather satchel at Carpenter's shoulder. May I have the bag please?

"He wants Amit's satchel," Kumar automatically resumed his role as translator. "He appears to be sincere," he added dryly.

The boxer grinned at Carpenter. "*Rujak gan, na? Phyan kan laew.*"

"He says, you know him – you're already old friends."

"Tell him he should come get the bag from his old friend here. I don't want to drop it and break what's inside. Tell him he should know it's valuable." There was a rough edge to Carpenter's voice, a layer of menace even he would not have recognized had the situation allowed time for reflection. Carpenter kept his eyes on the boxer, listening for movement behind him.

The man hesitated after Kumar's translation, then shouldered his way past Brother Joe, who turned to glare at him, hands bunched into fists, forearms swelling from the strain. "*Ai hea,*" Brother Joe hissed – only the second time,

Carpenter thought randomly, that he had heard him speak Thai. Profanity, apparently.

The boxer stiffened and whipped a backhand fist around to Brother Joe's ear that dropped him to the ground. In a single motion, Carpenter shrugged off his pack along with Kohein's bag and swung a brutal kick to the boxer's exposed liver. The man bent immediately in pain, clutching his side. Carpenter cupped the back of the boxer's neck in clasped hands and brought his knee up sharply. There was a sharp sickening crack as the bridge of his nose shattered. The boxer collapsed alongside Brother Joe, who sat up quickly, shaking his head, then added a massive forearm blow to the prone man's temple before scrambling to his feet.

"All right, now we got five to three. Much better. Kumar, try to stay between us, OK?" Brother Joe backed toward Carpenter. "Big knife, huh?"

Carpenter took a breath, deliberately suppressing contradictory sensations of joy and repulsion. "Can you hold off the guys behind us?" Carpenter moved forward balanced lightly on the balls of his feet. "Let me see what I can do about the knife."

"Listen, kid. Don't be stupid, OK? Let me do this. I've been in more bar fights than Carter has little pills."

But Carpenter was past him already, edging toward the two men blocking their way forward. The man with the machete raised it menacingly, but Carpenter could read the doubt in his eyes. His leader had gone down in a matter of seconds.

Carpenter took two quick steps toward the machete as if to confront him first, then shifted his weight to his right leg and sent a hard left kick instead into the stave man's midsection. He crumpled and lay squirming. The machete man sliced at Carpenter's leg, but it was no longer there. Carpenter had brought it back and down to serve as the foundation for a high right kick that connected with the machete man's jaw. Three down.

Carpenter heard a grunt of pain behind him. Brother Joe was locked on the ground with one of the attackers, ignoring the blows of the other stave man whose clumsy flailings were impeded by the thick undergrowth lining the narrow path. Carpenter sprinted back past Kumar whose eyes were wide with fear. The stave whipped past Brother Joe's head as he ducked to deliver another blow to the man on the ground. The force of the swing left the stave man unbalanced. Carpenter stepped straight into the man's chest, well inside the range of a blow. A short right took the wind from his solar plexus and bent him at the waist. An uppercut to the windpipe left him on the ground, struggling for breath.

Carpenter looked right and left. The second man from the train was nowhere in sight. Brother Joe scrambled to his feet, leaving his opponent gasping in the dirt. "OK, kid. I guess you got more experience than I thought. Thanks."

From in front, Kumar winced in pain. The accomplice from the train held a short blade to Kumar's throat. "*Toi lang, na. Rewrew.*" Back off, fast. Kumar's eyes were closed tight. A thin trickle of blood ran down the front of his neck and into his shirt. Kohein's bag lay in the middle of the path just a foot from where Carpenter stood with a panting Brother Joe.

"Hold on, kid. He wants the bag. Screw it, we tried." Brother Joe began to move back slowly. Carpenter retreated a step, considering options and struggling with a surprising readiness for extreme violence. Behind him, Brother Joe's beaten opponent had struggled to his feet and now held the sturdy club high in both hands, blood trailing down from nose and eyes, a murderous look distorting his swollen face. Carpenter and Brother Joe moved together reflexively to face him.

Then from the front again, another wince of pain. Carpenter swung back around, expecting the worst. Instead, he saw the bearded watcher from the temple pressing the bore of an automatic rifle to the head of Kumar's assailant. Kumar sat several feet away at a safe distance, but hunched over holding his chest. The watcher looked toward Carpenter and grinned as if greeting a lost comrade.

Carpenter stared, confused. "What..." he began to ask, just before a heavy wooden stave thudded against his skull from behind.

FIFTEEN

HER VOICE CAME FROM EVERYWHERE. *A gentle stream washing through his mind, cool and cleansing. Pain ebbed and disappeared. He floated on a jeweled cloud, cocooned in warmth and protection. "You hold a precious truth. Watch for it now, free from time and space. Look for what cannot be seen. Listen for what cannot be heard. Breathe. Let the universe unfold."*

He opened his eyes. The dawn sky shone pale blue and golden. Shimmers of diamond light rippled through a network of dewdrops clinging like tiny jewels to the spider's web stretched new across the cave's entrance. A small wind rustled the forest ceiling below, whispering promises of things both past and future. Crystal chimes drifted on the air and mixed with the beat of double-headed drums, conch shell and trumpet.

He watched. He listened. He breathed.

"He isn't moving. It's been over an hour."

"He's breathing easily. He seems to be talking to himself."

"Really? Can you make out what he's saying?"

"Just syllables… muttering. I think he's still seeing stars."

"He's been hit on the head. We'll be lucky if he can see at all by the time he wakes up."

"Let us be patient. Let him rest. The blow does not seem to have been as severe as yours. He should recover completely. A matter of time."

Her voice soothed and gentled, yet urged him on. "Your dreams are visitors from an unforgotten past. Sit, watch, listen, breathe."

Images rushed through his mind. Places, events, lifetimes. Faces… some familiar and repeated, some new then gone forever.

He was a quiet priest watching the dance of mind play as his inner warrior stirred and struggled keeping watch. Random drifting fragments of light coalesced into ghost memories. Visions formed and faded. Nightmare assaults. Panic and desperate resistance. Close combat. Pursuit. Slaughter by the thousands. Gut-wrenching fear. Grotesque carnage. Hands wet and slippery with the blood of a slain child. A survivor's relief. Victory and vengeance. Violent and benevolent Ashoka.

"He moved. His eyelids fluttered. He's still talking to himself. One moment he looks as if he's in pain, then he smiles, then it's pain again."

"Could you make out what he was saying?"

"No, nothing that sounded like English. Just mumbling. Something like, 'Ashoka' a couple of times. Nothing that makes sense to me."

"Could he be dreaming history? Ashoka once ruled an empire as large as Alexander the Great's. All of India and more. Slaughtered thousands including his own brothers, then cast himself as a great patron of Buddhism. Kind Father to his people, *et cetera*."

"But how would James know about him?"

"Probably in his university studies. He is quite well-read for such a young man."

"Maybe when he wakes up…"

"A long and terrible journey, my son, but not without joy or happiness. You have taken many paths. Some have led to peace, others to battle. You have fought and advanced, fallen and retreated. Worshipped and rejected belief. You have ventured forth to discover then sought to leave the world behind. You have loved and lost great love. And you have been betrayed by those you hold most dear… one especially, with whom one day you must reconcile. All paths are bound together. They cross again and again like the threads of a net. There is more to see. Sit, watch, listen, breathe."

A dizzying succession of sunrises and sunsets, a rush of days, years, centuries. A bright comet trailed its long tail across the night sky once, twice, three times as the world spun endlessly in space. Vengeful priest turned again to war; sickened warrior again to peace. He sought shelter in the high hills and lived alone.

He felt the Stranger's presence before he heard the rattle of pebbles and loose rock announce his approach. The Stranger was not old, though his face was weathered and his feet calloused from travel. He sat near the fire, grateful for its warmth and for the chance to share the Hermit's thin meal of rice and lentils.

He was a Jew. A refugee of sorts from the boot heel of Rome. He told the Hermit of his homeland and his travels. Imperial rule lay heavy on the land. Protest was dangerous, rebellion suicidal. The Pharisees had been co-opted and sought simply to retain their authority at the expense of their people's independence. The Stranger had spoken up in challenge. They threatened him not with Jewish law, but Roman justice. His association with malcontents became known. The Stranger saw no answer in violence, but found no other answer either.

The Hermit nodded at this. He too had slept in peace and woken to violence. He had freed himself to walk his own path, unhindered and alone. The Stranger had done the same, traveling east along the Silk Road. He had no faith in earthly rulers. Rome was a cruel father who took without giving.

The Hermit felt a kinship here. He told the Stranger of his own family's journey over centuries, of their escape from Babylon, their wandering search. He shared the story of the parchment and the stone. How the original writing on the scroll had been lost to time. How new words and new truths had been written over the old through exposure to other traditions, other wisdom... only to fade themselves to mere ghosts of meaning. And the message he took from it now: the illusion of beginnings and endings. How the end of one thing is simply the beginning of another.

The Stranger told of his own journey of many years along the great trade route. Buddhist monasteries dotted the path and monks had welcomed him into their caves and holy places. The Stranger had stopped wherever a teacher appeared. Some taught the chill power of mind and reason. Others taught simple compassion and daily practice. He learned to go beyond the limit of words, to see God as Being rather than a being.

But the Stranger's most recent encounter had left him uncertain and confused. In a mountain cave at the furthest point in his eastward journey, he had stayed with an elderly man in a cave in the mountains. His companion knew but little of the various languages used along the trade path, and tended toward silence anyway. He alluded to the Way of Heaven, a formless and eternal power flowing through all living and non-living things alike.

The Stranger sought to reconcile this vast and impersonal vision with God the Father of his own tradition. The Mahayana Buddhists offered an answer of sorts, recognizing an individual connection to all beings and a responsibility for their deliverance from suffering and sin.

But the old man had quoted an ancient sage in words that left the Stranger questioning his own journey.

> Without going out of your door,
> You can know the ways of the world.
> Without peeping through your window,
> You can see the Way of Heaven.
> The farther you go, The less you know.

"So perhaps, my mind, like your parchment, should be cleansed of presumption. Perhaps it is time to end this journey, as you seem to have done. Is there more to learn? Am I seeking or am I running away? Are we the children of God, or just the forgotten orphans of a father who never knew they existed... or cared."

"A question I should ask myself," the Hermit replied. "I remain now in one place as your sage recommends, but I have found no real peace here, not from my own angry mind."

"Surely there are more ways than one," the Stranger mused. "More ways of seeing and being. More paths to the Father... whatever, wherever He may be."

"Perhaps, though I myself have left most paths that take me through the world," the Hermit answered.

"And I have traveled all I could find."

"Yet neither of us has reached a true resting place, it seems. My dreams still trouble me now in this quiet place so far from all I know."

They conversed through the night. In the end, the Hermit listened and watched. The Stranger spoke equally of self-discipline and compassion. He seemed to grasp the meaning of the Buddha in a new way. He referred to him as the Son of Man and the Son of God, "... as are all men if only we could see ourselves completely and unapart from the Father Without End, from All That Is."

Sometime during that short night, the Hermit came to realize that in choosing one path, he had needlessly abandoned another. Choice allowed freedom, but invited illusion. Maya had visited again to deceive him with a false vision of duality, of beginnings separate from endings. Perhaps the only way to escape a world of suffering was to embrace it and work to change it.

The Stranger, too, came to a realization. His journey was not over, but his eastern travels had reached a turning point. This night, both understood, had linked the web of their lives and begun to spin them out anew. Both had fled the past, but neither had escaped it. Both would turn back now to confront it and create a new future. The Hermit would continue toward the dawn. The Stranger would follow the sunset toward a distant sea and home.

They sat together, no longer needing to speak, as the sky hinted at another morning. They watched. They listened to the world begin. They breathed.

SIXTEEN

CARPENTER BREATHED DEEPLY AND OPENED HIS EYES.

He lay on his back, a cylindrical pillow propped neatly under his neck for support, his throbbing head cushioned by soft silk and down. He blinked to clear his vision. A white vaulted ceiling, gleaming brass fixture suspended from the center, base set in multi-colored tiles overwritten with flowing black script... an unfamiliar calligraphy. Teak book shelves lining the walls. An open door letting out into what appeared to be a cloakroom or foyer.

Faces hovering over him swam into focus. Brother Joe, anxious and attentive. Kumar, looking pale beneath his brown skin. And several others in the background, white skull caps prominent on their heads.

"Ah, finally. Let us not crowd too closely. He seems to have survived."

Kohein's generous face appeared. "How are you feeling, my friend... my true friend? We have been waiting most anxiously for your return."

Carpenter started to speak, then coughed, swallowed and began again. "Is it morning? Did the Stranger leave?" His own words confused him. Images lingered, more real for a time than the reality he had woken to. He clutched at the dream, but the harder he grasped at it, the more quickly it faded. He felt it slip away. He began a third time. "Is that you, Amit? It's good to see you. Are you OK?"

"Yes, James, it is indeed I. But the question is are *you* OK? Is your vision clear?"

"I can see alright, but my head hurts pretty bad." He closed his eyes momentarily, then opened them. Pieces from his last moments of waking consciousness began to return, crowding out finally all thoughts of mountain paths and hermit caves. "What happened?" He shifted his eyes to look around the room without moving his head. "Is everybody alright? Joe, is that you? What happened to Kumar? He didn't look too good. Where's the guy from the temple, with the beard… and the gun?"

Everyone began speaking at once.

"Could I suggest the time-honored formula of 'one at a time'?" Kohein suggested quietly. The voices fell silent. "Thank you all. Please allow me to begin by saying that I am deeply grateful to you, James. More than you could possibly know. You have saved a treasure – possibly more than one," he added rather cryptically. "As to the man with the gun, may I introduce Mr. Hajee, my friend and colleague. He has been keeping close track of you since your arrival."

A familiar bearded face emerged from the back of the group. "*Sawadee, Misatuh Jame. Sia dai mai dai pongkaan dee, na? Kho thod na khrab.*" He added a *wai* to his last sentence, head bowed, a shamed expression showing.

"He greets you and offers his apologies for doing such a poor job of protecting you." Kohein translated. "Perhaps you could say something to indicate your acceptance?"

"Are you kidding? He saved our skins." Carpenter began to sit up to return the gesture, but sank back immediately. "*Mai pen rai, khrab! Mai tong kho thod leuy. Khob khun jingjing.*" No problem – no need to apologize. Many thanks.

Carpenter looked past Hajee to Kumar. "Brother Edward, what happened? I remember you were holding on to your chest. I thought maybe you were having a heart attack or something, then it all just went black."

"I am fine, James, thank you. And more importantly, thank you for your protection. You are the hero of the day. You, and Brother Joe here - who seems to have found a way to apply what he learned in his previous life in a rather more useful manner than simple linguistics." Kumar tossed an affectionate glance at Brother Joe. "I believe I may have mentioned that my heart does not function in all circumstances as it should. It has threatened to stop altogether on several occasions. But, thank God, not on this one."

"Scared me to death. I thought he was gone. But then…" Brother Joe's voice faltered at this last as emotion overwhelmed words.

Kumar finished the sentence for him. "But then, it turned out to be a false alarm. And now we are concerned most of all for you. Please take it slowly."

Carpenter turned his head toward Kohein. "Can I ask you something? Where exactly are we now… and where have you been since the train?"

"Ah, well, a most interesting story, as you might imagine." Kohein clearly was pleased to be able to tell the tale. "I am anxious to relate it all. But perhaps we can allow the doctor to examine you first?" He motioned the others back with a gesture. "You are in a mosque, James. *Matsayit Chiang Mai* or the 'Ban Haw mosque', to be exact. I have been here since your arrival. I have rather good friends here, you see... including Dr. Amnuay."

Kohein moved aside to allow a small man with a heavy oval face and thick, manicured hands to come forward. "Dr. Amnuay is one of the finest medical men in Chiang Mai," he announced with some pride. "Trained at Mongkut Medical School in Bangkok and at Columbia University in a place called New York. You may have heard of it?" Kohein smiled briefly.

"Of course, thank you. But, Amit, this is kind of crazy, you know? I just don't understand. It's making my head hurt all by itself."

"Indeed." Kohein's expression became serious. "I understand your confusion, believe me. I owe you a complete explanation." He looked quickly up at the others. "All of you, really, but especially you, James." He dipped his head toward Carpenter. "I have put you in danger, James, though it was not my intention. On the train I acted hastily on the simple impulse that you could be trusted... which, quite obviously, was more than accurate. Nonetheless, I have involved you in my business and have succeeded in harming both you and your friends." Kohein paused, sorrowful. "And, I'm afraid, the danger may not be past. I hope you can forgive me."

Carpenter felt a pang of guilt for pursuing the matter, but quickly realized the absurdity of his own reaction. He and Brother Joe and Kumar *had* been injured. The danger, after all, had been real. "I just want the whole story, Amit."

"And you shall have it, my friend. You shall have it, I promise. But may we first, as I believe it is said, have your head examined?"

****

"As far as I can tell, without the benefit of radiology, Mr. James appears to have avoided permanent injury. He has a concussion, to be sure, but his responses are sharp – excellent, actually... much better, in fact, than most people who have suffered lesser head trauma."

Dr. Amnuay packed his things and turned to Kohein. "He is quite lucky, you know. He is in extraordinary condition, and," he said with a smile back to Carpenter, "apparently extremely hard-headed. A few days' rest should do it, so long as he does not play the part of a baseball again anytime soon."

"Thank you, Doctor." Kohein was clearly relieved. "You know I appreciate your help... and your discretion."

Once the doctor had left the room, Kohein addressed them. "As I said, I owe each of you an explanation. Let me attempt that now. Please feel free to ask whatever questions you may have. I will try to be thorough." Kohein thought for a moment before proceeding. "There are some portions of the story, however, that I will reserve for James alone. His unwitting role in all this has left him most exposed to the dangers, I'm afraid."

Kohein waited for a comment before going on. "As you may know, James and I met and rode together from Bangkok, just two days ago as it turns out, though it seems much longer. I was carrying a bag containing several items of some value. As Kumar may have told you, I have been engaged in the jewelry trade in Bangkok for some years now. I sometimes carry merchandise with me.

"James and I had a very pleasant trip. He is a fine young man, as I'm sure you have noted already. And we seemed to share a bond of sorts from the beginning. I found him most agreeable. More important, I realize I trusted him implicitly... based, I must say, on rather limited experience – but there you have it."

Kohein seemed to be reviewing the story himself as it unfolded, surprised by what he discovered in the telling. "I was accosted on the train, near the stop at Lamphun. I know the attackers. I have encountered them before in my travels here in the North and in Burma. I have worked with them, actually, though that has proven a foolish mistake. As you all know, the area is rife with conflicting parties – each with its own militia, even small armies – and each, in one way or another, with a hand in the manufacture and transportation of heroin, among other illicit activities. It is virtually impossible to avoid dealing with these groups if one ventures into certain parts of Burma as I do."

Kohein paused here, looking somewhat abashed, then carried on. "I have been offered 'protection' at times, which for the most part, I have been able to decline, thanks to my friends among the *Hui*." Here, he nodded toward Hajee, who acknowledged the gesture with a slight bow. "But I have dealt with intermediaries... some more dangerous as it turns out than the principals themselves.

"All of these groups, for their own reasons, are of course interested in whatever may profit them, regardless of the source. I have dealt with each at one time or another. Of them all, the *Kuomintang* or KMT - remnants of the nationalist Chinese army - has perhaps the widest network of contacts. They travel regularly throughout the Golden Triangle to buy raw opium from growers and transport it to factories where heroin is made for shipment and sale. In their dealings with local villagers, they seem to have run across a journal belonging to an early British traveler – one James George Scott, the first colonial 'governor' of the area, which was ruled, of course, by the British at the time. They recognized that what they had 'found' was old, and possibly of value. So they brought it to me."

Kohein offered an apologetic smile. "Although they are clever, they are not all formally educated or conversant with English. They were aware of my interest in history and proficiency with languages, but placed no particular value in the journal itself. When I offered to look it over, they seemed unconcerned. The journal contains diary entries and a letter from Scott to a colleague in Chiang Mai. The letter describes a portion of Scott's travels in the Shan area of northeastern Burma near the Mekong during the late 1880s. It alludes to a cave and mineral deposits... potentially a very rich concentration of gems."

Kohein paused again, thoughtful. "I must admit I was excited by the journal and the letter – at least as much for its historical value as for any promise it might hold of actual treasure. The letter offers limited geographical references which I attempted to follow on my next trip across the border." He stopped and looked at each of the listeners in turn. "I found reason to believe the account is in many ways, quite accurate."

"But what about the two guys on the train? What was that all about?" Carpenter asked.

Kohein nodded. "The two gentlemen on the train represent another, smaller group of 'businessmen' in the region. They provide a certain intermediary function to the major players... procurers, if you will, of whatever may be needed or desired, so long as it is paid for. I made the mistake early on in trusting them with some of my transactions. Characteristically, my greatest mistake was in allowing my own excitement to banish caution. I sometimes leap well before I look, as you may already have noted. At any rate, I mentioned the journal and possible treasure in a gathering that included bigger ears, so to speak, than I realized were listening at the time."

"Whose ears?" Brother Joe's question held a note of challenge.

"Dangerous ones, I assure you, belonging to the head of the group. A truly evil man. 'Phi Rak', as he calls himself, is a rather mysterious personage of uncertain origins. His appearance is unusual to say the least and offers no clues to his nationality. 'Phi Rak', by the way, is Thai for 'Brother Love'." He bent slightly toward Carpenter. "The Thai words sound like 'peacock', by the way. I hope the title is not one you will hear aside from my remarks. Should you hear it, however, be forewarned."

Kohein straightened to address the group again. "For those unfortunate enough to know him, the title of 'Phi Rak' is particularly ironic given his indecent proclivities. This Brother Love has direct dealings with the KMT. After hearing of my tale, he offered to purchase the journal for a nominal fee. That sale, of course, was conducted without my knowledge or involvement."

Kohein paused here to search the faces of the others. "I must admit that I was loathe to relinquish the journal... even to its KMT 'owners'. The potential it represents has been difficult to ignore. Jewels are my business and livelihood, after all. But once I was able to think beyond my own narrow interests, I realized that in the wrong hands, the journal also represents a danger to those to whom it truly belongs."

"So it was Phi Rak's men on the train," Carpenter asserted.

"Yes, his men. They were aware that I might be keeping the diary in my satchel. They confronted me while I was by myself. Had you not come along when you did, I fear they would have taken it, and left me with a broken head as well. But because of your intervention, I was able to leave the train at Lamphun. Knowing they would pursue me, I saved the bag in the only way that occurred to me. I simply threw it back through the open window and onto our seats – trusting that you, James, would manage somehow on your own. I did not think, obviously, of the possible consequences. I'm so sorry ..." Kohein spread his arms and sighed. "I must admit that I am both ashamed and relieved to finally share the tale."

There was silence in the room. Kumar broke the spell. "But Amit, does this diary not belong now to your Brother Love character, regardless of his nature? Did he not purchase it himself? Is it right that you have confiscated it to use for your own ends?"

Kohein nodded, unoffended. "He did. And offered me a half-share in whatever profit it might bring. But there is more to the story, as they say. Bear with me."

The others leaned forward to hear.

"In following the course set forth in the diary, I was able to get close enough to the location it describes to learn that there are local tales similar to those Scott wrote about. I encountered a group of villagers on what appeared to be a deserted track. There was no sign of habitation nearby. They seemed a humble and rather superstitious folk. When I questioned them about mineral deposits in the hills, they acknowledged the possibility but told horrific stories of witches and dangerous guardian spirits. If they knew the actual site of a rich cave complex, they seemed afraid to visit it themselves and clearly were unwilling to share the location with outsiders."

"Were they the owners of the journal then?" Kumar asked.

"Possibly. They knew of it. And their legends are consistent with its contents.

When I mentioned it, they seemed anxious to know if I had it with me. There is no telling how they may have come to possess it. Scott appears to have tried to have it delivered to acquaintances in Chiang Mai. One presumes it was seized or sold before it reached its destination. The people I met likely had had it for generations. If so, they did not give it up lightly."

"How do you know that, and why keep it yourself?" Brother Joe persisted.

"Fair questions. Of course the diary does not belong to me. But neither does it belong to those who took it from its owners, or to the one who then purchased it. I believe it must be returned. Phi Rak will not approach the KMT to ask where the diary was found. He will not wish to share whatever it may yield. But if it should fall into his hands, he will find the location in question and those who guarded the diary will suffer."

Brother Joe kept on. "OK, that makes sense. I wouldn't want to wish those guys on anyone else, not after our little dance with them. But why did you wait to contact James here? And what's the connection with Mr. Hajee and the Ban Haw mosque? James mentioned you're Iraqi, but he also said you're Jewish. You don't usually find Jews in mosques..."

"Let me answer your last question first. The circumstance is, as you rightly point out, rather unusual." Kohein glanced at Hajee. "Jews and Muslims these days are not typically thought of as friends or allies. It was not always so. In my own country and throughout the Middle East, the two religions and their adherents co-existed reasonably well for centuries. The Prophet was not specifically anti-Semite."

"They don't seem to get along too well now."

"No, but it is only in recent times that we have seen such bitter conflict between Arab and Jew. Colonialism's legacy, in my view. Of course, the establishment of Israel and the dislocation of Palestinians are very much connected. There is blame enough on both sides to satisfy those eager purveyors of hatred who use it to take and hold power. But the fire that consumes the region was laid originally by the colonial powers with their capricious and self-serving divisions of the land. The nightmare of the Holocaust lit the match... and oil - most flammable - has fueled the flames."

Kohein paused and smoothed his mustache with a thumb and forefinger. "Forgive my digression. This history is rather personal for me, you must understand. But your question was rather more immediate." He glanced again at Hajee. "I met the *Hui* as a fellow trader. We both are middlemen, you see. Our economic relationship was quite natural. I needed product; they had access to its sources. That explains our initial connection. There was more, however, than either first suspected. I am a Jew from Iraq. They are Muslims who came from China. We both are minorities who have found a home here. Both have suffered persecution – whether individually or as a group. History has seen 'pogroms' against the *Hui* in China as it has of the Jews in Europe. We both have had to assimilate to survive. The experience has taught us a degree of openness and, for some of us, it has bred a reluctance to judge or condemn simply on the basis of difference."

Kohein looked thoughtfully around the room and its fine furnishings. "It was my Iraqi heritage, ironically, that offered a bridge to friendship. I speak and read Arabic, the language of *Hui* religious instruction. Hajee, my first real friend here, discovered this during one of our early ventures across the border. We found much in common. Suffice it to say that they respect my origins, and I theirs. Perhaps you will think it odd, but I teach Arabic to children here at the mosque when I am in Chiang Mai."

Kohein waited a moment for further questions. When none came, he gestured toward the foyer outside. "If you don't mind, gentlemen, I would like a moment alone with James. We won't be long."

****

The others shuffled from the room, leaving Kohein and Carpenter alone. "A momentous two days," Kohein began, taking a seat alongside the low couch. "I do hope they prove to be exceptions rather than a rule." He settled back in his chair. "I have had an opportunity to look through the satchel you so valiantly protected. Again, I thank you."

"I hope everything was there. I didn't open it, but I believe Paul Hemple did, while I was showering. I found it open and some of the stuff inside was spilled out, including the letter from George Scott you mentioned. I read it... sorry."

"Please, there is no need to ask pardon. As I said earlier with the others, you have saved at least one treasure."

"I guess the diary is pretty valuable, then?"

"It is... perhaps more than anything else the bag contained. But there was something else, something that I want you to know about and for which you have earned more than simple gratitude." Kohein bent forward and pulled the satchel onto his lap from where it rested on the floor. Unclasping the latches, he reached inside and produced a silk purse which he held out to Carpenter. "Open this, James."

Carpenter looked a question at Kohein, then tugged at the knotted drawstring and loosed the open end into his hand. A deep red glassy stone, the size of a large walnut, dropped into his palm. Its surface was smooth, almost greasy. Carpenter looked up at Kohein. "Is this a ruby?" he asked, simply. "It's a good thing this wasn't in the bag, too."

"Ah, but it *was* in there, my friend. An exquisite specimen. I acquired it on the same expedition I described to the others. The villagers I encountered pressed it on me at the end of our conversation to encourage me to return with the journal. I took it, obviously... I couldn't bring myself to refuse the offer. It is such a thing of beauty, but I realize now I can't rightly keep it as payment for something that was never mine. I hate to let it go, but I mean to return it with the journal if I can. At any rate, there are other stones in the area as well - certainly enough to satisfy my own desires and business needs." Kohein withdrew a second purse from the case. "This is one of the others. It is smaller, but not without substantial value of its own." He removed a raw gem a quarter the size of the first and laid it in Carpenter's hand. "This is yours, James. You have earned it."

Carpenter was dumbstruck. "Amit, I can't take this. I didn't do anything but keep your bag for you. I had no idea what was in it. This is too much, really." He held both rubies out to Kohein, who took the larger then gently closed Carpenter's fingers around the smaller of the two.

"No, James, this is yours. I insist. It has value, to be sure, but it is a single stone. Even this," he said, indicating the larger gem in his hand, "though extraordinary, is only one of many that may lie undiscovered in Scott's hills." Kohein leaned forward. "But no matter how many gems there are, no matter what size or quality, there may be an even greater treasure to be found."

"A greater treasure? How could that be?" Carpenter felt himself on the edge of a precipice, the sensation both strange and familiar. "I mean, if the place is full of jewels, how could there be a greater treasure than that?"

"You read Scott's letter. You may recall the legend he quoted... local talk of caves leading to the domicile of Indra, a net of pearls, clouds of jewels... odd dreams?"

"Yes. He mentioned a lot of weird things, but he dismissed them all. He didn't say he found the place, right?"

Kohein ignored the question. "When we met, you may recall a rather lengthy discussion – a ramble on my part, actually – regarding the origin of my name?"

"Yeah, I remember. It was fascinating," Carpenter nodded. "But what does that have to do..."

Kohein interrupted. "I believe I mentioned my interest in the Huayen School of Buddhism? Are you familiar with it?"

"Just a little, from school. Huayen is Chinese, right... with Taoist influences? I read something about them, but don't really remember much. Didn't they use the image of Indra's net as a metaphor for how everything is connected?"

Kohein's eyes shone. "Exactly! Indra's *jeweled* net. An infinite luminous web hung with precious gems at every intersecting node."

"OK. But, Amit, it's just a reference in Buddhist mythology, not an actual place."

Kohein shrugged. "Perhaps. But it is described in some detail in the Flower Garland *sutra* from the second century. Fa-Tsang, a Huayen sage, even offered a demonstration of it. He placed an image of the Buddha and a single candle in the center of a darkened chamber and surrounded it with polished mirrors. The reflections were infinite... a million, million Buddhas shimmering together in the flicker of a flame."

"Reminds me of sitting in the barber's chair as a kid looking at the reflections made by the big mirrors on the walls in front and behind and wondering if the reflections went on forever. A memorable image but really just a visual effect. I don't see how Fa-Tsang's demonstration was any different."

"It probably wasn't," Kohein admitted, "but the sutra also describes the acquisition of amazing spiritual powers culminating in a state of *samadhi* in which all things can be accomplished without obstruction... thought translated instantly into reality."

Carpenter recognized the same flight of conjecture he had observed with such relish in his first conversation with Kohein. He found himself resisting simply to maintain his own sense of balance. "This is all fascinating, of course, but I'm not sure where you're going with it."

Kohein offered an embarrassed smile. "Of course, you have witnessed my endless extrapolations before. But let me complete what may be a thoroughly absurd, though intriguing, string of associations." He clearly was eager to share his train of thought. "The *sutra* relates this ultimate level of consciousness to the image of Indra's net. It describes an infinite crystalline universe, all interconnected and harmonized like Indra's jewels and their reflections. It describes a world of endless, incomparable beauty. In such a world, all reality is so deeply interconnected that if one is able to penetrate and join with it, one literally *becomes* One, and all things become possible."

Carpenter started to interject, but Kohein held up a hand. "In the *sutra*, each manifestation of reality reflects all others located throughout the three stages of time – past, present and future – in the same way as each atom of creation is ultimately connected to every other."

"I get the images, but you leave me when you start to suggest that they are somehow more than metaphorical." Carpenter hesitated, considering his words carefully. "Forgive me – I don't intend to be rude here – but what you're saying strikes me simply as magical thinking."

"Yes, it does, doesn't it? And I would dismiss it as mere fancy were it not for one rather odd coincidence that I suspect you will recognize."

The sensation of standing on a precipice returned. "And what is that?"

"The reference to the three stages of time. Does it hold any special meaning for you?"

"Not particularly, why?"

"You mentioned that you had read Scott's letter. Do you recall his reference to dreams?" Kohein asked, intense now.

"Yes," Carpenter stepped closer to the edge. "He mentioned having strange dreams."

"And have *you* dreamed lately, James? *I* have. Dreams that transcend the *sutra's* 'three stages of time' – or at least the past and present."

Dream fragments surfaced in Carpenter's mind. Images of other times and places, of people and events both distant and familiar. At least two, he realized with a start, that had included Kohein or someone very like him.

The older man nodded slowly. "Yes, I see you have as well. You, by the way, have appeared in some of mine. I dismissed them at first, but they have become more frequent and more powerful... more recalled than imagined, I would say."

Carpenter abandoned skepticism. "What do you think it means?"

"I don't know, my friend. I truly do not. But I aim to find out if I can. There is a connection somewhere between the myth and the reality. Some strand of this 'net', if you will, seems to connect us. Some piece of it that is more than mere metaphor, though I have no idea what it may be."

Kohein's tone was earnest and excited. "I rejected your request to accompany me on my next trip, James, out of concern for your safety and for my own. I did not think I knew you then. But I know you now and I understand your considerable capabilities. Clearly you are able to take care of yourself. And after your encounter with Phi Rak's men on the train, your safety already has been compromised. I fear he is unlikely to simply forgive and forget."

"But what can you do about it?" Carpenter asked the question almost as if to slow Kohein's words.

Kohein held Carpenter's eyes with his own. "I was right to reject your initial request, but events seem to have overtaken us both. Now I invite you to join me, James. I trust you as I would my own family." He dropped his voice to a hoarse whisper. His black eyes burned, lit from within by the slow flame of intrigue. "Perhaps we shall find a treasure in jewels, my friend. And, who knows," he sat back and smiled, abandoning himself now to the mystery, "perhaps we shall find something vastly, infinitely more…"

Golden Triangle

SEVENTEEN

THE GOLDEN TRIANGLE COVERS THE MOUNTAINOUS AREA BEGINNING AROUND CHIANG MAI AND EXTENDING NORTH TO INCLUDE PORTIONS OF THAILAND, LAOS AND BURMA. Those three nations come together at a point near the town of Sop Ruak in Chiang Rai Province where the Ruak River empties into the Mekong. The land there is remote, steep and green. But the primary color is gold.

The Golden Triangle was the Afghanistan of its day. The bulk of the world's opium was produced there, and much of the refined heroin. Groups hungry for profit and driven to procure arms for a variety of liberation struggles competed to control the trade. Most notorious – or the two best armed - were the Shan Army and remnants of Chiang Kai Shek's Nationalist Kuomintang Army. The latter fled south and east into Burma after their defeat in the Chinese civil war that brought Mao Tse Tung and the Communist Party to power.

The American war effort in Vietnam produced strange bedfellows. It is widely accepted that the CIA was complicit in the transportation of opium and heroin for local allies involved in the drug trade in exchange for their support in the war against communism. Ironically, one of the early markets for Golden Triangle heroin was among American GIs in Vietnam where estimates of usage among troops there range from 10 to 30%. The heady mix of warfare, profit and politics turned the Golden Triangle into a lawless and often violent place. In 1968, it had become something of a no-man's land.

******

Carpenter and Hemple sat together near the front of the bus, staring in horror through the windshield as another large bus passed a slower vehicle on the narrow two-lane road and headed straight for them at break-neck speed. Carpenter gripped the seat between his legs and glanced around at the other passengers. Some chatted nonchalantly to neighbors. Others sat forward with wide grins watching the drama unfold as if from the safe distance of theater seats. Hemple's eyes were squeezed shut in prayer, his hands steepled, lips dancing in silent supplication.

We're going to die... and no one seems to mind. Carpenter tightened his hold and pushed back against the seat cushion preparing for the impact.

The two giant vehicles hurtled toward each other, both headed for a narrow bridge that separated them by no more than a hundred yards. Neither slowed. The blast of air horns drowned all other sounds as the drivers challenged each other for the right of way. At the last possible moment, the oncoming bus swerved sharply past the slower vehicle to complete its pass. Both buses reached the bridge simultaneously and veered slightly inward and closer together to avoid the concrete pilings at each end. Wind screamed as they passed within an inch of each other, horns blaring in defiance and celebration as they cleared the bridge at opposite ends. The passengers laughed and cheered at the performance, then returned to their separate conversations.

"Mother of God," Hemple gasped unselfconsciously and crossed himself. He kept it up until finally seeming to realize he was still alive. "I thought we were all going to die."

Nearby passengers glanced over to him, clearly delighted by the spectacle of a terrified *farang*. Carpenter struggled to maintain an air of unconcern, hoping to distinguish himself from his unwelcome companion. For a moment, he savored the sense of being part of a crowd rather than singled out as different. Reluctantly, he broke the link.

"You OK?"

"OK? I thought we were all going to die," Hemple repeated. "How can I be OK? How can *you* be OK?" Hemple shook himself. "Must be in the genes," he muttered, more to himself than to Carpenter.

"Excuse me?" Carpenter sat forward in challenge, sorry now for publicly acknowledging his connection with Hemple.

"I mean, you seem to have ice water in your veins, like *they* do," Hemple looked around toward the rest of the bus. "Didn't that at least *worry* you?"

Carpenter toyed with the notion of claiming indifference, but couldn't bring himself to deny the truth despite the obvious satisfaction it would bring. "Actually, it scared the hell out of me, Paul. I don't know how we survived." He leaned closer as if to confide. "And despite our common genetics, I found the general response on board rather inscrutable, if you know what I mean." He winked broadly at Hemple, who began to return the gesture before realizing Carpenter's intent.

"I am not a bigot," he insisted and turned away, hurt. "I'm here to help these people not to judge them."

"That's good, because some of 'these people' may be able to figure out when they're being lumped together under a single code – genetic or otherwise."

"Well, I don't see why you need to get so high and mighty. You just waltzed into this opportunity because of your uncle, not your faith. You're not even much of a Christian if you ask me." Hemple's embarrassment had begun a predictable defensive turn to resentment and indignation.

In truth, Carpenter realized, Hemple was nervous at the prospect of this trip. He had a *bona fide* letter from Father Wilkins inviting him to the mission, but had not met him directly. He couldn't claim a personal connection to the priest. He had pushed to be included in Carpenter's plans to travel by bus to Chiang Rai.

Carpenter had remained at the Ban Haw mosque for several days recuperating under the watchful eye of Dr. Amnuay. During that time, he had given serious consideration to Kohein's invitation, but decided finally that he could make no commitment to the journey before speaking to Father Harry first. Kohein had understood. Since he would be passing through Chiang Rai province near Sop Ruak before crossing into Burma, he had agreed to check in with Carpenter there before setting out. Meanwhile, he would stay close to the mosque or do business outside Chiang Mai only with Hajee or other *Hui* along for security.

After two weeks, no word had come from or about Father Harry. The only good news to be had was the arrival of a thermostat and two new tires for the Land Rover. Brother Joe installed the thermostat within a half hour. The tires took up the wayback and half of the rear seat. An unexpected load of medical supplies from Bangkok for Father Harry's Sangor mission rode the roof and took most of the remainder of the interior, leaving adequate space either for Carpenter or for his luggage - but not both. Kumar graciously volunteered to take the bus. Carpenter did the same and as the two argued politely, Hemple had approached asking again to be included.

Brother Joe had been adamant. He could barely tolerate the notion of Hemple joining them at the mission, let alone the prospect of suffering his company for several hours in the same vehicle. Father Anond finally intervened to invite Carpenter and Hemple to remain at *Suan Dok Gnam* through Christmas and New Year's before traveling north by bus. Brother Joe was relieved enough at the reprieve to end his challenge to Hemple's request. The plan was for Kumar and Brother Joe to return to the hill tribe mission at Sangor to wait for Father Harry. If he didn't return, they would drive down anyway to meet Carpenter and Hemple in Chiang Rai town in mid-January.

Carpenter had used the additional time at *Suan Dok Gnam* to make friends and work on his language. A month of rest had left him feeling completely healed and surprisingly comfortable with basic Thai. Hemple, on the other hand, had taken it upon himself to instruct Father Anond and staff in the proper celebration of Christmas. By mid-January, the priest gently but clearly suggested that Hemple's stay at *Suan Dok Gnam* should come to a conclusion while peace still reigned among the faculty. So it was that Carpenter found himself sharing leg space with Hemple on a narrow bench for the cramped and unexpectedly dramatic bus ride to Chiang Rai town.

Clouds of red dust filled the air as the bus pulled off the macadam and onto the broad area that served as the town's bus stop and market. The 'cold' season may have arrived, Carpenter reflected, but the heat still felt intense. A row of crude wood and bamboo stalls lined one end of the broad loading area. A small army of hawkers rushed to the steps of the vehicle as the passengers attempted to step down to the ground. Hemple emerged before Carpenter, squinting in the bright sunlight, red beard thrust forward like the bushy prow of a war ship. The crowd of sellers swayed backward in reaction then rushed forward as one, wares held out at arms' length as each small merchant jostled for access.

Hemple stood besieged, unable to move forward or around his bemused admirers. A teenager strode boldly up to measure himself against the stranger's high narrow form, his hand passing from the top of his own head to Hemple's chest so as to dramatize the outlandish size of the orange giant. A burst of appreciative laughter rose from the crowd as Hemple reddened further.

Carpenter slid quietly past Hemple looking for Brother Joe or Kumar. He saw the Rover first then Brother Joe next to it looking directly at him, his face a question mark of surprise and concern. Carpenter wondered briefly if there had been an accident of some kind or if word had come of a mishap involving Father Harry. He waved and started toward the Rover. Brother Joe nodded a response then bent to the window of the vehicle to speak with a figure seated on the passenger side. A large dark hand – larger and darker than Kumar's - emerged from the open window to grasp the outer door handle. The door swung open and two booted feet swung easily to the brown earth in a motion impossibly familiar.

Carpenter stopped short and stared as Reggie 'the King' Kingston rose smoothly from the vehicle, grinned broadly and remarked in an almost conversational tone, "Hey, little brother, you look like you seen a ghost."

EIGHTEEN

"HE SWORE HE KNEW YOU SO I BROUGHT HIM ALONG. Not that I could have kept him from coming. He's a huge son of a ..." Brother Joe looked an apology to the man dwarfing him at his side. "He's big." Carpenter simply stood, hardly believing what or whom he saw.

Reggie looked the same... kind of. Tall and very broad in the neck, chest and shoulders despite noticeable weight loss. Thick, vein-etched arms. Bear-paw hands. Skin a half-note ivory black and hair cropped short close to the skull above a high, ridged forehead. This much was familiar; other things weren't. Scarring above his right eye ran down and through it at the edge, leaving a trail of milky blue-white at the corner. And something about Reggie's expression had changed. The eyes were older, weary... like a thick shade had been clamped over some internal light. They no longer danced with mischief as if hiding a joke just beneath the surface. His once open face was almost grim despite the wide smile that greeted Carpenter now.

"Well, guess you're alive huh?" Carpenter felt a wave-set of emotions. Confusion followed closely by relief, then an overwhelming and almost comic sense of elation. "Jesus, Reg, how did you get here? I mean..." He struggled to find words. "I mean... actually, who gives a damn!" Carpenter stepped forward to embrace the dead man come to life.

"Long story, JC. Here's the short version. Copter to Burma, a little hide and seek in the bush, night march to the river, raft ride, a little overland detour to avoid river pirates, a quick hop across the river by fishing boat, truck with a timber poacher – then the Rover with the little guy there."

Reggie nodded toward Brother Joe as he wrapped Carpenter in a bear hug that lifted him a foot off the ground. He set Carpenter back down and held him at arms' length. His eyes narrowed. "You look good, A-Man. I needed to see that. Needed to know you're OK." He shook his head slowly, disbelieving. "Ricky's dead, man. Overdose. I helped kill him." The big man's eyes filled suddenly and his head dropped. He bit his lower lip trying in vain to contain a flood of emotion. "I helped kill him and I didn't even know."

Carpenter bent to find Reggie's eyes. "Hold up. What're you talking about? That's crazy, Reg."

"He OD'ed, man. Heroin... strong heroin. From here. Courtesy of your Uncle Sam, my boss." Reggie glanced up briefly then hung his head again. "We been helping push the shit, JC. Helping get the poppies grown, dealing with the fat cat manufacturers, helping transport product. And I been working for the Man the whole time, thinking I was saving lives. Trying to be a hero rescuing pilots from the bad guys 'stead of pushing dope. Like a blind man thinking he has perfect vision. So, yeah, I helped kill him, man. My little stupid-ass brother, the junkie. He's dead, man. Dead."

"I heard. I didn't know if you knew."

Reggie looked up, tears streaming down his cheeks. "Oh, I heard, all right. I heard and then I quit. I walked off the job. No more war, right? Isn't that what you were trying to tell me? I'm done, man. I'm fucking done!"

It was Carpenter's turn to hold Reggie. He folded his arms around him quietly as the big man's body shook with the grief he hadn't yet let himself feel completely. A small crowd gathered to watch from a distance, curious but unsure of how to interpret what they saw. A long minute passed. Reggie lifted his head, swiped a hand across his eyes and straightened. "Sorry, A-Man. I didn't know that was coming. Seeing you makes it real. You like a little brother and all." Reggie chanced a half-grin. "You even kinda look alike 'cept he better looking since he takes after me."

Reggie turned to look around at the audience. "*Set laew, na. Mai dai hen naa phyan tae naan, kae nan. Mai dtong mong si. Set laew.*" It's all over. I haven't seen my friend for a long time, that's all. Don't stand around staring, it's all over.

A small child, no more than four or five, had approached and stood just behind Reggie's knee. He reached up to tug on the big man's fatigues, tiny bare foot planted next to the outsized jungle boots. Startled, Reggie looked around at eye level as if to challenge the crowd, then noticed the child below him. His face softened. "*Arai, na, nuu?*" Yes, little mouse?

The child dragged a red checkered cloth from his khaki shorts and stretched on tiptoe to reach toward Reggie's hand – his brows knit, expression guileless. Reggie paused, then knelt to collect the handkerchief. He took it gently from the outstretched fist, looked long into the solemn eyes and dabbed his cheeks carefully before handing the cloth back.

"Thanks," he said, his voice quiet and composed.

"*Mai pen rai, khrab*," the child answered. He tucked the cloth into the pocket of his ragged shorts and offered a polite *wai* before retreating into the crowd. A small murmur of admiration passed through the onlookers. Several turned toward Reggie, palms together, heads bowed slightly to repeat the child's gesture of respect before moving off to their own affairs.

"What was *that* all about?" The voice was loud and abrupt, breaking the spell of the moment.

"Uh, Reggie. Meet Paul Hemple."

****

Chiang Saen lies almost directly due north of the provincial seat of Chiang Rai, a drive of some two hours in clear weather. The town itself is a river port perched on the south bank of the Mekong River and facing Laos on the far side. In 1968, the road was a narrow and erratically paved strip with sudden twists and occasional deep potholes requiring drivers to stay alert and react quickly.

The driver of the truck lying on its side in the oncoming lane clearly had not reacted quickly enough to avert disaster. As the Rover approached, its occupants could see only an inert pair of legs protruding from under the doorless cab of the vehicle like a macabre rendering of the demise of the Wicked Witch of the West. Gathered around the body of the truck and struggling desperately to lift it far enough off the ground to free the driver were several dozen villagers from a nearby hamlet, some barefoot or with rubber sandals and some wearing only *pha khawma* cloths. Off to the side on a small hillock, a badly injured young man lay across the lap of an elderly woman. His low moans gave evidence that he lived despite the terrible damage the accident had visited upon his torn and broken body.

"Jesus Christ... help us!" Brother Joe hit the brakes hard and pulled over as his passengers piled out of the Rover.

The villagers had succeeded in lifting the vehicle only a few inches off the ground and fought mightily to keep it there as two others clutched the driver's ankles and attempted to drag him free. Much of the truck's cargo remained secured to the bed, leaving the villagers stuck under an immovable weight with no free hands to change the stalemate.

Reggie was first to the scene. Seeing several medium-sized rocks by the roadside, he grabbed as many as he could and placed them strategically along the side of the truck to brace it up at the level the lifters had managed to create so far. Brother Joe arrived behind him with a heavy metal car jack that he wedged on its side beneath the truck to help hold it in place. The villagers quickly recognized the aim of these efforts. They parted to allow Reggie enough room to reach up to the canvas tarp covering the truck's cargo and slice through the thick cable holding it in place. Large bundles of heavy jackfruit and melons spilled from under the tarp as villagers dodged from their path.

With the load now lightened somewhat, Reggie, Carpenter, Hemple and Kumar joined the others to strain against the dead weight of the vehicle. From the ground close to the trapped driver, Brother Joe counted: "*Nyng, song, sam... ow!*" The volunteers heaved together. The truck rose another six inches as a collective gasp signaled that the lifters were near the limit of effort and endurance. Brother Joe pushed hard to right the jack and get it into place where it could lever the weight.

"Just another inch, goddammit!" Joe made no attempt to monitor his language. Even Hemple disregarded the epithet and put his energy instead into the weight of the truck. Cords of muscle and tendon stood out against Reggie's neck and back as if carved from a marble block. Next to him, knees bent, Carpenter gripped the underside of the truck and heaved.

"That's it! Got it!" Joe pumped the jack handle which groaned and held for the moment as two men near him pulled the still body of the driver from beneath the wreckage. "OK, careful now! At three, let go! *Nyng, song sam... Bloi dai, laew!*" The rescuers stepped back together quickly as the jack teetered for a few seconds and collapsed. The truck banged down against the rocks, slid onto the asphalt and rolled slightly sideways before quivering to a rest in the road.

"I don't know. I don't think he made it." Brother Joe shook his head and grimaced as he stood over the lifeless body on the pavement. Kumar bent to feel the driver's neck for a pulse and looked up to confirm Brother Joe's observation. Hemple hung back, shaken.

Carpenter looked over to the roadside and nodded toward the young man lying there wrapped in the old woman's arms. "He may still have a chance, if we can get him to a hospital ... fast."

Brother Joe motioned to the Rover. "I guess that's our ambulance, God help us." Clouds of steam were billowing from beneath the hood of the vehicle where he had left it running in his rush to pull over and help. "Let's get him in before she blows!" He began to recruit volunteers to help move the boy.

A babble of excited chatter pulled the group's attention back to the road. Headlights blazed from an approaching car a half-mile distant, headed for Chiang Saen. The vehicle, a polished dark blue 4-door Mercedes sedan, slowed as it approached. A group of men carrying the injured boy moved carefully to the front of the crowd, ready to place him in the vehicle as quickly and gently as possible. The gap in the single open lane narrowed as the villagers edged toward the slow-moving vehicle.

A long blast from a powerful horn shattered the sudden quiet. The Mercedes rolled slowly up to, then through the crowd. Carpenter stood near the front, helping to support the boy's body. The driver's face was turned away and obscured by shadow so that only the line of a scarf at his neck offered definition to the silhouette. The rear held two passengers, their faces pressed against the side window. One belonged to a young child whose anxious look seemed directed more toward the face next to his own rather than at the scene outside.

That second face, mask-like, seemed constructed rather than real as if made of some artificial substance other than flesh. It was completely hairless. The skull smooth and bald, the face devoid of brow or lash. Almost without wrinkle or line. The eyes were black and opaque, more like those of a fish than a man. A pale rubbery imitation of a human countenance.

The face seemed at first without expression. But as the big car rolled quietly past the ragged throng, the eyelids lowered slowly as if in pleasure and a slight, almost playful smile twitched at the corner of red lips. The face turned briefly away from the window to speak unheard directions to the driver. The vehicle accelerated suddenly through the remainder of the crowd causing villagers to leap back to avoid being run down. The pale mask returned for a moment to the window, smiling broadly now as the powerful sedan sped smoothly away.

Carpenter stood for a moment watching the vehicle disappear to the north. Mixed with shock and anger was something else. Disgust, certainly. But also a troubling sense of denial... denial that he had in fact witnessed what he had just seen.

"Did you see that? I can't believe it." Brother Joe was clutching Carpenter's elbow tightly. "But look, we gotta go if we can. A few more minutes and that baby isn't going to move at all." He waved a hand at the still steaming Rover.

As the men moved toward the vehicle with the boy, however, another murmur rose from the crowd. A second car was heading toward them from the north. At first, Carpenter thought the Mercedes might be returning, but soon made out a small, crowded Toyota. A spokesman from the village approached the vehicle as it slowed to a stop, explaining the situation in rapid language and gestures. The car carried the driver and his family – his wife and three children. The mother quickly stepped out with her brood and the injured boy was placed in the backseat. The older woman who had held him by the roadside climbed into the front. The vehicle backed rapidly, turned again north and headed off for Chiang Saen and whatever medical facilities could be found there.

The man who had spoken to the Toyota driver approached. *"Mai pen rai, na. Chiang Saen mee moa, mee rongbaan duay. Ja thug raksaa thinan."* The man bowed and *wai*ed deeply. *"Khob khun na khrab, khon jaidee. Khob khun jingjing."*

Kumar translated. "He says it's all right. There's a doctor and a hospital in Chiang Saen. The boy will be cared for." Kumar pressed his palms together to return the man's respect. "He thanks us for our kindness."

"What about the driver's family? The woman and children who were in the car... where will they go?" Carpenter looked to see them walking off with several of the villagers who had tried to rescue the truck driver.

"Mai pen rai, lok. Mae gap luk ja phak thi ban raow. Diow, phoa ja glap. Mai pen rai, yaa huang." The older man spoke directly to Carpenter, recognizing his concern.

"He says not to worry. The woman and her children will stay with them until the father returns. It will be OK."

"Did he say anything about the Mercedes?" Reggie approached after helping with some cleanup from the accident.

"Rujag rod mercedee mai khrab? Rujag khon hua laan, mai?" Kumar asked the villager if he knew the car and the bald man in it.

The villager hesitated, then spoke slowly through tight lips. *"Mai koei hen rod nan. Mai hen mee khon kangnai."*

Kumar looked confused. "He says he has never seen that car. I asked if he has ever seen the bald man inside. He said he didn't see a man."

Kumar turned again to the villager. *"Mai dai hen khon nan, jingjing, ry?"* You really didn't see him?

"Mong, tae mai hen mii arai manut."

Kumar nodded, understanding now. "He says, 'I looked, but I didn't see anything human.'"

NINETEEN

THE SMALL TOWN OF SOP RUAK IS PERCHED ON THE BANK OF THE MEKONG, upriver from the larger town of Chiang Saen. From Chiang Saen, a narrow track twisted west along the river's edge for another 10 kilometers. In dry weather, the surface was hard red clay. But rain had begun to pelt down shortly after the Rover left the scene of the accident. By the time they passed through Chiang Saen, the clay had turned to butter-thick mud. For more than an hour, the Rover struggled through the muck until it finally reached the short stretch of paved street that signaled the beginning of Sop Ruak.

The noise and strain of the journey kept conversation to a minimum throughout. Even Hemple was quiet after a fruitless attempt to discover who Reggie was and how he had arrived as he did. His effort brought a sharp rebuff from the big man who then managed to sleep through the bulk of the ride. Seeming to take the silence of his companions for a personal affront, Hemple sulked in self-imposed exile as far in the corner of the backseat as space would allow. Perversely, the rain stopped abruptly just as they reached the town. Brother Joe pulled over to crack his neck and fingers before turning to the others.

"So, this is metropolitan Sop Ruak. It doesn't look like much, but that's because you haven't been to the suburbs yet. How 'bout we stretch our legs here for a few before we move out again?" Without waiting for an answer, he opened the door and stepped onto the roadside, bending at the waist and rubbing his back.

Reggie came awake immediately and without transition. "We here already?" In a moment he was out of the vehicle and moving down the street poking his head into shops and speaking to merchants who were bringing their goods back out from where they had been stored against the downpour. Carpenter and Kumar followed, leaving Hemple sitting stiffly alone. Reggie was back by the time the others had gathered beside the Rover. "What's with him?" he asked, gesturing toward Hemple. "He waiting for an invitation?"

"Give me a minute, OK?" Carpenter opened the back door and slid in next to Hemple.

"What's up, Paul?"

Hemple ignored the question at first, then offered only a monosyllabic, "Nothing." He knew he sounded like a spoiled adolescent, but couldn't help himself.

Carpenter tapped his foot mentally, impatient at Hemple's artificial nonchalance. "Listen. We're going to walk around here for a bit. It might not be wise to stay in the car by yourself... even to make whatever point you think you're making here." Hemple's face was turned to the window, but Carpenter knew he was listening. "Reggie is a friend of mine... an old one. He's not going to work at being your friend or your enemy. Why don't you take a chance and join the rest of us? I know you'd like to be included, no matter what attitude you put out. Maybe nobody else knows it, but I do." Hemple sat, silent, eyes averted. "OK, suit yourself." Carpenter climbed out and joined the others.

Brother Joe cleared his throat. "OK, I'm for taking a little walk around. Anyone staying in the vehicle needs to lock up. We are standing almost exactly in the center of the Golden Triangle." He pointed toward the nearby river and the terrain across and beyond. Dense green foliage pushed up against the far bank and rounded, storybook hills rose behind. "That's Laos across the water. Upstream on this side, there to your left, you see that point of land at the mouth of the big creek? That's Burma, just across the creek, which actually is the Ruak River. The town is named for it. Thailand makes the third side of the triangle."

"The famous *Sam Liam Kham Thong*," Carpenter muttered the Thai name.

"Yeah. And famous mostly for drugs and warlords. This little town, my friends, is about as close to the Wild West as you're gonna see in the East. The law doesn't get real close up here and when it does it doesn't look too hard at what it sees." Brother Joe raised his voice to be sure Hemple understood. "So like I said, if you're staying here, stay in the car and keep the door locked, alright?"

Brother Joe started off with the other three behind. Within a few paces, they could hear the door slam. No one looked back, though there was no doubt that Hemple had had a change of heart.

Rain over, the street was beginning to fill with a wide array of humanity. Chinese shop owners in white strapped T-shirts and khaki shorts sat on stools outside their shops working straw fans close to their sweat-shined faces. Barefoot children played with marbles and tops on smooth concrete shop floors. Men sat at small tables under awnings attached to rough wood posts, drinking whiskey and soda and talking loudly in several languages. On the roadside, tribal women sported a variety of costumes with ornate jewelry adorning necks and ears, fingers and feet. Blue Meo in pleated skirts and elaborate embroidery. Yaw in black pantaloons, turbans and blouses with puffy red ruffles along the collars. Akha in tall head dresses spangled with silver Burmese rupees.

Just ahead at a small noodle shop, a group of tipsy men played a risky game of mumbly-peg with a 12-inch blade. All but one wore military gray. Half a dozen automatic rifles were propped carelessly against the wall. Two men stood facing each other, their legs splayed wide apart, feet planted in the damp clay beneath a rough canvas overhang. One was uniformed... another soldier. The other was outfitted in a rather strange array of civilian dress – formal white shirt with gold scarf, tight black slacks, red silk socks and pointy Italian leather shoes. He held the knife between thumb and forefinger, swaying awkwardly forward to gauge the distance to his rival's foot. He threw. The knife flashed through the air to quiver in the clay an inch beyond the other's foot. The soldier struggled to reach the point with his outstretched foot, but lost his balance and fell instead to a chorus of jeers and laughter.

The onlookers barely noticed Brother Joe as he walked quickly past. Kumar, head down, eyes averted, drew some interest. Carpenter and Reggie clearly were unique and earned a few catcalls in Mandarin. Hemple bringing up the rear became the focus of attention.

"You! You! Come play! You, red man!"

Hemple might too have cleared the cluster of players had he not stopped to address them in what sounded like a tone of irritated command rather than the shaky insecurity it masked. "I have no intention of playing silly games with any of you. You should be ashamed of yourselves drinking like this in public. Can't you see there are children all around you?" Hemple nodded toward the knot of children squatting on the floor inside.

All laughter quickly subsided. Those standing stepped forward. Those seated rose to face Hemple. The winner of the contest bent to retrieve his knife, heavily oiled hair spilling over his forehead, and slid in front of the others. He held the blade out toward Hemple, hilt first. "Hallo my goo' fren. Come, you play wit' me, OK? You good guy, huh, red man? Easy game."

Hemple seemed to shrink as he stood, realizing too late the effect of his comment. "Uh, no, thank you. I'm not very good at that sort of thing actually. You go ahead. Sorry." He made as if to move on, but two of the group stepped to block his way.

A smile crossed the winner's face. He toyed reflectively with his scarf, then turned to his friends to make a comment. All laughed loudly as the dandy turned back to Hemple. "No, no, mah fren'. You play now. Here, you go." The knife hilt pushed against Hemple's stomach. "You firt."

Hemple stepped back. His voice rose in pitch. "No, really. I don't want to play. Please."

The winner's faux smile took on a hint of menace. A ragged left eyelid drooped and twitched erratically as if in mock flirtation. "OK, I go." The knife flew from his hand to stick in the ground a quarter inch from Hemple's sandaled foot. A roar of laughter erupted from the group.

Before Hemple could react, a large dark hand swept the knife from the clay and in a single fluid motion embedded it in a wooden awning post 15 feet away. A hollow, knocking sound echoed for a beat as the weapon quivered in place. Reggie straightened with a wide smile, voice warm and booming. "My friend here is no good at this kind of thing. But I love it."

The dandy stepped forward. "You no play. I say dis one." He pointed to Hemple.

Reggie grinned broadly and leaned down closer to the smaller man's face. "And I say, *we* play... you and me, little buddy."

The dandy looked uncomfortable now and glanced back toward the others who had retreated a step since Reggie's sudden appearance. "No unnerstan." His expression betrayed both rage and caution, but he held his ground with a resigned sigh as if he had no other choice than to stand firm.

"In that case, *Ni hwei shwo Junguo hwa ma? Wo hwei shwo ydyar.*" Do you speak Chinese? I speak a little. Reggie's posture and tone exuded both good humor and lethality.

Silence. The direction the moment would take hung in the air like a hummingbird and then just as quickly veered away from confrontation. A soft voice rose up from the rear of the shop. "He actually speaks a number of languages... and all of them badly."

The dandy stiffened and remained still.

"Please forgive the poor fool. He's been drinking and doesn't know when he's had enough."

The cluster of soldiers parted to reveal the source of the voice. The bald man from the Mercedes sat at a table in the rear of the shop. One narrow hand rested on the table near a clear glass of tea. The other moved back and forth affectionately along the shoulders of a small boy who sat cross-legged at his feet.

"Please forgive us. We've had a rather traumatic afternoon. There was a terrible accident down the road and we were unable to stop to help. It left us all feeling rather desperate." He remained seated and seemingly relaxed. Long fingertips ran up and down the boy's neck.

"Desperate, my ass." Brother Joe stepped forward and advanced toward the interior of the shop. The men standing nearby moved forward. Several snatched up weapons.

Carpenter found himself between the two groups, addressing a foreign but alarmingly familiar face. He struggled to contain his own rage, yearning to do violence but trying at the same time to prevent escalation. He managed a nearly polite smile. "Yes, we noticed you passing. You'll be pleased to know that another, better equipped, vehicle came along shortly after your departure. A small family stopped to help. They didn't seem to have more pressing engagements."

What had been a condescending smile disappeared from the bald man's face. His eyes seemed to go dead as they bored directly into Carpenter's. "Good fortune for us all, then. We were able to make our appointment with the Colonel here." He gestured toward an older man in military dress seated opposite him at the table. "And you were able to do your good deed for the day. May your actions serve to protect you... in your next life."

He stood now and came forward. His body was long and unusually thin and wrapped entirely in white. Billowy Indian shirt, sharply creased pants and immaculate jacket whispered slightly against each other with the movement. As he passed the dandy, he backhanded him brutally without so much as a glance. The man went down and remained on the ground, a thin trickle of blood running from the corner of his mouth. He dabbed at it with his scarf without taking his eyes from the bald man.

"Let me offer my apologies, gentlemen, for this entire misunderstanding." The ghostly figure surveyed the group, then fixed an appraising stare on Hemple. He stepped past Carpenter without a word and offered Hemple his hand. "And please, my friend, please do accept my sincere and heartfelt apologies." He pointed delicately at the cross hanging at Hemple's chest. "I see that you, too, are a brother in the Lord and clearly a leader among your people, if I am any judge of character. Please forgive the drunken foolishness of my well-intentioned but deeply ignorant companion. Your admonitions were both appropriate and courageous. Thank you."

Hemple hesitated, surprised, but quickly recovered himself to stand taller and with exaggerated dignity. "Not at all. Simply doing the Lord's work as best I can for the sake of the children."

"Ah, yes. I am a firm believer in taking care of the least of us. As He said, 'Suffer the little children to come unto me', isn't it?" His lips formed a thin smile as he turned to the others. "So, perhaps we can forget this most un-pleasant encounter and hope for better circumstances should we meet again?"

Reggie pressed forward to stand eye to eye with the bald man. "You best hope we don't meet again, friend."

The bald man threw his hands up in mock surprise. "Oh! Such bitterness! Let us hope we are not so fated then." He turned back into the shop. Glancing over his shoulder at Carpenter, he winked and added in singsong tones, "And sweet dreams, my young friend. Sleep well."

Carpenter laid a restraining hand on Reggie's chest and motioned the group toward the Rover. As if dreams could be sweet after this day. As if sleep could come easily at all.

TWENTY

BACK IN THE ROVER, HEMPLE WAS STIFF WITH SELF-CONSCIOUS PRIDE. "That was completely unacceptable. It's a good thing I am not a violent man... and that there was another among that drunken lot who was willing to help avert conflict."

Reggie turned in the seat, eyes wide in disbelief. "Hold on. Are you saying what I think you're saying? You don't get that that fish-eyed pervert was playing with you?"

Hemple's chin jutted out defiantly. "All I know is that he appears to honor faith and to be conversant with the Word. Had he not intervened, the situation could have turned ugly."

"And you don't call that ugly?" Reggie turned back around. "You're on your own next time, pal. You're lucky I have a knack for picking the underdog. The uniformed guys were KMT. Opium fighters, probably soldiering for Lo Hsin Han. They could just as easily gutted you as play footsie. There's no law to protect you here. Just whatever misguided hero happens to be around. And your pale 'friend' there is with *them*."

Hemple started to protest. A long arm flashed out to grab him by the collar. "Why don't you just keep it buttoned until you get permission to speak again, OK? I don't want to regret that we saved your sorry ass."

Hemple did as he was told.

Brother Joe had driven west along the river almost to the end of the town, then turned left toward the hills along a red clay trail pitted with mud holes and runnels. They passed at first through small plots of cut and stubbled paddy, stalks blackened from post-harvest burning. As the trail began to ascend, thick woods closed in for a time then gave way to a sight both breathtaking and macabre. Just past a steep switchback, Brother Joe pulled to the side of the track to allow his passengers to step out of the vehicle to view the scene.

On either side of the trail, the forest had been cleared for miles. In place of tall teak and Thai redwoods, a cloud of white blooms rose and fell along the curve of the hillside. Fist-sized blooms on tall dark green stalks stretched to the horizon across the red-brown clay. Here and there patches of wild mustard punctuated the landscape with splatters of rich butter yellow.

"*Papaver somniferum*. The opium poppy... beauty and beast." Brother Joe shut off the engine and climbed down to join the others. "Pretty, huh?"

"What an extraordinary sight. Magical, even peaceful." Carpenter felt at once both disturbed and strangely moved.

"And deadly." Reggie stared out across the acres of white.

Brother Joe offered a brief overview. "Not long till harvest, either. The blooms will be replaced by seed pods twice as big as walnuts. The farmers will slash each one with a three-bladed knife in the morning and by evening each cut will give up a bead of white milk like rubber sap. That's raw opium. It'll turn brown and sticky. The farmer comes back around and scrapes the stuff onto a flat blade and adds it to a mound of product ready to sell to the traffickers to use to make number 4 heroin."

Reggie turned to Hemple. "Those KMT guys you were playing with in town. People like that."

Hemple saw an opportunity to agree and find common ground. He nodded knowingly. "I hate the traffickers. The devil can have them and the weak-willed addicts too, as far as I'm concerned."

He was on his back before he could take a breath. Reggie's fingers dug into his throat until Hemple's face turned the color of his beard. Before anyone could move, Reggie eased his grip. He bent to press his face close to Hemple's. "You want to preach about the devil? You poor bastard, you think you know what you're saying. You don't. I've seen the devil." Reggie stood to look down at Hemple, his voice softer. "And you know what? When you catch up with him, you may find he looks a lot like you."

Reggie turned away, his jaws working and chest heaving. Carpenter moved to stand quietly next to him. Hemple pulled himself up from the ground, indignant but otherwise silent.

"Well, you sure do have a way with people, Paul." Brother Joe turned back to the Rover. "I think we've lost the magic of the moment. Let's move."

The trail twisted upward almost to the top of a low ridge overlooking the river behind them to the north. The Rover eased into a rough settlement. Small wooden huts huddled on either side of the road. Pigs and chickens picked their way along, oblivious to the vehicle. A few barefoot children ran laughing by the side of the car as it moved slowly through the village.

"Here we are – Ban Sangor. Home sweet home." Brother Joe pulled the Rover through a white wooden gate and into a small compound composed of three thatched buildings and a small field of grass. "This is Father Wilkins' mission... minus the Father, wherever he may be. The village is Akha – hill people. Opium cultivators. Some Christian, but mostly a little of this and a little of that. The name '*Sangor*' is local Thai dialect. It's a contraction of *chang* and *gnu* which in northern Thai become 'Sangor' for short. *Chang* means 'elephant' and *gnu* means 'snake'. There's a lot of both up here... so don't step on anything and don't get stepped on. Welcome."

****

The Rover was unloaded and the travelers settled in. Four of the five sat around a simple square table topped with split bamboo strips in what served as kitchen, den and bunkhouse. Outside, a swath of orange lingered through the green silhouettes of the forest canopy. Oblivious to the sunset sky, Hemple paced uneasily, unsure as to whether he had yet been granted permission to enter and join the others. Ever watchful for an open door or a face at a window, he strained to hear the conversation inside while scanning constantly for snakes in the short grass beneath his feet.

Over the table inside a single kerosene lantern hung from a redwood ceiling brace, its harsh light creating a tableau of shadow dancers against the bamboo walls. Reggie spoke, picking up the narrative of his own journey. "I didn't get it at first. There wasn't any reason to. We got dropped into hot spots to pick up pilots where they weren't supposed to be. Officially, there isn't an air war in Laos... not unless you're on the ground under the bombs."

Carpenter sat silent with Brother Joe and Kumar at the edges of the table.

"So, the missions were to pick up the pilots or what was left of them before the *Pathet Lao* got there. We got a lot of them out, too. But then two things happened around the same time. We got the call to go in for an extraction. But this one wasn't Air Force. It was Air America... which is spelled 'C-I-A'." Reggie looked over at Brother Joe and Kumar. "You follow me?"

They nodded.

"So when we get there the bird has holes all up through its belly, but the pilot and both crew are alive. So far, so good. But, here's the deal..." Reggie's dark face shown amber in the yellow light. "The plane is full of opium cakes." Reggie looked around as if expecting a challenge. "I mean, *full*, man. Each one was a couple of kilos. Brown and sticky. Wrapped up in banana leaves.

Ready for processing as it turns out. Like they used to do just across the river there." He nodded in the direction of the Mekong.

"Ban Khwan, a village on the Lao side of the river. At least, it was. They destroyed that motherfucker, believe me." Reggie pointed north and west. "Right over there. You probably could have seen the lights from this side if you were standing on the riverbank. Big heroin factory with cookers from Hong Kong making very pure number 4. And, get this," Reggie leaned forward, spreading his broad hands flat across the tabletop, "the operation was owned by a friendly Lao general, name of Ouane. Right-hand man of Phoumi Nosavan, a big politician. Helping us fight for freedom and democracy and all that while doing a little business on the side."

"You were there?" Carpenter believed, but needed to understand.

"Man, I saw the Ban Khwan battle go down. Watched some of it from a chopper while they were killing each other off. But that was last year. The pick-up I'm talking about was only a couple of months ago, just before I heard about Ricky. We land and the spooks tell me all about the dope as we're getting them out of there. They want us to pack as much of the shit into the copter as we can. What're they gonna say? 'Just picked up a little smoking material for ourselves while we were visiting the countryside?' No way, so they tell me the real story. Turns out they move this shit for the hill people who make a little money off it and agree to fight against the commies in exchange."

"So you rescued a plane-load of opium?"

"That's right... which is not exactly why I volunteered, you understand. My granddad died up in Burma back in the '40s building a road across the Himalayas so we could supply Chiang Kai-Shek against the Japanese. I was following in his footsteps, you know. The good fight. The good soldier." Reggie's jaws clenched. "Like my dad, too. He died in Korea and left my mom pregnant with Ricky. Left me to help out... be the man of the house for her and my little brother, right?

"I knew your granddad was in the war, but I guess I never really thought much about the details."

"Oh yeah, he died building the Ledo road with a bunch of other black GIs – not that they got any credit for it. But he set the tone for the rest of us... for me and daddy, at least. Anyway, when I get back to base from this 'rescue op', there's a letter waiting for me. It's not even from my mom, man, it's from her pastor. All formal and apologetic. Ricky is dead from an overdose but doing fine otherwise up in heaven... blah, blah, blah." Reggie straightened and shook his head. "And me just back from helping make a shipment for the Man. Me, the good soldier. The big brother. The pusher..."

Pin-drop silence around the table. Reggie's face gleamed in the lantern light. Kumar's eyes were wide, the whites standing out in the deepening gloom. Brother Joe shook his head over and over as he pounded the table softly with a tight fist. Carpenter held his breath and sat motionless.

"So I decided to quit... just disappear. Go on a mission and not come back. Get lost in the line of duty. A few weeks later, we get a call to fly out wounded from a firefight. It's another gang war over who gets the drugs. KMT against Khun Sa, the Shan warlord. Both of them our great allies. Fighting each other like they did last year over there in Ban Khwan. But get this... it wasn't Laos, it was Burma. Nobody mentioned it out loud, mind you, but when you cross the Mekong where it's running north to south, you're in Burmese space... no matter where you're supposed to be."

Reggie checked the faces around the table to be sure they understood. "So, we're supposed to help bring out some of the injured KMT troops since they're the friends of the month. KMT... and one American. A 'civilian'. So I gear up and move out. But I don't come back. Just disappear in the smoke and fire. Let 'em miss me, mourn my brave passing... poor bastard. And that's how I became officially Missing in Action."

Reggie's expression bore a hint of challenge. "And I don't have any apologies to make. I found my way here through some very hairy terrain based on what JC had written me about his fellowship gig. Met up with Joe here and the rest is history." Reggie sat back, empty. "And that's about as far as I planned. That is, until I got here. Until I heard about this Father Harry of yours." He leaned forward again to prop his weight on his elbows. "You say he's missing? And according to JC, he used to be OSS up in Burma? Hooked up with the KMT after WWII?"

"That's what my mother told me," Carpenter confirmed.

Reggie paused for effect. "I think I know where he is, or at least where he *was*. I think he may be the American we were supposed to pick up. Turned out he was a no-show. Pilot kept asking, 'Where's the priest, where's the priest?' Pretty big coincidence, if you ask me." Reggie's face split in a broad smile. "Someone had to go find him and that was my job, so I had the perfect opportunity to disappear." Reggie looked around the table. "I think I may owe him one."

TWENTY-ONE

THE KEROSENE LAMP STILL BURNED DIMLY OVER THE ROUGH TABLE AT THE END OF THE ROOM. So much had happened in a few short days. The world had changed. Reggie was alive. Father Harry was probably somewhere in Burma, if he was alive at all. Carpenter was sure he would find sleep impossible, but his thoughts began to drift and take new shape as his lids got heavier and closed ever more frequently. Sleep lifted him and he floated into it seamlessly without any sense of change.

The sun dipped below a tall horizon highlighting contrasts in light and shadow. Thick clouds glowed from within like living things, spilling rich shades of gold, orange and bronze across the world as if an unseen hand had borrowed the colors of sky and earth from a giant's pallet. The flanks of the mountain were sunset red against a snow-white crest and deep blue folds of sky. Below, abandoned now by the sun, jagged outcrops of gray stone rose like the backbones of ancient beasts to punctuate a monochrome scale of boulder and gravel and pebbled moraine. For Hindus, this mountain was Meru itself, center of the universe, crystal dwelling place of Shiva. For Bon shamans, it was the seat of all spiritual power. And for Tantric monks like himself, Mt. Kailash represented the perfect union of emptiness and bliss.

He spied the group in an open spot near the river as he rounded a turn. He paused a moment to lean on his thick staff and watch from a distance. They were camped by the Zangpo that ran east through mountain gorges to the Brahmaputra and at last into the sacred Ganges itself. His was a secret mission... to hide a special 'terma' - a secret treasure - so that its message could be rediscovered and revealed as needed in later times by a special 'truth finder'. That this 'terton' would indeed appear one day had been foreseen by the master himself.

But the Guru had given him no physical terma to conceal. He had directed the monk only to seek a hiding place near the sacred mountain, assuring him that the way to conceal the treasure - whatever it might prove to be - would become apparent as he searched. Guru had embraced him at parting as if in farewell.

"Do not be trapped by the one you appear to be. When you are lost, you will be found. What is hidden will be revealed." Confused but obedient, the monk had set out trusting that the meaning of the instruction ultimately would come clear.

As he approached the camp, the monk's attention was drawn to a single solemn figure standing stiffly erect at the center of a kneeling crowd. Leading his flock in prayer. The priest noticed the stranger's approach. His voice rose to a crescendo, then fell silent as all heads bowed. The priest straightened his bowed head, looked up and walked slowly to the stranger without abandoning the drama of ritual. He held his head high, chin forward, red beard preceding him more in challenge than in welcome. *"Greetings and Shalom, friend. Allah u akhbar - God is Great."*

The monk bowed in response, noting the odd mixture of Hebrew and Arabic which bespoke multiple antecedents and twisted journeys through time. He recognized these people now though their original identity had been much altered by experience. Refugees from Zion. A tribe of wanderers related somehow to the same ancient peoples as his own.

"I am Aaron, priest and leader of this small flock." The priest waited for acknowledgement.

"And I am a simple monk, follower of the Amitabha and his servant the Vajra Guru Rinpoche. I recognize you from your dress though not your reference to Allah."

The priest's face clouded. *"There is of course but one true God. Allah is only the latest name we have learned for Him whose name is not to be said aloud. God is great, though others who professed to follow him could not find room in their hearts for us."* The beard rose and jutted forward another inch.

The challenge in the priest's words was a surprise. Custom held that travelers be welcomed, not judged. The monk breathed deep to let his first angry reaction subside. *"Alas, I cannot claim your clarity. I am merely a seeker who has found little of which to be certain. I do know, however, that a warm cup of tea would be most welcome if you have it to share."*

"Of course. Please forgive our Aaron's lack of hospitality. He appears to have forgotten his manners. I am Malka." A very old woman, white locks partly covered by a thick blue shawl, appeared from behind the priest. *"You are most welcome here, my friend. We are all but seekers on this earth, no matter what truths we carry... be they hidden or revealed."*

The monk reached to touch the leather bag at his shoulder with its gem and its ancient scrap of hide that held so much but revealed so little. *"I would claim* kinship as a fellow seeker at the very least. Perhaps a seeker of the one true God as your Aaron has stated, if God be the deity within and around us all."

Aaron's neck stiffened in response. Before he could answer, Malka took the monk's hand in her own and led him toward a makeshift hearth. "So quickly we advance to discourse," she smiled. "Come, sit and rest. Take tea with us." She poured a cup. "What brings you here, friend? Few encounters are mere accident, you must know."

He felt an immediate comfort with her. Without further thought, he reached inside his shoulder bag and withdrew the parchment and the jewel. "You see clearly and with wisdom. This is no accident. I see that we share a common past. My father gave me these. They have passed from hand to hand for countless generations. Both are said to be relics from the original Temple, before it was destroyed by Babylon. I was told that this scrap of parchment was cut from a scroll there before the pillaging began. It is perhaps from the Torah itself. If so, it is centuries old but remains somehow intact, though the writing has faded to a blur. The story has it that the scrap bears written wisdom gleaned from all the travels our family has undertaken since the beginning. I have kept it as my father decreed, though in truth it may be no more than a simple piece of hide."

The monk passed the parchment to the old woman who took it carefully into her hands and held it with a reverence that belied its ragged appearance. "I can feel the power in this, my son. There is truth hidden here, if only in its history. One need not read it to know it."

'Truth hidden here.' The monk repeated the phrase to himself and heard his teacher's voice speak the words. Perhaps this scrap was the terma he carried. It had been in his possession all along. "Wise words," he acknowledged. "There is indeed power in this... power beyond what I had recognized myself. You have led me to the meaning of my own mission. Perhaps you would help me complete it?"

"If I can. If we can." The woman glanced again at Aaron who had leaned into the conversation now. "How may we assist you?"

"Keep this parchment. Take it with you. It is to be hidden for a future seer - a terton - to find. If it is like the others my teacher has bequeathed to the future, it should be placed in a cave or some other remote place."

"This is blasphemy" Aaron snatched the parchment from his mother's hand and held it out toward the flames. "You are too ready, old woman, to be tainted by magic and superstition. To be lulled by the influence of complete strangers." He glared openly at the monk. "There is only one truth and it is written elsewhere, not on this filthy scrap of skin." Aaron bent to lay the parchment in the fire.

At once the monk was on his feet, heavy staff ready to crush Aaron's fingers. Monk first, yes, but warrior as well to protect what must be protected. Yet before the blow could land, the old woman's hand had plunged into the flames to rescue the scrap. She held it up intact, edges slightly charred. Her voice was controlled even as she admonished Aaron. "This is not yours to sacrifice like an innocent bird of the field. If God is great – and He is – then He is greater than any of us can know. His works are a mystery not to be dismissed as mere superstition. Not even by a priest of our people. Not even by my own son."

She turned to the monk, with sad eyes and gentle tone. "Forgive us. We cannot protect this treasure of yours, not even if it carried our own salvation. My son is trapped in a bound truth that can no longer grow even if the God he claims to know so well were to ordain it Himself. We are refugees here – welcomed at first in our former home by the very one who then betrayed us."

She cast an affectionate and pitying glance at her son. "Aaron was taken in, you see, by a clever mentor who seemed so like the father he lost long ago. I too was glamoured by this pale demon and failed to warn Aaron until it was too late. We were flattered by pretty words, then punished for what were made to seem our own ugly deeds. We became children of Allah as well as Yaweh... one father, two names. Our 'protector' welcomed us at first as weary wanderers only to lead a mob against us as foreigners and exiles. Aaron's belief has grown hard and angry."

Aaron shrank back in tight-lipped silence.

The old woman sat without saying more for several minutes. She appeared to be discussing some weighty point within herself. She turned to the monk who sat again at her side. "I am convinced that you have come across us here for a reason. Why else would we meet in so remote a place... seeming strangers, but with a deep and enduring connection stretching back through distant time. I feel I have known you all my life yet we have only just met." She peered into the monk's eyes. "Perhaps your teacher's instructions are more literal than you have guessed. We have found you and you have found us here, now. You bear treasures yourself. And you, yourself, are their hiding place." She faced the fire again, her hands working as in conversation. At last, she nodded as if in agreement and turned back to him. "I believe you are meant to join us, my son... to travel as one of us. Whatever of value you carry will be ours to protect until it finds its way to wherever it must go next."

The woman's words penetrated and merged with the guru's instructions. He knew in some irrefutable way that he had reached his mission's destination – itself the beginning of another journey. "But will Aaron allow me to join you?"

"Only if you accept the one true God!" Aaron rose to his feet. "I will not tolerate an unbeliever in our midst! I have never deviated from the path of righteousness!"

"Perhaps God challenges us to seek a wider truth than what our meager understanding has shown us so far." His mother's gentle voice offered suggestion with the power of command.

The monk offered the parchment to Aaron with an open hand. "I will honor your truth. Let it be written here.... whatever you wish to add to what it already contains."

Aaron drew a blackened stick from the fire and without a word wrote in large letters across the width of the hide, 'Allah u akhbar.' "Will you erase this?" Aaron challenged. "Those who taught us the phrase forgot it soon enough." He pushed the parchment away with a satisfied smile.

The monk recalled his teacher's parting advice. 'Do not be trapped by the one you appear to be.' He began to understand. "I will carry it forward... a gift to the future."

After a rest of several days, the group broke camp and moved eastward again. The monk walked with them, his step surer now as he moved through the light of the shadow cast by the holy mountain at the center of the world.

TWENTY-TWO

LIGHT BEGAN TO DIM THE SHADOWS. A hint of gray crept through the tangle of trees and vines to trace the faint edges of dawn. Carpenter lay for a time watching the day emerge, then rose from the narrow cot and stepped past his sleeping companions to the doorway. Images of rock and snow gave way to the sights and sounds of the waking forest. The dreams, more frequent now, were themselves less surprising than their increasing intensity. A woman's voice echoed through his mind. The dreams were changing his sense of the world, of himself.

Was Reggie's sleep similarly haunted? He had stepped from the gloom like a ghost and sent them running with his revelation about Father Harry. The drama that had begun only weeks ago of Carpenter's own volition had picked up speed and overtaken him like a river in flood. There seemed to be no alternative but to go with it and try to keep afloat.

The sun burned a path of gold through the dense bush surrounding the compound. The sky was pale blue now with thin brush strokes of orange and pink cloud. Carpenter closed his eyes, stretched and breathed the damp air of vegetation. Bird song thickened and grew in volume. And something else. The distant sound of a motor approaching from the direction of the river and the town.

Inside, the others had begun to move around. By the time the vehicle arrived, they had all gathered by Carpenter to watch it pull up. Kohein clambered down from the passenger side of a mud-spattered Jeep, a broad smile on his purple lips. "Ah! I see that I have failed to catch the proverbial worm despite my efforts at an especially early rising. Good morning!" He stepped forward to embrace Carpenter and offer his hand to all but Hemple, who stood apart from the group as if separated by an invisible barrier. "I trust you have not eaten yet. We had hoped to prevail upon your hospitality should it include an invitation to breakfast." Kohein pumped Kumar's hand as he spoke, his good nature infectious. He turned to gesture toward the Jeep as Hajee stepped down from the driver's side.

Kumar responded with a smile. "Of course you are invited. Though there may not be enough to satisfy your prodigious appetite."

"Only two extra mouths. We travel alone to avoid easy detection. Hajee by himself is worth any number of others. He is quite expert in jungle survival. He has accompanied me on nearly every trek I have made into what we might call the 'less charted' areas of the region. He will be with us on this next journey." Kohein's face took on a more serious expression. "And it is that journey, of course, that has brought me here."

"Why don't we take this up inside over whatever fare we can manage," Kumar gestured toward the main house. "There have been a number of developments since we last spoke… not the least of which is the rather unexpected appearance of Mr. Kingston – a close friend, as it turns out, of James. A military man… at least until recently."

Reggie stepped forward to grasp Kohein's hand with an oddly familiar warmth. "Just 'Reggie' will do. Recently self-retired from the U.S. Army Special Forces." This last was added in a nonchalant tone that belied Reggie's direct gaze. "You would be the man with the Burmese mission. JC likes you, so you must be OK."

Kohein's hand reappeared from Reggie's swallowing grip. "I am Amit - indeed the very man of whom you speak. The 'man with the mission', as you say." Kohein glanced at Carpenter, adding, "And thankful that I have been vetted already by young James. It seems he and I are old friends, though rather recent acquaintances."

"Reggie is a friend from the States, Amit." Carpenter stepped forward. "We've known each other since grade school, when he first helped me adjust to life in the schoolyard."

"Saved your narrow ass, if the truth be known," Reggie grinned. "But speaking of truth - not to mention consequences - I'd say we have a good bit to talk about."

"My sentiments exactly," Kohein replied. "Perhaps we can beg at least a cup of tea as we talk?"

Inside, the men gathered around the same rough table at the opposite end of the room from the sleeping area. Yellow sun leaked through strips of vertical bamboo siding to cast narrow bars of dark and light across the interior. Dust motes rose glowing from the packed dirt floor to float slowly in and out of existence in the heavy air. Kohein, Kumar, Brother Joe and Carpenter faced each other on crude chairs across a large communal basket of sticky rice and a red lacquered plate piled with tangerines, pomelo and bananas. Hajee stood behind Kohein sipping instant coffee from a chipped cup. Reggie leaned on the back of Carpenter's chair, the muscles of his forearms and biceps standing out as if in stone bas relief.

"My aim is to travel in a small band." Kohein held a white can over his mug and waited patiently as a thin rope of sweetened condensed milk twisted slowly into his tea. He sipped, added a large lump of coconut sugar to the mixture and dabbed at his mustache. "On most trips, I have joined a large *Hui* caravan with Hajee and his colleagues. This time, however, is different." He glanced up sharply. "There is more danger now to all involved. More than typical... which is to say, a great deal. This is not a case of simply being prepared for the mere possibility of danger."

Kohein's eyes made a slow tour of the gathered company. Kumar sat as upright and attentive as an obedient student in a classroom. Brother Joe leaned forward on an elbow, chewing thoughtfully on one of a bunch of finger-sized bananas clutched in his other fist. Carpenter listened intently, sensing that for all of them this was more a briefing than an invitation. Hemple leaned against the doorway at a distance, seemingly unconcerned, but with his head cocked toward the conversation.

"Oh, no," Kohein continued. "The danger this time is quite real, and completely of my own doing, I'm afraid. We will be pursued by men who wish me harm and are prepared to inflict it in ample measure on whomever accompanies me. The only way it will be avoided is by eluding pursuit altogether. I expect they will do their best to watch from afar, undetected, until the destination is revealed and whatever treasure it holds can be seized. They want what I carry, but also what they may find by following me. I hope some of you will join me, but I accept that you may not ... and respect whatever decision you make. Though he may suspect it, Phi Rak has no reason yet to consider us as united in this enterprise."

Carpenter spoke first. "The last time we met, there was only one issue. I needed to ask Father Harry if he was OK with me going with you. Things have changed since then." He looked back over his shoulder toward his friend, "...Reggie?"

"Right," Reggie straightened. "Well, first off I'm here, which changes things all by itself. I mentioned retiring from Uncle Sam's forces. Fact is, I am either AWOL or MIA depending on what the official word is now. Wherever JC goes, I go. And I got my own priorities. So you're gonna have to deal with all that up front."

Kohein simply watched and listened.

"Next thing, JC and the Brothers here have another agenda that you don't know about. Their Father Harry is also Missing in Action and I think I have a rough idea of where he may be... though not whether he is alive or not. Your thing is not the only concern any more and it seems like everybody's got a dog in the hunt." Reggie leaned to grip Carpenter's chair back again. "Like I said, I go with JC. If you plan to head north, maybe we can join up. Tell you the truth, I'm not much worried about these dangerous dudes you're talking about. Personally, I'm more worried about Uncle Sam the Pusher Man." Reggie stood again and folded his arms across his chest, ready for a challenge.

"This is a new development to be sure." Kohein placed his cup gently on the table. "My original intent was to include James only, if he was willing. We would be most fortunate, to say the least, to have your assistance as well, Mr. Kingston. I hesitate, however, to expose anyone else to the risks I have created." Kohein lifted the cup again, then set it down without drinking. "But that decision is no longer a simple one, nor mine alone to make. In fact," he laid his palms flat on the table to either side of his tea, "I am coming to believe that our paths have been converging for some time. I have the distinct feeling that we already belong together... already are a crew of some kind despite our differences and what seems in many cases a rather shallow acquaintance."

"What do you have in mind?" Reggie's question was direct and unembroidered.

"Let me tell you where I am headed," Kohein offered. "Then tell me if that direction is not also the same you would pursue in search of the Father. If they are different, I shall move on now. Time, as they say, is of the essence. But if our paths are congruent, then so must be the aims. Should that be so, let us make all haste to get started together, today."

"Makes sense to me." Reggie looked to the others for confirmation. He clearly had assumed the lead.

"You say you know where this Father Harry may be?"

Reggie nodded. "Our orders were to fetch him from the Shan States, at roughly N20°55' E100°18'. That's eastern Burma, north from here - about 50 miles as the crow flies. We picked up a radio signal when we got close. If you know the area, it's pretty rugged and remote – not much there. Not far from China and Laos – maybe 40 miles south of Yunnan and a few west of the Lao side of the Mekong. Hilly country like here, but steeper and higher. Deep valleys, dense shade with narrow ridges and green slopes and lots of little streams. Good for growing poppies and good for hiding."

Kohein seemed unsurprised. "The compass coordinates I have are between

N20°50-60' E100°15-20', as written down nearly a hundred years ago by a British adventurer. James will understand the source." Kohein took a long sip of his tea. "In other words, roughly the same area, Mr. Kingston."

A hint of a smile touched Reggie's broad face. "Looks like we may be in business, Mr. Kohein. And like I said, you can call me 'Reggie'."

"Before we go further, perhaps we should consider priorities and the practical risks involved in this venture." Kumar's gentle voice commanded attention. "Our paths may converge, but our final destinations may differ. Suppose we reach a crossroads, do we split again or must we choose one or the other? There may not be time for lengthy discussion should we reach that point."

"Certainly safety and welfare must be paramount. My original aim was treasure, to be honest. To return one and perhaps find another. If that proves possible, I shall be delighted. However, if forced to choose, I would consider the safety of your Father Harry – of any one of us, really - a much higher priority. I would hope, however, that you might share my aim of finding the people and the place where this belongs." Kohein reached into his shoulder bag to produce Scott's diary. "At some point on this journey, I shall try to accomplish that aim – with or without assistance beyond that offered by Hajee." A rueful expression came over Kohein's features. "In truth, regardless of our purposes, once we set out together, I'm afraid we will be pursued by a common enemy. This will occur even if we travel separately. Our pursuers already have encountered James and Brother Joe, much to their regret. They may even have been watching for me in Sop Ruak, though I saw no sign of them this morning as I passed through."

"Of course, that only means they stayed hidden," Brother Joe ventured.

Kohein lifted his mug and drained the last of his tea. "You are right, of course. But they are not simply devious. I hesitate to say this about fellow human beings, but these men are different... especially their leader. Make no mistake. I mentioned him to you once before. He will stop at nothing to get what he wants. He seems to derive a certain satisfaction from others' pain – particularly if he inflicts it himself or helps cause it. I sincerely hope you will not have the opportunity to meet Phi Rak yourselves. He has no capacity for remorse. I dealt with him originally out of foolish ignorance and without considering all possible consequences. I did not think beyond the fact that he was so well spoken and could put me in contact with providers of gems. Since then, however, I have learned a good deal more about him."

Kohein's eyelids narrowed. "Be clear on this. Phi Rak deals in whatever commodities bring the greatest return. He began by trafficking in children, buying or stealing them from poor villages and selling them for the sex trade in Bangkok. That likely accounts for his assumed title of 'Brother Love'. From that enterprise, he and his partners have branched out to all sorts of illicit activities including the export of local opium and heroin. They are well connected with all parties in the drug trade including Khun Sa and his Shan Army and Lo Hsin Han and his KMT forces. Phi Rak's network is not large, but it is wicked." Kohein leaned back to study the faces around the table. "If he sees us as a group, he will deal with us all in the same manner, without compunction or restraint."

Reggie shrugged his broad shoulders. "I'm in. We do this together. I've already been called," he added somewhat mysteriously.

"Count me in, too. We gotta find Harry and we'll be headed the same way." Brother Joe spoke through a mouthful of banana as if agreeing to a walk in the woods.

Carpenter simply nodded. Before he could reply further, Kumar spoke up.

"I am willing as well. I fear I have little to offer, however, beyond an acquaintance with languages and with the peoples of the area generally. I would not wish to become a liability to more able-bodied souls." Kumar looked to Kohein apologetically.

Kohein seemed ready with his reply. "No one is more familiar with the people, customs and history here, except those who are native. Your knowledge, your presence itself, would add an element of comfort for me, my friend, that goes well beyond any other kind of prowess. I hesitate only at the risk involved for you. I know that your heart is strong in all ways but the physical." Kohein hesitated, pulling at the corners of his mustache. "No, Kumar. If you are willing to come, I welcome you. But," he leaned closer, "how about our friend Paul over there? What do we do with him?"

"F... uh, I mean leave him here to save souls until we get back. Talk about danger. If he comes along, I'm afraid I'd kill him myself before any bad guys even showed." A small vein pulsed across Brother Joe's forehead. "I mean it. Look at him over there, pretending he doesn't give a hoot about what we're saying and taking it all in like some kind of spy. I don't like him and I don't trust him."

Hemple covered his hurt with an indignant cough. The taste of rejection was familiar. He fought to hide his reaction, striking a tone of well-rehearsed outrage. "I'm not interested in joining your little club. I would of course go through whatever was needed to help poor Father Harry, but it sounds to me like you are more interested in planning a criminal activity than rescuing a man of God. I'll have nothing to do with it."

A moment passed, then Kumar's quiet voice rose again. "I'm afraid it isn't quite so simple, Paul. Certainly, you can refuse to join us. I believe, like Brother Joe, that it would be better if you did not. The question remains, however - as Amit has perhaps indelicately put it - of what precisely to do with you."

Hemple pushed himself angrily from the wall and crossed to the table. Stripes of sunlight passed over his rigid frame to lend his movement the unreal herky-jerky quality of a silent movie caricature. "I beg your pardon? I've endured your ridicule and your silent judgment without any complaint. Your complete lack of Christian charity. And now you want to deny me even the simple shelter of this God-forsaken spot as if I were a beggar or a common thief? Unbelievable." He stopped just short of Kumar, who remained seated, though Brother Joe did not.

Kumar gentled Brother Joe with a hand on his forearm. "As I said, Paul, the situation is rather more complicated than you seem to understand. If Amit is correct in his assumption that he is being followed, then this place may not be safe for you." Kumar tilted his head to the side as if considering whether Hemple would understand the next statement. "If you remain here, Paul, you may well endanger our few teachers, the children and indeed the entire village." Kumar shook his head slowly. "No Paul, I believe you must go with us or at least leave when we leave. If that decision lacks charity, I can only apologize and hope you may understand."

Hemple stood trembling for a moment over Kumar, then turned abruptly away and walked back to his post at the door. "Whatever you say. I am willing to make some sacrifices for the less fortunate, but I will not join your adventure." He looked away from the group and into the darkness of the room, determined to show no vulnerability.

"Let me be the first to second that," Brother Joe tossed over his shoulder before returning to his breakfast. "You nearly got us all killed back in Sop Ruak with that hairless pervert and his drunk chauffeur."

"I beg your pardon!" Kohein started from his seat, struggling to calm himself before continuing. "When did this encounter occur?"

"Just yesterday," Carpenter replied. "After we reached Sop Ruak and just before we started out for the mission here."

Kohein's expression was fierce. "Can you describe these men? You say there were two of them?"

Reggie spoke. "Three, actually. There was a kid with them too, a young Thai kid maybe seven or eight. The guy Joe referred to as the chauffeur was all duded up and drunk and playing with knives. But the big guy in the back was the top dog."

"Big guy? You mean the 'hairless' one?" Kohein nodded as if already knowing the answer.

"Yeah. I mean he was tall and skinny. But he was, I don't know, 'big' in a different way. Like you wouldn't want to cross him unless you could, uh, well... kill him." Reggie's voice betrayed a note of apology. "Listen, I've been killing people for a while. I probably shouldn't have said it like that, but it's pretty much what I felt."

Kohein dropped his voice. "So, it appears you already have met Brother Love. God help us."

****

Silence reigned around the table as Kohein's revelation sank in. He paused for some time, considering his next words. "Well, then, we must assume Phi Rak knows Hajee and I are here. We are his primary focus. He surely observed our arrival in Sop Ruak and our departure this morning. He likely is waiting for our return to the town along the only road available. This is no surprise. In fact, I suspected something like this. So I have a different plan in mind."

Kohein lips betrayed a sly smile. "I propose we band together and leave Phi Rak waiting in Sop Ruak while we continue on together over the Sangor ridge above us, then loop back north toward the river. There is no real road over the ridge, of course, but there is a cart track that the Rover and Jeep both should be able to negotiate. Phi Rak is not likely to expect us to take that route, even if he is aware of the track. He will wait for some time in Sop Ruak before coming here to investigate. His aim, I am sure, is to follow Hajee and me all the way to our destination before revealing himself and taking whatever treasure may be found there."

Expressions around the table showed confusion. Kumar gave voice to the concerns. "I have walked the track you refer to. It may be wide enough for the vehicles as you suggest, and I know there is a small road in the valley on the other side of the ridge that winds back north to the river. It ends near the Ruak River just west of the town, near its junction with the Mekong. But that also is very near where Phi Rak now waits for you. If we take it, will it not deliver us directly into his arms?"

"That is of course a risk. And once he sees us together, then we all become his prey. But I believe the risk is worth taking." Kohein's gaze swept the others at the table. "Phi Rak will watch the road to Sangor for my Jeep, since he knows now that we have taken it to come here. We have the chance to elude him while his attention is thus diverted. But even if Phi Rak sends someone here to verify our presence, precious time will be lost as he then pursues us over the ridge." Kohein sat back smiling. "Either way, we should reach the Ruak well before Phi Rak is aware that we are closer than he suspects. And... " Kohein's smile broadened now, "the Ruak River flows into the Mekong. I have arranged to have a boat waiting for us there. The Ruak will take us into the Mekong within a few minutes. We will then head across the river for the Lao side before Phi Rak has any notion of where we may have gone. We can wait for nightfall or proceed as soon as we have a sense that the way is clear."

Brother Joe spoke up. "OK, maybe everybody else gets what you're talking about, but I don't. Can you, like, draw me a picture or something?"

"Of course." Kohein withdrew a notebook and pencil from his satchel and tore off a blank sheet. "Let me show you." He drew a curving line that bent up and back down from left to right across the middle of the page. To this, he added another wavy line beginning in the middle of the page and weaving its way up toward the top. "Forgive my meager drawing skills. This curving line in the center of the page running east to west is the border between Thailand and Burma – a 'B' here - and then between Thailand and Laos – 'L' - further to the right. Everything below the curved line is Thailand – 'Th'."

Kohein drew a small triangle where the two lines met. "This triangle is the Golden Triangle itself. The second line extending north is the Mekong River."

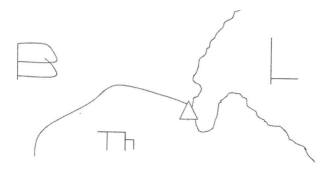

Kohein placed the point of the pencil at the top of the triangle. "Sop Ruak lies here where the Mekong joins the three countries. Above Sop Ruak, the Mekong divides Burma and Laos. If you go far enough upriver, you come to China... Yunnan province, to be exact, which is on the northern border of Laos. Do you follow me so far?"

Reggie placed a thick finger at the top of the triangle. "So, if that's Sop Ruak on the river, we're down here a hair south." He traced the left side of the triangle down from Sop Ruak. "Somewhere along here. This is just below the summit of the ridge you're talking about, right?"

"Precisely." Kohein bent to the crude map. "Our ultimate destination lies up the Mekong in northeastern Burma in the Shan States. The easiest, though most exposed means to reach that area is by boat, which, as I mentioned, waits for us near Sop Ruak as we speak. My plan is to slip past Brother Love and across the river to a densely forested area quite near Ban Khwan until we are sure of our safety."

"Ban Khwan?" Reggie interjected. "Where the Opium War was fought last year?"

"The same."

"I was just telling these guys about it last night. The Lao air force ended up bombing the shit out of both sides – even though the general who sent them in was in business with the KMT *and* the Shan Army. They leveled the place."

Kohein nodded. "Yes, a terrible battle... though it settled nothing. For our purposes, however, Ban Khwan offers certain advantages. The conflict devastated the site, so it is deserted now. The forest nearby is thick, however, and should offer good cover." Kohein's eyes widened in mischief. "Once our Phi Rak recognizes that we have evaded him, he doubtless will set out on the river in pursuit. But with luck, we will be so far ahead of him by then that he will have no chance of finding us again." Kohein lowered his voice conspiratorially, "You see, he has only what he may have been told by the KMT, and I happen to know that their sense of the original location of the journal is vague at best. So he will have only a broad sense of the proper direction, but nothing more specific. I have the journal and the coordinates. He will need someone to guide him or he will be lost altogether."

Carpenter frowned. "Hold it. But *we* don't really know where we're going either, right? I mean you know generally, but not exactly either."

Kohein hesitated for moment. "I have been to the general area myself, so we have an advantage in that regard. And I believe we may have others as well." He turned to Reggie. "Do we not, sir? Have we not been 'called' as you rather cryptically put it earlier?"

Reggie held Kohein's gaze for a still moment. "You, too?"

Kohein nodded slowly. "Me, too."

Carpenter spoke up, "Would you mind sharing whatever secret you seem to be talking about?"

Reggie answered simply, "I think me and Amit had a Martin Luther King moment. Mine was last night."

Kohein nodded in response. "And to borrow a phrase, we had a dream... possibly the same one, it seems. Reggie was in mine. I saw him choose a path in the forest."

"In mine, you and Hajee both seemed to know where to land a boat, though I didn't see you together for some reason. I don't know that I could tell the spot myself, but in the dream, I had a sense of where to go after we landed."

Kohein nodded again. "The dreams evidently fit together... as do we."

Reggie shrugged, almost apologetic. "Yeah, it sounds crazy, but I'd say that between the three of us, we have a pretty good idea of where we're headed."

"You mean, you actually believe you can locate the village where the journal was found and the spot Scott was looking for?" Carpenter realized his question sounded more incredulous than he actually felt. His own dreams had become too real, too strong to dismiss as pure imagination.

Kohein translated for Hajee. All three nodded together.

"OK, there's something going on here that we haven't been talking about. Who else has been dreaming? And I don't mean regular dreams. I mean like the ones you're talking about now. Like the one I had last night." Brother Joe pressed, anxiety showing. "Mine didn't have anything to do with directions, but it was awful... a primitive sacrifice."

"But I had a similar dream! As you say, nothing to do with direction but certainly involving some of us." Kumar's head bobbed in agreement.

"Jesus... save us." Brother Joe stared first at Kumar, then at Carpenter. "So me and Kumar both had the same dream, OK? And *you* were the sacrifice." He went on, voice shaking. "Did you have it too, James? It was terrible. Everybody but Reggie was there in some form or another. Even Paul." Brother Joe threw an angry glance at Hemple across the room. "I watched the whole thing, but I couldn't stop it. I'm sorry, James."

"My own dream last night was different, but I'm pretty sure I've had the one you're talking about. Many times, unfortunately. It's a nightmare I can't seem to escape."

Kumar added, "Yes, a nightmare... and much more vivid than most dreams."

"You were tied to an altar of some kind and they set a fire and ..." Joe swallowed hard, "and Father Harry was holding a knife over you and someone that looked like that bastard Brother Love was whispering to him."

"In my dream, the man with the knife was a priest, but also my own father," Carpenter felt himself again at the edge of a precipice.

There was silence around the table. Brother Joe exchanged a glance with Kumar then pushed forward. "Well, the truth is you look a lot like him, James." He let out a deep breath. "There, I've said it. I saw it the first time I laid eyes on you in Chiang Mai. Everybody who knows Father Harry can see it. We just didn't want to think about it too much."

"Somrak, the cook at *Suan Dok Gnam* noticed," Kumar added. "She told you in Thai that you looked like the Father. She was referring to Father Harry, though I don't believe you took her meaning."

Carpenter felt himself begin to float over the group as if watching from above. His vision shrank and tunneled as if he were watching the conversation through the wrong end of a telescope.

"James? James! Are you all right?" Kumar's voice echoed as from a distance.

Slowly, Carpenter's awareness returned to the present. As the moment renewed itself, a familiar voice - a woman's - seemed to speak to him from inside his own head. "*Such is the yoga of life. Do not flee the truth. Lean into it as you would the pain of a simple stretch.*"

TWENTY-THREE

CARPENTER WAS THE FIRST TO BREAK THE ANXIOUS SILENCE. "I'm OK, really. This isn't even as weird as the whole collective dream phenomenon." He took a deep breath. "Now that I've heard it out loud, I guess I'm not so shocked... not even as surprised as I thought I would be if I ever discovered who my real parents were... or are." Carpenter looked down at hands that lay folded in his lap. "I always thought I'd find out somehow when I came here. I don't know why." He looked up. "But then maybe I do. My mom always talked about her brother – Father Harry – like she was apologizing for him. Like maybe sending me to them wasn't the kind of good deed everybody else seemed to think it was. Not that they didn't love me, or him, for that matter. It was just, I don't know, like there was a secret behind it that she wouldn't tell but couldn't hide."

Carpenter paused, sifting through uncounted numbers whose sum had never been consciously tallied until now. "But this doesn't really change anything. Father Harry is still missing and we're still looking for him. Just looking for more than I thought. More than any of us thought, as far as that goes. And the clock is still ticking, right?" Carpenter nodded to Kohein who paused reflectively then proceeded as before.

"Yes, well. The clock is indeed ticking as you say. But I find myself rather at a loss for words... a rarity as you surely have guessed by now." Kohein pulled thoughtfully on his mustache. "This quest of ours has taken on a depth and variety of meaning I could never have imagined at the outset." He gave a wave of his hand intended to include everyone in the room. "Each of us would appear to be a part of it. We seem bound together in ways we can only suspect. My belief is that whatever course we pursue must include us all." Kohein watched the faces around the table. "Your thoughts?"

A murmur of assent rose from around the table. Reggie straightened. "Yeah, I think we're all in. Except maybe Red, here. What about it Paul, are you with us?"

Hemple stiffened as if offended by the large man's tone of familiarity. "Obviously, I must leave. That much is clear now that Kohein has exposed all of us in this way."

The others began to protest, but Kohein cut them off. "What then do you propose to do?"

"I refuse to join this escapade. Leave me here and I'll simply walk out."

"Where will you go, Paul?" Kumar's voice was gentle but clear.

"I don't believe that is any of your business," Hemple snorted.

"Ah, but it *is* our business, unfortunately. Whatever you choose to do will affect us all. Perhaps you should join with us at least for a time."

Hemple stepped closer into the room. "I'll have nothing to do with this goose-chase. I am sorry for Father Harry, despite his obvious failings as a young man. I had hoped he would be different. Be that as it may, I clearly don't belong with the rest of you." Hemple nudged a large backpack with his foot where it lay on the floor. "Most of my belongings are still in there. I can be ready to go in a few minutes. You decide yourselves. I'll wait outside." He banged through the door without another glance.

"Let him walk out from here. The Love Brother can do whatever he wants with him." Reggie made no attempt to hide his disdain.

Carpenter voiced concern. "Yeah, but what if Phi Rak gets to him before we cross the river? Our only chance is to escape his notice before he can follow us."

Kohein turned to Carpenter. "Precisely, James. But Sop Ruak is nearly two hours away by foot. Paul will be carrying a heavy pack. We should be able to make it over the ridge and to the river well before he reaches Sop Ruak. But we must leave now."

A motor coughed and died, then coughed again. "The Rover!" Brother Joe jumped to his feet. "That little bas…" He ran to the door and leaped out followed by the others.

Hemple was behind the wheel of the Rover, struggling to shift gears without letting the engine die. Before Brother Joe could reach the driver's door, the vehicle's tires spun crazily in the soft earth, spraying him with clods of thick clay. "Stop! Stop, you worthless…" Joe leaped for the door handle, slipped and sprawled face-first on the ground. Hemple shook his fist in the rearview mirror as he tore out of the compound and headed downhill toward Sop Ruak.

Brother Joe lay for a moment pounding the dirt, then pulled himself to his feet without pausing to brush his clothes. "I guess we better get moving, huh?"

****

The party hurried to pack. Carpenter pushed a change of clothes and two extra T-shirts into his backpack, leaving his suitcase behind. Brother Joe stuffed a cloth shoulder bag with fruit and baskets of cooked sticky rice. Kumar added candles, mosquito coils and matches to his own woven sack.

Reggie bent to open the tall duffel-pack he had arrived with and extracted a brown sheath. The handle of the same slim blade he had used at the accident site showed at the top. He eased it out a little ways to check its narrow black length before strapping the sheath to his right side where it clung close to his waist. As Reggie bent again to his pack, Carpenter noticed the butt end of what appeared to be some sort of gun protruding from the neatly packed contents. A tremor of dread tinged with excitement rippled through his chest.

"OK, OK... are we ready yet?" Brother Joe's voice was sharp with frustration and anxiety.

Carpenter took a last look around. The unfinished meal and the personal items scattered about told a clear story. Even if their pursuers arrived without having met Hemple first, they would know the cottage had been abandoned in haste and its occupants possibly not far ahead on the other side of the ridge. Still, that shouldn't pose a problem so long as the party could maintain its lead. Carpenter slid past Kumar who held the door and surveyed the room himself before joining the others.

Outside, the Jeep was running. "I guess we'll just have to squeeze, gentlemen." Reggie tried to make himself small in the rear seat with Brother Joe as Carpenter and Kumar joined them there. Hajee drove with Kohein next to him in the passenger seat in front. The Jeep backed and turned with a squeal of tires, then swung left out of the compound and toward the summit of the ridge.

****

Hemple watched from the undergrowth as the Jeep loaded up and departed. He hadn't really thought much beyond his dramatic exit from the building, but outside he couldn't miss the key in the Rover's ignition. It was a sign, not a sin. At first, he considered going back for his pack, but there was no time for that. Once he had the Rover, he reasoned, he could simply wait at the bottom of the ridge for the others to leave, then return on foot to retrieve his own belongings. It wouldn't take long. He waited for the sound of the Jeep's motor to fade before he emerged from his hiding place. He crept quietly into the compound and up to the door of the main building. Unlocked. He pressed his ear close against it listening for any sound inside. Nothing.

He slipped in. The remains of breakfast lay on the table hosting a few hungry flies. His pack rested on the floor where he had left it. He bent to pick it up and turned. On the wall near the door, he noticed something hanging from a peg. A rosary. An old one. The smaller beads were a dark green interspersed with larger pink stones at each decade. More pink beads surrounded a large, elegantly cut crystal at the center of the circlet. He reached for the string of stones almost automatically and held it up to the window. Heavy. The green beads were jade. The pink, probably marble. Light danced through the large crystal piece like fire, glinting blue and pink and white-gold. Perhaps more precious than mere crystal. A powerful tool for prayer that should not be left idle or exposed. He could use it to pray the rosary for Father Harry's safety. Hemple removed his own heavy cross from his neck and hung it on the peg. Grasping the jade rosary, he crossed himself and kissed the large stone before placing the circlet around his neck. The weight gave him comfort, like the embrace of a loving parent.

Hemple shouldered his pack and peeked out carefully before emerging from the building. No one. The teachers were in their quarters or away from the compound altogether. He hustled out of the gate and down the track he had driven a short time before. He walked past the low houses of the villagers as if on a mission, head high and confident, sidling away from the skinny, yapping dogs that rushed at him from behind bamboo fencing and danced away as he passed. In 10 minutes he was back at the Rover and headed toward Sop Ruak. From there, he could find a boat to take him downriver on his way to home base in Vientiane.

****

The Jeep followed the steep track to the top of the ridge, then down a narrow and deeply rutted footpath on the other side. The vehicle struggled over the rugged ground and descended slowly in a series of bone-jarring bumps and scrapes for two rocky kilometers. A flat valley stretched out below in squares of brown and ocher left by the recent rice harvest.

The lane widened at the bottom where it joined a red dirt track lined with the tread marks of other motor vehicles. Hajee turned right and headed briefly east before winding north again past bare fields. Here and there an ox-cart lumbered slowly along laden with straw. Women with winnowing baskets swayed rhythmically at their work. Heads turned and hands pointed whenever the car was spotted with its odd cargo of strange and tightly packed humanity. The hills shrank behind them as they approached the river. The narrow clay road joined another, larger artery to the west of Sop Ruak town where a small group of villagers squatted at the intersection. Curious faces surveyed the Jeep as it drew to a stop.

"The road to Mae Sai," Brother Joe, sardined between Reggie and the rear wall, struggled to get an arm free to point left. "They're waiting for the pickup-bus. Three *baht* to the Burmese border from here. Let's hope the bad guys don't come this way. We're about as inconspicuous as a pack of dogs at a cat convention."

The Jeep turned right onto the packed surface of the Mae Sai Road, heading back toward Sop Ruak. Kohein turned toward the rear. "Not far now. Less than a kilometer, then we will look for an opening on the left."

"Better not be much further than that. Sop Ruak itself isn't more than a kilometer from here." Brother Joe's anxiety level was rising.

"*Cha cha noi. Thi ni.*" Kohein addressed the silent Hajee and pointed to the left side of the road. Slow down. This is it. Vegetation grew thick and unbroken but for a narrow opening near ground level where a subtle gap interrupted the wall of interwoven branches.

"That's it?" Brother Joe asked, eyebrows raised in doubt.

"Yes.... quickly now. Several of us must hold back the bushes while Hajee pulls off the road. If we are careful, we will leave little sign of our passing." Kohein stepped down from the left front. Reggie and Carpenter disentangled themselves from the back to join him. Together, they parted the bushes at the gap, leaning against them to allow the Jeep to push its way through. Past the initial thicket, the opening was less a track than a partial clearing that sloped gently down through a tunnel of moss-covered trees to a wall of tall grass.

"Gentlemen. I give you the Ruak River and our *hang yaw*." Kohein pushed through the stalks to the edge of a stream nearly 30 feet across. Five feet below him, a narrow canoe-like wooden boat floated on a rope next to the bank. From pointed bow to flat stern, the shallow craft stretched nearly 30 feet along the brown water. Mounted at the stern was a huge naked engine from which a 10-foot propeller shaft protruded backward like the fragile appendage of some prehistoric wading bird.

The literal meaning of '*hang yaw*' is 'long-tail'. A *hang yaw* boat is so named for its long propeller, which typically is driven by an automobile engine supplying considerable thrust. Such craft draw little water and are made for speed. They also respond dramatically to sudden shifts of weight. Of the five men already aboard, only Hajee weighed less than 140 pounds. As Reggie stepped carefully into the middle of the craft near the packs, its sides dipped uncomfortably low in the water as it wobbled radically from side to side.

"We must pay close attention to our own movements," Kohein warned from the bow. "The water is slow here but will have more force once we enter the

Mekong itself. Let us stay low and be as still as possible for the crossing. If we can make the Lao side undetected, we will be relatively safe." He turned to Hajee at the stern. "*Pai dai laew, na!*" Hajee nodded and pushed off from the bank.

The boat nearly capsized as Reggie shifted his weight to find a place for his legs and feet. "Whoa, damn!" The others held their breath and the *hang yaw* moved out into the stream.

Hajee did not engage the engine, but used a stout paddle to steer them along the bank with the current through tall rushes and low-hanging branches. Here and there they passed wicker fish traps lying with mouths agape just below the water line, woven in such a manner as to allow fish to enter but not to escape. Carpenter found himself distracted by the ingenuity of these low-tech devices and tilted the boat dangerously as he reached down to touch one as they passed.

The boat glided silently east toward the town and the confluence of the Ruak and the Mekong. After less than a kilometer, the thick vegetation crowding the left bank gave way to a grassy sliver of land that came to a point where the smaller stream joined the larger. "On your left, Burma. On your right, Thailand," Kohein sounded oddly like a tour guide. As the *hang yaw* cleared the point, the Mekong came fully into view. Across the expanse of its coffee au lait waters, the Lao shore showed green and thick and a hundred yards away. "And that is Laos, the third side of our Golden Triangle. The trick now will be to reach it without getting wet." The engine rumbled behind them. "Hold tight, keep low and be still!" Kohein's voice was just loud enough to be heard above the throaty whine of the engine. Hajee twisted the throttle and the *hang yaw* leaped forward into the thick churn of the Mekong's muddy current.

The boat cleared the point and veered left toward the middle of the river. Halfway across, Hajee maneuvered the propeller to turn left again upriver and west for 20 minutes. A long flat island came into view near the Lao shore. "That's our spot," Kohein pointed past the sandbar. "You can see the site of Ban Khwan just upriver." The *hang yaw* maneuvered past the shallows and scraped through a dense overhang to bump hard against the bank.

Reggie shifted carefully in his seat. "Looks familiar." He gave a bitter laugh. "Nothing like the safety of a war zone."

TWENTY-FOUR

HEMPLE HAD BEGUN TO MASTER THE ROVER'S LETHARGIC STEERING. From the foot of the ridge, the road stretched in flat loops toward the town. So long as he anticipated the curves well in advance, he could wrestle the vehicle through them with fair ease. He passed an occasional feeder track running through the fields on either side, but made good enough progress to know he would have plenty of time to reach Sop Ruak and negotiate a boat ride downriver to Chiang Saen. God willing, he should be able to be on an eastbound bus before dark and well on his way toward Vientiane.

His mission, of course, had not ended as he had hoped. His plan was to establish a connection with Father Wilkins, from all appearances a kindred soul. The priest was known in several remote villages in western Laos. He could help win the confidence of locals so that the International Voluntary Service would re-think its decision to terminate their association with Hemple. Instead of being fired, Hemple would lead the way for IVS' expansion into new areas. And IVS resources could help Father Wilkins' missionary efforts. A win-win for everyone and a new chance for Hemple to show his value to those who just couldn't see it. And should his efforts go further, bring opportunities for personal advancement, well, one should not shrink from responsibility. Perhaps he would even be rewarded with a promotion. The doors could open again to work in Burma. Maybe the match with Father Wilkins was one made in heaven, despite the Father's youthful folly. Hemple felt generous and expansive.

If only he could have gotten to the Father directly. Hemple had pushed what he characterized as a solid connection with Father Wilkins to his IVS superiors in Vientiane. The letter had helped. Yes, he had embroidered a bit on the Father's invitation to make it seem more the shared vision Hemple was sure it would become. Communism in Laos was at least as great a challenge to the true faith as its Buddhist tradition. And consider China. The communists there already had destroyed decades of missionary work. Father Wilkins would understand. He had been there.

The Americans he had met in Vientiane knew about Father Wilkins, though they didn't say much. Hemple knew the Father had been OSS before he was a priest, that he had fought the Reds in China for the Nationalist cause and in the Burmese Shan States after WWII. He likely fought them still. There had to be CIA connections. And the priest's trips into eastern Burma surely suggested more than one kind of missionary work. But no one claimed to know the real purpose of those Burmese trips – even the men who were privy to information about covert operations. Hemple had hoped to learn more and make his special knowledge work for him with the IVS doubters who didn't feel he was relating well to the people.

Hemple looked carefully up and down Sop Ruak's main street as he pulled the Rover to the side next to the town wharf. No sign of this boogie man Brother Love the others had been so afraid of. He had had no problem with the man himself, anyway. Kohein was the target. Hemple remembered the earlier encounter now with a degree of pride. He had maintained his dignity and won the respect of a man even Reggie Kingston could not intimidate. The street was rather empty for midday. Hemple turned to search the shadows for signs of activity.

"Well, well. What a complete surprise! Not the Rover, of course, but you, my friend... and without your companions!" Hemple whipped back around toward the voice coming from the Rover's left passenger side. Brother Love stood at the open window. He had somehow materialized there despite Hemple's close inspection before stopping. "Perhaps you would join us for a drink or meal?" Brother Love opened the passenger door to lean in as he spoke.

"Uh, no... thank you. I am on my way actually and haven't got much time."

"Leaving us then? How unfortunate. I had hoped to have a chance to further our acquaintance." Brother Love slid easily into the passenger seat. "The earlier 'incident' left us scant opportunity for conversation. But I sensed a bond between us despite the rather juvenile antics of the others."

"Yes, definitely. Very juvenile." Hemple stammered a reply then paused, at a loss. "Um, well... I guess it turned out alright in the end."

Brother Love leaned toward him, eyes wide with sincerity. "My thoughts exactly! And due in no small part to your quiet strength, if I may say so." He relaxed back against the seat. "But perhaps I embarrass you. Forgive me. At the time, I found your demeanor deeply reassuring. It gave me courage to intervene with my own man. Thank you for that."

Hemple was beginning to feel more at ease. What was the big deal about this man? Clearly yet another example of Kohein's misguided judgment. "It was nothing, really. You played an important part yourself. I doubt I could have managed the situation on my own."

"Nor could I." Brother Love radiated warmth and humility. "But this leads me to ask again if you wouldn't stop for a meal with us before you leave. The opportunity may not present itself again." A string of beads at his neck had found its way into his hand. He fingered them as he spoke. "I know you are also a man of faith. Perhaps you will share something of your story? And, please, call me Phi Rak. I've become quite used to the name. It does describe what I consider to be my own small mission in life."

****

The five sat on the bank above the *hang yaw* tethered below and watched the river for signs of pursuit. An occasional *sampan* poled by fishermen worked its way up or down the river. Two clumsy riverboats towing empty *hang yaw* chugged their way north along the far bank, ragged awnings fluttering lazily in the breeze and ancient engines burbling a steady drone. No threat. No pursuit.

On landing, Reggie and Carpenter had explored the vicinity to assess their situation and, as Reggie put it, to establish a perimeter. Together they had peered through the foliage to the empty remains of Ban Khwan village, once the site of a timber mill doubling as a heroin factory. After their return, conversation had dwindled as each man turned anxious attention to the river. One or another rose periodically to check for intruders, but found none. The place was no longer a crossroads of activity. No inhabitants, no foot traffic. Each man seemed lost in private thoughts.

"How long do you think it will take us to get where we're going?" Carpenter broke the silence.

"Rather difficult to say. Our destination is roughly 70 kilometers upriver on the Burmese side, then some more on foot. But the last portion likely will be up and down, so it is difficult to estimate travel time. We should have no difficulty finding our way, though the specifics are not entirely clear..." Kohein paused, searching for words.

"We'll know when we get there," Reggie broke in. "I floated down the river for a while when I first 'went missing'. I'll probably recognize the spot where I set out, but we'll have to take our time or we could miss the place. Kohein and Hajee will know." Reggie's brows arched up. "But the truth is, we can't really say where we're going, can we, Amit?"

Kohein took in a mouthful of breath as if to answer, then simply dipped his head in agreement.

"So we can't really say how long it will take to get there. You understand A-Man?"

Carpenter nodded and Reggie continued. "We'll have to keep a steady watch on the Burma shore. But when we get to the place, there won't be any doubt. Right, Amit?"

Kohein breathed out. "If dreams can be believed, then yes."

"Maybe you'll have to go into a trance or do some sleep-walking or something." Reggie turned back to Carpenter. "I'd say we could make it in three or four hours, maybe before dark, if we leave soon, move pretty quick and don't swamp the boat." He turned to scan the river again. "That is, unless we get guests. *That* particular development could slow us down considerably."

****

"Fascinating. I understand now how you might find yourself in such company." Phi Rak laid down his rice spoon and nodded slowly, rapt. "And I would like to help, if I may. This Father Wilkins sounds like a fine man, but surely is in grave danger if not... I hope you'll forgive me... if not worse."

"No, I think that's accurate. Something happened to him or he would have made the pick up Reggie referred to." With gentle urging from Phi Rak, Hemple had explained the circumstances of Reggie's appearance and offered background on each of his former companions. He felt a certain, not undeserved pride to possess such a wealth of information.

"You have told me a great deal about your friends, yet rather little about yourself. I suppose I should not be surprised by such humility. Yet, I am curious about your work and how you came to be here."

"There's not much to tell, really. I didn't feel comfortable at college. The campus was not particularly welcoming for a Christian and committed anti-communist." Hemple looked up from his plate. "I had heard about IVS while exploring the possibility of applying to the Peace Corps. I read something by John Steinbeck – the author – after he was in Laos last year. He talked about Pop Buell and his work to help the Hmong people. It seemed both unselfish and unashamedly righteous. And he had begun with IVS. So I applied and was accepted. I've been in Vientiane for nearly a year now." Hemple omitted reference to his trouble 'fitting in' as a volunteer.

"So, you do not reside here in Thailand?"

"Oh, no. I actually came here to meet Father Wilkins and learn more about his mission. We have corresponded, but I haven't actually met him yet. I was hoping to get his help in establishing new projects. IVS - and the U.S. government, of course - generally want to help the people of Laos, especially the Hmong hill tribes and General Vang Pao in their struggle against the *Pathet Lao* communists." Hemple felt almost as if he had achieved a promotion in his work as he tossed out the names of the central players in the sad drama that was Laos.

Phi Rak's lips drew together as he shook his head from side to side. "An amazing... no, a noble mission for such a young man. Your father must be very proud."

Hemple stiffened. "Actually, my father doesn't know much about my work, and probably cares even less. He left my mother when I was still very young."

Phi Rak's brows knitted in reflected pain. "How sad. She must be a very strong woman."

"Oh, yes. She has been a rock for me. And the Church has been hers. My father, on the other hand, hasn't bothered so much as to keep in touch." Hemple restrained a bitter sigh.

"Well, he has missed a rare opportunity to know an extraordinary man... one who just happens to be his own son." Phi Rak placed a hand on Hemple's forearm. "Those of us who are not so fortunate to have children of our own would be more than proud to be able to claim you, believe me."

Hemple wasn't used to such demonstrations. His mother loved him certainly, but was not comfortable with displays of affection. Yet, he found Phi Rak's gesture both tender and compelling. It was hard to believe this same man was in fact the beast Kohein made him out to be. Still, there were doubts. He had, after all, passed by the accident scene without offering assistance. And there was the child.

Hemple hesitated then plunged in. "I wonder if I could ask you something... several things actually?" He reddened slightly. "But as you have pointed out, my information about you and other things has come from a single, possibly tainted source."

Phi Rak nodded his understanding. "Kohein."

"Yes, exactly! I don't really trust the man. He appears to be a smuggler, perhaps worse. I'm not sure what to believe, but he certainly has described you in less than flattering terms."

Phi Rak's lashless eyes flashed fire for a brief moment, then cooled quickly to a look of quiet concern. "I would hope you could feel comfortable asking me anything, Paul. Whatever you need to know. Please be frank."

Hemple decided to abandon caution altogether. "Kohein claims you are a criminal involved in all sorts of illegal activities, including the exploitation of children. I noticed the young boy with you when we met yesterday..."

Phi Rak's body jerked as if struck by a bullet. "My word! Will he stop at nothing to poison my name and cleanse his own? Let me tell you the true story." He took in an injured breath. "I have worked for years for the welfare of poor children, especially in this region. I bring aid and resources to their families and provide whatever assistance I can to help them survive and thrive. In that sense, my work, my mission if you will, is not so different from your own. The boy you met yesterday is a case in point. Like you, he was abandoned by his father. His mother is gravely ill. I have succeeded in finding a home for him while she is treated at a hospital in Chiang Rai. When we passed the accident scene yesterday, we were coming from the hospital. I was hurrying to meet a man who had offered to help pay for her care. I dared not stop, considering the urgency of the need. The boy is now in a loving home."

Phi Rak searched Hemple's eyes. "That is the truth. Nothing less, nothing more."

Hemple swallowed and finally looked away, embarrassed now at having questioned the man's behavior or motives. "Kohein claims you are following him to recover a stolen journal. He says it belongs to someone else and that you will harm him if you find him."

Phi Rak snorted in disgust. "And do you believe this, Paul?"

Hemple lowered his eyes. "No, not now. I believe he must be lying to cover his own greed."

"Exactly! Greed! This is the primary driving force for our friend Kohein. The truth is just the opposite of what he claims. He stole the journal from those men you saw with me yesterday. Not good men, mind you. They are involved in the drug trade, I'm afraid. But not completely evil, either. They offered to help me with the boy and his mother in exchange for whatever I could do to help them locate their property." Phi Rak's stoic expression dared to be challenged. "Given the circumstances, it seemed a reasonable bargain."

Hemple felt small and ashamed. "Thank you, Phi Rak. I appreciate your telling me the real story. Somehow, I'm not surprised. I'm sorry for questioning you like this."

"It is never wrong to seek the truth, son. Never. I take no offense." Phi Rak patted Hemple's arm again. "I do hope to locate Kohein and warn your less discriminating companions of his real intentions. We saw him head toward Sangor this morning. Perhaps you saw him there?"

"Yes, he was there, but he isn't there now."

Phi Rak leaned close. "Really? Do you know where he is?"

"Yes. He is headed toward some place in Burma. The place where the journal came from. And..." Hemple lowered his voice as if to avoid being overheard, "... and where Father Wilkins may be too. They are all trying to find him."

Phi Rak shook his head in frustration. "Then they have managed to elude us. If only we could follow them, perhaps we could kill two birds with a single stone, so to speak." He squeezed Hemple's arm and drew back with a sigh of regret. "But, we would need to know how to find them."

Hemple's voice rang with conviction. "I can help with that."

****

"It's been an hour. If we wait much longer, we'll lose whatever head start we have on them." Reggie finished a thorough cleaning of what looked like a large pistol or small machine gun and placed it carefully back in his pack. He was anxious to move and it showed. The others looked aside nervously, trying to ignore the brutal intrusion of the weapon into the surface calm of the riverside and their own anxious thoughts.

Kohein broke the silence. "I agree, though we certainly expose ourselves on the river. It will be hard to hide from any pursuit. We may need to pull to the side at some point and wait until sunset. But either option holds risk. There can be danger both on the river and on its banks." He deferred to Reggie's judgment with some reluctance. "But you are the expert in these things now. I am out of my depth."

"I've seen enough of the view from here. Let's get going before that creep shows up." Brother Joe scooped up his bag and stood ready on the bank above the *hang yaw*.

Carpenter roused himself from thoughts of Father Harry, and his mother and father back home. He had had little time to reflect since the conversation in Sangor. In truth, he felt completely out of balance since the revelation concerning Harry's identity... and his own. And the dreams in their intensity and content made the world spin further. Waking reality had been invaded, distorted. It was changing into something else completely outside his control.

And he felt himself changing as well. Becoming someone at once new and familiar... and no longer young.

"Yeah, ready!" Carpenter shook himself and pushed to his feet, hoping that action would banish the ghosts of dreams.

TWENTY-FIVE

THE MEKONG RIVER BEGINS ITS 3000-MILE JOURNEY TO THE SOUTH CHINA SEA in a remote part of the Tibetan plateau in what is now Qinghai Province in western China. It begins as glacial melt trickling into Lasagongma Creek at 17,000 feet in the heart of the Kunlun Mountain chain, a range of peaks that stretches thousands of miles from northern Tibet to the eastern sands of the Gobi desert. The mountains were pushed up a million years ago when the earth's Cimmerian plate – which encompasses what have become Iran, Afghanistan, Tibet, Indochina and Malayasia - collided with Siberia. The river and the lands that form its basin are ancient.

The river has many names. In much of China, it is the *Lancang Jiang*. West and south where it crosses into Tibet, it becomes the *rDza Chu*. Re-entering China in northern Yunnan Province, it may be called the *Za Qu* or the *Meigong Le*. In Burmese, it becomes the *Me' Kaung Myit*. In Thai and Lao, it is the *Mae Nam Kong* or Mekong, and in Cambodia, the *Mehkong Thonle Thum*. By the time it drops its tons of silt on the Vietnamese delta, it is the *Song Cuu Long* ('Nine Dragons River') or *Song Me Kong*. The sound 'mae' as it is pronounced in Thai and Lao connotes 'mother'. The word 'kong' and its variations appear to have begun with the Sanskrit for 'Ganges' in reference to that sacred water.

The Mekong and its basin define diversity in every sense. The variety of trees, orchids and other jungle plants rivals the richness of the Amazon. Snakes, insects, fish, rodents and other mammals abound. The Mekong Giant Catfish, at nearly 9 feet and over 600 pounds may well be the largest freshwater fish in the world. The huntsman spider is the world's largest with a leg span of 25 inches. The King Cobra at 13 to 18 feet in length is the world's largest venomous snake, capable of injecting enough venom in a single bite to kill 20 people. Although the 'dragon millipede' is not large, it is exotic for its hot-pink coloration and ability to produce its own supply of hydrogen cyanide to discourage predators. The Laotian rock rat, once thought by scientists to have gone extinct 11 million years ago, actually is alive and well in this remote region.

The river's exceptional biodiversity applies to its human population as well. Qinghai Province is an ethnic melting pot where Tibetan, Han Chinese, Mongols and Turkic peoples like the modern Uigers have mixed and struggled for centuries. It was a battleground for much of China's Tang Dynasty as various Tibetan kingdoms challenged Chinese control until becoming part of China proper in the early 20th century. The river flows through southwest China's Yunnan province where Mongol warriors overcame the kingdom of Dali in the 13th century and settled among the dozens of tribal peoples who still compose more than a third of the province's population.

Leaving China, the Mekong serves as the east-west border between the mountains of Myanmar and Laos until it joins the two with Thailand at the Golden Triangle. All through that portion of its journey, the river drains an area whose abrupt, vertical terrain has created a multiplicity of tribal groupings, each with its own language and customs, defined as much by the elevation of their settlements as by location. Separated by steep hills and narrow valleys, these peoples have traditionally been isolated from each other and from the outside world.

In the complex weave of the world's mythology, the mountains where the river originates are said to be the domain of Hsi Wang Mu, the 'Spirit Mother of the West', who some link to the Queen of Sheba. In that multi-layered tale, the queen left her throne to her son Solomon and fled east where she attained enlightenment as the 'Queen of the West' and influenced the development of Taoism in China. The Queen of Sheba is a powerful occult figure in legend, celebrated as much for her power as a woman as for the few details history offers of her actual life. She appears as Bilquis in the Qu'ran, as Makeda in Coptic Ethiopia, and under various other names further south in Africa.

High on the Tibetan plateau, hidden in the deep folds of the Kunlun range where the Spirit Queen of the West holds court, the Mekong begins its twisted journey to the sea veiled in mystery and wrapped in the power of the female spirit.

****

Brother Love glassed the far side of the river through a slit in the awning of the first of two riverboats carrying him and his crew slowly past the barren site of Ban Khwan. The vessels chugged steadily upstream hugging the Burmese shore, disappearing for all but the most watchful eyes into the sporadic traffic of the river and its lazy rhythms. "They are moving. Slow down, you fool!" The engines slowed by half as Brother Love drew the folds of the awning close together again. "Now we simply watch and follow."

Phi Rak looked forward. "Somchai!" he hissed to a block of a man standing in the bow, his boxer's face a network of scar tissue. "Signal Meng Ti to speed up a bit and pass them, staying on this side. We'll take turns passing and falling back. Remember, we are working vessels. An occasional stop is not out of the ordinary and should arouse no suspicion."

The boxer spoke briefly into a walkie-talkie. In the lead boat, the dandy, Meng Ti, listened and ordered his boatman to speed their progress to try to keep pace with or move past the *hang yaw* on the far side of the water. He held the walkie-talkie to his thin lips. In the second boat, the boxer nodded and handed his device to Phi Rak.

"What?" Phi Rak's greeting was a short, irritated bark. He listened, then waved his hand in annoyance. "Of course, if they speed up, they will lose us for a time. But *that* is why, my stupid Meng Ti," Phi Rak enunciated each syllable as if speaking to a child, "that we went to the trouble of procuring the two *hang yaw* we are towing behind us. Perhaps you've noticed the one following you?" Phi Rak sighed dramatically. "Just do what I tell you to do and we'll be fine. Don't think for yourself... it isn't pretty." He extended the walkie-talkie toward his minion without an acknowledging glance.

Phi Rak turned with a forced smile toward Hemple who sat behind him fingering the awning aside for a view of Kohein and his companions. Phi Rak slapped the awning from Hemple's hands. "Are you a complete idiot? The idea here is to avoid being noticed." His words cut with the same dismissive tone Phi Rak had used with Meng Ti.

"I... I'm sorry. You were doing the same thing, so I thought it was safe." Hemple was startled and taken aback.

"There *you* go! Thinking!" Phi Rak tilted his head to the side as if studying some curious specimen. "Not a good idea for you, Paul." Phi Rak turned to shout at the others in the boat. "Not a good idea for any of you, do you understand me!"

He swiveled again to address Hemple. "You see, Paul. You are not here to think. Actually, there is precious little reason for you to be here at all, truth be told. You already have served your purpose. You have most generously helped us locate your erstwhile friends. So you have very little if anything to offer now. Certainly not your amusing little 'thoughts' ".

Hemple started back as if struck. He struggled to make sense of Phi Rak's statement. "I don't understand. You asked for my help in returning the journal and stopping Kohein." Hemple's posture began to stiffen. He shook his head back and forth, frowning in recognition. "Lies? Did you tell me nothing but lies? How dare you!"

He felt the slap almost before he saw it. Brother Love's hand struck Hemple's face fast and hard. Hemple's head jerked to the side. Before he could say another word, a second slap followed the first. Then another and another. Phi Rak's voice was mildly surprised, reasonable, eerily disconnected from the violence of the blows. "I don't recall asking for your opinion, Paul. Do you see what happens to mouths that fall open but have nothing interesting to say?" The pale face relaxed into a mask of calm civility. "So, unless you have something further to add...?"

Hemple wiped his mouth with the heel of a widespread hand, trying to hide the hot tears welling from his eyes. "Well, I'm glad we could have this little talk, Paul." Phi Rak offered an immaculate white handkerchief, solicitous now. "I appreciate your understanding."

Phi Rak sat back in his seat with a thoughtful smile and an expression of patient command. He called out to the boatmen. "Now that's a very nice pace. Let's stay with it, shall we? Thank you all so much... so very much."

✸✸✸✸✸✸✸

The late afternoon sun spread antique gold across the dark surface of the river. The *hang yaw* kept to the middle of the stream and moved at moderate speed to avoid standing out to anyone watching from either shore. The water was flat and smooth. Steep hills climbed from high banks on either side, their deep green contours interrupted occasionally by bare limestone cliffs. Wood and bamboo structures dotted both sides of the river. Fishermen poled *sampan* up and down the shores. On the Lao side, a group of laughing children splashed in the water as if war had never visited their land or touched their lives. Five passengers sat in file along the length of the boat, heads shrouded in *pha khawma* to hide their distinctive appearance. At the rear, Hajee steered, the driver's end of the long propeller shaft tucked comfortably under his right arm.

Kohein turned from the bow. "It would appear that we have successfully evaded detection. Congratulations, gentlemen."

"Yeah, except for those two riverboats that keep passing and stopping. Have you noticed that they don't really do anything when they pull in? Nothing loaded or unloaded. The same two guys get out and act busy while we pass them. What do you make of that?" Reggie's reply was part question and part challenge.

Kohein addressed Hajee at the rear. "*Hajee hen mee arai plaek kap rua, song laem nan mai?*" Hajee nodded a short answer. "Hajee has noticed something odd as well."

"Maybe we should speed up... leave them behind? I'd guess we can outrun them, if we need to."

Kohein spoke more urgently to Hajee. *"Pai rewrew na! Nii dee kwaa."* Speed up. Let's lose them.

The engine roared to life. The bow rose sharply as the boat leapt forward. The passengers grabbed the gunwales to keep balance. Behind them, the river-boats shrank, then disappeared behind a large sandbar. Hajee kept the pace for another twenty minutes before slowing again. Kohein and Reggie both nodded to show their approval.

"Perhaps we should pull in now until dark?" Kohein suggested.

Reggie's reply was quick. "Yep. At least as long as it takes to check them out if they chase us. Let's find a spot where we can cover the boat and watch. Then we can decide whether to wait till dark or move on."

Hajee maneuvered the longtail to the right shore. Before long he pulled into the mouth of a small creek thick with overhanging branches. The warm light of the late afternoon sun disappeared into shadow. The air was heavy with the smell of vegetation and decay. Swarms of insects swirled in and out of the rare beams of sunlight that penetrated the dense growth.

"Be careful in here. Lots of snakes. They like trees and water, both. Look above and below you before you grab anything or take a step." Reggie used an overhead branch to pull the boat up onto the steep bank before jumping off to clear a path through the thicket away from the creek. Carpenter helped Kumar work his way up the bank. Kohein followed close behind. Hajee and Brother Joe brought up the rear after pushing the boat further into the dense bush. The group stopped at a relatively open area ten feet from the river where it was visible through a screen of vines and bamboo. They waited.

The sound reached them first. The whine of big engines rose from the distance followed soon after by the sight of two *hang yaw* racing full bore upriver within fifty yards of each shore. Three men sat in the far craft, one at the rud-der-prop, the other two scouring both sides of the river with binoculars. Paul Hemple sat in the middle of the second boat, nearest the watchers on the Lao side, beard mashed against his face by the wind and flanked by two more of Phi Rak's men.

"Everybody down... now!" Reggie hissed. Each man dropped to the ground without a word. "Stay still. They're going too fast to see much except move-ment." Reggie quickly drew a pair of camouflaged binoculars from his pack. After a quick look through the thick foliage, he handed the glasses to Car-penter. Once the two boats had passed, he asked, "What did you see?"

Carpenter lowered the binoculars. "Looks like Paul has found new friends.

And the driver is one of the guys from the train. Did you recognize him, Amit?"

Kohcin nodded. "Yes, I don't need binoculars to recognize that scarred face. It belongs to Somchai Nuonerng. Formerly a kickboxing champion. Now employed in the service of Brother Love. I believe you have met him on two previous occasions."

"Well, I guess that eliminates any doubt about whether they're following us or not. Too bad."

"Yes, 'too bad' indeed." Kohein's voice was tight with disappointment. He turned to Reggie. "Our next step?"

Reggie thought for a moment before answering. "They'll be back once they figure they passed us. We need to make sure our boat is completely out of sight before we do anything else."

"Me and Hajee can take care of that. We've already made a start." Brother Joe spoke briefly to Hajee and the two moved off to the creek. The sound of branches being broken and cast across the boat could be heard for several minutes as Reggie continued.

"The light is fading. It'll be almost dark by the time they come back. They'll move slow, close to the banks." Reggie pursed his lips and sniffed absently as if working out a simple math problem. "If we lay low, they may miss us in the dark. Down between these mountains like this, it gets *real* dark, real fast. If we pull away from the river and don't use any light, it will be next to impossible for them to see us, no matter what they do."

"It will be equally impossible for us to see anything, will it not?" Kohein's anxiety showed.

"Yes, except for this." Reggie produced a dark green pen light from a hip pocket. "It has a very narrow beam and we should be able to conceal it from anyone on the river if we only use it in quick bursts."

"So, do we just wait till morning and run then, or try to slip out of here in the dark?" Carpenter couldn't see an advantage either way.

"Well, there *is* another option besides waiting and running."

"And what would that be?" Kohein canted his head to the side, confused.

"We could take the fight to them."

Carpenter frowned. "How do we do that… without getting killed?"

"Well, first of all, *we* don't all do it. That *would* get us killed for sure. I was thinking more along the lines of a commando attack. Just me. Nobody else."

"No way!" Carpenter was on his feet.

"Quiet, A-Man! Let's keep this down to a roar, OK? We don't know how far away they are or how much sound may carry along the water."

Carpenter crouched and proceeded in a hushed tone. "Listen, you just got here. Just back from the dead. I'd like to keep it that way."

"I appreciate that, little brother. I really do. But the fact is that I'm the only one here that's trained to do this kind of thing. And I'm good at it." Reggie nodded to himself and looked around to the others. "Very good."

"Granted, with one exception." Kohein interjected. "Hajee is a quiet man. But he is an excellent jungle fighter. Do not underestimate him. He will want to be involved, but will wait for instructions rather than pushing his way in."

"OK, maybe we can use him too," Reggie agreed.

Carpenter rose and started to speak again. Kohein tried to calm him with a restraining hand. Turning to Reggie, he asked, "What do you have in mind specifically?" Then back to Carpenter, "Perhaps we could simply hear Reggie's plan before we reject it? In the end, we will have to agree to do something."

Carpenter swallowed a reply and held his tongue.

"Here's the deal. *They* are chasing *us*. They are the aggressors. They have numbers and resources. That means they won't be watching for a counter." Reggie leaned forward and dropped his voice further as if to conceal the scheme. "Look at the sky." He gestured toward the river where the water had gone from gold to brown as the sun dipped behind high ridges to the west. "By the time they come back downriver, it'll be well past sunset. Like I said, they'll come slowly, close to the bank on either side of the river. They'll be looking for a light where there isn't any settlement. They'll hug the shore and use a spot of some kind if they have one. *They* will be after *us*." The corners of Reggie's lips ticked up in a slight smile. "They wont expect *us* to be after *them*."

"So?" Carpenter challenged, "They'll be right, won't they?"

"Not if we're waiting to take their boat."

Faces were blank around him.

"Look, the little creek where we pulled in is a perfect place to wait in the water. We'll hear them coming – you can't disguise the sound of a boat engine."

"Then what?" Carpenter's concern still showed, but so did a spark of interest.

"Simple, A-Man. Ambush. I take their boat. They go for a swim... or feed the fish."

Silence for a beat, then Kohein spoke up. "So, if this scheme proves effective, we will have a second boat. What then?"

"Sabotage their equipment." Reggie looked around the group. Noting the puzzled expressions, he explained. "Listen. My guess is that Phi Rak's riverboats are already tied up somewhere downstream – probably about where they lost us. He knows we're somewhere above that point and won't be foolish enough to try to sneak back down. He and most of his people will probably camp on the bank and make a fire to keep the critters and the bugs away. I'm guessing their boats will be exposed, vulnerable and not hard to find. Are you following me so far?"

Kohein and Carpenter nodded their understanding. Kumar simply waited patiently.

"I'll use the *hang yaw* I 'borrow' to make it downstream. I'll wait long enough to give their second boat time to get back and tie up. It will be full dark by then. There's not much moon, if you've noticed. I'll drift in and get close without being heard or seen. Believe me, I've done this kind of thing in hairier situations than this. If there's no one on board the riverboats, I'll just cut the mooring lines and off they'll float down the river. Meanwhile, you take our own *hang yaw* and head upriver. Come dawn, you look for me. If you see me without a tail, you holler and we go on together. Phi Rak will still be trying to find his ride."

"Hold it. All that's fine if you can just creep in and send their boats floating away. What if there's someone on board or they notice what's going on?" Carpenter put in.

"I brought a few toys with me that could come in handy."

"Toys?" Kohein wrinkled his brow.

"Two grenades... which gives us one per riverboat. We disable one, we've diminished the threat. We get both, and that takes care of the pursuit altogether."

The group was quiet for several beats, then Kumar spoke up. "So there are at least two levels of risk involved. There is the risk to you, Reggie, which clearly is our greatest concern. Then there is the risk to them. Your plan calls for violence. I understand that and while I could not undertake it myself, I can accept that it may prove unavoidable to assure your own safety, much less ours." He looked at the others then spoke as if to remind them. "We know that Paul is with them. While he is not a pleasant man, we do not know that he is there of his own accord. Is it right to risk harming him along with those who in fact may be his captors rather than his cohorts?"

Brother Joe emerged from the bushes near the creek. "That's a risk I'd be willing to take... that is, if I hadn't made the mistake of joining up with Gandhi here." He gestured toward Kumar. "There's this 'Thou shalt not kill' thing. He takes it seriously... so I guess I do too, when my better self is in charge."

"Phi Rak would not hesitate to kill us all if it served his purposes." Kohein broke in. "But Kumar, regrettably, has a point. Suppose Paul is a captive. Do we simply leave him?"

"Like I said, that possibility warms my heart... until I really think about it." Brother Joe squatted and slapped at a mosquito on his neck. "And if the alternative is to wait here all night in the dark, I know what I'd vote for."

Carpenter hesitated. After a moment, he nodded. "Let's get their boat."

Kohein was thoughtful. "I am in favor of Reggie's plan as well, with a reservation that comes as something of a surprise to me as a rather devout coward."

He took a breath as if to steel himself. "You see, I must admit that I have been consumed with the possibility of considerable treasure... enough to change my life significantly. Up to now, I have convinced myself that my interest is more than simply material and that our purpose is just. But my actions have endangered you all. I have not truly put anyone's welfare before my own desire." Kohein wrestled with himself to continue. "And I must admit to a very powerful desire to find and possess." He pushed on. "So, if it is possible to simply abandon this dangerous enterprise, I can commit this...." Kohein withdrew the journal from his satchel, "...to the river and put an end to it all right now."

An embarrassed silence followed until Kumar's quiet voice broke in. "Oh, to be able to undo all our past mistakes with one sweeping gesture! But of course we cannot. We can only let experience teach us." Kumar grasped Kohein's hand with both of his own and slowly moved the journal back to its place in Kohein's bag. "I believe the die have been cast, my friend. Turning back is no longer a realistic option, no matter what we may face. There seems to be no alternative but to continue."

Kumar turned to the others. "I would ask only that we proceed not according to what Brother Love and his followers might do to us if they have the opportunity, but what we choose to do ourselves regardless of what their motives or actions may be."

"That sounds like a 'Do unto others' thing', right?" Brother Joe offered.

Kumar's smile blossomed white against his dark countenance. "Ah, but you do have such an economical way with words, Brother." He turned back to Kohein. "So, to be succinct, I vote 'Yes' for Reggie's plan as well."

Reggie stood and brushed off his knees. "OK. Hajee and I are gonna think this through. Meanwhile, let's move away from the river where we can't be heard or seen. And keep your voices way down from here on out. We may not want to hurt them, but you better believe they won't be playing by those rules if they find us."

TWENTY-SIX

THE TWO *HANG YAW* RODE THE CURRENT BESIDE PHI RAK'S RIVERBOAT. In the first, Meng Ti and two others stood ready to follow Kohein's escaping *hang yaw*. In the other, the scar-faced boxer and a mate looked up awaiting orders as Phi Rak faced Hemple on the larger vessel. "I wonder if your friends have any concern for your welfare, Paul? Would they rescue you if they had the opportunity? Don't you wonder? Wouldn't you like to know? I certainly would." Phi Rak's voice held an equal measure of feigned compassion and real contempt.

"They are no friends of mine," Hemple struggled for a brave show of dignity. "No more than you have proven to be." He looked down and lowered his voice to a near whisper at these final words, aware they could bring retaliation.

"Poor, poor Paul. Betrayed and abandoned by all."

"By all but my Lord," Hemple muttered softly, almost to himself.

"Yes, well, there surely will be ample opportunity for you to experience true martyrdom in the next few days. I shall see to it myself... as a personal favor to you." Phi Rak lifted his chin in a show of mock nobility. "My own small attempt to make up for whatever disappointment our relationship may have caused." His voice took on a harder edge. "Meanwhile, you will take a ride upriver with Somchai." Phi Rak nodded toward the boxer in the boat below. "Your friends surely are hidden somewhere there. When they see you with us, perhaps they will worry about you."

He paused, with a doubtful shake of his head. "But perhaps not. Either way, your presence may prove confusing and make it easier to apprehend them." An amused smiled followed. "They must be quite lonely by now... with night approaching and only the mosquitoes to keep them company."

****

The forest was alive with sound. The chirp and croak of frogs and lizards. The telltale 'tookae-tookae' for which the foot-long *tookae* lizard is named. Twilight brought an increase in bird song and the click, buzz, drone of thousands of insects. And swarms of mosquitoes.

"Great!" Brother Joe slapped at the back of his neck and the top of his head. "The one thing a bald head is good for is to feed mosquitoes!"

Reggie was kneeling nearby with Hajee, spreading various contents of his pack on the ground between them. He reached down and produced a small bottle. "Here, try this. It works." He tossed the insect repellent to Brother Joe who used it and passed it on to the others. "Go slow," Reggie warned, "we need to make that stuff last."

Kumar pulled a green mosquito coil from his own pack. "I don't suppose we can risk using this? The smoke is relatively effective at close range. I have a number of them. A fire, of course, would be better."

Reggie considered the prospect. "Maybe you can light some coils later after we get the boat and I'm gone. Forget about the fire. Even if I can get down the river, we don't know who's gonna come back up. And in case it isn't me, there's a few items I'm gonna leave here with you." Reggie pulled a short, ugly weapon from his duffel. "This is a CAR-15 Colt Commando submachine gun. It's light, powerful and fast. It's also reasonably accurate if you know what you're doing... which you don't, except for Hajee. I'm gonna leave it with him. If we keep faith with Kumar, we'll have a couple of prisoners to guard instead of a couple of bodies to donate to the river." Reggie shrugged his concern. "I'm willing to try the peace thing, but it complicates the whole deal... and makes it more dangerous for all of us. If push comes to shove, I'm shoving. You understand?"

Kumar offered a silent nod of acceptance.

Reggie paused to acknowledge the gesture and went on. "Me and Hajee have a plan. When the time comes, the rest of you please get way back and lie low. Don't interfere. We need to focus on what we're doing, not on protecting anyone else. Got it?"

****

Hemple's back hurt. He had been sitting for at least two hours on the hard board seat of the *hang yaw*. He had barely moved the whole time. He couldn't swim... not well enough to fight a river current. And he knew what could be in the water. King Cobras were strong swimmers. So were foot-long stinging centipedes. And there were fish big enough to swallow a man. Hemple had no desire to repeat the Jonah experiment, though he assured himself that his faith would be equal to the test should it come to that. They had seen nothing on the trip up the river. Hemple hadn't really looked. The leader, the one with the battered face, threw Hemple an occasional disgusted glance whenever he pulled the binoculars away from the mass of scar tissue surrounding his eyes.

They raced upstream for more than an hour. Kohein and the others had a head-start. But even then they should not have outdistanced Phi Rak's men by this much. Meng Ti, the oily one from the mumbly-peg encounter, was in charge of the other boat. He came alongside for several minutes and discussed options with Somchai, the boxer. They waited for a time as Meng Ti tried to raise Phi Rak on the walkie-talkie. Apparently it didn't work in this narrow space between high hills.

They separated again. Meng Ti took the Burmese side. Hemple's boat hugged the Lao shore. They started very slowly downstream, stopping to check out each small tributary along the way. Kohein and his crew were bound to be holed up in one of them. Hemple said a silent prayer asking for deliverance, but not specifying from whom or how.

****

Darkness fell abruptly after a brief but spectacular sunset over the high green hills across the river to the west. The sky lit turquoise and pink with fingers of red and gold stretching from one narrow horizon to the other before disappearing into a single enclosing blackness. The volume of forest chatter increased. A lower pitched drone rose up from beneath the swell of night sound.

Carpenter noticed it first. "Is that an engine?" Talk stopped.

"Yeah," Reggie whispered. "The *hang yaws* are on their way back. One is probably on the other side of the river. Pull way back and lie flat. Don't look toward the water. Open eyes are like magnets."

They moved back through the undergrowth to a spot just behind a small hillock. Reggie and Hajee spread branches over the prostrate forms of the others, then moved off toward the river. The wet gurgle of a *hang yaw* engine at low idle grew as the boat approached.

Brother Joe slapped his thick hand hard against the top of this head. He whispered, "Sorry. I might survive this if the bugs don't suck my brains out first."

Kumar's face was hidden by the night, but clearly held an amused grin. "Not to worry, my friend. Consider how well you've done without them up to now."

****

Yet another small creek, thick with overhanging vegetation and the likelihood of serpents. No wonder the devil appeared as a snake to Eve. The air had grown so dark and close that Hemple could hardly breathe. Somchai peered into the blackness and called to his driver to pull in even closer to the shore. The bow nudged through the branches at the creek mouth.

The boxer swept a bright flashlight beam in and around the narrow channel. Nothing moved. The *hang yaw* turned its nose upriver against the current and low-throttled to hold steady as the boxer stood to seek signs of movement in the forest.

****

Reggie stripped down to nothing but a *pha khawma*. Hajee lay flat in the shadows near the bank behind a thick growth of bamboo, the matte-black of the CAR-15 hiding its surface in the night. He steadied the retractable butt against his shoulder with the muzzle pointed into the dark toward the water and the approaching longtail.

Reggie unsheathed his combat knife and cut a handful of branches from the trees overhead. He placed the blade's thin length of black steel carefully between his teeth. Holding the branches in one hand, he slid silently down the creek bank into the water. The *hang yaw* was no more than 50 yards away.

Reggie sank to his knees in the mud. Foul-smelling gas bubbles rose invisibly to the surface. He held still and listened for the steady chug of the *hang yaw* engine. Using vines that drooped to the surface from above, he pulled himself toward the mouth of the creek. He clutched the overhanging vegetation together with the branches he had cut to form a dark cocoon over his head where he stood in the water. Concealed, he waited for the *hang yaw* to get close.

The boat swung its nose back upriver at the creek and moved into the clump of vines and branches at its mouth. A light swung into the foliage illuminating white swathes of darkness and further obscuring the unlit shadows to either side. Reggie ducked under the surface as the light swept over and past. With a few strong strokes, he was past the boat's bow feeling his way along the flank furthest from the shore. Still submerged, he snuck both hands up and over the gunwale and pulled down with all his considerable might and heft - once from below water and again as he rose from it and leaped aboard in a single fluid motion.

The boat dipped heavily and swung away from the shore as the driver struggled to regain control. Hemple screamed and held tight to his seat. The boxer grabbed wildly for a branch, lost his footing and plunged sideways into the river. His flashlight clanged hollowly against the bottom of the boat as his body struck the water. The boatman reached for a gun near his feet while working to keep the *hang yaw* afloat. A slim black blade tore through the fleshy space between his thumb and forefinger and imbedded itself in the bottom of the boat. Reggie danced to the rear like an acrobat, kicked the knife free from the driver's pinned hand and delivered a single blow to his head that swept him from his perch and into the water.

Hemple keened and rocked in place as if unaware of what was happening around him. Hajee appeared on the bank, a flashlight in one hand and the Colt in the other. The light caught the driver then the boxer as they instinctively grabbed for the side of the boat. Reggie scooped up the flashlight and gun from the floor of the *hang yaw* and trained both on the figures in the water below him. He motioned the two men to the shore with the weapon and stood balanced in the *hang yaw* as they pawed their way up the slick bank to kneel before Hajee.

"*Gniep loei!*" Hajee's harsh whisper cut through the insect buzz. "*Yaa phood, yaa den, na*". Quiet! Don't speak. Don't move. Hajee kept the ugly snout of the Commando pointed at the two captives.

"Wait there." Reggie grabbed the prop-rudder and headed the boat into the creek mouth. Hemple sat rigidly in place as Reggie pulled the boat up onto the bank. He directed the light at Hemple's back. "No more squealing, Paul. It's over. Climb up there where I can see you. You'll excuse me if I don't trust you with the boat."

TWENTY-SEVEN

THE BOXER AND THE BOAT DRIVER SAT SHIVERING AND BOUND TOGETHER AGAINST A TREE TRUNK THIRTY YARDS FROM THE RIVER, illuminated by a thin beam from Reggie's light. Green vines were wrapped awkwardly around their torsos and knotted their hands loosely together in their laps. Tall shadows climbed into the trees behind them and perched like buzzards waiting for carrion.

Reggie, dry and clothed, sat on a log facing the prisoners, the confiscated pistol pointed toward their feet. Hajee sat at his side, CAR-15 across his knees. Paul Hemple sat somewhat apart from the captives, left hand alternately twisting strands of beard and fingering a jade prayer bead at his neck. The remainder of the band sat in a rough semi-circle facing Phi Rak's men, backs to the water to help conceal the needle of light.

Kohein broke the silence. "So far, so good as I believe you are fond of saying. Your plan has worked out quite well, Reggie, despite our various misgivings." He looked around at his companions. "Wouldn't you agree?"

A small chorus of assent rose in response.

"I assume that we proceed with the next stage of Reggie's scheme. An old question remains, however. What do we do with Paul? Is he prisoner, ally, or neither?"

Hemple stiffened and began to speak. Reggie held up a hand. "Shut up for now, Paul. You made enough noise on the river already. We're lucky you didn't call the other boat over." He glanced around at his comrades. "If it was up to me, I'd shoot all three of them and move on."

Hemple half-rose and Reggie jerked the pistol toward his head. "Yes?" Hemple sat back down.

"Clearly, Paul has put himself in this position and endangered us all in the process. Perhaps we should hear from him nonetheless before we decide how to deal with him?" Kumar's question, devoid of challenge, seemed for that very reason to carry more weight.

"OK. I hear that. What have you got to say for yourself, Paul? All we know is that the last time we saw you, you were stealing a car and headed Phi Rak's way. I'm sure you can explain that, right?" Reggie's voice held no menace beyond that posed by his sheer physical presence.

Hemple hesitated as if unsure of permission to speak. "All right," he admitted. "I did borrow the Rover, but I did not steal it. I intended to leave it in Sop Ruak once I found a way to get back to Vientiane."

"So what happened?" Brother Joe growled the question. "How did you end up with these two," he gestured toward Phi Rak's men, "and out on the river looking for us?"

Hemple hung his head and mumbled a reply.

"Speak up, dammit... sorry." Brother Joe looked at Kumar sheepishly.

Hemple raised his head again as if Brother Joe's slip had restored a measure of self-confidence. "I didn't think Phi Rak would be interested in me alone... just Kohein and possible you others. He saw me when I arrived in Sop Ruak despite my efforts to go unnoticed. He forced me to join him. Against my will. He forced me into the boat with these men. I had no choice." Hemple swallowed hard to summon courage. "I apologize for taking the Rover. I admit I didn't see Phi Rak as a real danger. I wasn't thinking clearly, but I have been punished. My judgment may have been poor, but I have nothing to do with Phi Rak. He is a liar... a twisted, evil man." Hemple flushed and stopped abruptly. He held a hand to his mouth as if to prevent more words from issuing forth.

"I don't think Paul represents any threat to us... at least not intentionally. I mostly believe him. We shouldn't treat him like a prisoner, just an accidental danger to himself and others." Carpenter pushed to move the discussion on. "Let's get clear on what we need to do next and start doing it."

"Amen, A-Man." Reggie looked to the others. "Are we good with letting Paul live like a normal person, since we're stuck with him anyway?" Silence served as consent and Reggie continued. "OK, we have two boats now. Phi Rak still has the advantage in terms of men and supplies and boats. But like I said, if we can eliminate the boats, we eliminate the pursuit."

Reggie paused to calculate. "Since we have these two here to watch, we need to make sure we outnumber them. That means it makes most sense for Hajee to stay here and help keep guard. I'll take the extra longtail and head down-river and see what I can do about Phi Rak's transportation." Reggie seemed to expect an argument. He turned to Carpenter. "It'll be safer than what we just did. I'll do it right before dawn when it's still dark and most of them are asleep."

Kohein started to hold back a protest, then went ahead. "You are clearly the most qualified of us for this business. But, again, I am responsible for this danger. If the plan is as straightforward as you indicate, perhaps I ..."

Reggie cut him off. "Listen. You're right; it won't be complicated... for me. But it's not the kind of thing you try without some experience, alright?"

Kohein bit off a reaction, then stopped and looked away.

"OK, so that's settled," Carpenter interjected. "But what about the other *hang yaw*? After it gets back, they'll be expecting that one too." He nodded toward the creek and the boat it concealed. "When it doesn't show, won't they be just a little curious?"

Reggie nodded. "Sure, but I doubt they'll expect we've captured it. They'll wonder what happened, but they'll be thinking of other possibilities. Anyway, they'll only have two real choices. Either they go back out in the dark to look for their guys, or they wait till morning. I'm betting they'll wait till morning. If they don't, I'll hear them before they see me. I'll just let them pass and do my thing. Like I said, it will be a lot easier than taking the *hang yaw* was. And that worked out alright, didn't it?"

"OK. You've been right so far. I don't doubt you can pull this off too."

"Good. Thanks for the vote of confidence... and for the worry." Reggie looked around the group. "We should try to get some sleep. Hajee can watch our friends here. The Commando is loaded. It shoots fast and there's forty rounds in the mag. I think they understand the risk of trying to escape." He turned to Kumar. "You still have those mosquito coils?"

"Yes, of course. And we definitely could use them. Brother Joe has very little blood left at this point," Kumar said with a straight face.

"If we fire up a bunch of them, we'll be able to save on batteries. We only have two flashlights and I'll need one with me."

Kumar rummaged in his bag and began lighting coils. Heavy pungent smoke rose from the red glow at the end of each. Reggie dropped the captured flash in his pack and held his hand over the lit end of his own as eyes adjusted to the darkness. After a few minutes, he switched the light off altogether. "I don't know about you, but I'm getting some shut-eye. Joe, why don't you stay up for a while with Hajee just to be safe. Here..." he handed the pistol over. "Wake me if there's a problem. I sleep good, but I sleep pretty light."

Carpenter lay on his back watching pieces of sky through the tangle of branches overhead. He glanced at Hemple a few feet away. Their eyes met briefly. Hemple's darted away. Carpenter turned again to the night, lids growing heavy. A random fragment of Shakespeare drifted through his mind. To sleep, perchance to dream. If only sleep could be purchased without the cost of dreams.

TWENTY-EIGHT

FROM SOME DISTANCE, THE ECHO OF HARSH VOICES REBOUNDED FROM HOL-LOW STONE. Blurred images swirled in the darkness behind closed lids then resolved into angry faces.

The Malka and the young Aaron faced each other. The Queen and her son, the Priest. No longer simply names for individuals, but formal titles for leaders of the People.

The tribe's survival was again at stake. But at what price, the Malka asked. "Shall we sell our souls to survive and in doing so become truly lost? Better to leave this comfortable place and risk losing our way on the earth rather than in our own hearts."

The young Aaron's voice thundered. He would hear none of leaving. The People had wandered long enough. They had carved a paradise here in the heart of the Changshan mountains. "To leave now would be to sacrifice all. We can play one side against the other. Or, even better, ally with both sides and avoid association with the loser. No one knows these steep paths like we do. Kublai Khan will pay dearly for the knowledge. If he wins, then we gain a place at an emperor's side. If he loses, we vow everlasting loyalty to the invincible Kingdom of Dali."

"And betray those who offered us refuge when we had no home? No, I cannot follow your lead in this, my son."

"Old woman! You would sacrifice us all for nothing. Barbarians rule this world. Let them butcher each other and leave the feast to us!"

The cave walls echoed with the cheers of many men.

"It is a poisoned feast you invite us to, my son. No good can come from deceit or denial. We are who we are because we have learned and grown. Not because *we tried to hide from change. Yes, we know these mountains and their many paths. We can leave in safety without compromise."*

A chorus of approval rose from the women surrounding the speakers.

The Aaron's pale advisor stepped out from behind the priest. "Witch! You lay claim to righteousness, but you lust only for power. Your son, the truly righteous one, leads us now. You counsel cowardice, the weakness of womankind. We are who we are, not who we may some day become!"

Another low murmur of male assent.

The Malka sighed, despairing, and tried another tack with the Aaron, ignoring his advisor. "And what of your father? How do you propose to betray his friends without betraying him as well? Do you believe the Khan will treat him gently because he has taken the same monk's robes as the Dali royals?"

The Aaron surveyed the gathering and spoke to them more than to her. "I do not see my father here, do you, old woman? Yet you would have us guess at how best to follow his wishes. And so you ask us to forego the one advantage we have in these hills rather than use it to strengthen ourselves."

"I ask you only to be true, not false."

"And I ask you to leave if you cannot support my decision! I am the Aaron. I shall decide!" The advisor tugged on the Aaron's sleeve and whispered. The Aaron nodded gravely and stood tall in his gilded robes, red beard thrust forward in defiance. He held his mother's eyes with his own then turned away, stiff with self-conscious dignity. "I have spoken. The choice is yours."

Most men followed to cluster around the Aaron. Most women remained.

The confrontation had been brewing for generations. Change or stasis. Certainty or risk. Belief or learning. Once argued patiently, the debate now was cast by the new Aaron as a matter of Right or Wrong, of Truth or Falsehood. And finally in a manner almost absurd... of Man or Woman.

The Malka spoke to the crowd surrounding her, tears pooling in tired eyes. "I will leave. Those who wish to come may join me. We will cross the river together. Find a new home. To those who wish to stay, I say 'shalom', peace be with you." She folded her hands before her face and bowed slightly to the gathering. She turned to go.

One man stood separate from the two groups, hand thrust into the folds of his shoulder bag. "Mother, please! A word!"

The Malka stopped. "Yes, my son?"

"Where shall I go? Do I stay with my brother or follow you?" He gestured toward the Aaron standing nearby with his followers. "I cannot abandon my father, even if he has left us."

"I understand, my son. The two of you are tied together in ways beyond blood. He responds to you as to no others. Now you may save yourself or wait for him without promise of deliverance... without any certainty that he will return at all. A difficult choice, but one you are capable of making on your own. One that you must make." She sighed heavily. "I will go tomorrow, west and south across the Meigong Le. Away from here. I have dreamed a vision of another place, not so different from this one. A place in the hills where we can seek and thrive on our own terms. You are welcome to join me, but not obligated. I will love you no matter."

He reached into his satchel to produce a scrap of parchment. "Then take this. It will be safer with you. One day it may reveal something beyond a blot and a smudge."

The Malka folded the scrap away in her robes without another word, but her hand emerged bearing a single gleaming jewel. "And this I would leave for your father who gave it to me these long years past. It is partner to the parchment. I fear I shall not see him again in this life." She offered him the jewel.

He considered her extended hand, but refused. "Better that you give it to him yourself, mother, should he see fit to find you. It is he that has forsaken you ... and us," he added bitterly. "Sacrificed us for his new faith."

She held his gaze, her eyes moist with sadness and compassion. "He seeks, believing that a new faith, a new practice, will bring a final answer to all questions. Visions of salvation have closed his eyes to the life he has." She paused then, as if considering whether to proceed. "You should know that he is like your brother in this. The Aaron clings to what is past, your father to what may yet be. Both are blinded by belief."

She embraced her son for a long moment. Turning to leave, she stopped and stood silently as if listening to an internal voice. Finally she looked back. "If you and your father do not come now, you will find me when you are in need of healing. Call to me then, my son, and I will bring you home."

He looked into her kind eyes, then to his brother standing apart. The Aaron turned to glare back at him with an expression of contempt, or jealousy... or both.

TWENTY-NINE

CARPENTER OPENED HIS EYES TO SEE HEMPLE LYING ON HIS SIDE A FEW FEET AWAY, just awake, and staring at him with an intensity that belied the moment. A thrill of recognition swept through both men. Carpenter pushed himself to his elbows. "Was that you?" He caught himself. "I mean, did you just have a dream... an angry dream?"

Hemple started as if struck, then turned quickly away, ignoring Carpenter's question. Anger, confusion, fear rippled across his bearded face like clouds in a fast moving storm.

Carpenter watched Hemple for a moment for some other response, then sank down again. Dreams invaded and re-ordered waking reality. Who was Paul, really? Who was he, Carpenter? And who was the woman... his mother? An ache crept into his chest. A mixed sense of warmth and sadness lingered there like an echo in a hollow cave. Images hovered with the sound of her parting words, "... when you are in need of healing. Call to me then, my son, and I will bring you home."

The harsh cough of a motor broke into his reverie. A few yards away, Reggie sat up abruptly and shouted, "What's that?"

Brother Joe stood and rubbed an eye with a fist, pistol still trained on the two captives sitting against the tree. "I don't know. Sounded like an engine starting." Hajee was on his feet and running toward the river.

Reggie stood now, completely awake. He looked around the rough circle of men. "Where's Amit?"

"Um, he stepped away to take a ... you know, to use the facilities," Brother Joe stammered.

Reggie stared into the blackness. "When was that?"

"A few minutes ago, I guess."

Reggie scooped up his flashlight and headed into the dark following Hajee. The two returned within minutes. "One of the longtails is gone. So is Amit."

"Impossible! He wouldn't just run off." The dream state fled Carpenter's mind.

Reggie trained his light on the ground around them and then on his own pack. "No, but he might decide to be a hero. You heard what he said about this whole mess being his fault." He held his pack out as if to offer evidence. "The flashlight and the grenades are gone."

Hajee clearly understood. Alarm spread across his face. "*Gae pen khon mai khid maak. Tadsin rewrew… te tadsin mai khoi chalad. Pai yiam Phi Rak taen raw.*" He isn't one to think too much. He makes hasty decisions… bad ones. He's gone to visit Phi Rak in our place.

Carpenter rose and stumbled over something at his feet. Kohein's bag lay open next to him on the ground. He bent to retrieve it, knowing what he would find. The journal was balanced at the top of the bag, a clumsily scribbled scrap of paper on top. "Hold it! There's a note here. Shine the light on it."

Reggie stepped over and held the beam to the paper in Carpenter's hand. "What does it say?"

Carpenter squinted and read aloud. "My fight, my risk."

Reggie shook his head. "I made it sound too easy."

Hajee spoke rapidly and gestured toward the river.

"He's right. We gotta go get him before he gets himself killed or captured. And we need to leave right now." Reggie slid his knife in and out of its sheath.

"Hold it! You can't go alone. It's going to be a lot more dangerous now with Amit ahead of you. He may be trying to do the right thing, but he could rouse Phi Rak's whole camp." Carpenter grasped Reggie's arm.

Reggie patted Carpenter's hand once then pulled away. "Listen, Hajee's going no matter what. Just look at him. He'll swim if he has to." He spoke to Hajee, who handed Carpenter the Colt. "You'll need that. It's ready to fire… just point and pull." Carpenter started to protest. Reggie held up a hand. "If we leave now, little brother, we might be able to get to Amit before he reaches

Phi Rak. But we gotta move." He shouldered his pack. "We'll take the other boat. Guard these two and shoot them if they try anything. Might as well light a small fire so we can find you. We'll be back for you as soon as we can... hopefully without company."

Reggie motioned Hajee into the darkness toward the river and was gone.

****

The fire's sputter and glow created dancing ghosts of thick smoke in the humid air. Captives and captors were arrayed around it in various stages of wakefulness. Nearly a half hour had passed since Hajee and Reggie had left to catch up to Kohein. The prisoners slept leaning against the tree behind them. Carpenter sat cross legged on the ground opposite alternately watching them and trying to study the weapon in his lap. He had no experience with guns. Brother Joe sat on the ground to Carpenter's left, shaking his head every few minutes, struggling to stay awake. Kumar was on the near end of a log to Carpenter's right, black eyes alert, a sheen of sweat making his round face a mask of reflected red and gold. Hemple, still unable to look at Carpenter, perched as if in exile on the far end of the log, away from Kumar and nearer the sleeping boxer.

The boxer snorted in his sleep and shifted against the tree. Hemple slapped at a mosquito and expelled an irritated breath. "This is completely ridiculous. We'll be eaten alive before morning."

Brother Joe started momentarily and slowly dropped his head again toward his lap.

"May I use some of the insect repellent Reggie brought?" Hemple spoke to Carpenter without meeting his eyes.

"Sure. Just don't use it all up."

Reggie's pack lay near the fire across from Hemple, who rose to retrieve it. Kumar leaned quickly forward. "Not on their side of the fire, Paul! Careful..."

Too late, Hemple had stepped in front of the sleeping prisoners, taking the shortest route to his object. As he passed before them, the sound of distant explosions cracked through the buzz of insects and hiss of flame. Hemple froze. He looked first in the direction of the river, and then turned back toward the others. "Did you hear..." Before he could finish the sentence, Hemple went down hard, legs swept from beneath him. The boxer kicked Hemple's prone form into the fire with both legs and stood, pulling the last of the vines from his wrists and arms where he had worked them loose.

Hemple screamed and tried to rise, but cringed as his hands contacted red-hot embers. Kumar dove immediately into the fire, pulled Hemple free and wrapped his own body around him to smother the smoke spouting from Hemple's shirt. Carpenter jumped up and attempted to aim the Commando across the fire, but dropped the muzzle to avoid Kumar and Hemple. The boxer snatched at his cohort's bindings and leapt out of the firelight toward the river.

Brother Joe jerked awake, let off a shot after the fleeing pair and joined Carpenter to give chase. The boxer and his companion stood at the river's edge silhouetted dimly against the moving current. Carpenter pulled up abruptly, slipped in the wet mud of the bank and went down. The CAR-15 made a short splash as it hit the water. Without hesitating, the captives leapt for the river and disappeared. Brother Joe stood on the bank moving the mouth of his pistol back and forth across the black water, but seeing nothing.

"Are you OK?" Brother Joe asked Carpenter without looking over to him.

On his feet, Carpenter nodded shortly. "Not that it does us any good now."

They turned back to the fire. Hemple crouched nearby, shirt smoldering and a look of panic stretched tight on his face. On the ground next to him, Kumar lay curled on his side, unmoving, hands clutched to his chest. Tears streaked Hemple's face and he seemed to plead with Carpenter and Brother Joe as they bent over Kumar's limp body.

"He was just trying to save me... just trying to save me."

THIRTY

"WHAT HAPPENED?" Reggie stood, chest heaving as he looked down at Kumar's silent form on the ground near his feet.

"They got away. We heard a blast and one of them kicked Paul into the fire and then… well, it went downhill from there. Both Phi Rak's men ended up in the river and Kumar ended up like this." Carpenter gazed at Kumar's still figure and clenched his teeth. "He was trying to protect Paul."

Hemple's response was almost a shout. "It wasn't my fault. I was fetching some insect repellent and one of them tripped me. They weren't properly bound. *That* was the problem."

Reggie dismissed him. "Doesn't really matter. Kumar is in bad shape and we need to do something. We can't go downriver. Kohein has seen to that. There's no telling what happened down there. We turned back when we heard the explosions." He gestured to Hajee. "If it was up to him, he'd go after Amit himself. But we only have one boat and he understands that too. And we don't know what happened to Amit. He may be dead or taken. He could even be on his way back upriver. Doesn't matter. We can't hide here… this place is blown. We gotta move out and the only direction is upriver unless we want to hike."

"We can't carry Kumar far. It's got to be the river. But how do we know we can get help for him that way? We're in the middle of nowhere." Brother Joe knelt anxiously beside Kumar holding a wet cloth to his head.

"He needs healing." Carpenter spoke almost to himself. "I think we'll find it if we keep going."

"You talking about some kind of faith healing, A-Man? I don't have a lot of faith about our chances upriver."

"I had a dream last night. Another one like the ones we've all been having."

Carpenter glanced sharply at Hemple, who looked quickly away. "Look," he continued tentatively, as if questioning his own perception, "It ended with a woman saying that if I need healing, she would show the way. Something like that." He omitted the rest. "Well, we definitely need healing now." He searched the faces in the group, stopping at Reggie's. "You said Hajee and Amit dreamed the destination we're headed for and you have a sense of where to go once we get there. Kumar needs help... right away. We've got to follow the dream message and hope we aren't all crazy."

"We don't have a lot of other choices, do we." Reggie's response was a flat statement.

"Kumar is the only priority as far as I'm concerned. We can't do a thing for him here. I'm for trying whatever the kid says." Brother Joe nodded toward Carpenter.

"Hajee?" Reggie turned to the quiet man and explained the situation.

Hajee grimaced and swallowed. "OK," in reluctant English.

"If Amit has managed to stay alive and free, he'll know where we're going. He's had the dreams." Reggie pursed his lips and let out a breath. "So, I guess we're committed... whether we know what we're committed to or not."

****

Kohein cut the engine on the *hang yaw*. His only plan was a simple one... to follow Reggie's. He crouched and glided silently up to the two riverboats without arousing any response from the single drowsy guard. The bulk of Phi Rak's crew was indeed ashore, leaving a lone sentry aboard just one of the riverboats as Reggie had predicted.

The two larger craft were tethered together. The first was anchored to the shore. The second drifted at the end of a thick rope downstream from the first with Phi Rak's one remaining longtail tied to it. Kohein held on to the line joining the two larger boats and sliced it through. He watched the second spiral with the current for a dozen yards before it struck a partly submerged log. Though the boat with its *hang yaw* in tow continued to spin on and out of sight, the collision produced a hollow boom that sounded across the water like a muffled cannon shot.

On board the first riverboat, the guard jumped to his feet shouting. With one hand, Kohein clawed frantically at his shirt for a grenade while holding tight to the severed end of the rope with the other. Starting the boat's motor would require a third hand... impossible. He let go of the line, pulled out a grenade and tossed it. Nothing. Too late, he realized he had not pulled the pin. His own boat had begun to drift downriver. He snatched the second missile, pulled the pin and threw it as far as he could toward the riverboat. As it thudded against the deck, the guard jumped. The explosion, loud and brilliant in the night, was followed almost immediately by a second as the unprimed grenade was touched off by the blast.

Kohein stood, transfixed by the spectacle as pieces of what once had been a riverboat splashed into the water around him. Coming to his senses, he bent hurriedly to the *hang yaw* engine. It kicked and sputtered. He pushed the gas bubble as he had seen Hajee do and tried again. The pungent odor of gasoline filled his nostrils. The engine coughed repeatedly but refused to start. A bright beam of light fixed him against the dark water. A sharp crack echoed from the bank and a bullet flew past his head.

"Ya ying, na! Raw jap man laew!" Don't shoot! We have him. Phi Rak stood on the shore, his long body silhouetted against the light in his hand. "I would be delighted to shoot you now if you wish, Kohein, but I am hoping you may yet be of use before we offer you passage to the next life." Phi Rak's voice was strangely controlled given the drama of the moment. "Stay there. We will help you ashore."

The longtail was beached. Kohein's hands were bound tight in his lap. A fire blazed close behind him, so close that Kohein could feel it heating his back and neck. Phi Rak loomed overhead, then bent to within inches of Kohein's eyes. His breath was rank as if a recent grave had been opened and the dead exhumed. "I must say, you surprised me. I didn't expect actual heroism on your part... just a certain infatuation with the chase and the pot of gold. You are a curious if impetuous fellow, my friend."

Kohein sat wide-eyed but silent.

"So, you have little to say for once. How novel!" Phi Rak cocked his head to the side and stood. "Well, all I really need from you is the journal. Had you simply responded to my generous offer, we wouldn't find ourselves in this present fix, would we?"

Kohein said nothing.

"But, of course, you do not have it with you, do you?" Phi Rak spoke with an exaggerated air of rationality and understanding. "But knowing you as I do, I suspect you have a sense of the destination it describes. Yes?" Again, Kohein did not answer. Phi Rak's right foot caught him in the chest and sent him backward into the fire. He could not stop himself from screaming. Rough hands quickly pulled him free, but not before his back and neck had blistered from the heat.

"Ah, so sorry." Phi Rak mocked gently. "I forget myself. It is only fair to offer you a choice rather than simply consigning you to the flames." He waited. "Can you guide us or would you rather begin your cremation ritual here? I know you are an admirer of the Buddhist rites." Phi Rak nodded and smiled sympathetically. Pain seared through Kohein's back. He could smell the odor of his own singed hair and skin.

"What will it be, my friend? We offer you free choice. This, despite your un-provoked attack."

Finally, Kohein spoke. Taking a place in the remaining *hang yaw* would reduce its capacity by at least one of Phi Rak's men. "I will go with you, though I cannot guarantee my sense of direction. I have only that... a sense."

Phi Rak stood silent for a moment, one hand propped on an elbow, the other holding his chin thoughtfully. "Then a sense will have to do. We will see where it takes us in the daylight. And if we are disappointed," he smiled en-couragingly down at Kohein, "well, we can always build another fire."

****

The dim glow of low embers shrank and disappeared behind them. Hajee steered the narrow craft into the current and upstream at moderate speed to avoid running aground. Reggie shined his light ahead to scout for obstructions and debris. Joe and Carpenter squatted near Kumar who lay stretched uncon-scious along the bottom of the boat. Hemple sat stiffly nearby, darting quick glances down at Kumar and over at Carpenter every few minutes.

The heavens overhead, at first thick with bright stars against a black and moonless void, began a subtle transformation. A note of gray crept in and starlight began to fade. The dark shape of high hills emerged in the east against a hint of pink and pale yellow. The river ran brown and the steep rounded contours of Burmese mountains to the west began to show against the early dawn.

"Do you think we already passed the spot?" Carpenter continued to study the west bank closely as he spoke to Reggie.

"Not yet. But don't ask me how I know, 'cause I don't." Reggie nodded at Hajee. "But I bet he does." Reggie turned to scan the river behind them. "So far, there's no sign of pursuit... or of Amit by himself. So nothing has changed except we have some light now." Reggie looked down at Kumar and bit his lower lip. "How's he doing?"

"Alive. That's about all I can tell. Looks like a heart attack." Brother Joe crouched next to Kumar on the floor of the boat. "I used to tease him about his heart being too big for such a little guy. Now it's really true and there's no smart-ass comment that will change anything." He gently swabbed Kumar's forehead and swiped a thick hand across his own eyes. "That scar-faced bastard better hope I never see him again."

"Is there, uh, anything I can do?" Hemple spoke without looking at Brother Joe or anyone else.

Brother Joe looked up sharply. "It'd be too easy to say you've already done enough… and Kumar would give me… grief for it anyway. So, no." Then his face softened. He forced his eyes up toward Hemple's. "But thanks for asking. I know you didn't mean this to happen."

Hemple swallowed hard. He glanced once in Brother Joe's direction then quickly away. "I'm sorry. He was a good man."

"Still is, goddammit! The best!" Brother Joe stifled a sob and bent toward Kumar as if speaking to him only.

The awkward silence was broken by the sound of the engine as Hajee gunned the motor to increase speed. He stood periodically to look ahead, then swiveled to scan downstream. The river itself had narrowed somewhat. Its banks rose steeply on either side to merge with the vertical slope of the land. Dark limestone cliffs rose sheer from the river in odd angles to form high, al-most comically rounded figures against the dense green of the forested hill-sides. Occasional falls gushed white from the rock and splashed foaming into the stream. Signs of habitation appeared now and then, but the steepness of the terrain offered little purchase for construction, no matter how simple.

"Hold it!" Reggie rose to point to the Burmese shore. "See that little level spot next to the cliff? That's where I put in when I started downriver." Hajee slowed the boat as Reggie rummaged in his pack. After a moment, he pulled out a compass. "Let me get a reading just to be sure." Reggie scrutinized the device. He shook it twice then looked up. "Well, it's acting up for some rea-son, but I have N20°50' something by E100°15' something. The needle keeps swinging around, but the numbers are about what they should be. We must be close to where the fight was and to the pick-up spot. So I guess we just follow our noses from here on."

The engine roared back to life.

Carpenter felt a deep sense of unease as the vertical banks closed in further for a time. He searched the heights on either side of the river for hidden threats. The trapped feeling persisted until the close stretch opened unexpectedly at a sharp bend. On the left, a low sandbank protruded light brown above the surface of the river. Behind it in a deep cove, water cascaded down the face of the hill from a deeply shadowed opening in the stone some 30 feet above the river.

"*Nan si!*" That's it! Hajee's shout somehow was no surprise. He slowed the boat and pointed it toward the shore.

Below them, Kumar stirred and moaned. Brother Joe looked up excitedly. "You hear that? He may be coming around!"

"Now if we can just get him some medical attention, maybe we'll get through this." Reggie moved past the others to the bow, stepping gingerly past Kumar, who had begun to move his head side to side and murmur occasionally as if in conversation. Reggie's eyes searched the bank and the dense growth on the hillside. Water striking rock echoed in the narrow space to fill the air with musical vibration. A small smile played around the corners of Kumar's mouth. To the left of the falls, the cliff fell away in a V-shaped cleft through which a short stair-step path wound into the bush.

Reggie looked down at Kumar. "Maybe he knows something we don't." He blew a breath out through puffed cheeks. "I don't know where we are... but I think we're here."

The Caves

THIRTY-ONE

SHAN STATE, THE LARGEST OF ALL BURMESE PROVINCES, is so named for the Shan or *Thai Yai* which make up the majority of the people in this otherwise ethnically varied region of hill tribes and opium poppies. It rises abruptly from the central plain of the country to stretch across a mountainous plateau bordered on the north by China's Yunnan province, on the east by Chiang Mai and Chiang Rai in Thailand and for a short distance by Laos just across the Mekong River.

The hills of Shan State are dotted with caves, many of which contain religious artifacts of indeterminate age and are the subject of local myth and magic. The most famous is the Pindaya complex which runs for nearly 500 feet through the heart of a limestone ridge and attracts a host of pilgrims each year. Among the 8000 images of the Buddha found inside are some 70 unexplained figures related to Tibetan Mahayana traditions... an anomaly. Where a single, dominant way of seeing the universe holds almost complete sway, another apparently has crept in.

Pindaya's age as a place of worship and repository of Buddhist iconography is not known. Some claim the cave site dates to the time of India's great patron of Buddhism, King Ashoka, which would place it somewhere in the 2nd or third century BCE. In legend, a hidden path at the end of the underground complex leads through a magic doorway to the ancient capitol city of Bagan, some 200 miles distant. No one has discovered such a portal.

What *is* known is that many of the hills of eastern Burma are hollow. Few outsiders know what they contain.

******

Dawn lit the cove and painted the face of the rock a light shade of orange as the *hang yaw*, engine silent, swung past the sandbar and onto the shore. Bird song mixed in the air with the crystal tinkling of the cascade to fill the space with natural melody.

"Yeah, this is definitely it." Reggie peered into the forest as he jumped ashore with Carpenter and began to pull the boat further onto the narrow beach.

Brother Joc, Hemple and Hajee followed. The five strained to haul the craft completely from the water, feet sinking deep into mud. Together, they carefully lifted Kumar from the hull and laid him in a patch of soft reeds back from the pool at the foot of the falls and near the path they had seen from the river. The morning sun already was warming the small open space where they gathered. Near the water, a thick stand of bamboo bent and swayed in a light breeze. Long vines draped themselves down the face of the cliff. Orchids clung to the rock on both sides of the falls, pink and red blossoms sprouting from spiked leaves against a mossy background of varied green.

The forest crowded around them in staggered heights on all sides save the cove and the river. Shorter plants stood at four and six feet, elephantine leaves spread wide to absorb dappled sunlight. Above them, small trees rose thirty to forty feet, trunks adorned with clusters of more flowering bromeliads. Still higher, the giants of the jungle towered a hundred feet and more to make a roof of their broad leaves and shade for the profusion of life below. The path snaked away into the forest through tall grasses, whose gray-white beards seemed to move in time to the crystal splash of the falls.

"Quite a spot." Brother Joe looked up from Kumar's side. "Now that we're here, where do we go?"

"We take that path. It's exactly like what I saw in the dream. There's only one anyway, so it's not like we have too many choices," Reggie added with a shrug.

"Maybe we should check it out before we try to move Kumar," Carpenter suggested.

"For sure." Reggie already had begun to plan. "But first we'd better hide the boat. Now that it's daylight, Brother Love may not be far behind and he'll be making time." All five wrestled the *hang yaw* deeper into the high weeds and grass.

"Somebody will need to stay with Kumar... and watch for Amit or whoever shows up." Carpenter chewed his cheek, thinking out loud. "I don't know how long we'll need to follow this path to get a fix on where we are and what to do."

Reggie shrugged. "All I saw was the path, not where it went."

Carpenter knew – just sensed it really - that the path would lead where they needed to go. "I'm pretty sure we're on the right track," he offered, trying to sound confident.

"Me too," Reggie's tone betrayed no doubt.

"I'm staying with Kumar." Brother Joe was clear.

Hajee, watching the exchange, understood the decision at hand. Carpenter couldn't understand what he said, but caught the meaning. Hajee would wait and watch for Kohein. Brother Joe made sure. "So me and Hajee will stay here. Maybe Paul, too, in case we need to move Kumar in a hurry."

Hemple fought back a surge of fear at being left behind. "I don't see what help I can be. I'd rather explore the path with those two." He gestured toward Carpenter and Reggie.

Brother Joe replied with forced patience. "Look, if Phi Rak shows, we may need to carry Kumar to a safer place. Reggie and James can move faster without you and deal with whatever they find a whole lot better by themselves."

"I don't think we'll be that long anyway, but I agree with Joe. Let me and Reggie see where the path goes. It must go somewhere. We'll be back as soon as we can."

Hemple struggled against unbidden resentment. He tried to stop himself, but couldn't. He reddened slightly and muttered, "You're not any faster than I am. I beat you up the stairs at Doi Suthep."

Carpenter saw the reflection of the Aaron's jealous face, but put it from his mind. He ignored Hemple's remark. "So, we have a plan. We'll be back as soon as we scout the path." He shouldered his pack and Kohein's satchel and with Reggie leading the way, moved into the bush.

Bright sun defined the trail through the grass for the first few hundred feet then gave way to forest shade as the track left the open and twisted into the canopy. Here, as at the cove, bird song echoed through the space to create a cathedral-like feeling of sanctuary. The path sloped gently higher for some minutes, then twisted sharply up along the side of a narrow ridge. Carpenter and Reggie moved quickly toward what appeared to be an opening above them where the green dome of the forest was replaced by a patch of clear blue. They emerged from the thicket onto a flat outcropping above the falls and the cove where they had landed. White water rushed from the rock from some hidden opening in the cliff and arced gracefully to the pool below. From this height, the river rolled and twisted like a single giant sinew wrestling its way south along the body of the land.

Before them, the ridge reached upward toward a startling sight. A pale rocky peak, much higher than all around, rose above its tree-topped companions to stand alone, framed by a bank of white cloud. The mountain seemed to shimmer in the sunlight, as in a mirage or a dream. To the left, a vista of rounded hills and shallow valleys stretched for what seemed like miles to the far horizon. On the hillside beneath them, a cluster of thatched buildings spread into the near valley. A side trail split off here to wind its way down to the village. Neither man spoke. For long minutes they shifted their gaze from the river to the valley and to the peak high above.

Carpenter nodded at the peak towering over them. "Is it real?"

For a moment, Reggie could only shake his head in response, a token of amazement rather than confirmation. "You know, the elevation around here shouldn't be that high. Most of these hills are only a few hundred feet higher than the river, maybe a thousand at most. Steep, but not huge." He pointed to the peak. "But that's a good two or three thousand feet higher than anything else around. I never saw it on a map of the area. Basically, it doesn't belong here."

"But there it is," Carpenter stated flatly.

"Yeah, there it is alright." Reggie shook his head again, then turned away from the peak and back down toward the village. "Look!" He reached out a long arm and pointed. Below, an elephant climbed the path toward them, a small figure perched on its neck. "Do you see that?"

The animal mounted at an unhurried pace. An elderly man grinned up at them from just behind the animal's ears. A home-spun cotton shirt draped loose over baggy dark pantaloons. A woven, striped cape was knotted at his throat and hung in red and black to his knees. A cotton sash tied at his waist held a wide machete blade. Next to it, a grass carrying basket hung from a twisted grass string and dropped from a shoulder. An embroidered skullcap clung to the top of his cropped gray head. Gaining the high ground, the man spoke a single word and the elephant kneeled to allow him to dismount. He climbed down nimbly to stand, breathing regularly, before the two strangers. A broad smile lit his face as he greeted them, palms together: "*Shalom, Namaste, Allah u Akhbar.*"

Neither Carpenter nor Reggie could muster an immediate response. After a long moment, both returned the man's greeting with palms together. "Jesus Christ!" Reggie whispered, unbelieving.

"Ah!" the man nodded enthusiastically and smiled even more broadly. "OK! Jesus Christ!"

****

Hemple sat frustrated and anxious in the shade fanning himself with a fat leaf broken from a nearby bush. "They've been gone a long time. Shouldn't one of us go see what's happened?"

Brother Joe sat near Kumar, hand on his friend's chest to feel his heartbeat. "That's probably the fifth time you've asked that, Paul. We don't need to lose anybody right now. If you take off, there'll only be two of us here to watch out for Kumar. Why don't you just sit tight?"

"That's what I've been doing," Hemple argued. "And we could sit here until dark and still not know where we are or what to do."

Brother Joe gave in with a disgusted snort. "Listen, if it will stop you whining, why don't you go ahead and check out the path for a little bit. Just don't get lost and don't be too long."

Hemple stood immediately, relieved to have regained a sense of control. "Well, that seems reasonable. I am very comfortable in the woods, despite what James may think."

Brother Joe simply waved him off and looked away.

Hemple pushed through the grass. As he neared the taller growth, the brush seemed to crowd closer around him. The track continued, but wound back and forth through dense vines and choking vegetation until it brought him to the V-shaped confluence of two streams. The path divided here. One branch crossed the nexus of the waters on a series of large stones, then continued on the far side following the creek on the left. The other stayed right to follow the nearest stream where it disappeared upwards into the foliage. The ground between the two rose through the trees to form a sharp ridge.

The choice was confusing. Which fork had Carpenter and Reggie followed? Hemple looked for signs of their passing, but could detect none. He considered turning back, but resisted. He would not give Brother Joe the satisfaction.

He stayed to the right, following the path along the side of the stream. After another quarter mile, the creek veered to the left where another, smaller flow emptied into it. Another choice. The path also branched here, the broader track crossing the water to proceed along the course of the smaller stream. Surely Carpenter and Reggie would have stayed with the broader path at this point. Hemple balanced to cross on the river rocks and forged ahead into the forest. Just a few more minutes, he told himself. Then I'll turn back and make sure I haven't missed them.

****

"Does he speak English?" Carpenter wondered at his own reluctance to treat the situation, and the person, as real.

The old man clapped his chest. "*Mizo.*" Noting the confusion on the two strangers' faces, he spoke again. "*Chin, tae phood Thai Yai pen, na.*"

Reggie answered Carpenter's question. "I don't know what tribe he's from, maybe some kind of Chin. There are all sorts of them in the north and west. But if that's true, I don't know what he's doing here. He seems to speak a form of Thai. *Thai Yai* or Shan is the majority tribe around here. So I can communicate with him some."

"What's with the elephant? And how come he greeted us like that? Instead of something in Thai or Burmese or whatever?"

"Don't know, but those could be confusing questions even if I knew how to ask them."

"OK, ask him if there's a doctor around here."

"Got it." Reggie worked at communicating. The man nodded understanding and replied.

"Sounds like he's sort of a healer himself. His basket there is full of herbs." Reggie asked something else. "He says he's the *Sao Faa* here… which means something like 'Sky Lord' in *Thai Yai.*" The man spoke again. Reggie listened, struggling to comprehend. He turned to Carpenter. "OK, this sounds crazy, but I think it's what he said: 'I can help your friend, though the white priest would be better. But he can't help now.'"

"What? White priest? And how does he know about Kumar?"

"Man, I don't know." Reggie shook his head. "The main thing is he's all we got at the moment. I say we ask him to help and figure out the rest later."

"Right." Then, almost as an afterthought, "The woman in the dream said to come if we needed healing. She said she would guide us."

"Well, maybe she has. Let's get this *Sao Faa* or whatever we call him to Kumar and find out."

****

Hemple stood at another crossing, struggling to recall the details of his hike so far. Had he stayed consistently to the right or had he always chosen the broader path? Or was it some combination of the two? Perhaps he had moved on too quickly. Maybe time to turn back. He couldn't let the others know that he had lost his way.

****

Brother Joe jumped to his feet as Carpenter and Reggie emerged from the forest followed by an elderly man and, more startling, a large elephant complete with prominent tusks and chewing lazily on whatever it had pulled from vegetation along the path. "What is this?" Brother Joe took an involuntary step back. "We need a doctor, not an elephant!" Recovering his composure, he added, "So who is this and does he know where there's a real doctor?"

"He's some kind of lord and healer, as far as we know. His village is just over a ridge less than a mile from here." Reggie sounded doubtful. "I don't know what he can do, but he's as close to a doctor as we're going to find around here."

The *Sao Faa* greeted Hajee and Brother Joe as he had Carpenter and Reggie earlier. Hajee responded immediately with a stream of words Reggie and Joe found difficult to follow. He and the *Sao Faa* conversed for a time, then Hajee whispered to Reggie. "Hajee says this guy is for real. That he was told to expect us and that we carry something that belongs to his people." Reggie went on, "By the way, Hajee was shocked that the guy used an Arabic phrase, a Moslem greeting, really, but he doesn't know why or how. Or why he said, 'Shalom' or 'Namaste' either, or why he's wearing a skullcap."

"Doesn't matter now." Brother Joe was impatient to tend to Kumar.

Before more could be said, the *Sao Faa* stepped forward to kneel beside Kumar. He placed a wrinkled brown hand over Kumar's chest and closed his eyes. He breathed deeply and seemed to whisper to himself as he rocked slightly back and forth. He stopped and opened his eyes. Kumar began to mumble. Brother Joe's pulse jumped and he knelt beside the *Sao Faa* to bend his ear low to his friend's lips. "Kumar! Brother Edward! I'm here. I hear you, man! Talk to me!"

The *Sao Faa* reached into his basket and produced a small bundle wrapped in a single dark leaf and fastened together with a sliver of bamboo. He removed the skewer and spoke without looking up from where he knelt. Hajee translated and Reggie explained. "He says Kumar's heart is damaged but may be OK if it isn't stressed further. He says his spirit seems to be struggling to revive."

The *Sao Faa* spoke again and looked inquiringly at Hajee. Reggie seemed to understand right away. "He needs a cup or container of some kind. I've got one." Reggie stooped to the pack at his feet and withdrew an army-green tin cup which he offered to the *Sao Faa*. The man smiled at Reggie then rose to walk over to the edge of the cove. He slid sideways along the cliff face, toes gripping the slick rock, and held the cup to the water spilling from above. Returning, he emptied the contents of his leaf-pouch into the cup, stirring it with the bamboo stick. He knelt beside Kumar again and offered the cup to Brother Joe at his side. Brother Joe cradled a heavy forearm under Kumar's head and held the cup to his lips. A trickle ran down Kumar's chin, but his lips drew together as he managed a small sip. Brother Joe moved Kumar up another few inches. "Go ahead, man. Take another."

Kumar responded with a faint attempt to drink. He swallowed, rested, then sat forward a bit in Brother Joe's arm. He repeated the effort until he had drunk half the cup. Kumar's eyes opened suddenly. He swiveled his head toward Brother Joe and the *Sao Faa*, then grimaced and closed his eyes again. "I am so very tired!"

Brother Joe let out a deep sigh as if he had been holding his breath. "Man, Kumar... oh, man. You're gonna be alright, you hear me? Just keep drinking this stuff, OK?" Brother Joe held the cup to Kumar's lips until the liquid was drained.

Kumar rested for a minute longer among the blue and red ink of Joe's tattoos, then pushed himself slowly to a sitting position. He looked around him, an expression of wonder on his face. "A bitter brew, though refreshing." Kumar's eyes swept over the small and anxious gathering. "I have been away. Forgive me."

"Don't try to talk too much, OK?" a worried Brother Joe urged.

"I am OK, Brother. I am." He looked past Brother Joe and the others to the elephant grazing in the tall grass. "I have been traveling and am perhaps still lost in dream. Is that an elephant? Are we at Indra's gates? And where is Paul?"

****

Hemple clearly didn't know where he was. Everything looked the same. He couldn't tell if he had been here before... couldn't really tell one place from another at this point. It had seemed so simple when he set out. But the forest was deeper and thicker than he had expected. He hated to admit it, but he was lost and alone... again.

He began to shout, to scream. "Help! Can anyone hear me? Help, please! I'm right here!"

THIRTY-TWO

THE RIVERBOATS WERE GONE. One wrecked beyond repair and the other with its *hang yaw* too far downstream to chase. Never mind. They were stolen anyway. Time now was key. Phi Rak selected the men he would take with him and instructed the others to follow if they could. Kohein was bundled aboard the remaining longtail and tied to his seat near the bow.

"Hope that you can guide us, my friend. Otherwise, we will be forced to perform your cremation ritual at the riverside, much as the Hindus do. This stream could well prove to be your Ganges."

Kohein stared straight ahead and watched the brown water pass under the nose of the craft.

"Fast, now that we have the light!" Morning had barely lit the sky before they were under way. The *hang yaw* raced through the water with its crew of eight. Phi Rak's white-clad figure perched stiffly erect at the bow point scanning the shore like a bird of prey. "Look to the right!" Phi Rak detected the remnants of smoke from a recent fire where no habitation could be seen. "Over there!"

Meng Ti swerved to the Lao shore. Before they had gained it, the boxer and his cohort stepped into view at the river's edge.

"So, our erstwhile comrades appear." Phi Rak's voice dripped with sarcasm. "Closer, but don't land yet." The *hang yaw* idled a few yards off the bank. Phi Rak called out, "So what happened here?"

The boxer growled a response in Thai and pointed to the helmsman of his lost craft.

"Ah, a critical error in judgment." Phi Rak held his chin and nodded judiciously. "Such a shame. Unfortunately, we have no room to spare here." He looked over the boat and its crew. "You there," he pointed to one of his men. "Over you go!" When the man hesitated, Phi Rak drew a .45 caliber automatic from the folds of his long shirt and pointed it with menace. "I don't recall having made a request. Jump or be thrown... whichever you prefer."

The man stared briefly at the muzzle of the weapon and jumped. On the shore the helmsman grinned and began to descend toward the boat. Phi Rak swiveled and shot him in the head. The body slumped and slid down the muddy bank. "Now we have room for one. Come aboard, Somchai, you idiot. Lucky thing that you are less expendable than your friend there."

Meng Ti maneuvered the longtail closer to shore. The boxer, face impassive, jumped aboard. In the water, the expelled crewman stood waist-deep and awaited instructions, trying not to touch the body floating face down next to him. The boat hung idling, nose pressed into the current. "Well, my brainless one, what do you wait for?" Phi Rak spoke without looking back at Meng Ti, who clenched his teeth and gunned the engine.

Phi Rak seemed unaffected by the *hang yaw's* sudden burst of speed. He sat calmly in place, holding the hot pistol delicately in a silk handkerchief well away from his white garments, scrutinizing the shoreline. Without turning, he addressed Kohein behind him as if continuing an uninterrupted conversation. "You see, my dear Kohein, the merest misstep may cost you your life." Phi Rak pocketed the cooling weapon and wiped his eyes with the handkerchief as if overcome with mirth. "I do so hope you choose to cooperate. But then, we shall be amused regardless."

The *hang yaw* sped upstream for over an hour without further conversation or incident, slowing only occasionally to examine a suspicious location before racing on. When the channel began to narrow, Phi Rak withdrew a compass from a white pocket. "And what coordinates are we considering, Kohein?"

"Somewhere around North 20°50' and East 100°15'. Scott's numbers were not reliable. His compass ceased functioning altogether at one point."

Phi Rak studied his own instrument. "As is mine, now. Interesting. Perhaps we draw near?"

The *hang yaw* entered a close section between high cliffs on either side. Kohein felt anticipation build. As the boat emerged from the passage, he experienced a pang of recognition at the cove and the falls. But no sign of his friends. Perhaps they had missed the spot. Perhaps they were safe. "Here! This is the place!" Kohein's voice echoed against the rock wall. Meng Ti swung the boat to the left and into shore.

"I assume you are certain of the location?" Phi Rak's voice held quiet menace.

"As certain as I can be, not having been here before myself."

"Well, then, we'll look around and you can lead us on." The crew dragged the boat from the water. Phi Rak stepped lightly off. "Check the area," he ordered. Within minutes, the hidden longtail was discovered. "Ah! Well done, Amit!" Phi Rak surveyed the scene. "So far, so good, my friend. Lead on."

Kohein pointed to the single path into the forest. "Scott offered no clear directions, but there is only one track here. I daresay the others took it before us. There seems to be no other choice."

"Then onward, chop-chop!" Phi Rak shooed his men forward with an impatient wave of his hands. They moved single file into a tangle of woods. Thick vines hung across the path and hampered the advance. Stinging nettles sprang forward where men struggled to clear a path. "Not the most welcoming environment, I should say. I hope you know what you are doing here, Kohein."

Kohein could not explain the hard going. Surely Carpenter had come this way already? "I can offer very little advice beyond what I have given already. This is new to me as well."

"How sad for you, then."

A half-hour of slow progress yielded only deeper shade and wilder tangle. Angered now, Phi Rak made no effort to disguise his impatience. "Another hundred yards, Kohein, and we will stop to build a fire." Just then, a muffled shout rang through the wood. "Stop! What is that?" Phi Rak commanded silence.

Kohein masked his recognition. "I don't hear anything."

"Someone is calling for help. Over there beyond that stream. Perhaps we are not the only ones to find the going difficult here. Could we have stumbled on your friends?" Phi Rak smiled broadly. "Well at the very least, we can have some fun on this wild goose chase you've led us on, Kohein. A barbecue would be pleasant."

THIRTY-THREE

THE ELEPHANT LIFTED KUMAR AS GENTLY AND AS EFFORTLESSLY AS IF HE WERE A CHILD. He sat astride the animal's neck with the *Sao Faa* holding him from behind. With the others following on foot, they made their way slowly through the forest, up the ridge and down into the village below. Kumar asked to stop and rest at several points from the simple effort of holding on, but seemed to continue to revive. By the time they reached the village, he was alert and relatively at ease. What he saw amazed him.

A great mix of tribes. Eng, Akha, Loi, Palaung, Lahu, Lissu, and Wa – these from the Shan region. But also Chin, Kachin, Karen and others he barely recognized. Animists, Buddhists, Christians. A young Paduang girl, elongated neck stretched by four thick silver rings, sat in the sun next to a matronly Akha mother whose bangles, bells and chains glinted as they moved with her headdress. Turbaned Karen women in white squatted to chat with black-clad Lahu and Yaw. Men costumed in baggy green or blue pants worked side by side with others in black. Some wore only *pha khawma* loincloths as they toiled in the sun. Naga men, feathers protruding from cotton turbans, long woven cloths strung with bells and draped over their shoulders front and back like homemade sign boards, chopped bamboo with hand-forged machetes. It was a riot of color, language, sound and movement.

"I thought you said this was a Shan village," Kumar called down to Carpenter, who walked beside the elephant on one side.

"I'm not even sure the *Sao Faa* is Shan, just that he speaks *Thai Yai*." Reggie replied from the other side. "I just assumed this was a Shan village. Have you ever seen anything like it?"

"Never. And I have spent much of my life among these various peoples. I cannot explain this." Kumar turned back to the *Sao Faa* to ask how the village had come to be populated with so many different tribal folk. He listened to the reply, then questioned the *Sao Faa* as if for clarification. He nodded, sure of the response, though puzzled by it. "He says all these people are here because 'the mountain called'."

As they moved through the village, young children ran to greet them, calling out in a mix of languages. Adults looked up surprised from their work and chattered back and forth at the spectacle. After a hundred yards, there was a change. The mix of men, women and children was replaced by a cluster made up entirely of men – all dressed like the *Sao Faa*. The elephant stopped among them at a small thatched structure standing a few feet off the ground on stout wooden stilts. At the *Sao Faa's* shouted, *"lohng,"* it knelt while Carpenter and Reggie helped Kumar to the ground. The *Sao Faa* led them up to a small, bamboo-floored hut. Removing their shoes, they ducked into the dark interior. Kumar was shown to a red and blue woven mat where he stretched himself wearily as if having completed a long journey.

"Thank you all. This was very nearly my last gasp, so to speak." He leaned back against a large triangular pillow that served to cushion him in a sitting position. "I can tell you this. While I was 'unconscious' as you put it, I was quite aware of other things... dreams perhaps, but clear and lucid images. Many scenes, many lives... all bound together by various strands of obligation and feeling. We were all there in various ways throughout. And this," he continued, "is part of it, though not now a dream, I think. The elephant does not seem at all out of place." Kumar looked to the *Sao Faa* and then to Carpenter. "I believe you have something for him?"

Carpenter dug into Kohein's satchel which lay at his feet and produced Scott's journal. He held it out to the *Sao Faa*. "Yours, I believe?" He rummaged further in the case and extracted a small pouch. "And this."

The *Sao Faa* held palms together in gratitude. Accepting the journal and the pouch, he nodded and smiled while speaking at some length to Kumar. He loosened the strings gathered at the top of the pouch and poured the large red stone it contained into his open hand.

Kumar spoke without rising. "He thanks you for the return of these things, though their value lies more in the act of restoration than in the items themselves. He points out that few here can read the words in the book, though it does hold legendary significance for some. And the ruby, of course, as magnificent as it is, is but one of Indra's countless jewels... whatever that may mean."

The *Sao Faa* continued, then looked to Kumar to translate. "The real value of these items is to bring us here, together, to restore balance... to reconcile word and meaning, past and future, men and women, father and son." Kumar spoke with a question in his voice as if unsure he had translated accurately. "I confess that I do not really understand what the *Sao Faa* is saying, though

I believe the translation is correct in a literal sense."

Carpenter leaned forward excitedly. "What did he say again about 'father and son'?"

"It seems he believes that the journey to return these items serves to bring father and son together."

"Can he tell us anything about Father Harry?"

Kumar asked. The *Sao Faa* smiled in response. "He seems to have expected the question, James. He refers to a 'white priest' dressed in black. He simply calls him '*Khun Phoa*', 'Priest' or 'Mr. Father', I guess you'd say."

"Can he describe him?"

Kumar asked, then looked long at Carpenter. "Oh, yes. He looks very much like you, James."

Reggie broke in. "Where is the Father now? Does he know?"

"He apparently was injured not long ago when a large bird was attacked as it tried to land near here. He isn't sure who the attackers were... but they shot the priest where he waited for the bird. He was badly hurt, but not killed."

"That's our guy!" Reggie exclaimed.

"Where is he now" Carpenter asked, anxious.

The *Sao Faa* pointed up toward the ceiling and replied. Kumar nodded almost as if nothing more could surprise him. "He is up there, inside the mountain, in the caves." Kumar sat forward. "It seems he needs you, James."

****

"Please! I'm here. Don't leave me behind!" The voice held a note of despair as Phi Rak and his men approached through the snarl of undergrowth.

"Keep shouting so we can find you!" Phi Rak's response was encouraging and hopeful.

"Here! Over here! Thank God, you've come!"

Phi Rak stepped into view beside the stream where Hemple sat on a low rock fingering a rosary, shirt and face drenched in sweat. "Well, God may have been involved, but I'd rather take the credit myself, Paul." Phi Rak looked around the small clearing with an off-hand air of self-assurance. "It brings me great joy to find those who have lost their way. No challenge too great and all that."

Hemple reacted in terror. He began to look sharply around for a way out before realizing the futility of the effort. "You!" was all he could manage.

"Yes, me... and mine. One of whom I believe is a comrade of yours... or at least closer to it than you may count me and my assistants." Kohein stepped into the clearing with the rest of Phi Rak's men.

"Hello, Paul. This time I am the one who has managed to be captured by the enemy." Kohein's tone was tired and apologetic. Behind him, the boxer gave a push and Kohein sprawled at Hemple's feet.

"Well, what an interesting coincidence. You both seem to have been in the frying pan *and* the fire," Phi Rak quipped, noting the burn marks on the two men's clothes and bodies.

"Thanks to your lackey there," Hemple replied, nodding toward the boxer. Kohein remained silent.

"I hope you have learned that playing with fire can be dangerous. Fortunately, I am here to see that nothing is harmed by your reckless antics." He held his hand out to Hemple. "Give me the pretty necklace, Paul, before you damage it."

Hemple stuffed the beads into his shirt. "Never! This is part of a holy sacrament! You would defile it!"

Phi Rak smiled without mirth, his eyes dead and cold. "You waste my time, Paul. I will have your head as well as the necklace if you persist." He gestured behind him. "We don't really have time for a chat, do we Meng Ti?"

Meng Ti came forward holding the same long blade with which he had threatened Hemple in Sop Ruak. "You want keep you head, red man?"

Hemple drew the rosary over his head. "It's not a necklace," he muttered bitterly as he handed it over to Phi Rak. "It's a tool for prayer. It belongs to the kingdom of God."

Phi Rak held the rosary at arm's length, admiring the stones. "And worth a king's ransom, I would say." He fingered the central jewel. "This alone makes the trip more than worth the effort and expense." He lifted the gem high to capture the light and examined it for a long moment before casting a delighted smile at Hemple. "And now it belongs to the kingdom of brotherly love...

nearly divine as you so rightly point out." Phi Rak gently slipped the rosary over his head. "I feel closer to God already. Now… Meng Ti, perhaps you can persuade Paul to help us further?"

Meng Ti advanced, knife snaking slowly right and left. "Where you friend go?"

Hemple exhaled. "If I knew that, do you suppose I would be here calling for help?"

"Let's see how loudly you *can* call, Paul. It may help stimulate your memory."

"No, please! I don't know where they are. I tried to follow James and Reggie, but I lost them!"

"And who else is with them?" Phi Rak raised an eyebrow.

"Hajee and Brother Joe and Kumar, but Kumar is sick – unconscious – because of your men." Hemple looked around for the culprit.

"I believe discipline has been delivered for that indiscretion." A slight smile played about Phi Rak's lips as he stroked the rosary beads through his shirt. "But where are these friends of yours now, I ask." All expression left his face as he motioned again to Meng Ti. "See what you can drain from him."

"Wait!" Kohein spoke up from where he lay on the ground. "Paul can offer you nothing. If he had seen any of this beforehand, he wouldn't be lost now."

Phi Rak turned inquisitively to Kohein. "Then you have, as you say, seen this beforehand? How might that be, my fat friend?"

Kohein blew a breath through his mustache. "Some of it, but only in a dream."

"A dream? How quaint! Rather a fragile source, I should say. Would you care to stake your life on it… and Paul's?"

Kohein hesitated, considering. "It's all I have. I suspect that neither of us will survive your attentions, regardless of what we do. But there is no reason to hurt Paul now. And, unless I am mistaken, I am your only alternative to wandering in this thicket by yourself as Paul himself seems to have been doing."

"Ah! A most logical suggestion, if from an irrational source. We will see where you take us." With a gesture, Phi Rak waved Meng Ti away from Hemple. "We can always return to this game. Lead on."

THIRTY-FOUR

CARPENTER AND REGGIE LOOKED DOWN AT THE VILLAGE BELOW. Tiny figures bustled back and forth among the structures and open areas that defined the settlement. The *Sao Faa's* house was discernible in miniature along the main track. In it, they knew Kumar would be well taken care of by Brother Joe and Hajee and by the *Sao Faa* himself. Turning to the mountain, they followed the path with their eyes as it wound its up way along the ridgeline and into a dense patch of green that stretched halfway to the summit. Reggie glanced at Carpenter and raised his eyebrows in question. Carpenter nodded a reply and they set out.

After a few hundred yards, the trail entered the trees, leaving the broad panorama of hills, valleys and water behind. The ridge steepened and narrowed to a single slim vein of earth. The trail snaked along its spine, tunneling through the trees amid alternating pools of light and shade. As they ascended, what had been a faint tinkling reminiscent of the cove and its falls below grew in volume to match the chatter of birdsong overhead. A soft wind pushed gently at their backs and the scent of jasmine, lavender and wild blossoms mingled in the cool air. Carpenter and Reggie exchanged glances but neither ventured to speak until the path ended at the foot of a flight of stone steps carved into the side of the mountain. The steps wound through an archway of branches and flowering vines to disappear into the foliage above.

"Almost like a church or a temple," Carpenter breathed.

"Like a dream," Reggie answered.

Carpenter led upwards through an enchantment of green illuminated here and there by the white gold of a noonday sun. At first broad and gradual, the steps began to grow in height and come closer together until Carpenter found himself reaching up with both hands as if scaling a wall. He looked ahead. The stairway stretched up at a steep incline for another hundred feet to a point where the forest gave way to bare stone. On either side, silver falls shot from openings in the cliff face and plunged down into the jungle and out of sight. Far below and to the east, a telescoped version of the river meandered through the landscape like a miniature diorama. Opposite, a procession of round hills marched westward toward the slant sun trailing afternoon shadows like black scarves.

****

The way back to the path did not seem difficult. Kohein simply led the troop along the course of the nearest stream until it joined another. Following that, he emerged just downriver from the cove.

"I hope you will be able to do better than this, Amit," Phi Rak warned.

Kohein pushed through to the opening at the cove and turned back up the path. They followed it this time without difficulty to the outcropping overlooking the river on one side and the village on the other. Kohein felt a pang of anxiety in his gut as he looked down at the dwellings below. "The village looks deserted. We should just keep going up the side of this mountain."

"Perhaps. But we may find something of value down there as well. Your hesitation itself suggests that we would be wise to visit the village first."

Kohein led the way down and into a humble array of derelict huts. Only a few ill-clad adults stared at them as they made their way along the main track. One, a wrinkled old man naked save for a faded *pha khawma*, stepped forward from beneath a small dwelling to brace Kohein. "*Tongkan arai thi ni?*" What do you want here?

"The natives don't appear to be friendly. Let's accept his gracious invitation to look inside." Phi Rak started toward the short wooden steps. The old man stepped into his path. Phi Rak stopped, surprised, then pushed him roughly to the ground and moved on. Behind him, Meng Ti grimaced but followed.

Brother Joe appeared at the door holding a pistol. "Stop right there! Just turn around and go... now!"

Phi Rak looked up from the foot of the steps, amused. "Well, another surprise! We've been looking for you, you know." He turned to smile warmly at his followers. "But I must say I am a bit discouraged by the reception." He gestured toward Kohein and Hemple. A knife appeared at Hemple's throat, a rifle at Kohein's head. "So, are you sure we are not welcome? We could simply dump this baggage with you and leave as you suggest. Or better, we could dare you to use that weapon you seem to have borrowed ... and to live beyond your first shot. You may get lucky - we have only three guns of our own. Your choice, of course."

"Don't listen to him, Joe! He isn't to be trusted!" Kohein risked Phi Rak's wrath.

Brother Joe seemed ready to take the dare. Kumar's voice rose weakly from inside. "Don't be tempted, Brother. We all are in your hands now."

Brother Joe glared a challenge at Phi Rak, then threw the pistol to the ground. "If it was only Paul, I'd be tempted to shoot the bastard and take my chances." He offered Kohein a mirthless smile. "Glad you're alive, Amit, though I can't say I'm too happy to see you under the circumstances."

"He has been our honored guest, you know. And who may be yours, I wonder? Let us have a look inside." Phi Rak motioned behind him and two men scurried up the steps to push past Brother Joe. Phi Rak followed.

Kumar lay on his back alone inside. The journal and Kohein's gem-pouch rested near him on the floor. "I believe these are what you have come for. They are yours. There is no need to harm anyone."

Phi Rak stepped inside and gathered up the pouch and journal. "And where are the others?"

"They have gone up the mountain. Their interest has nothing to do with yours. Do not follow them. It is not safe for you."

Phi Rak laughed softly to himself as he opened the pouch and extracted the ruby. "A second treasure... and so soon!" He patted the rosary beneath his shirt. Tucking the pouch and its contents into a pocket, he picked up the journal and began to leaf through it. Scott's letter fell from the pages. Phi Rak plucked it from the floor and paused to read. Finished, he looked up, his face suffused with a strange light. "So this is indeed the place. And, I would assume, the mountain holds the extraordinary treasure Scott hints at here." Phi Rak shook his head sadly. "And you would deceive me so that you and your companions could have it all for yourselves, eh?"

Phi Rak stepped to the doorway to shout orders, then ducked back inside. "But I bear no hard feelings toward you. In fact, to demonstrate my generosity, I shall give you the chance to participate in the discovery." His face hardened. "Get up! You shall all join us to lead the way. You can be our buffer. And you can help carry our find back down to the river when we are done. After all, you should see the end of this journey before meeting your own, yes?"

****

Carpenter scrambled hand over hand for the final ascent. The incline was so steep as to hide the top from view until his eyes had cleared the last step. He stopped suddenly at what he saw. Reggie drew up level with him from behind. They stood on the upper stairs for a long moment, hands resting on a flat stone floor that formed the base of a fair-sized opening in the cliff face. A line of carved symbols was etched across the top of the opening to hover over whomever bent to approach.

Six-sided stars stood out in bas relief at either end. Inside each, left and right, a winged figure with a bearded man's upper body flanked octagonal webs surrounding circles of one-eyed *yin-yang* figures. Next to them, simple crosses rose from the rock beside paired crescents and stars. These stood sentinel to the central motif - a figure with four arms seated on a royal elephant.

On the ground below, a massive golden Buddha stood facing the steps, a single ruby embedded in its forehead, one hand upraised, palm out in a welcoming posture intended to allay all fear. Carpenter and Reggie pushed themselves over the lip of the staircase and stood silent at the foot of the Buddha. Neither spoke. A cool breeze emanated from the dark hollow behind, carrying the light scent of flowers.

Reggie looked a question at Carpenter who proceeded past the image into shadow. There, the roof of the hollowed area sloped back and down to a small oval mouth, roughly three feet tall and nearly five wide, its interior black and impenetrable. The source of the breeze and the fragrance.

"I don't suppose you're planning to go in there?"

"I don't see any other route to follow. And it looks kind of like an entrance."

"An entrance... right. I avoided tunnel duty to stay away from entrances like this. It's like letting yourself be blinded. Gives me the creeps – always has." Reggie held his lower lip between his teeth.

"I can scout it out and come back for you," Carpenter offered.

Reggie sighed and bowed slightly. "We both go, little brother. But you and your skinny butt can take the lead." He handed his flashlight to Carpenter. "Only turn this on when you have to. It's about out of juice."

Peering into the black mouth of the opening, Carpenter could see no more than a few feet. Rock walls crowded in from both sides and the ceiling slanted slightly downward toward the floor as it disappeared into the murk ahead.

He started forward on hands and knees with Reggie close behind. The cave tunneled straight back for at least thirty feet before the lowering ceiling forced both men to their stomachs. Carpenter shined the light ahead. The opening appeared to grow even smaller with no sign of an end, though the breeze and the fragrance it carried grew stronger as they proceeded.

"I don't know how much of this I can take, A-Man. Looks like it just peters out."

"That's what it looks like, but it feels like it goes somewhere. There's still a breeze coming this way from inside. If it gets too small to go on, we can just back out and re-think the whole thing, OK?"

Reggie forced a note of confidence into his voice. "Sure… go ahead. But this hole is starting to feel like a suit a couple sizes too small. It gets much smaller, I'm gonna be stuck."

They bellycrawled forward a few feet, then a few inches at a time for what seemed like hours but could only have been minutes. Carpenter began to feel the ceiling scrape his back as he slid forward. The walls hugged his shoulders, elbows and hips as he squirmed against them in the dark. He could spread his feet no more than a foot apart. Despite the breeze, the coffin-like closeness of the space began to feel like an airless trap. Carpenter shined the light ahead again. Black and tight.

"That's it, JC. If I push in any further, I don't think I'll be able to get back out." Reggie's breath rasped as he struggled for self-control. "I'm not even sure I can go backward now." The light blinked and began to fade. "Shit! Turn it off, man. Quick! We gotta have some light in here or I'm gonna go crazy!"

Carpenter snapped off the light. He spoke into the dark ahead, unable to turn to address Reggie. "Listen, I'm smaller. I'm gonna try a few more feet. You take the light." He struggled to find a position in the narrow channel that would allow him to move the flashlight from his outstretched hand to his friend behind. Impossible. Carpenter spoke into the darkness. "OK. It's too tight for that. Let me see if I can squeeze into some place where I can get you the light." Reggie's silence was less a response than a sign of simple endurance.

Carpenter pushed ahead, moving his flattened body with the tips of his shoes, holding the flashlight ahead of him in the dark like a relay baton. The ceiling seemed to hold him in place for a single panicky moment then fell away abruptly as he slid forward to move on elbows and knees, then to a crawl. The tunnel floor arced up and into a broad opening, filled with soft light. "Reggie! I made it! It gets bigger and there's light up here. I think you can make it!"

Reggie's exhaled breath echoed through the tunnel rock. "I can't see anything, JC. I don't think I can move any further."

"Don't try to back out yet! I'm gonna turn around and come back. I can pull you through."

"Better hurry, little brother. I'm going kinda nuts here."

Carpenter moved forward until the width of the cave broadened enough to allow him to turn around. He headed quickly back into the tunnel, sliding the last few feet through a space little larger than his own frame. He reached forward and stretched. "OK. I'm here and my hand is out in front of me. Try to reach me."

Carpenter could hear Reggie grunting to comply, his breathing fast and shallow. "Can't find you, man!"

Carpenter flipped on the flashlight. Reggie's face, beaded with sweat, glistened a few feet away then began to fade. "Grab the light!" Carpenter watched Reggie's hand close over the luminous end of the tube just as the light went dead. "OK! You push and I'll pull. This is the narrowest part. It opens up further in. Make yourself as small as you can."

Reggie struggled to unstrap the knife from his hip, but could not reach his own waist. "If I get stuck in here, you're gonna need to find a way to put me out of my misery, 'cause I'd hate to have to try to figure out how to kill myself." Reggie pushed with desperate strength as Carpenter pulled. Carpenter could hear the bigger man gasp with effort and pain as he scraped through. Once his shoulders cleared, Reggie moved so quickly that his head butted Carpenter's. "Sorry, man. I think I'm OK now. I can see the light – like, really. Thank God."

When the passage widened sufficiently, Carpenter turned around to face forward again and both men moved quickly to the end. They could hear the sound of chimes now joined by the chanting of female voices. The scent of fresh blooms filled the clean air. They pushed themselves out of the tunnel and to their feet.

They stood silently and stared. The space was huge and alive with light... a giant geode illuminated from within by some warm and hidden source that spread a deep glow through a world of crystal color and texture. Fingers of gold and silver, jade and turquoise curled upward to a high, arched ceiling where needle-sharp stalactite clusters of diamond, sapphire and ruby hung like ingeniously crafted chandeliers. Veins of precious and semi-precious stone ran across the vaulted ceiling in shades of red, green, blue and pink. Here and there, great pillars of gem and rock spiraled up from the floor, joined at the waist by a twin from above. Throughout this vast display – balancing and enhancing it all – intricate carvings scrolled across open surfaces of marble and onyx.

The chamber narrowed at the far end to another tunnel, this one broad and lit by flaming torches inset into sconce-like niches in the rock. Chanting swelled from the tunnel and grew in volume. A column of robed figures, all women, filed into the chamber and gathered to surround the two men in a semi-circle. On some unseen cue, they stopped together and parted at the middle. A tall woman with strong Asian features stepped forward. A streak of bold white ran through her black hair at the temple. A proud nose hooked down past deep-set eyes and high cheekbones toward a generous mouth and gentle smile.

She stepped forward, robed arms outstretched to Carpenter. "Welcome, my son. Finally you have come."

THIRTY-FIVE

HE KNEW HER. He knew her voice and face and feel.

Not simply from the illusion of dream. He knew her immediately and deeply and with a clarity that defied logic and reached beyond conscious memory to tighten his throat and constrict his chest. He felt his face flush and tears stream down his cheeks. He stepped into her embrace as a drowning man grasps a rescuing hand, as a lost child burrows into the shelter of a parent's arms. He felt her warmth but not her touch.

"Mother…"

They stood knitted together in silence for a full minute as Carpenter's sobs of relief quieted and questions began to form in his rational mind. Gently he drew back to gaze into her eyes. "But, who are you?" He shook his head as if rejecting the question. "How do I know you? And why are you here? Why am *I* here? What is this place?" He shook his head again, unable to match the comfort he felt with the bewilderment it engendered.

"I am Johara." Her voice was the voice he had heard so often of late in sleeping and waking dreams. "You know who I am, but that realization must be alarming, even frightening in this strange place and under even stranger circumstances."

She stepped back to examine him, her eyes taking in his full measure. Delight shone clearly on her face. "I am Johara," she repeated. "Your mother. This place is your home, your first home… this time." She moved her head side to side as she searched his face in wonder. "You were born here. You lived here with me, with *us*," she nodded at the knot of people gathered behind them, "for the first months of your life. Before the ambush. Before I lost you." Her voice wavered slightly. She reached a slender hand to touch his cheek. "I am so sorry, my son. I could not save you without leaving you behind." Tears gathered in her eyes even as Carpenter struggled to make sense of her words.

"But... but, what happened?"

"I hope that may be explained by both of us... your father and I."

"My father."

"Yes. He is here, though barely living. This is why I have called you. You are our last hope to restore him."

Carpenter's face had grown pale. He felt light-headed and confused. She noticed and directed him to a stone bench carved into the side of the jeweled wall. Reggie followed awkwardly, unsure of what to say or do. She turned to touch his arm. She smiled up at him, then bowed. "I believe they still call you 'king', do they not?" Reggie started at the title, but remained silent. Johara did not seem to expect a reply. She straightened and spoke soothingly. "I know this must be as strange for you as it is for James... perhaps more so. I will attempt to explain shortly. Would you care to sit for a moment?"

Reggie nodded dumbly and sat next to Carpenter.

"You have dreamed," she stated simply. They nodded. "But these 'dreams' – did they not feel more like visions or memories than dreams?" They waited for her to go on. "By now, you must know they were more than the musings of a tired or drifting mind. They are images of past times, earlier experiences. Recollections from the lives of ancestors, of other versions of yourselves. Memories that usually cannot be touched lest we be trapped by what has been rather than create what may be." She paused, watching their faces. "But here... I offer arcane philosophy rather than practical comfort. Simpler explanations are in order."

She sat between them. "Our stories stretch far beyond the arc of a single lifetime. We are more than what we seem – even to ourselves. There are ways to access these 'memories' and to help others access them. This much we have discovered over the years." She examined their rapt faces. She nodded as if to herself. "We have been calling you... sending 'dreams' that might awaken and beckon. Not without reason. We have been together before and will be again, but we seek to avoid intrusions into current lives. Events, however, seem to have overtaken us. My decision – and it was mine alone – was to call you to us. There are limits to what we can do – to what any one of us can do." She shifted to look into Carpenter's eyes. "I cannot reach your father by myself."

Carpenter searched her face, struggling to understand.

"This is hard, I know. I see that the experience threatens to overwhelm comprehension. There are larger purposes at work, beyond my own understanding as well. What I do know is this." She laid a hand on Carpenter's shoulder, her touch lighter than air. "Your father is wounded. He made his way here with the help of friends who laid him at our threshold, unable to enter themselves. He was brought in and attended by the few sisters who remain."

Johara stopped here as if considering how far to pursue this piece of her explanation. With a subtle shake of her head, she continued. "He was not conscious then… is not now. He hovers at death's door, but refuses to enter. He has called your name. We have done what we could to preserve his life and to make him comfortable." She stood to face them, beckoning to follow. "But if he is to be truly healed, my son, it must be by your hand alone."

THIRTY-SIX

HAJEE CROUCHED IN THE BUSHES NEAR THE *SAO FAA'S* HUT AND WAITED. They apparently had forgotten about him. Silence can render one nearly invisible, he thought to himself. And invisibility would serve him well.

Invisible. Were the tribesman standing all around truly invisible to them or were Phi Rak and his men simply oblivious? He watched as Kumar and Brother Joe descended the short steps from the hut followed by Phi Rak and the one who liked playing with knives. Hajee could play such games too… if necessity required.

The group headed out along the village path and up the hill with his friends in the lead. Kohein and Hemple, then Brother Joe with Kumar grasping his forearm for support. Four of the pale one's lesser minions followed with weapons trained ahead, then the boxer and Meng Ti and finally Phi Rak himself, pacing proudly like a herder of goats. Hajee waited until they had crested the hill then slid from cover and followed through the brush.

They halted at the top. To Hajee's eyes, the trail ran smoothly along the spine of the ridge. But the group hesitated and looked to Phi Rak for guidance as if uncertain how to proceed. Finally, two of the men took the lead, holding machetes and apparently looking for a way through foliage Hajee could not see. They looked to each other in confusion, then back to Phi Rak, who urged them on with threats and curses. Finally, they began to swing their machetes almost at random, with nervous eyes on their surroundings. A bird of prey screeched from a tree, swooping low over their heads. Machetes cast aside, they hit the ground shaking.

"Move on, you cowards!" Phi Rak's angry shouts drove them again to their feet.

Hajee moved past the main group and to the right, skirting the trail and clinging to the side of the hill above the cove. He held a short blade by his side, looking for an opportunity to attack or simply to reduce the number of potential opponents. None presented itself.

Thick clouds obscured the sun. Pools of dark shadow replaced gentle shade on either side of the path, whose edges seemed to crowd in like curious ghosts. Hajee continued to flank the group as it proceeded along the ridge. They moved more quickly now, as if the going had become easier. Hajee could detect only an occasional crack of a machete as the party advanced. The ridge narrowed and he dropped behind.

"What's this?" Phi Rak's voice cut again through the still air. They had reached a stone stairway cut into the side of the mountain. The two men leading the troop stopped, glancing nervously up through the trees and fingering protective medallions at their necks. Phi Rak drove them forward. Hajee stayed back as the group began to follow the steps. When they had twisted out of sight, he ran lightly up to follow, staying back just far enough to avoid detection.

The group paused again at the foot of a much steeper incline. The stairs rose ladder-like into and past the surrounding trees to emerge against the bare rock above. Water streamed from cavities on either side to cascade down toward the jungle and the river below. The leaders hesitated, then plunged forward. The others followed in single file, each man bent low to balance on the steps ahead.

Hajee avoided the stairs altogether and climbed instead along the cliffside. Just below a flat area at the top, he found a space where he could both hide and observe as the group crested the lip. He peeked over the edge to watch. An open area fronted what looked like a large cave entrance over which a number of symbols had been carved into the stone. A golden Buddha stood facing the stairs, hand raised in the 'do not fear' *mudra*. Hajee ducked back and listened.

"So, this clearly is an entrance of sorts. I assume the demon figure is some sort of guardian, wouldn't you say?" Phi Rak had stepped forward to address his captives.

"Demon?" Hajee recognized Kohein's voice. "Are you referring to the Buddha figure?"

"Don't play the fool, Kohein. Guardian figures are just what they appear to be."

"As you say." Kohein's reply was subdued. He glanced at Kumar, who responded with a raised eyebrow.

The sound of feet slapping stone interrupted them from behind. Phi Rak swiveled, brandishing his pistol. "Quick, Somchai. Your men have run off!" The boxer, looking back toward the standing image, advanced cautiously to the edge as if afraid of attack from the rear. "Down there, you fool!" Phi Rak thundered as he stepped to the edge and fired three swift shots at the fleeing figures below as they disappeared into the forest cover.

"Cursed with cowards and superstitious fools!" Phi Rak swung angrily back to the others before assuming a mask of calm indifference. "They see what they believe and fear what they see." He appeared to dismiss the men and the incident. "So, Amit, what do you make of the carvings overhead?"

"Clearly they are religious symbols, but rather unusual here where you would expect to find only Buddhist or animist images."

"The first is clear enough," Phi Rak mused, stepping forward again and squinting up at the rock above. "The pattern repeats itself starting with what certainly is a Star of David. What is that next to it?"

Kohein continued. "That is the *Faravahar*, a Zoroastrian icon. But native to Iran or Afghanistan, not here."

"And the next?"

Kumar interjected. "That appears to be the Taoist symbol for the *yin* and *yang*... the complementary forces - positive and negative, male and female - that inform all creation."

"Quaint. The others are familiar – the Christian Cross and the Crescent and Star of Islam."

"An unholy union." Hemple muttered low, barely audible in a rising wind.

"Shut up, Paul." Phi Rak dismissed him without so much as a glance. He continued to address Kumar. "How about the figure in the middle?"

"Indra. Both Hindu and Buddhist. For Hindus, the king of the Gods."

"So, we have uncovered a refuge for religious fanatics. Hopefully a storehouse of treasure as well." Phi Rak peered into the deep shadows at the rear of the cave. "You!" He ordered his two remaining minions in Thai. "Check for an opening behind the ogre."

Hajee peered over the lip of the rock again to see Phi Rak's men disappear behind the Buddha figure. Even from his perch some twenty feet away, he could see the darker shadow of a low opening in the rock to the rear. Phi

Rak's men walked to it and continued past as if it were not there. They stopped at a tall slit in the rock to the right of the smaller cave mouth.

"Go ahead... in you go. Let's see what we have. Take Somchai's light." The two men looked at each other nervously before obeying the command and sliding sideways into the fissure. Five minutes passed, then ten. Neither man reappeared.

"Imbeciles!" Phi Rak's anger was tinged now with a shade of uncertainty. "So, we will follow together. Meng Ti, give your torch to Hemple there. Paul, you may lead the way."

Hemple drew back from the wall toward Phi Rak. "I... I can't. I have trouble with tight places... and it's very dark. I can't do it."

Phi Rak leaned down to growl into his ear. "Ah, but you must and you will. You will lead us, or you will try flying from the edge of this cliff." Phi Rak smiled and waited, then leaned in again to whisper. "Which do you prefer?"

"Please! I have a terrible feeling about this. Let someone else go. Please!" Hemple shrank away from the wall and from Phi Rak.

"I will go. I am a bit wide in the beam, but small enough I think to squeeze through." Kumar stepped toward the fissure.

"I'll go. Kumar isn't fit for this." Brother Joe elbowed Kumar aside. Kohein moved forward as well and all three vied for a moment to lead the way.

"Silence!" Phi Rak roared, brandishing his .45. "Paul will exercise his natural leadership. If he can make it forward, so can the rest of us. But if he would rather try a loftier option, then Meng Ti and Somchai can help him into the air... gentlemen?" Meng Ti and the boxer grabbed Hemple's arms and moved him to the edge of the cliff. Hajee shrank back into his crevice.

"Which will it be, Paul? Land or air?" Phi Rak snickered. "I believe you are destined to be the first to explore the mystery, whichever you choose. Will you lead us to discover what is inside this mountain? Or will you attempt to prove that man can fly? Your choice." His voice went cold. "Now, make it!"

Sweat streamed from Hemple's face. "I don't know how far I'll be able to go," he warned.

"Further, let us hope, than our last pair of adventurers." Phi Rak nodded and Hemple was pushed toward the gap in the wall. He gasped for breath and stepped inside, flashlight held at arm's length before him.

"Now, the rest of you." Phi Rak flourished his weapon again. Brother Joe, Kohein and Kumar followed Hemple into the rock. Meng Ti sidled in, but the boxer backed away muttering to himself. The muzzle of Phi Rak's automatic bore into the back of his head. He shivered and stepped through. Phi Rak kept the weapon pointed straight ahead and ducked inside after it.

Hajee pulled himself over the lip and onto the flat. The Buddha figure seemed to smile down at him from above. He walked around it to the rear to examine the oval entrance, then moved along the wall to the right. He frowned and stepped back to view the entire surface. The oval opened darkly to his left. To the right, nothing. There was no fissure. The bare rock stared back at him in naked mockery of what he had witnessed. He stood for a moment more, wondering if his eyes had betrayed him, then bent low to crawl through the oval entrance and into the mountain that had swallowed nine men whole.

THIRTY-SEVEN

"WE ARE WHAT REMAINS OF A TRIBE ONCE UNITED, then divided between those who would risk change and those who held tight to what they knew."

Johara was leading them along a passage more sculpted than dug and whose muralled walls seemed lit from within. She spoke quickly as if hurrying to squeeze a lifetime of narrative into a single exchange. Carpenter and Reggie walked to either side, still stunned and struggling to comprehend.

"We trace our antecedents to the fall of Jerusalem. We have wandered eastward since that time, stopping for years or decades or generations along the way, adapting and changing with each new place and people. Changing that is, until we stayed too long in one place and began to resist further metamorphosis." She glanced at Carpenter. "Your most recent dream? It was of that split... not so far from here, just across the river in what has become Yunnan."

"Yes, I remember that dream in detail. And I've had others too. Wandering or exploring, or running from death and destruction. But not with a whole lot of success."

"And I've had my own," Reggie added quickly.

"Yes, you both have dreamed. And your friends, those who come here now, have been visited as well. They all are needed in some way, so all have been called." Before either Carpenter or Reggie could question this last observation, Johara turned left into a passage leading further into the mountain. Noting their puzzled expressions, she continued. "I will try to explain. Let me first complete this part of the tale, for it is connected."

Neither man spoke, so she rushed on. "There was a split and the tribe parted ways. Some of us, mostly women, came here led by our Malka, the queen... in a sense, a direct relative of mine... of ours." She glanced apologetically at Carpenter. "The Malka located this place in a dream-trance and brought us here safely through violence and chaos." Johara paused, looking from one to the other. "You must understand, we have been seekers from the beginning. We have acquired considerable knowledge in our long journey through the world and over time... knowledge that many would consider 'magic'. The Malka saw this place and the way here despite the danger. She led us to safety, and cast a spell to enfold and protect us from the world outside."

Johara's eyes fixed for a moment as if seeing the events she described. "But the spell, intended as a blessing, proved a curse as well. The Malka could not overcome the bitterness of her own loss. She decreed that no one could enter these caves but our own people, not even those we left behind. There was a single exception. If any required healing, they could be helped until well enough to leave. All others were barred entry until such time as the Aaron, the priest who had cast her out, entered in humility and denied the one who had caused the rift."

"The Aaron...?" Carpenter began, seeing Hemple's face in his dream.

"... is trapped by his own choices now." Johara completed the sentence without further explanation and sighed as if in regret. "All that was long ago. We were indeed protected as the Malka intended. We thrived in this mountain for years, but our numbers inevitably dwindled. Eventually, we were gripped by the same fears that had divided us before. Safe from outsiders, we became opposed to change itself. Not unlike those we had left behind, we began to deny what in fact are the inevitable transmutations that life demands."

Carpenter broke in. "Forgive me. I don't want you to stop, but this is more than I can get hold of."

"Me too... way more," Reggie's face reflected both awe and confusion.

"Of course. There are so many strands knotted together."

"Mother, I don't understand all this... probably can't. But I need to know how it's connected to my father. And... " he couldn't hide the note of desperation in his voice or the pain he felt deep in his chest. "And why didn't you keep me before?"

Johara bent her head and blinked back tears. "As I said, it would be best that your father help explain what happened to us. It was not my intent to lose you. It was beyond my control. Explanation may help you to understand, but the past cannot be changed... only the future, by what we do with each moment." She turned to face him. "That is how these threads are bound together, my son. It is why you are here... to heal more than a single wound."

Carpenter's face showed his confusion.

"I told you that we came here from another place in another time after a deep division split the tribe. Our Malka foresaw that a time for reconciliation would come. The Aaron somehow would find us, leading the way. He would bear a *terma* to light the path. Our *terton* would appear and use it to reveal the truth that has been hidden in plain sight."

"I don't understand what any of that means," Carpenter began to object.

She stilled him with the merest semblance of a touch on his arm. "Listen, my son. This is your story as well as mine. We have carried certain artifacts with us since the destruction of our temple. Items from the temple itself ... a gem and a scrap of parchment from an early scroll. We – actually, individuals from a singe line - carried these things for hundreds of years without knowing their meaning beyond the connection they represented to our own origins."

"And what does that have to do with me?"

"Centuries ago, in what is now called Tibet, we learned from a teacher who thought to send messages to the future. He hid them in what was then the present, so they could be discovered later by one he called a '*terton*' or 'truth finder'. These *terma* were treasures of various kinds, each offering a truth that would be of value to the finder and to the world in which he or she lived. Ancestors of yours – I will call them that – carried these *terma* until joining the tribe. The items then became part of our common heritage. They remained with us here until I gave one of them - a jewel - to your father."

"To my father?"

"Yes. We were in love. He was a young soldier in the great war against the Japanese. Then came civil war in China. He remained here and in China to fight against what he saw as a dire threat." Johara paused, a slight grimace touching her lips. "Change frightens and threatens, even from across a sea."

She buried the thought and went on. "I first saw your father on an outing from the mountain. He did not see me, of course. I watched him from a distance. I must admit I loved him immediately, before we had even spoken to each other. But my mother, the Malka then, forbid that I make myself known to him. As I said, the only 'outsiders' who were allowed to know us were those in need of healing. They could enter our world, but only for such time as needed to assure their recovery. And then upon leaving, they would be glamoured in such a way as to prevent their return and our discovery."

Carpenter found himself intrigued now despite a lingering resentment. "And my father was allowed to enter?"

"Yes, he was badly injured and brought here to be tended to. Just as he was again not long ago. He remained that first time for several months." Johara's voice grew wistful. "We were young. We fell hopelessly in love. But he cooperated when told he must leave. He is a man of honor. But he promised to return to find me as soon as he could. He did not know I carried his child... you. Before he left, I took the jewel – the *terma* – from where my mother kept it and gave it to him. Perhaps I thought it would help him find me again, though it did not. So he came to possess one of the treasures and I, more fortunate, came to have you... my son, and our *terton*."

She gazed up at him with deep affection. "So, you come not only to me and to your father, but to a great chasm between an entire people. The time for reunion has come... time to restore the balance we lost so long ago. Time to free ourselves from the past. So I give you this." Johara reached into her robes and withdrew a yellowed and ancient piece of parchment. "The other *terma*, my son. It bears some truth we have not yet deciphered on our own. It is for the *terton* to discover."

Carpenter took the hide in both hands and turned it over and over. The markings were old and so faded as to be indiscernible in any language. "I don't know what to do with this. I can't read it, if that's what you expect."

"I cannot tell you how to access the *terma*. I know only that we have carried it too long now ourselves, waiting for its answers to be revealed. Our journey has been hard and this poor scrap grows heavy."

Johara looked up at the high ceiling in its carved and sculpted splendor. "We have made a beautiful sanctum here. We created this sacred place with our own hands over hundreds of years." She turned back to Carpenter. "But I'm afraid we have succeeded finally in constructing our own handsome tomb. We have been captured and preserved by our own handiwork and decisions. Perhaps you can deliver us from ourselves."

****

"If you can't find your way in this labyrinth, we might just as well leave you in the dark, Paul." Though threatening, Phi Rak's words held a hint of desperation. "I don't intend to wander in this maze forever. Do you hear me!"

Hemple mumbled as he squeezed forward sideways through the tight space. The walls had closed in since they entered and every step seemed to draw them further into a menacing darkness.

"I can't hear you! Speak up, Paul!"

Hemple slid an arm up his side to wipe oily sweat from his eyes. The close sides of the tunnel allowed barely enough room even for this simple gesture.

As he struggled to touch his own face, the flashlight dropped from his hand and blinked out. The world went completely black. The air seemed to empty from the passage as well. Hemple's breathing immediately became labored. Panic welled just below the surface. "I can't see anything! The light is out! I can't find it!" His comments came out as a shout and a whimper, but he was past caring. This was more than he or anyone could bear.

"We will turn around when I say so and not before. Time is wasting, Paul. If you cannot lead us, you are of no use to me. This tunnel will be your final, humble home. Feel your way forward or die where you are!"

"Then kill me now. This is worse than any coffin." Hemple flattened his palms against the walls as if to prevent them from closing in.

Phi Rak started to reply, then held himself. His tone became gentler, soothing. "I thought you were a man of faith, Paul. Where is your faith now? Has God abandoned you?"

Hemple's silence was the only answer.

Phi Rak waited. "We aren't going backward, Paul. You must lead us, lead us into the mysteries of this place." Still no response. Phi Rak pulled the rosary over his head and draped it over the muzzle of Meng Ti's shouldered rifle until the smaller man had grasped it firmly in hand. "Paul! I am sending you an emblem of your faith. Something you can hold on to... literally." He urged each man in succession to pass the rosary forward. As it advanced from hand to shoulder and on, the central gem seemed to catch the faint reflection of a farther light. "Paul! Take this as a sign! And He said, 'Let there be light and there was light'." Phi Rak grinned in the dark at his own cleverness.

Hemple felt the beads at his shoulder. A dim but distinctive glow showed from the largest stone, offering a measure of illumination to the passage and suggesting the reflection of a light source further on. Hemple clutched at his shoulder and closed a hand tightly over the reassuring weight. The rosary! He slipped it carefully over his head. His frantic breathing eased. A new confidence grew within. He looked forward and began to move again.

THIRTY-EIGHT

THEY CONTINUED IN SILENCE ALONG THE WIDE CORRIDOR, Johara slightly ahead. The muffled drag of her heavy robes against the stone floor scraped a counterpoint to the faint sound of rushing water that seemed to come from beneath their feet. Every hundred yards or so, they passed smaller cavities in the rock. Chimes, drums and the sound of women's chanting voices issued from most, though the inhabitants remained invisible. The passage led to another, even broader walkway that intersected it at an angle. They turned left at the junction and followed the main artery toward what Carpenter felt sure to be the very center of the mountain.

Eventually the avenue opened onto a large, well-lit cavern with a single portal at the opposite end showing only darkness beyond. Near it, pillows and bedding covered the base of a niche carved into the wall. A broad-chested man of middle age lay stretched and unmoving along its length. His skin was pale and hung rather loose about his neck. Thick, steel-gray hair cropped short framed a high forehead. Large, rugged hands lay clasped as if positioned by someone else atop a blanket too short to cover his feet.

Carpenter stopped and stared. "Is this...?"

"Yes. Your father... or what would be him if he were to awaken."

Carpenter hung back almost as if to approach was to accept some undeserved punishment.

"It's on you now, A-Man. You been looking for a long time. Now you found what you were looking for." Reggie's voice was soft but insistent. Carpenter felt a large hand push at his shoulder. "Go on, man. He don't look too good... and he ain't getting any better while you stand here."

Carpenter stepped forward a few feet. The body shivered slightly beneath its thin cover. Carpenter's eyes widened and he advanced to the side of the shelf that served as a bed. He stood with his arms at his side, unsure of what to do. "Say something, man. He moved when you did. Let him hear your voice. Go ahead, now." Reggie pushed Carpenter gently forward and backed away into a side corridor.

Carpenter swallowed and bent to whisper. "Harry... Harry Wilkins?"

Startling green eyes blinked open. Carpenter froze and stared as if looking into a mirror and seeing some older, future version of himself. A powerful mix of emotions welled up and threatened to overtake his more rational mind. He had thought about this meeting all his life... wished for it, feared it, resented it.

The figure coughed and struggled for a breath. "James?" At first more a croak than a question. Then again, "Is it James... son?"

Relief washed over Carpenter like a cool bath, followed almost immediately by something else. Something less noble, but undeniable.

"James?" Father Harry repeated and turned slightly toward him, grimacing with the effort. "Is that you son? Where am I?"

Anger welled in an unbidden rush despite the frailness of the figure lying before him. Carpenter fought back feelings of betrayal and rejection. Nightmare images crowded his consciousness. Images of fire and struggle and blood. A tall figure crowned with horns stared down at him as he lay bound and helpless on a bed of dry branches. His face felt hot and flushed with old, red rage. He spoke without thinking. "How can you call me son?"

The older man flinched and worked to suppress another deep cough through clenched jaws. Emerald eyes penetrated Carpenter's own, pushed past meager defenses. Harry swallowed and forced words through cracked lips. "Am I back here again, son? You are my son, you know," another slow breath, "... a fact." He turned his head back into his pillow, facing only the rock overhead. "A fact I would never undo... only my own failure as your father."

He strained to turn again toward Carpenter, to look at him directly and without pretense. "I'm sorry, James... for everything. For sending you away. For sacrificing you to my own needs and fears." His chest heaved as if bearing a great weight. A long sigh wheezed through lips pressed tight against something more than pain. He struggled for a breath and pushed on. "I am ashamed, please believe me. I know there is no way to undo what I have done. I wish there were, but there isn't. I'm sorry. I'm no true father. Of course I have no right to call you 'son'." Harry sank back again, exhausted and defeated... but alive.

Carpenter hesitated, then held out his hand. Harry reached for it awkwardly. Their fingers touched briefly and rather formally. Carpenter could feel Johara's presence at his side. Harry showed no sign of recognition. A flood of more complicated emotions rose to mix with Carpenter's initial reaction. Reluctant sympathy for the man whose own shame so engulfed him. Relief to hear an absolution of sorts for the blame he had carried himself for so long. And the hint of another feeling for the man who seemed to love him, however imperfectly. The man and not the idol. The reality and not the dream.

"You're safe, Harry. You're back in these caves... with my mother."

Harry tried to rise to his elbows, excited. "Is she here?"

"You can't see her? She's standing right next to me."

Harry turned his head, eyes casting wildly about, then losing their light. "No. She's still gone... still gone." A look of such anguish came over his face that Carpenter felt moved to lean closer.

"Listen. She's here. Really. Maybe your eyesight is bad. They've been taking care of you. You were shot. Somebody brought you here. They saved your life."

Harry strained against a flood of pain. "Not worth much." He turned his face away. "No good as a husband. No good as a father."

Carpenter tried to respond. "Listen she's here, just take my word for it OK? And look, I... I'm just not used to saying 'father'. I was calling my own dad ... you know, your sister's husband ... by his first name by the time I turned 13."

Harry drew a few short breaths for strength. He spoke looking straight up at the rock overhang above. "It's ironic, you know. Everyone else calls me 'Father Harry' without a second thought." He turned to Carpenter and allowed a shy smile to creep into his eyes. "At least I can see *you*. I can't tell you how happy it makes me, James, no matter what you call me." He struggled again against a deep cough. "I owe you at least an explanation. Not an excuse, an explanation."

He looked around the chamber, aware now of where he was. "I've been here before, you know. It's where you started, where you lived until we lost you... and you lost your parents."

"I *have* parents, Harry." Carpenter felt his resentment rise again. "You took care of that. Your sister is a good mother and my dad is OK too. He's had to deal with an angry teenager for a lot of years."

"Thank God they could take you."

"Why did they have to? What happened? Was it because you were a priest? Is that why you didn't keep me? Was it shame at sin or fear of being caught?" Carpenter tried to keep the blame from his voice, but 'why' hung in the air like a specter that everyone saw but no one acknowledged.

"I guess shame and fear played a part." Harry winced and tried to find a comfortable position. "I'll try to stick to the bare bones. I don't have a lot of energy... or a lot of time."

"You're shot."

"I know. In the chest and back and leg. Don't know how I got here, but if it takes getting shot to get back again, then it's worth it... especially if she's here somewhere."

Harry looked around again, then rested a moment before going on. "That's how we met, you know. After the war, I was helping Chiang and his people, the Nationalists. Worked out of Chun King, but I spent a lot of time across the border here in Burma, where I had been when we were fighting the Japanese. The KMT were in retreat and some ended up here, chased by Mao's soldiers. There were battles and I was hurt."

"But why was a priest fighting at all?"

"Oh! You didn't know? I wasn't a priest... not then. That all happened when I lost your mother."

"Lost her?"

"I'm getting ahead of myself." Harry seemed to be gaining energy as he spoke. He raised up a bit against his pillows. "Here's what happened. I joined up with a new outfit after the war. The OSS. It turned into the CIA later, but it started here. I'd been a soldier in the war, but I stayed on after. I'd learned some languages and, I don't know, I guess I felt comfortable here in a way. But I got shot in a skirmish near here ... would have died then if your mother hadn't rescued me. She brought me here and we... we fell in love."

"She told me. And she got pregnant."

"You talked to her? Where is she now?"

"Right over there. You just can't see her." Johara had retreated from the niche. "She's there, honest."

Harry pushed on. "Yes, she was pregnant, though I didn't know. I don't think she knew either at first."

Johara spoke from the shadows. "Not when he left, not definitely." She sighed, remembering. "But when you were born, James, I wanted your father to see you. And I wanted to see *him*. I knew he remained in the area."

"There was no way I was going to leave without her." Harry looked about him as if he had heard Johara's words. "I was in love and I was going to stay as long as it took to find your mother and marry her and take her back to the States. That, at least, was what I was thinking at the time."

Johara nodded, unseen. "I knew he wouldn't leave me, especially with our child." She sighed deeply again. "So, one night I stole away from the mountain with you bundled up with me. I intended to show you to your father. Perhaps to run away with him." She glanced shyly at Harry. "A young girl's dream."

It was almost as if Harry could hear her now. "Your mother found me, of course. But we were attacked. She ran off making as much noise as she could to distract the enemy. Probably saved both our lives that time. The bravest person I've ever known."

"What happened to me?"

"You were with me. I was holding you when the ambush came. There were a lot of rounds fired and a couple of explosions. I lost your mother in the dark, but I had you." Harry's face darkened as he recalled the event. "We fought them off, but there was no trace of her in the morning. No sign at all and no word from her."

Johara was quiet for a time, pondering a response. "I ran to keep them on my trail, hoping eventually to make it back to the mountain. My mother, the Malka, was a great healer and capable of real miracles."

"But you were OK?"

"I came here," Johara replied simply without elaboration.

"What's that?" Harry asked. "Who are you talking to?"

Carpenter hesitated, unsure how to answer. "I was asking if you were OK."

"I'm much better now, thanks. Seeing you has given me new life, James."

Harry took up the narrative again. "I couldn't find your mother. We weren't out of danger, so I took you to safety in Chun King, then came back to search for her again. Spent weeks at it. I finally accepted that she was gone. I was crazy with grief. I had you, but all I could think of when I held you was her. To tell you the truth, I didn't want to keep on living." Harry stopped for a time, overcome with emotion or fatigue, or both.

"But then a priest in Chun King helped me see things differently. I decided to join up. I wasn't fit to raise you, as far as I could see. I had let your mother down and I was sure I'd do the same with you. So, I wired my sister and you and I both went to the States. I went to seminary and you went to your new family." Harry looked up guiltily. "I didn't tell anyone who you were. But I kept up with you through my sister. I left you, James, and I'm sorry. I couldn't bear to keep you. Couldn't bear my own shame."

Carpenter felt a flood of feeling with each revelation. He sat and listened, unable to speak himself.

Harry rested a few beats then went on. "When I finished seminary, I went to Thailand, to the North, and started making trips into this region as well." He cast a sad smile toward the ceiling. "I guess I always held out some hope that I'd find her some day, somehow." He looked back at Carpenter. "But I didn't. I didn't find her. Still haven't." He swallowed a short burst of pain. "But meanwhile, I've done some good. Helped start schools, clinics."

"There's one in the village below here. They helped a friend who was hurt."

Harry's face was blank for a moment. "I don't think it's near here actually... but who knows? I'm not really sure where I am anyway." He dismissed the confusion and went on. "I've been able to bring medicines and medical supplies to supplement what the people in these caves apparently have been providing all along... training local folks in the healing arts. Your friend was lucky."

"I don't think it was luck," Carpenter smiled at Johara, who nodded her agreement.

Harry pushed himself up on an elbow, stronger. "So, that's the story. I had hoped to tell it to you while you stayed with me in Chiang Rai after we set up the internship. My plan was to make one more trip up here and do some reconnoitering for my old friends in the CIA before you arrived. There's been some Red Guard activity in the area and things are getting a little crazy with Mao's 'Great Proletarian Cultural Revolution' across the border. I told my buddies I'd check with my sources in the area. But I managed to stir up a hornet's nest. We were attacked and you pretty much know the rest."

Harry dropped back down and closed his eyes. "I wanted it to be different, James. I really thought it would be." Carpenter had taken a seat at his side. "I guess I wanted it so bad I fooled myself into thinking I could explain it all to you and make it come out right." He closed his eyes again. "Stupid... and too late."

Carpenter studied the tired face of the one man he had vowed never to forgive – the man he had spent a lifetime hating without ever knowing. He felt something familiar lift from his chest and shoulders. He resisted, clutched at it as if losing a friend. Anger had smoldered and warmed him like a winter's fire for as long as he could remember. He clung to it for a moment longer, then let it go. He reached for Harry's hand and covered it with his own.

"Yeah, pretty stupid." He squeezed the hand. "But not too late, Father... Harry. Not too late."

Indra's Net

THIRTY-NINE

THE LIGHT GREW BRIGHTER AS HE PROCEEDED. Whether it was a reflection or something else didn't matter to Hemple. It was light. An answer to his prayers. He continued leading the way for another hundred yards. The cleft opened gradually to allow easier passage. He was able to walk facing forward. His anxiety eased another tick. Rounding a turn, he could see an opening ahead. "We've made it! I can see a way out!" Hemple couldn't keep a note of triumph from his voice despite the circumstance.

"Well done, Paul. I knew you were the one to lead us." Phi Rak pushed Meng Ti roughly forward. "Move on, you oaf. It's close in here."

The notch was narrow but negotiable. Hemple climbed through and waited for the others. Somchai followed quickly. Kohein backed out holding Kumar's arms to help him through, then Brother Joe, both hands under Kumar's shoulders. Meng Ti emerged, jaws knotted in anger. Phi Rak slipped out as easily as a ballet dancer despite his height, white dress somehow unsullied. They were in a broad corridor of deeply carved and richly veined stone. Wall torches added to the ambient glow from some other, indirect source of light. Phi Rak commanded silence. From somewhere ahead, voices rebounded faintly along the rock walls mixed with the subterranean sound of rushing water.

Phi Rak bent to the side of the passage to examine its marbled surface. He stood, eyes lit with delight. "Well, this appears to have been worth the effort, eh? Shall we proceed?" He shooed the others along with an impatient flutter of skeletal fingers. "Wait!" The group halted at the order. "We should mark the way back to this spot." Phi Rak turned toward the opening in the wall through which they had just emerged. The etched surface stood blank.

"*Hai pai nai wa?*" Where is it? The boxer's voice quavered slightly as he pushed his way to Phi Rak. He ran his hands along the wall searching for what clearly was not there. "*Mae, phi lok!*" Haunted. He stepped away from the wall and seemed to shrink into himself.

"Nonsense. A simple illusion of some kind." A worried frown passed quickly across Phi Rak's face before he shoved the boxer forward. "Let's move!"

They paused at a junction where another corridor joined on the left. Phi Rak started to order the boxer to scout it before continuing, but spoke instead to Meng Ti who disappeared briefly into the passage and returned to declare it empty.

"Do you hear the chanting?" Brother Joe whispered to Kohein and Kumar.

Both nodded.

"I don't think they hear it." Joe pointed with a forefinger pressed against his stomach to conceal the gesture. "This is weird."

The way before them seemed to lead further into the mountain before widening into a large chamber with several smaller corridors off to either side and a much larger opening at the far end. Carpenter sat near it in a niche in the rock next to an older man who lay among a heap of blankets. "James! Harry!" Brother Joe began to rush forward but stopped abruptly as Phi Rak's voice echoed from the stone.

"Far enough! Let's be sure it's safe before we venture any further, shall we?" Phi Rak's pistol prodded Brother Joe's back. "James! What a surprise to find you in such an odd place. I hope you won't mind our intrusion?" Carpenter rose abruptly from where he sat next to his father and started forward. "Uh, uh! Careful now. It would be a shame to see anyone hurt, wouldn't it?" Phi Rak retreated a step, turning the automatic toward Carpenter then back again toward Brother Joe. "Not to mention the unpleasant boom a gunshot would make in these stately surroundings."

Carpenter stopped, fists clenched at his side. "What do you want here?"

"Oh, just a small portion of this exquisite wealth." Phi Rak opened his arms wide to take in the ceiling and walls. "And, of course, directions to the exit."

"It would be wise to exit now." Johara's voice emanated from just beyond the large opening, calm and barely audible.

"Ah! And who is this" Phi Rak squinted into the darkness beyond the gap. "James failed to mention other company."

"I am of this place." Johara's voice sounded from just beyond the chamber.

"A native! Excellent. Do show yourself." Nothing stirred. "As you wish, but your assistance will be much appreciated once we finish our business here.

We don't plan to stay long. Just long enough to harvest some of the mineral riches that are so clearly abundant here."

"It is not safe for you here." The voice echoed from the dark. Somchai, edging away, brushed against Phi Rak, only to be pushed violently back toward the voice.

Phi Rak called out dismissively. "So we've been told." His gaze searched the surroundings. "But you see, there is the matter of my fee."

"Your fee."

"Yes, for my time and effort, you see. A generous sampling of various gems will do. Conveniently packaged for transport by my associates here, of course."

Brother Joe spun around to face Phi Rak, a vein pulsing prominently on his forehead. "I'm not your associate, you freak! None of us are!"

Phi Rak's response was immediate and blindingly fast. The pistol whipped twice across Brother Joe's face before he could fall. Phi Rak raised naked brows and addressed the others. "Are there any further comments before we proceed?" He waited politely. "I thought not." He danced lightly across Brother Joe's twisting form and tapped Meng Ti's shoulder. "Perhaps you would be so kind as to investigate that area before we continue?" Phi Rak gestured toward the opening that seemed the source of Johara 's voice. "Find our mystery woman." His eyes swept the chamber again. "The outsized soldier doesn't seem to be here, nor does the little bearded one. Find them, too." Meng Ti unshouldered his rifle and held it before him like a lantern as he exited into the blackness beyond the opening.

Phi Rak looked to Father Harry. "So you must be the famous hand of the Lord, the scourge of communists and heathens alike ... a pleasure. You may call me Brother Love. I am something of a professional colleague, really. I too am in the business of saving souls." Brother Love covered the smile on his lips with a free hand, "...or at least redistributing them according to their fair market value."

"I'm Harry. I've heard of you. So, apparently there are much worse things in this world than communists and heathens. I'd take either, frankly... over you."

Phi Rak's face folded into a pout that mutated quickly to a mask of pretended outrage. The game clearly had its appeal. "And you a priest of the one true faith...tsk, tsk." Phi Rak turned to Hemple with a look of deepest shock. "What do you say to that, Paul? To hear you speak, this Father Harry is something of a saint. Surely he can't approve of the Godless Reds or the ignorant savages?"

Hemple took the bait. "He is a patriot and a man of faith." Hemple approached Harry's bed. "Paul Hemple, Father. I've been looking forward to meeting you for a long time."

Harry stifled a weak cough. "Pleased to meet you."

"Thank you for your letter. It's what brought me here. I hope we still will have a chance to work together someday. There aren't many in this part of the world with your stature or your faith."

Harry searched Hemple's earnest face for a moment, then closed his eyes to summon energy for a reply. "Paul... may I call you Paul?"

"Of course."

"I appreciate your enthusiasm, but I'm not feeling so special right now. Just hanging on to whatever scraps of life and faith I can."

Hemple was confused. "But you have to have faith in God ... and His Church."

"Oh, I have plenty of faith in God. I just hope He has some left in me." Harry grimaced with a spasm of pain. "But to tell you the truth, son, I don't really have what I'd call 'faith' in the Church. I just work for her. She's as flawed as the rest of us."

Hemple reddened. "Excuse me, Father, but that borders on blasphemy." He reached inside his shirt and withdrew the rosary. "Isn't this yours? I know you pray the rosary."

Harry blanched. "Where did you get that?" He struggled for a breath. "Never mind, I know where. What are you doing with it?"

Hemple straightened, offended. "I was protecting it! Saving it for you!"

Harry shook his head wearily. "Then I guess I should thank you. But it isn't mine. I was just keeping it for someone else. It belongs here."

"How utterly fascinating! It's rather sad that we don't have time for the complete story." Phi Rak stepped forward holding the .45 before him. "But I'll have the necklace and thank you both for keeping it for *me*."

Hemple drew back and doubled his hands protectively across the rosary at his chest. "It's *not* yours! Don't even touch it!"

Phi Rak pressed the gun barrel against the side of Hemple's head. "But I do claim it, you see. Not for some abstract purpose, but simply because I want it." He eased the weapon away to allow Hemple to remove the rosary, then fingered the beads lovingly one by one. "My own motive is pure and uncomplicated by theology." He took a step back and placed the rosary around his own neck.

Meng Ti's entrance ended the exchange. He strode over to Phi Rak and whispered his report. Phi Rak's brows arched in surprise. "There seems to be an extensive complex of tunnels and chambers just beyond this opening... as well as a dark and sizeable hole in the ground." He stepped toward the opening and called into the dark. "We can't see you, whoever you are. But perhaps you can direct us to whatever passage leads to the space you have set aside for the treasure accumulated in your most ambitious excavations."

"You mistake stone for treasure."

Phi Rak continued unperturbed. "Yes, perhaps so. But I beg your indulgence, nonetheless. For one who seems to value people over mere stone, my request should be an easy one for you." He trained the automatic on Carpenter. "I can't see you, but apparently you can see me. Do you see this?" he cocked the weapon. "I will offer you a simple choice. Either you show me where your precious rubble is stored, or we will begin to offer sacrifices to whatever gods may dwell in this place."

Phi Rak swung the gun over to Harry and gestured with it toward the chamber's opening. "James, would you be so kind as to help that poor man from this room so that he may prepare himself as our first offering? And Kohein, help the dwarf." He nodded toward Brother Joe, who sat on the floor rubbing his temples.

An answer rebounded from the dark. "You will receive what you ask. Follow me." The sound of steps rang out against the stone.

"Excellent. My assistant will accompany you." Phi Rak jerked his chin in the direction of the receding steps. Somchai shrank back. Phi Rak aimed at his head, then moved the gun slightly to the right and fired. Splinters of rock burst from the wall next to the boxer's frightened face as a violent boom bounced through the hollow space. Somchai threw a wild glance at Phi Rak, unholstered his own firearm and rushed through the opening.

Phi Rak called after in mock falsetto, "Ta, ta! We will await you both near the sacrificial pit! Don't be long - we may become impatient!" He waved the others toward the opening and barked a terse order to Carpenter, "Carry the priest if he can't walk, James. We'll put him out of his misery soon enough."

Carpenter offered Harry a hand, but the older man could not stand. Carpenter gathered him in his arms and carried him like a child from the chamber. "I won't let anything happen to you," he whispered as he moved through the opening and into the much larger space beyond.

The sight was dramatic. The cavern was huge and circular and unlit. Dark seemed to exude from a great open crater in the center more than fifty yards across and deep enough to appear bottomless. The ceiling rounded and disappeared into gloom high above. A lip perhaps six feet wide extended around the entire circumference of the cavity, quartered precisely by four broad streams that poured over the side in opposing cascades of white water. The nearest emerged from the rock less than twenty feet to the right. At least a dozen tunnels opened onto the lip at regular intervals, each outlined in dim radiance from somewhere deep inside.

Phi Rak ushered the captives to the edge of the depression. "Please make yourselves comfortable, gentlemen, while we wait. Sit. Let your legs dangle with your backs toward me." Phi Rak and Meng Ti stood near the wall at a safe distance.

Time passed slowly. A quarter hour went by, and another. Phi Rak began to pace. "I will not wait forever, woman!" His voice rose and echoed through the hollow space. "I know you can hear me! Do not try my patience!" He turned to Meng Ti. "Check the entries to these tunnels. Listen for sounds of activity. See if you can tell where they went." When the smaller man hesitated, Phi Rak swung the gun in his direction. "Do you have a question?" Without answering, Meng Ti spun to obey, eyes burning resentment.

They waited in an eerie silence broken only by the sound of water rushing into the pit and the occasional swell of chanting or crystal chimes. These latter elements seemed to go unnoticed by Phi Rak, who strode up and down along the lip of the cavern fingering the rosary beads at his throat and muttering to himself. Meng Ti's return offered only a moment's break in the tension. He had listened at each tunnel entrance and called for Somchai. There had been no response.

"Enough!" Phi Rak's voice boomed and echoed from the stone walls. "You trifle with the lives of those you seem to hold most dear. Perhaps they mean nothing to you?" He cocked an ear to the darkness, listening for a response, then shouted a challenge, "So, you choose death for the priest? So be it!" Phi Rak approached the edge of the pit. "Stand up, James. You will be our executioner."

Carpenter rose slowly and turned to face Phi Rak, the muscles of his lower legs tightly coiled and ready. Harry lay a few feet from the edge, his shallow breathing rasping a counterpoint to the roar of the falls. Phi Rak raised his weapon. "Pick up the priest and hold him over the edge. If anyone is watching, I want them to be sure of what is about to happen."

"No." Carpenter's reply was flat and clear.

"No? Did I hear you correctly?" Phi Rak's attempt at an amused smile twisted into an ugly grimace. "You do understand, do you not, that I can just as easily have you take the priest's place?" He jacked a round into the pistol chamber for emphasis.

Carpenter stood his ground. The others now were on their feet and spreading quietly apart. "It ends here. You can shoot me. But I'm not sure you can shoot us all." He looked to each side, then back at Phi Rak in challenge.

Phi Rak extended the pistol toward Carpenter. "Sorry, my dear, but I believe I can. And I will, if you hesitate a moment longer." His lashless eyes narrowed to black slits. "Do as I say!"

Without a word and apparently without fear, Kumar stepped in front of Carpenter and advanced slowly toward Phi Rak. "It is a shame, you know, that a man of your intelligence uses it so rarely." He slowed to whisper as he passed Brother Joe. "Do not mourn for me, my friend. It is my time." He continued on, looking directly at Phi Rak, his face betraying little emotion beyond a sort of nervous dignity as he walked. "You really have placed yourself in a most vulnerable position."

Phi Rak's next move ignited a flurry of action. With Kumar only a few feet away and the others beginning to mill closer, he raised the pistol and fired. The shot boomed through the cavern. Kumar dropped immediately to the ground and lay still. The others stood unmoving for a moment more.

Brother Joe and Kohein broke the tableau and rushed to kneel next to Kumar. Carpenter stepped forward and with snake-like speed kicked the weapon from Phi Rak's hand and into the pit. It clattered and careened off the rock as it fell. Phi Rak shrank back and called to Meng Ti who rolled Harry roughly toward the pit with his feet. Carpenter swung away from Phi Rak, dropped Meng Ti with a vicious blow to the back of his knees and kicked his weapon too over the edge. Before he could turn to face Phi Rak again, Carpenter felt the taller man's long fingers push against the small of his back.

Carpenter fought for balance but could not recover before he was propelled over the edge. He fell only a short distance before striking a rock outcropping some eight feet below. Stretched out on his stomach, Carpenter stared down into blackness, his chest tingling with the adrenaline rush of fear and anger. He pushed himself to his feet and sought a way up the face of the rock, but found no immediate purchase.

Above, the melee continued. Phi Rak moved quickly to the edge to gloat over Carpenter's demise, taking little note of Harry sprawled nearby. Stepping back, Phi Rak felt legs and arms tangle in his feet as Harry grunted with the effort to bring him down. Phi Rak bent to strike the priest. The rosary slipped over his head, across Harry's torso and began to drop over the edge. Phi Rak rescued it with one hand, the other clamped to Harry's throat.

The priest's breathing slowed and his grip weakened. Phi Rak stood and pushed the priest toward the drop with one long leg. Harry hung on the rim struggling to right himself, then seemed to surrender. He looked down into the gloom. His eyes met Carpenter's and locked for an instant on his son's face. Harry spoke, but the words were lost as he hurtled past Carpenter's outstretched arms and into the void below.

A delighted smile began to spread across Phi Rak's face as he watched from higher up. The rosary hanging loose from one hand suddenly went taut and the smile disappeared. Phi Rak clutched the central gem reflexively and jerked. Another hand gripped the jade beads at the other end. Phi Rak looked up to see Hemple's face set in grim determination.

"This is Father's! You won't have it!" Hemple wrapped his free arm around Phi Rak's chest and struggled to throw him to the ground. The scuffle stirred up a cloud of dust and sent a shower of pebbles rattling into the pit. Hemple, showing surprising strength, seemed to be gaining an advantage when Phi Rak swiveled his hips and sent Hemple over the edge. But Hemple's grip on the beads held fast. Phi Rak teetered on the brink, then lost his balance and slid feet-first over the edge of the pit, joined to Hemple by his own stubborn hold on the rosary's central stone. The two hung suspended over the abyss linked by the rosary and supported only by Phi Rak's desperate, one-handed grasp of the rim.

Neither spoke. Phi Rak grunted with the effort to hold on above and below. He managed to gasp an order to Meng Ti. "Quick, you idiot! Grab hold!" Meng Ti stood unmoving only a few feet away. Phi Rak repeated his command. "Now! I'm losing it!"

"Hold on!" The shout came from within the nearest chamber. Reggie flew from the entrance like a man possessed. Disregarding Meng Ti, he slid on his belly to the cliff's edge and reached a thick arm down toward Hemple. "Grab on! Fast, man! He's about to go!"

Hemple clutched the rosary with both hands, eyes shut tight in fear or prayer or both. "Paul! You got to grab my hand! Right now!" Hemple seemed to recognize the voice and opened his eyes to stare up into Reggie's face.

He hung frozen, eyes wide in terror, then let loose of the rosary with one hand to reach frantically for Reggie's. "Reggie?" He managed to utter the big man's name once before the rosary chain broke. Beads scattered and ticked against the cliff side like some frenzied form of Morse code. Hemple's scream seemed to rush up briefly before following him into the depths.

Phi Rak whipped his newly freed hand to the cliff edge, spilling the rosary gem on the verge. "Here, take this. Now hurry and pull me up!" Meng Ti slowly bent to retrieve the stone before stepping forward. "Finally!" Phi Rak hissed. "What have you been waiting for?" Meng Ti edged closer and stared down at Phi Rak's upturned face. He watched his pale master strain. A short laugh burst from his lips as he raised a booted heel and brought it down with crushing force on the boney fingers... once, twice, three times... mashing them into the stone. Phi Rak shrieked and disappeared into the shadows.

Reggie sprang up and looked wildly around. "JC! Where are you, man? JC! Talk to me!"

"Down here, Reg!"

Reggie glanced at Meng Ti who stood immobile, staring down into the pit. He moved quickly past Brother Joe and Kohein where they knelt next to Kumar and sprawled to pull Carpenter up. "You OK?"

Carpenter stood brushing at his shirt and jeans. "Just a few bumps. There's a ledge. I could pretty much see everything from there, but I couldn't get back up." Carpenter tried to continue, but stopped. He squeezed his eyes shut. Reggie glanced nervously over his shoulder at Meng Ti, who had not moved.

"He's gone, right? Your father?" Reggie clutched Carpenter's shoulder.

"Yeah, he's gone." Carpenter looked up. "I tried to save him, you know. And he tried to save me." Carpenter shivered as if just remembering. "And Kumar started the whole thing. He wasn't afraid."

"Yeah, well, he didn't make it." Reggie gestured behind him to where Kumar lay curled on the ground. "He's gone too." Reggie stared for a moment at the still figure and the two men kneeling nearby, then roused himself. "But we still need to save ourselves, if you know what I mean." He turned to face Meng Ti. "He's still here, though he did take care of Brother Love. And there may be others somewhere."

"Just the boxer. He went after Johara… followed her voice. They haven't come back."

"OK. So let's finish this." Reggie took a few steps to the side before starting toward Meng Ti. "Hey, slick! Look over here! Toss me your knife… I know you have it somewhere." Meng Ti looked confused. He brought his right hand to his face and opened it to gaze at the stone that glowed now in his palm. His brows knitted together in a mixture of fear and delight.

"That's Harry's… and my mother's." Carpenter stepped forward in challenge. Meng Ti closed his hand tightly over the gem and backed away. Carpenter leapt. Meng Ti ducked to snatch at his boot. The stone dropped to the ground and rolled to a stop at Kohein's side. Meng Ti rose, knife in hand, but unsure whether to advance or retreat.

Kohein lifted the jewel to eye level. Its dull blue glimmer illuminated the whites of Kohein's eyes and cast a sheen across his features. "My God! Such a treasure." Kohein lowered his hands slightly to look around at his friends. "This is beyond all value." He drew the gem close again, eyes widening at its growing luster. "We cannot let this be lost!"

"Nothing is truly lost." The voice seemed to rise from the crater's depths. "A thing may be lost only to one who believes he possesses it."

Kohein lowered the jewel and searched the shade. "Where are you?"

"Here, nowhere, everywhere." The response reverberated melodically through the chamber and twined in harmony with the soft swirl of song and crystal tune.

"Mother? Johara?" Carpenter looked around him almost frantically. "Are you there? Have you returned?"

"I have never truly left you, my son. Though my time here now is past."

Kohein closed the gem tightly in his hands. "What would you have me do?"

"The gem is for the *terton*, who holds its partner."

Kohein slowly, reluctantly, released his grip on the stone and looked to Carpenter. "That must be you, James." The jewel glittered, lit from within. Kohein cupped it carefully in his palms and held it out to Carpenter like a sacred offering. Meng Ti started forward but stopped immediately as Reggie blocked the way, his own black blade a mute warning against further movement.

Carpenter reached into a pocket and withdrew the parchment piece. Kohein laid the stone across its yellowed surface as if performing some understood ritual. Carpenter stood and waited. The gem spread a weak glow across the parchment. Nothing else happened. Carpenter moved his open hand up and down and to either side. Still nothing. He picked up the gem and rubbed it across the parchment without success. "There must be some secret to this," he said almost to himself. He squinted at the dull markings on the hide, trying to read them or at least to decipher a letter. "I can't do this." Carpenter shook his head in defeat. "Either I'm not the right person or I can't figure out the puzzle. I'm sorry."

"You are the *terton*. You hold the key." Johara's voice echoed through the chamber.

Carpenter tried again to elicit a reaction from the gem and the parchment. He switched them between hands, dropped one then the other and picked them up again in different order. Still nothing. Carpenter looked at his friends. "I'm sorry. I can't think of anything else to do. We may need to find our own way out of here… unless we get help." He shook his head slowly. "I'm done trying to make sense of this. At least I found my father. At least we found each other." He searched the shadows for a sign. "And you, mother! Can you hear me? You have the only magic here! I'm nothing special … I'm just another person!"

There was no answer from the still darkness. Carpenter closed his eyes briefly in disappointment and breathed a deep sigh. "These obviously don't belong to me. They belong here." He looked an apology to his friends and tossed the gem and parchment into the pit.

Neither fell. Instead, both spun weightless to the center of the rift and hung suspended high over the abyss. The parchment spread itself slowly beneath the gem whose radiance bloomed and deepened. The cavern began to fill with light.

For the first time, the ceiling became visible, its curved surface alive with detailed paintings of animals and gods, angels and devils rendered in a broad spectrum of rich color. Crystal points of light dripped from veins of silver to reflect the brilliance of the central stone where rays of impossible luminosity began to multiply and extend in all directions. Along each radiant beam, smaller replicas of the central gem appeared to reflect its luster and that of its sisters and brothers in infinite profusion. Diamond brilliance danced back and forth between the jeweled nodes to give the whole the appearance of constant shimmering movement. The walls and ceiling of the cavern seemed to drop away as gem-like cells articulated themselves along the length of each golden ray. A symphony of pure and crystal sound spread through space like the music of creation itself.

The parchment shone golden. Its dull markings deepened to coal black, then to silver. Script began to flow from the hide surface out over the void in a stream of language and song. Letters flowed along luminescent strands of light in a host of tongues - Hebrew, Sanskrit, Pali, Chinese, Aramaic, Arabic, Tibetan and a hundred more – each written on the air and sung by an unseen chorus. Verses from the Torah, the Avesta, the Rig Veda, the Pali canon, the Tao Te Ching, the New Testament, the Qu'ran, all blended in a single celestial voice that transcended literal meaning and rippled across the filaments of light in waves of revelation beyond words.

"The Net reveals itself." Johara's voice rose joyful above it all.

Each man had fallen to his knees, quaking in some mixture of fear and reverence. Near the cliff edge, Meng Ti rocked back and forth, hands clasped prayer-like in supplication or remorse. The luminous glow of the jeweled net cleared to near transparency. Faces, scenes and events flashed along its vast surface like dreams or memories made manifest in holographic detail.

A sacrifice on a hilltop in fire and blood. The fall of the Temple and the sack of Jerusalem. A battle on the field of Jericho… a king's defeat and punishment. A massacre at the Persian Gate. Peace and contemplation in Persepolis followed by fire, destruction and death. Bloody war to win an empire and religion to salve the wounds. Loss of family, of wife and children. Retreat from a cruel and painful world. Re-entry. Innocence and innocence lost repeated through a hundred epochs. Change, rejection, growth, acceptance, evolution. Again and again and again. Carpenter watched, both actor and audience, fascinated and repulsed, proud and ashamed.

The Net told every tale, every experience, every changing reality shaped by the past and poised to create a new future. Beside him, Reggie cringed at the sight of the fallen at Jericho and the torture that followed. Three figures walked a muddy jungle road. Reggie called out to his father and grandfather and, finally, to his brother Ricky. He swore and wept and laughed to see them all. Kohein watched a plump priest linger too long at an altar while soldiers threatened just beyond temple doors. He cast an apologetic glance at Carpenter before bowing his head in prayerful meditation. Brother Joe knelt beside Kumar's body and stared in wide-eyed wonder as his mirror image knelt in ancient military garb beside the silent form of another beloved teacher.

Before them all, Meng Ti cried out in pain and stood shaking his head in terrified rejection, hands held protectively to shield his face. He spun as if to run, then turned slowly to face the vision. He stood straight as a soldier, arms at his side. A calm came over his face. He bowed slightly as if acknowledging a greeting and stepped from the edge of the cliff and into the void.

The images reflected in the Net shrank and coalesced into a three-dimensional web of silver light that vibrated in harmony with the rise and fall of sound and pulsed in cadence with Johara's voice. "The *terma* have revealed their treasure. We are delivered from the traps we have woven for ourselves from the fabric of our beliefs and expectations and pain."

Johara appeared shimmering in the center of the web, arms spread wide. Father Harry materialized at her side, Kumar at the other. All along the radiant strands of the Net, chanting figures emerged linked together by light and by touch. Men and women, young and old, of every race absorbed by the tribe in its centuries of wandering. An amazed Hemple appeared, eyes casting wildly around in a mixture of alarm and recognition as Harry reached out to pull him close. Johara turned to lay a gentle hand on his trembling shoulder, then back again to address the others. "We thank you. All of us." A flood of affection swept through Carpenter, who could only respond with a gulp and a nod.

The montage blurred at the edges. Phi Rak's angry face flashed forth from jeweled points at the perimeter. Meng Ti, bent in anguish, advanced and retreated among a host of new and disturbing reflections that jerked and twitched like puppets along spokes of electric light. Carpenter managed to speak. "But we defeated Phi Rak! How can he survive to share the Net with you?" Anger crept into his voice. "He killed Kumar! He is nothing but evil."

"He ended my time, James. Nothing more, nothing less." Kumar looked down to Brother Joe. "Know this my friend and be at peace." His familiar voice gentled and soothed. His hands opened to include everything around him. "This is all of Creation, James. All of it. Not simply what we want or hope for... but what is."

"But it should be perfect! Like God or heaven, right? What about goodness and justice and mercy? What about victory in the end?"

Kumar's smile was both kind and sad. "There is no end, James, and no beginning. There is only becoming. Even God is becoming, you see. Creation is... well, creating. It evolves point by point, moment by moment. It is the sum of our choices, James... good and bad, right and wrong and in between. This is the terrible, wonderful reality. We are linked, all of us, to everything. We create the future ourselves as does every other atom of Being. Heaven or hell, these are simply aspects of experience. They are what we make them. Everything is."

The silence was broken only by the sound of chanting and chimes and the rush of water into the chasm. A slight tremor shuddered through the rock floor. Dangling crystals clashed and tinkled dissonance overhead. "Time is short. You must leave now... as must we. This space will close." Johara's voice rang through the chamber as the Net began to pulsate.

"But we've only just met, finally. There's so much I want to know... about you, about Harry... about myself." Carpenter pleaded, knowing even as he spoke that the effort was futile.

"We have met many times, my son. We will again. But now is not that time." Johara's tone took on a note of command. "Now you must leave or give up this portion of your journey... and that of your friends'."

"Go ahead, James. Like Kumar said, we're linked. We can create our own future in spite of the past. This is not the end for us, son. I thank you for that.... I love you." Harry's figure throbbed and began to fade.

"There is a passage just below the stream to your right, below where it empties into the chasm beneath us." Johara looked down into the darkness. "You may reach it from the ledge where you fell, James. There are steps carved from the cliff wall. Take them to the opening beneath the falls. There will be a watercourse. Follow it. Do not turn back."

The radiating spokes of the Net began to turn slowly about the center, a giant spider's web of light, a wheel within a wheel within a wheel. Johara's figure and the images of all around thinned to haze. "Do not turn back," her voice repeated as the web spun faster and faster and finally blinked out leaving only the dark and the sound of rushing water. What had started as a quiver became a quake. The ground below their feet shifted and buckled. Stalactites dropped from above to shatter against the side of the pit or drop soundlessly into its depths. Carpenter stood staring into the air above the depression.

"We gotta go, A-Man." Reggie nudged him with a forearm and pushed him toward the rim. "We *really* gotta go!"

Carpenter shook himself. Kohein and Brother Joe stepped to his side. "How about Kumar's body?" He looked around the empty space.

"Gone, James." Brother Joe smiled up at him, a firm grasp on his upper arm. "He's gone, but not really, you know?" Brother Joe gave a gentle tug. "Reggie's right. It's time to get out of here." A large crystal shattered at their feet, shards bouncing painfully against their legs. "Maybe even past time..."

They dived for the rim and scrambled for the steps in the stone.

FORTY

REGGIE LAY FLAT HELPING EACH MAN DESCEND THE CLIFF EDGE TO THE OUT-CROPPING BELOW. When all were safely down, he swung easily over the rim to land next to Carpenter. "OK, now what?"

Carpenter bent to search the cliffside with his hands. "Here! There are steps! Hugging the cliff wall, he extended his left foot out and onto a slender file of small extrusions that graduated down to and under the near falls. He moved carefully along the stretch of stone, dropping to a small ledge just below the cascade. Overhead, the stream gushed into the abyss. He waited as the others joined him.

A dark gap in the rock opened just below the falls. "This must be it... the exit." He leaned to view the interior and withdrew his head. "It's completely black. Can't see a thing." A deep rumble shook the cavern and shards of stone broke away from the ledge where they stood.

"Doesn't really matter at this point." Brother Joe stood closest to the edge. "I say, go." A cascade of rock dropped away from the roof and plunged into the pit. Without a word, Reggie pushed past Carpenter and into the notch. Carpenter followed, then Kohein. Brother Joe, nervous hands on Kohein's shoulders, slipped through last just as the ledge itself dropped away.

They huddled in inky blackness. Reggie barked a quick order. "Stay in line and keep moving. There's no going back now." He reached overhead and to the sides to touch the rock. "This isn't very big. Keep low. I can't see where it goes or how high it is."

They moved blindly through the narrow passage, hands trailing along the sides and ceiling to feel their way. The tunnel was smooth to the touch, but low and close. Occasional tremors ran through the rock, causing them to pause now and then to steady themselves. They proceeded for a hundred yards before Reggie stopped them. "OK. I hear water ahead and the tunnel is getting shorter." Reggie took a deep breath. "JC, I need you to take the lead here. I'm starting to freak."

Carpenter squeezed past the bigger man and moved forward in a crouch. Within a minute, he was forced to a crawl. He had crept only a few feet more on hands and knees when the floor seemed to disappear. "Hold it! There's a gap here!" The sound of rushing water filled the cavity. Carpenter stretched onto his stomach and reached down only to withdraw his hand and forearm dripping wet. "There's a break in the path. The tunnel drops about three feet into a stream. A fast stream." He felt along the sides and ceiling. "Everything feels smooth, but it's slippery... probably too slippery to crawl through."

The rock quaked again and a low rumble shook the small space. "We don't have a lot of choices here, James!" Brother Joe called from the rear.

Reggie grunted through clenched teeth. " I can't move, A-Man. Feel like I'm stuck. Can't see... can't breathe."

The passage was too narrow to turn in. Carpenter spoke as calmly as he could manage. "We gotta move forward, Reg. We can't go back and we can't stay here." Another rumble coursed through the rock as if to underscore his last words.

"I know, I know," Reggie muttered, trying to convince himself. "It's tight spaces like this. Makes me feel blind. It's closing in... "

Kohein had been silent throughout, but spoke now with gentle authority. "I completely understand. I too am claustrophobic. But I have a way to deal with it... a fool-proof method."

"Better tell me quick."

"Since you can't see anyway, just close your eyes. Join me. I am in an open field. A fresh clean wind is blowing in my face. The sun is bright and clear."

"Clean wind, bright sun. What else you got?"

"Now make that your mantra. Say it over and over. Block everything else from your mind." Kohein's voice was calm and reassuring. "Clean wind, bright sun. Clean wind, bright sun. Those are your only words and your only thoughts. They are what you see and what you feel."

Reggie repeated the phrase out loud. "Clean wind, bright sun..."

"Alright, James. This would be an opportune moment to cast our fate to the wind... the 'clean' wind, so to speak."

"Go for it!" Brother Joe's voice was sharp and urgent.

"I'm ready," Reggie added.

Carpenter felt his way over the drop, hands pressed against ceiling and walls, feet plunged to his knees in water. He took a step, then another before slipping helplessly onto his backside and into the rushing stream. A startled cry escaped his lips as he slid along the smooth floor with the torrent, grabbing uselessly at slick ceiling and walls and gaining speed as he descended with the flow. Tepid water drenched his legs and back and washed over his stomach to bathe him completely in an oddly comforting warmth. He laid back to avoid colliding with the roof as the canal narrowed. Behind him, a sequence of startled shouts announced each man's parallel experience. A final epithet echoed against the solid walls as Brother Joe took a seat in the flood to follow his companions.

The incline was gradual at first. Carpenter slid swiftly through the dark trying and failing to stop his body's progress. His emotions swung between claustrophobic terror and giddy elation. Behind him one or another of his companions echoed his own feelings with cries of terror alternating with high-pitched squeals of something like laughter.

The slope steepened and he picked up speed. Fear overcame all other feelings. In the close blackness, he could not gauge his pace. He felt as if his body would be shattered at any moment against solid rock. Instead, the pressure of his back against the smooth stone disappeared suddenly and he was catapulted outward into nothingness. He felt himself drop and looked up into a night sky. Before panic could overwhelm him, he plunged feet first into deep water and sank well over his head. His feet touched muddy bottom. He pushed off, uncertain of where he was or even if he was badly hurt. His head burst from the surface and he gulped sweet air.

Reggie surfaced next to him, clawing at the water. Then Kohein appeared, then Brother Joe. Each man's expression showed a mixture of confusion and relief. Brother Joe was the first to speak. "Where the hell are we?"

Kohein expelled a deep sigh. "I have no idea. But we do seem to have rejoined the great river of life."

"The Mekong, in fact." Reggie's breathing had begun to return to normal as he tread water. "We're in the cove where we landed. Check it out." The cliff face revealed itself in silhouette against a blue-black sky. Behind them, the waterfall shone white as it plunged noisily into the water.

"So we're not dead, right?" Brother Joe's question seemed genuine.

"Hard to say, but I don't think so." Reggie looked toward the shore. "But I might drown if we stay here too much longer." He started toward the river-bank with a few long powerful strokes. The others followed close behind.

The sound of rapid feet pounding on earth greeted them as they made the shore. Hajee burst from the shadows and ran nearly frantic to the bank where they lay exhausted. He went immediately to Kohein and cupped his hands around the older man's face as if to reassure himself. He looked around to the others with an expression of delight writ large on his dark face. He spoke rapidly and with an uncharacteristic animation.

"He says he thought we were dead. He's been watching us from inside the mountain... watched us until we disappeared into that 'escape' hatch Johara directed us to." Kohein translated without rising from where he lay.

"He was inside too? Where was he?" Carpenter sat up.

Hajee spoke at some length, before Kohein held up a hand to stop the flow. "He followed us inside and stayed out of sight looking for a way to help. When Somchai followed Johara, he went along too. He took a separate passage that ended up connecting with the one they took. He could see Johara fine, by the way. She kept making turns and calling out to Somchai. He got quite agitated." Kohein conferred briefly with Hajee, then continued. "Hajee saw her simply disappear somewhere deep in the labyrinth. Disappear as in 'into thin air'. I would not credit that description had we not already witnessed scenes equally beyond belief. When Johara vanished, her voice just stopped. Somchai, as you say, 'lost it'. Hajee made his way out through his original entry point when the trembling began. He left Somchai wandering the passageways. Hajee seems to feel that was an acceptable outcome."

Hajee pointed over Kohein's head to a point above the cove and its cliff. Kohein listened and explained. "He has been waiting for us, hoping we would make it out as well. He apparently thought we had not until he heard my rather distinctive cry of terror as I shot out from the falls and into the cove. He has a fire made where we can dry out and rest until morning. He cautions, however, not to be shocked at what we see."

"As if anything could ever shock me again," Brother Joe blurted.

They followed Hajee along the path and up the hill to the bluff overlooking the village on one side and the river on the other. They stopped and stood at the top of the incline. The mountain was gone. In its place a rounded hill rose perhaps another 500 feet to match the outlines of its neighbors. Bright stars dotted the sky where there had once been an imposing edifice of stone. Below to the left, darkness occupied the area that should have been lit with village fires. It too was gone.

"So, was this whole thing some kind of mass hallucination?" Before anyone could reply, Reggie simply added, "Never mind. Don't even try…"

Hajee's fire offered a measure of light as they gathered grasses and fronds for bedding. Before they lay themselves down, each man clasped the other's shoulders as if to verify by touch the reality of an unreal experience… as if, indeed, to confirm their own existence.

Carpenter lay down next to Reggie. "What now?"

"What now? A-Man, whatever comes next. That's all I can say." Carpenter could hear the big man's head rustle the grass as he shook it. "Whatever it is. Whatever we make it."

On his back on the crude mound, Carpenter could hear the river murmur past in its long sweep to the sea. The fire nearby warmed and comforted. He lay quiet in its soothing glow. He looked up into a deep and endless sky. Stars clustered thick as jewels.

He watched. He breathed. He slept without dreaming.

SELECTED BIBLIOGRAPHY

To write a story that covers such a wide range of times and places of course involves considerable research. Karen Armstrong's body of work has been compelling and useful. Among others that I found helpful in this project are the following:

Capra, Fritzjof (1975). *The Tao of Physics: An Exploration of the Parallels Between Modern Physics and Eastern Mysticism.* Berkely, CA: Shambhala Publications.

Dalai Lama (2005). *The Universe in a Single Atom: The Convergence of Science and Spirituality.* New York: Morgan Road Books.

Eliot, Sir Charles (1935). *Japanese Buddhism.* London: Rutledge & K. Paul.

Fairbank, John K., Reischauer, Edwin O., & Craig, Albert (1973). *A History of East Asia Civilization.* Boston: Houghton-Mifflin.

Hall, D.G.E. (1968). *A History of South-East Asia* (3rd edition). New York: St. Martin's Press.

Humbach, Helmut, & Ichaporia, Pallan (1994). *The Heritage of Zarathustra: A New Translation.* Heidelberg: Universitatverlag C. Winter.

King, Rev. M. L. Jr. (1963). *Letter from Birmingham Jail.* Handwritten by Dr. King on April 16, 1963, this letter was first published in the June 12, 1963 edition of **The Christian Century** [Source: reprinted in *Reporting Civil Rights, Part One - (page 777- 794) - American Journalism 1941 - 1963.* The Library of America.]

McCoy, Alfred W., & Read, Cathleen B. (1972). *The Politics of Heroin in Southeast Asia.* New York: Harper & Row Publishers, Inc.

Scott, J.G. (1896). *The Burman: His Life and Notions.* London: Macmillan and Co. (Available on-line courtesy of University of California Libraries via Google Books.)

Spiro, Melford E. (1967). *Burmese Supernaturalism: A Study in the Explanation and Reduction of Suffering.* Engleside Cliffs, NJ: Prentice-Hall.

Watts, Alan (1964). *Beyond Theology: The Art of Godsmanship.* New York: Pantheon Books.

Wu, John C.H. (translator, 1961). *The Tao The Ching by Lao Tzu.* New York: St. John's University Press.

APPRECIATION

Many friends and fellow authors read and commented on **Indra's Net** and helped nurture it toward completion. Among those are Brenda Bryant, Cheryl Jones, Rick Cook, Bob Snodgrass, Pete Kooken, John Hooe, Lee Brooke and Myo Thant. Friend and writer Burt Weissbourd offered valuable feedback. Author Mark Edmundsen provided unfailing encouragement. Ann Barnett applied her characteristic vigilance to proofing - any mistakes readers may note are mine alone. Gretchen Long's cover and interior design work was also characteristically excellent. Special thanks to my wife, Sharon, for her sharp eye and wit as an editor and her patience as a friend and partner.

THE AUTHOR

Brad Bryant spent a year in 1968-69 teaching and living with a Thai family in Northeast Thailand as a fellow of Yale University's Five Year B.A. Program. After graduating *magna cum laude* in Southeast Asia Studies, he returned to Thailand in 1972 to teach at Ruam Rudee International School in Bangkok and to head the Pearl S. Buck Foundation's work with the children of American soldiers. All told, he

The author in central Burma (Heho).

spent 6 years in Southeast Asia during the Vietnam era, traveling extensively throughout the region and learning Thai, Lao and a bit of Mandarin. He has spent more than 30 years in the child welfare field and has published extensively in the area of foster care and adoption for children with histories of trauma and abuse. **Indra's Net** is his first novel.

17787355R00162

Made in the USA
Charleston, SC
28 February 2013